Praise for
TOMORROW AND TOMORROW

"One of the field's most inventively readable practicing scientists . . . provides his customary sterling performance. . . . Sheffield clothes the most advanced speculations of modern science in alluring forms of beauty and danger."
—*The Washington Post Book World*

"Charles Sheffield shares Verne's spirit of scientific adventure that has taken men and women to the bottom of the sea and the other side of the moon, and will someday take them to the end of the universe. . . . This is truly a love story of the ages."
—*The Orlando Sentinel*

"Ambitious, elegiac, and ultimately satisfying."
—*San Francisco Chronicle Book Review*

Tomorrow & TOMORROW

Charles Sheffield

BANTAM BOOKS

NEW YORK   TORONTO   LONDON   SYDNEY   AUCKLAND

TOMORROW AND TOMORROW
A Bantam Spectra Book

PUBLISHING HISTORY
Bantam trade paperback edition published January 1997
Bantam mass market edition/January 1998
SPECTRA and the portrayal of a boxed "s" are trademarks
of Bantam Books, a division of Bantam Doubleday Dell
Publishing Group, Inc.

ISBN 0-553-57889-8

Published simultaneously in the United States and Canada

Bantam Books are published by Bantam Books, a division of
Bantam Doubleday Dell Publishing Group, Inc. Its
trademark, consisting of the words "Bantam Books" and the
portrayal of a rooster, is Registered in U.S. Patent and
Trademark Office and in other countries. Marca Registrada.
Bantam Books, 1540 Broadway, New York, New York 10036.

PRINTED IN THE UNITED STATES OF AMERICA

OPM   10 9 8 7 6 5 4 3 2 1

Acknowledgment

Parts of this novel are drawn from the novella, *At the Eschaton,* by Charles Sheffield, published in the collection *Far Futures* (Tor Books, 1995).

PART ONE
Love and Death

Chapter 1

The Edge of Doom

Time: The Great Healer, the Universal Solvent

*A*nd if time cannot be granted?

When Drake finally received a clear medical diagnosis after months of secret terrors and false hopes and specialist hedging, Ana had less than five weeks to live. She was already in a final decline. Suddenly, after twelve marvelous years together and a future that seemed to spread out before them for fifty more, they saw the world collapse to a handful of days.

It had begun simply—more than simply. It had begun with nothing, a red car in the driveway when he did not expect one. Ana's car.

He had been passing the house almost by accident, on his way from a teeth-cleaning appointment to a meeting at the new concert hall. Like everyone else, Drake had complained about the acoustics, and the hall managers had called him in to be more specific.

The grace period for construction changes without extra charge would end in less than thirty days, and they were worried.

Well, he could be specific, very specific, about bass absorption and soggy midrange sound and resonant high frequencies. But Ana should not be home. She had a rehearsal in the afternoon. She had told him when she left that she planned an early lunch with the pianist and clarinet player, and she would not be home until about six o'clock.

Car problems? The Camry had been balky for the past week.

He parked in the drive and went inside, noticing the puddle of water on the blacktop and vowing for the hundredth time to have it resurfaced. Ana was not in the kitchen. Not in the dining room or den or living room.

He felt the first twinge of anxiety as he ran upstairs. His relief when he saw her, fully clothed in blue jeans and a tartan shirt and peacefully sleeping on their bed, was surprisingly strong.

He went across and shook her. She opened her eyes, blinked, and smiled up at him.

He bent forward and kissed her lightly on the lips. "Are you all right?"

"I'm fine, love. Except I feel so *tired.*"

"Did you stay up late?" Drake had been downtown to hear a performance of one of his own recent works, and glad-handing his public afterward had kept him out until after midnight.

Ana shook her head. "I was in bed by ten. I've been feeling this way a lot recently. Weak and feeble. But never as bad as this."

"It's not like you. Why don't we give Tom a call?"

He had expected her to say it wasn't necessary, that all she needed was a little more relaxation—Ana, between singing engagements and teaching, drove herself hard.

To his surprise, she nodded. "Would you call him for me?" She lay back and closed her eyes. "I just want to lie here for a little longer."

Drake had worried from that moment on, even if at first no one else seemed to. Tom Lambert was a close friend as well as their family doctor. He came over the same evening, grumbling about what other patients would say if they thought he made house calls.

He examined Ana for a long time. He seemed more puzzled and curious than concerned.

"It could be simple fatigue," he said when he was done. He accepted a small Scotch in a large glass and added lots of ice. The three of them were sitting in the den. Tom raised his glass to Ana before he took a sip. He sighed. "All I can say is, if it is anything, then it's something that I've never seen before."

"Do you think we should just forget about it?" Ana asked. She was sitting on the couch with her feet tucked under her. Drake, studying her now rather than simply accepting her presence, decided that she seemed thinner. "You know, take two aspirin and wait for tomorrow."

"Forget about it?" Tom sounded shocked. "Of course not. What sort of doctor do you think I am? I want to send you to a specialist."

"Of course." Ana's tone was teasing. She and Tom had had the argument before. "Today's typical physician: can't possibly tell you what's wrong with you unless you see at least four other doctors—who of course all get their fees. If you people were musicians, nothing would be written for anything less than a quintet."

"Sure. And if you people were doctors, you'd only perform with hundreds of people watching. Anyway, don't change the subject. I want you to see a specialist. I'm going to make an appointment for you to see Dr. Kevin Williams."

"But if you don't know what it is," Drake protested, "how do you know what sort of specialist she needs?"

Tom Lambert seemed slightly embarrassed. "I said I'd never *seen* anything like this, in my own practice. But it doesn't mean I don't have ideas. Kevin Williams specializes in diseases of the blood and lymph systems. He's head of a group at NIH. He's a friend of mine, and he's damned good. Don't worry, Ana."

"I wasn't going to. I don't believe in it. Drake's the worrier in the family."

"Then don't you worry, either, Drake. We'll get to the bottom of this." Tom nodded, and when he spoke again it was as though he was talking to himself. "Yes, we will. And we'll do it quickly."

Tom did his best. Drake never doubted that for a moment. Ana saw Dr. Williams the next day, then there came a bewildering succession of other doctors and tests in the following two weeks. Ana's teasing remark to Tom was an understatement. Drake counted twelve different physicians, not counting the individuals, many of them also MDs, who administered the MRIs, IVPs, myelograms, and multiple blood workups.

Tom said little, but Drake knew in his heart that there was a big problem. Ana's lassitude continued. She was definitely losing more weight. She had been forced to cancel her teaching and her near-term concert engagements. One morning she was sitting at the kitchen table, pale winter sunlight slanting through onto her fair hair. Drake noticed the translucent, waxen sheen to her forehead and the pattern of fine blue veins on her temples. He was filled with such dread that he could not speak.

The grim biopsy result, when it finally came, was no surprise. Tom delivered the news himself, one drizzly evening in early March.

"An operation?" Ana, as always, was calm and rational.

Tom shook his head.

"How about chemotherapy?"

"We'll try that, naturally." Tom hesitated. "But I have to tell you, Ana, the prognosis is not too good. We can certainly treat you, but we can't cure you."

"I guess that's it, then." Ana stood up, already a little unsteady on her feet because of muscle loss in her legs. "I'm going to bring coffee for all of us. It ought to have perked by now. Cream and sugar, Tom?"

"Uh . . . yes." Tom looked up at her unhappily. "No, I mean, cream, no sugar. Whatever. Anything is fine."

As soon as Ana was out of the room he turned to Drake. "She's in denial. That's natural, and it's not surprising. It will take a while for her to adjust."

"No." Drake stood up and went across to the window. The last heavy snow of the winter was melting, and fresh green shoots of spring growth were poking through. A few more days would bring bloom to the snowdrops and crocuses.

"You don't know Ana," he went on. "She's the ultimate realist. Not like me. Ana's not in denial. I'm the one that's in denial."

"I'm going to prescribe painkillers for her," Tom continued, as though he had not been listening. "All the painkillers she wants. There's no virtue in pain. In a case like this I don't worry about addiction. And I'm going to prescribe tranquilizers, too . . . for both of you." Tom looked toward the kitchen, making sure that Ana was out of earshot. "You might as well know the truth, Drake. There's not one damned thing we can do for her. Forget the chemotherapy. If it buys more than a few weeks for Anastasia, I'd be surprised. I feel that medical science is still in the dark ages about this disease. As a doctor I have to worry about you, too, Drake. Don't neglect your own health. And remember I can be here, night or day, whenever either one of you needs me."

Ana was coming back. She paused on the threshold, holding a tray of cups, coffeepot, cream and sugar. She smiled and arched an eyebrow. "You two all done? Safe for me to come back in now?"

Drake looked at her. She was thin and fragile, but she had never been more beautiful. Beautiful and brave and loving. At the idea of living without her his chest tightened. He felt as though he could not breathe.

Ana was his life, without her there was nothing. How could he ever bear to lose her?

Chapter 2

"O! call back yesterday, bid time return."

$\mathcal{T}$om was gone before ten o'clock. He could tell that Ana, who had been putting on her best front just for him, was exhausted.

Ana went off to bed as soon as Tom had left. Drake followed, half an hour later. She was already asleep. He lay down beside her without undressing, convinced that would be a waste of time. His mind was too active for any form of rest.

He closed his eyes. He imagined Ana, as she had been when they'd first met.

He always told people that he had loved her before he even saw her. The occasion of their first meeting was an end-of-term examination. Drake, as Doctor Bonvissuto's star pupil in musical composition, had been taking a test alone, in a small room next to Bonvissuto's austere office.

It was not the ideal setting for concentration, but Drake had been through the routine several times before. While he was setting down the parts of a fugal

theme provided by his teacher, Bonvissuto was inter-
viewing would-be choral scholars and students in the
next room.

The test material was not inspiring work, and Drake
could do it almost automatically, using sheets of lined
score paper and a pencil. Bonvissuto scorned computers and all other aids to the rapid writing out of
music.

"You think you need computer to write fast, eh?" He
had scowled at Drake on their very first session together. "Handel, he write *Messiah,* every note, in
twenny-four day. You do as good in two-three month, I
don't grumble. You want computer to help? Fine. Provided you write more and *better.* Better than Bach. Better than Monteverdi, better than Mozart. They had no
computer."

From Bonvissuto, that counted as mild comment.
But he meant what he said. Drake slaved away at the
test, without benefit of centuries of technological development, while in the next room a succession of young
men and women came and went.

Most of them, Drake knew, arrived prepared to sing
as Brünnhilde or Tristan or the Queen of the Night.
Bonvissuto would have none of it.

"Something sim-ple. Not the grand opera. The simple song, the folk song. You sing that real good, a cap-
pella, *then* maybe we think about Verdi an' Mozart an'
Wagner."

They would sing unaccompanied, often off-key and
loud. And Bonvissuto would comment, equally loudly.

"What key did you think you were in at the end
there? And what *language*? Did you ever hear about dic-
tion? This song is in *English,* for Christ's sake. Listening
to you it could have been in Polish or Chinese or anything."

Bonvissuto reversed the traditional pattern. When
he was angry and excited, the Italian accent disappeared. In its place came perfect English and a Kansas

twang. The same thing happened during his lessons with Drake, who had once been unwise enough to mention that fact. The teacher had winked at him and said, "Whoever heard of an Italian from Kansas? Whoever heard of a *composer* from Kansas?"

Drake finished writing out the fugue, turned the page, and went on to the final question. "Provide a suitable melody to go with the given accompaniment."

He looked at what followed and realized that the question was going to be a snap. He knew the original piece. He was looking at the piano part of "Erstarrung," the fourth song from the Winterreise song cycle. All he had to do was write out the vocal part. The accompaniment happened to be given in A-minor, up a tone from the version that he was most familiar with, so he would have to transpose; but that was trivial.

He read the question again to be sure. "*Provide* a suitable melody." It didn't say, "*Compose* a suitable melody of your own." And he certainly could not improve on Schubert.

As he wrote in the vocal line he heard the door open again in the next room. There was a mutter of conversation, then a single chord, E major, on Bonvissuto's piano.

A woman's contralto voice began to sing, "Blow the wind southerly." It was a strong, true voice, slightly husky in the lower register and with just a touch of an attractive vibrato on the high notes. Drake paused to listen. After the final note there was a pause, then again a single chord on the piano. It confirmed what Drake already knew. The woman had finished exactly on E natural, in the key where she had started. She had been right on pitch all the way through.

Drake heard another muttered sentence or two spoken in the next room, then the door opened and closed again. He waited, writing in the last few bars of the exercise. Surely Bonvissuto hadn't sent her away, just like that, without talking to her some more. Drake wanted to hear her sing again.

On an impulse he collected his answer sheets, stacked them neatly, and walked across to the connecting door. He turned the doorknob and went through without knocking.

He braced himself. Anyone who entered Bonvissuto's office uninvited could expect a hot welcome.

The expected blast did not come. Professor Bonvissuto was not there. Alone in the room, standing by the piano and staring at him uncertainly, was a slim, blond-haired girl.

He stared back. Her hair was cut a little lopsided. She wasn't very tall, maybe five four, and her pale blue dress didn't look quite right on her. Drake, no connoisseur of clothing, did not realize that it had been intended for someone a couple of inches taller. But the most striking thing about her, far more significant than clothes, was her age. She looked about fifteen. It was hard to believe that the mature contralto voice he had heard came from her.

"Are you next?" she said finally. "I thought I was the last one. He won't be long."

He realized that he had been staring, but so had she. She must assume he was there for a vocal audition. He thrust his sheaf of papers out toward her. "I'm not here to sing. I was taking an exam. I'm one of Professor Bonvissuto's students. Was that you?"

"What me?"

"Singing. 'Blow the wind southerly.' "

"Yes. Why?"

"It was good." He wanted to add that it was wonderful, heart-stopping, soul-searing. Instead he said, "Where is he?"

"The professor? He went to register me. I didn't think I'd be accepted, and it's the last day to sign up. He said he could push it through."

"He can. He knows how." Drake, not knowing what

to do next but reluctant to leave, sat down on the piano stool.

She asked from behind him, "Do you play?"

"Yes. Not very well." He was convinced that he could feel her critical stare burning into the back of his head. Music was full of prodigies: tiny infants picking out chord sequences, concert performers under ten years old, composers who wrote great works in their teens. And here he was, over eighteen and still a student. He wanted to blurt out that he had started late, that his family had been too poor to think of music lessons, that he had come to music only when he found that, almost against his will, melodies arose in his head to go with poetry that he was reading.

He couldn't say any of that. Instead, to hide his self-consciousness, and with "Erstarrung" still in his head, he began to play the restless, uneasy triplets of the song's introduction.

"I've heard that a couple of times," said the voice behind him. "But it's a man's song. Do you know 'Gretchen am Spinnrade'?"

" 'Margaret at the spinning-wheel'?" Drake was much more comfortable with the English translation. He paused for a moment, then began to play a steady, pulsing figure.

"That's it," the girl said at once. "Did you know that Schubert wrote it when he was only seventeen?"

"I know." It was a possible criticism, making the point that Drake was a lot older than seventeen and had done nothing. But before he could say more she went on: "It's a little bit high for me. But I can handle it. Start over."

After the four brief figures of the introduction she began to sing, *"Mein Ruh is hin, mein Herz ist schwer."* "My peace is gone, my heart is heavy." Drake, understanding the German words only vaguely but feeling the strong musical rapport between them, put all his mind into his playing, sensing and adapting to her vocal line.

They performed the whole song. After the final slowing chords on the piano there was total silence. He turned and found a smile on her face that matched his own delight. Before they could speak, a sound came from the doorway: four steady hand claps.

"You know, don't you, the penalty for playing my Steinway without my permission?" Bonvissuto walked toward them. "What are you doing in here, Merlin?"

Drake picked up his exam papers and held them out. "I finished."

"Yeah?" Bonvissuto skimmed the sheets for a couple of seconds. He snorted. "I told Leila Nielsen, using 'Erstarrung' was one dumb idea, you were sure to know it. No matter. Plenty of stuff you *don't* know for next time." He smiled sadistically. "How's your Webern?" And then, before Drake could reply, "Go on, go on. Out of here, both of you." He waved his hands at them. "Merlin, we'll discuss your test tomorrow morning. Werlich, I registered you. You're legal. You come in at one tomorrow, we'll work on your middle register. Now, go. What you waiting for?" And then, when they were almost out the door, "Since you two are going to be performing in public together, you'd better practice. You need polish."

Drake knew her name, or at least part of it. *Werlich.* And she knew his. They stood in the corridor, staring at each other.

"Did you hear that?" she said at last. "Performing together. Do you think he meant it?"

"I don't know." Drake had played before small groups only. The idea of a public concert froze his blood. "But he usually means what he says when it's about music."

She held out her hand. "I'm Anastasia Werlich. Ana for short."

"I'm Drake Merlin." He took her hand and felt an

odd compulsion to admit his secret. "It's actually *Walter* Drake Merlin, but I really hate *Walter*."

"So don't use it. You didn't pick it. I'm not too fond of *Werlich*." She frowned. "How much money do you have?"

The question threw him. Did she mean in the world, or in his pocket? Either way, it was an unsatisfactory answer.

"I have four dollars."

She nodded. "All right. And I have nine. So I'm the rich one. I buy you a Coke."

"I don't drink Coke. Caffeine doesn't agree with me. It gives me the jitters." Drake wondered why he was saying something so terminally stupid. Here he was, keener to continue a conversation with Ana than he had ever been with anyone, and he sounded like he was freezing her off.

But all she said was, "Sprite, then, or 7UP," and she steered them off toward the cafeteria at the end of the building.

They talked through the rest of the afternoon and all evening, so absorbed in each other that the presence of others in the cafeteria was totally irrelevant.

It had pleased Drake at first to learn that she was as badly off as he was. Her fluent German and knowledge of the world came not from an expensive private-school education in Europe, but because Ana was an army brat, whose tough childhood had dragged her from school to school all over Europe and most of the rest of the world. Like him, Ana was poor, too poor to attend a university without a scholarship.

And then, after just a few hours together, money or the lack of it didn't matter.

What did matter was that they were so keen to talk and listen to each other that Ana came close to missing her last bus home. What mattered was that when they were at the bus stop she said, with the directness that she would never lose, "I've been waiting to meet you since I was five years old."

What mattered was her face, gray eyes closed, upturned for a brief good-night kiss. When the bus drove away Drake felt the deepest loss of his eighteen years. He knew, even then, that he had found the girl he would love forever.

That first day set the pattern for all their time together. They were with each other every moment that they could manage. When Ana had an out-of-town performance she would return home on the earliest possible flight. When commissions or premiere performances took Drake away to New York or Miami or Los Angeles, he chafed at the obligatory dinners and cocktail parties that were part of the deal. He didn't want free dinner and drinks or extravagant praise of his talents. He wanted to be with Ana. Even in the early days, when they were desperately poor, he would go without dinner so he could take a taxi rather than a bus, and be home an hour sooner.

Drake recalled one day when Ana was involved in a major traffic accident on the Beltway. He was in bed with a fever of 102 when a telephone call came in from a total stranger, telling him about the accident but assuring him that Ana was all right.

He did not remember getting out of bed or dressing or driving to the scene. He recalled only the terrible feeling of possible loss, of doom hanging over him until he had his arms around her. Her car was totaled, and he didn't notice or care. He had been consumed with the fear of losing her.

And now . . .

Drake looked at the illuminated face of the bedside clock. It was past midnight, almost one o'clock. He rose, went through to the bathroom, and flushed the prescription for tranquilizers that Tom had given him down the drain.

There would be opportunity for sorrow later. Now

he had work to do, and little time to do it. He needed all his faculties, unblurred by drugs. For twelve years he and Ana had done their thinking and planning together. It couldn't be like that this time. She needed all her strength to fight her disease. It was up to him.

He didn't know what he would do, or how he would do it. He only knew he would do *something*.

Ana was his life; without her there was nothing.

He could not bear to lose her.

He would not lose her.

Ever.

Chapter 3

Second Chance

$\mathcal{T}$hree and a half weeks of his efforts proved futile. After the first half-dozen tries Drake learned how to dispose ruthlessly of false leads. Unfortunately, before each one could be rejected it had to be explored. And there were so many: homeopathy, acupuncture, bipolarized interferon, amygdalin, ion rebalance, meditation, chelation, Kirlian aura manipulation, biofeedback, quantum energy . . .

The list seemed endless, and hopeless. Whatever else they might do, they would not cure Ana.

By the fourth week it was obvious that Drake had to do *something*. Ana, though she never complained, was failing fast. He was approaching the end of his endurance. He had been sleeping only a couple of hours a night, making his data-bank searches and long-distance telephone calls when Ana lay in drugged sleep. He had canceled or postponed all commitments, except for one short television piece that could not wait. He disposed of that in a desperate seventeen-hour session, hearing as he worked at his computer the far-off voice of Professor Bonvissuto: "You think you write fast and good, Merlin? Maybe. Mozart, he write the overture for *Don Giovanni,* full score, in one sitting."

When Ana was awake they spent their time in an opiate dream world, touching, smiling, savoring each other, drifting. Except that Drake had taken no drugs and he could not afford to drift. Or wait.

At last it crowded down to a single desperate option. He would have liked to discuss it with Ana, but he could not do so. If she knew what he had in mind, she would veto it. She would make him promise, on her dying body, that he would abandon the idea.

So. She must not know, must never even suspect.

When he had done all that he could and was ready for the final step, he called Tom Lambert and asked him to come over to the house.

Tom arrived after dinner. It was fantastic weather for early April, with daffodils, tulips, and hyacinths bursting into blossom after a cool spring. Life and energy seemed everywhere except inside the darkened house. Ana was sleeping in the front bedroom. Tom gave her a brief examination and led Drake into the living room. He shook his head.

"It's going faster than I thought. At this rate Anastasia will pass into a final coma in the next three or four days. You ought to let me take her to a hospital now. There's nothing you can do for her, and you need the rest. You look as though you've had no sleep for the past month."

"There'll be time enough for sleep. I want her to stay here with me. In fact, it will be necessary." Drake placed Tom in the window seat and sat himself down opposite, knee to knee. He explained what he had been doing for the past week, and what he wanted Tom to do in the next few days.

Lambert heard him out without a word. Then he shrugged his shoulders.

"If that's what the two of you want to do, Drake, it's your call." There was a pitying look in his eyes. "I'll help you, of course I will. And I agree, Anastasia has nothing at all to lose. But you realize, don't you, that they've never done a successful freeze and thaw?"

"On fish, and amphibians—"

"Don't kid yourselves, Drake. Fish and amphibians mean next to nothing. We're talking *humans* here. I have to tell you, in my opinion you are wasting your time and money. Just making the whole thing harder for yourself, too. What does Ana have to say about it?"

"Not much." It was a direct lie. The idea had never been discussed with her. But how could he make a decision, this one above all, without telling Ana? Drake forced himself away from that thought and went on. "She's willing. Maybe more for my sake than hers. She thinks it won't work, but she agrees that she has nothing to lose. Look, I'd rather you don't mention this to her. It's like—like assuming she's already dead. I'll prepare the papers. And I'll get Ana's signature."

"Better not wait too long." Tom's face was grim. "If you're going to do this, she has to be able to hold a pen."

"I know. I told you, I'll get her signature."

After Tom left, Drake wandered out into the back-yard. It was still warm outside, with the promise of summer. But spring was a mockery, an unkind and cruel joke. He roamed from one flowering border to the next. They had created this garden with their own hands. When they moved into the house, seven years ago, the yard had been badly neglected. It had been nothing but weeds and bare earth. He had done most of the work, but it had been according to Ana's design and under her direction. These were *her* walkways and flower beds, not his. How could he bear to look at them, if she was gone?

After five minutes he went inside. He had to check all the legal procedures one more time.

• • •

Three days later Drake called Tom Lambert again to the house. The doctor went to the bedroom, felt Ana's pulse, and took blood pressure and brain-wave readings.

He emerged stone-faced. "I'm afraid this is it, Drake. I'll be very surprised if she regains consciousness. If you are still set on this thing, it has to be done while she has some normal body functions. Another three days . . . it will be a waste of time."

The two men went together into the bedroom. Drake took a last look at Ana's calm, ravaged face. He told himself that this was not a last farewell. At last he nodded to Tom.

"Go ahead." He could not tear his gaze away from her face. "Any time."

Time, time. A waste of time. To the end of time. Time heals all wounds. O! call back yesterday, bid time return.

"Drake? Drake? Are you all right?"

"Sorry. I'm all right." Again he nodded. "Go on, Tom. There's no point in waiting."

The physician made the injection. Working together, they lifted Ana from the bed and removed her clothes. Drake wheeled in the prepared thermal tank. He laid her gently into it. She was so light, it was as though part of her was already lost to him.

While Tom filled out the death certificate, Drake placed the call to Second Chance. He told them to come at once to the house. He set the tank at three degrees above freezing, as instructed. Tom inserted the catheters and the IVs. The next stages were automatic, controlled by the tank's own programs. Blood was withdrawn through a large hollow needle in the main external iliac artery, cooled a precise amount, and returned to the femoral vein.

In ten minutes Ana's body temperature had dropped thirty degrees. All life signs had vanished. Ana was now legally dead. To an earlier generation, Drake Merlin and Tom Lambert would have been judged murderers. It was hard not to feel that way as they sat in the silence of the bedroom, awaiting the arrival of the Second Chance team. Tom was filled with pity—for Drake. Ana was now beyond pity.

Drake's thoughts and plans were fortunately beyond his friend's imaginings.

He had a hard time with Tom Lambert and the three women who arrived from Second Chance. Not one of them could see a reason for Drake to go over to the Second Chance preparation facility with Ana's body.

Tom thought that Drake couldn't face the idea that it was all over. He urged his friend to come home with him and have a drink. Drake refused. The preparation team didn't know what to make of it as he hovered close by them. He seemed like a ghoul or some sort of necrophiliac, yet the look on his face showed he was clearly suffering. They carefully explained that the procedures were very unpleasant to watch, especially for someone so personally involved. They agreed with Dr. Lambert. Drake would be much better off leaving everything in their experienced hands and going home with his friend. They would make sure that everything was all right. If he was worried, they would be sure to call him as soon as the work was finished.

Drake couldn't tell them the real reason he wanted to see the whole preparation procedure, down to the last grisly detail. But by simply refusing to take no for an answer, he at last had his way.

The head of the team then decided that Drake wanted to come along because he was afraid that some element of the job would be botched. She explained the whole procedure to him, kindly and carefully, on the one-hour drive to the facility. They were sitting together in the rear of the van, next to the temperature-controlled casket.

"Most of the revivables—we much prefer that term to cryocorpses—are stored at liquid nitrogen temperatures. That's about minus two hundred degrees Celsius. It's almost certainly cold enough. But it's still about seventy-five degrees above absolute zero. All measurable biological processes become imperceptible long before that. However, there are still some chemical reactions going on. The laws of statistics guarantee that a few atoms will have enough energy to induce biological changes. And mind and memory are very delicate things. So for people who are worried about that, we make available a deluxe version. That's what you bought. Your wife will be stored at liquid helium temperatures, just a few degrees above absolute zero. That's supersafe. When it's so cold, the chance of change—physical or mental—goes way down."

And the cost, although she did not mention the fact, went way up. But cost was not even a variable to be considered from Drake's perspective. When they arrived at the Second Chance facility he hung around the preparation room, ignoring all hints that he should wait outside; and he watched closely.

The team members became more sympathetic. They were now convinced that he was simply terrified that a mistake would be made. They allowed him to see everything and answered all his questions. He was careful not to ask anything that sounded too clinical and dispassionate. The main thing he wanted was to *see,* to know at absolute firsthand what had been done, and in what sequence.

After the first few minutes there was in any case not much to see. He knew that all the air cavities within Ana's body had been filled with neutral solution, and her blood replaced with anticrystalloids. But then she went into the seamless pressure chamber. The body was held there at three degrees above freezing, while the pressure was raised slowly to five thousand atmospheres. After that was done, the temperature drop started.

"Back in the eighties and nineties, they had no idea of this technique." The team leader was still talking to Drake, perhaps with the idea that she might make him feel more relaxed. "They used to do the freezing at atmospheric pressure. There was a formation of ice crystals within the cells as the temperature dropped, and it was a mess when the thaw was done. No return to consciousness was possible."

She smiled reassuringly at Drake, who was not reassured at all. So they didn't know what they were doing in the eighties and nineties. Would they claim in twenty more years that people didn't know what they were doing *now*? But he had no alternative. He couldn't wait for twenty years, or even twenty hours.

"The modern method is quite different," she went on. "We make use of the fact that ice can exist in many different solid forms. Ice is complicated stuff, much more than most people realize. If you raise the pressure to three thousand atmospheres, then drop the temperature, water will remain liquid to about minus twenty degrees Celsius. And when it finally changes to a solid, it isn't the familiar form of ice—what is usually called phase 1. Instead it turns to something called phase 3. Drop the temperature from there, holding the pressure constant, and at about minus twenty-five degrees it changes to another form, phase 2. And it stays that way as you drop the temperature still farther. If you go to five thousand atmospheres pressure—that's what we are doing here—before you drop the temperature, water freezes at about minus five degrees and adopts still another form, phase 5. The trick to avoiding cell rupture problems at freezing point is to inject anticrystalloids, which help to inhibit crystal formation, then by the right combination of temperatures and pressures work all the way down toward absolute zero, passing into and through phases 5, 3, and 2.

"That's what we are doing now. But don't expect to see much except dial readings. For obvious reasons, the pressure chamber is made without seams and without observation ports. You don't get pressures of five thousand atmospheres, not even in the deepest ocean gulfs. Fortunately, once you have the temperature down below a hundred absolute, you can reduce the pressure to one atmosphere, otherwise the storage of revivables would be quite impracticable. As it is, we have many thousands stacked away in the Second Chance wombs. Every one of them is neatly labeled and waiting for the resurrection. That will come as soon as someone figures out a way to do the thaw."

She glanced at Drake, aware that her last comment might have been the wrong thing to say. The official position at Second Chance was that *everyone* was revivable, and that the organization had full control of all the necessary technology. In due course everyone would be revived.

Drake nodded without expression. He had researched the whole subject in detail, and nothing that she had said so far was news. In his opinion it would be as hard to revive the early cryocorpses as it would be to get Tutankhamen's mummy up and moving again. They had been frozen with the wrong procedure, and they were being stored at too high a temperature.

But who was he to make that decision? They had paid their deposits, and they had the right to sit there in the wombs until their rentals ran out. He had started Ana with a forty-year contract, but he thought of that as just the beginning.

He had brought with him a copy of Ana's medical records. He added to it a full description of everything he had seen in the past hour or two, copied the whole document, and made sure that a complete set was included with the file records on Ana. When Ana's body was finally taken away for storage he went back to the house, fell into bed, and slept like a cryocorpse himself for sixteen hours.

It was time for the next step. And it was not going to be easy.

When Drake was fully awake again, fed and bathed, he called Tom Lambert and asked to see him—at Tom's home, rather than his office. He accepted the hefty drink that Tom prepared, after one look at him, for "medicinal purposes," and laid out his plans.

After he was finished Tom walked over to Drake, poked the muscles in his shoulders and the back of his neck, pulled down his lower eyelid and stared at the exposed skin, and finally went to sit opposite him.

"You've been under a monstrous strain for the past few months," he said quietly.

"Very true. I have." Drake kept his voice just as calm.

"And it would be quite unnatural for your behavior or your feelings to be completely normal. In fact, if you seem normal now, it's only because you have completely walled in your emotions. You certainly don't understand the implications of what you are proposing to me."

Drake shook his head. "This isn't new. It's only new to you. I've been thinking of this since the day I gave up on all other options."

"Then that was the day you put the lid on your feelings." Tom Lambert leaned forward. "Look, Drake, Ana was a wonderful woman, a unique woman. I won't say I know what you have been through, because obviously I don't. I do have some idea of your sense of loss. But you have to ask yourself what Ana would want you to do now. You can't let the past become your obsession. She would tell you that you still have a life of your own. Even without her, you have to live it. She would *want* you to live it, because she loved you." He paused. "Let me make a suggestion . . ."

While Tom was talking, Drake found it harder and harder to listen. The room felt dull and airless and he had trouble breathing. Tom Lambert's words came from far off. They didn't seem to say anything. He forced himself to concentrate, to listen harder.

". . . of your work. You are still a young man. Forty to fifty good years ahead of you. And already you have a reputation. You are one of this country's most promising composers, and your best works still lie ahead. Ana may have performed your work better than anyone else, but there will be others. They will learn. With your talent you owe it to the rest of us not to cut your career off before it reaches its peak."

"I have no intention of doing so. I will compose again. Later."

"You mean, later after *that?*" Tom was frowning and shaking his head. "Suppose there is no later? Drake, take my advice as both your doctor and your friend. You desperately need to get out of your house, and you need to take a vacation. Go off on a cruise somewhere, take a trip around the world. Expose yourself to some new influences. I know how you must feel now, but you should give it a year and see how you feel *then*. I guarantee you, everything will seem different. You'll want to live again. You'll give up this crazy idea."

The breathless feeling was fading. Drake again had control of himself. He waited patiently until Tom was finished, then nodded agreement.

"I'll do as you say. I'll get away from here for a while. But if it turns out that you are wrong—if I come back to you, in, say, eight or ten years, and I ask you again, will you do it? Will you help me? I want you to give me an honest answer, and I want your word on it."

The tension drained visibly from Tom Lambert. He snorted in relief. "Ten years from now? Drake, if you come back to me in eight or ten years and ask me again, I'll admit I was completely wrong. And I promise you, I'll help you to do what you've asked."

"An absolute promise? I don't want to hear some day that you changed your mind, or didn't mean what you said."

"An absolute promise. Sure, I'll give you that." Tom laughed. "But I'm not worried that I'll ever be called on it. I'll bet you everything I own that after a year or two have gone by, you'll never mention that promise again. Hard as it seems to believe today, you'll be living a new life, and you'll be enjoying it." He walked over to the sideboard and poured himself a drink. "I'd like to propose a toast, Drake. Or actually, three toasts. To us. To your future. And to your next—and greatest—composition."

Drake raised his glass in return. "To us, and the future. I'll drink to those. But I can't drink to my next work, because I don't know when I'll create it. I have lots of other things to do—for one thing, you told me to get out of town. I'm going to do that, right away. But don't worry, Tom. I'll be in touch when the time is right."

Chapter 4

Into the Abyss

There were two problems. The first was easy to define but hard to solve: money.

In the early days, Drake and Ana had been very poor. As a result they talked about money quite a lot. She would glance through their joint checking account book, with its zero balance, and groan. He would laugh, with more worry than humor, and once he quoted something he had just read by Somerset Maugham: "Money is the sixth sense that enables us to enjoy the other five." He added: "I guess that leaves us six senses short."

Unfortunately, neither groans nor quotations produced income. Money, or the lack of it, seemed important, as important as anything in the world except music and each other.

Career success brought a change of attitude. Ana had her teaching and her concert appearances, Drake had pupils and occasional commissions. Their needs were modest. They bought a house, a big old-fashioned brick Colonial with four bedrooms and half an acre of fenced yard, expecting that someday they would need all the space for an expanded family. Neither of them wanted to travel or be wealthy. Wordsworth was quoted rather than Maugham: "Getting and spending, we lay waste our powers."

Now all that was past. Drake needed money, lots of it. He had to make sure that Ana could remain safe within her icy womb for the indefinite future, until she could be safely thawed and her disease cured. Then her life would begin again. There were a few things he couldn't guard against, such as a total collapse of the world to barbarism, or the rejection of all present forms of currencies and commodities. Those were risks that Ana—and he—would have to accept.

The other problem was more subtle. According to Tom it might be a long time before a cure was found for Ana's rare and highly malignant disease. As he pointed out, something that killed only a few people a year did not get the attention of common cancers and heart diseases, which ended the lives of hundreds of millions.

Suppose that a cure was not discovered for a century, or even for two centuries. What knowledge of present-day society would interest people in the year 2200? What must a man know or a woman be, for the inhabitants of that future Earth to think it worthwhile to revive them? Drake was convinced that even when a foolproof way of resuscitating the revivables was discovered, most bodies in the cryowombs would stay exactly where they were. The contracts with Second Chance provided only for maintenance in a cryonic condition. They did not, and could not, offer a guarantee that an individual would be thawed.

Why thaw anyone at all? Why add another person to a crowded world, unless he or she had something special to offer?

Drake imagined himself back in the early nineteenth

century. What could he have placed into his brain, then, that would be considered valuable today, two hundred years later? Not politics, nor art. Knowledge of them was quite adequate. Certainly not science or any technology—progress in the past two centuries had been phenomenal.

What would the people of the future want to *know* about the past?

He decided that he had lots of time to ponder his own question; time, which had been denied to Ana. It would be foolish to hurry, when he could plan and calculate at his leisure. He set a goal of ten years. That would still allow forty of the shared fifty that he had looked for and longed for. But he was quite willing to stretch ten to fifteen if he had to.

If it did take more time, it would not be because he allowed himself to be distracted by other activities. His only diversion was to estimate the probabilities that everything would work out as he hoped. Always, the odds came out depressingly low.

While he was trying to decide what he needed to learn, he still had to solve that difficult first problem: making money.

He decided to visit his old teacher. His relationship with Bonvissuto had passed through three distinct phases. At first there had been absolute awe of the professor's musical skill and encyclopedic knowledge. Bonvissuto seemed to know, and be able to play by heart at his cherished Steinway, his own piano transcription of any work by any composer. After three years of study, Drake's attitude changed. He still respected and admired his mentor's learning, but in matters other than music he came to think Bonvissuto a bit of a comic figure. He could not ignore the elevator heels, red carnation buttonholes, dyed-brown shoulder-length tresses, unreliable Italian accent, and relentless romantic activity.

It was Ana, in Drake's final year as Bonvissuto's student, who revealed to Drake another side of their teacher.

"Can't you see how much he envies you?" she said, as they sat one afternoon poring over a marked-up score of *Carmina Burana*.

"Who?"

"Bony. Who else?"

"*Me?*" Drake put down the score. "Why on earth do you think he would envy me? He knows ten times as much about music as I'll ever know."

"He does. But just the same he envies you—for the same reason as *I* envy you. He teaches music. I perform music. But you *create* music. Neither of us is able to do that. Can't you see the look in his eyes, whenever you bring him a beautiful original melody? He's delighted, yet sad. It must kill him inside, to be so gifted and yet be missing that one essential spark."

Ana's insight led Drake to a final opinion of his teacher. The professor could be sarcastic and short-tempered. He was certainly vain, and a dedicated womanizer. But he loved music, with a passion and a strength and a devotion far beyond anything else in life.

And again it was Ana who stated it best. When a discussion of Haydn's "English" songs was interrupted by a telephone call from Bonvissuto's current flame, she said to Drake, quietly and with real affection for their teacher, "Listen to him. He tells Rita—and Charlene and Mary and Leah and Judy—that he loves them, and I think he really does. But he'd trade the lot in for one new Haydn symphony."

Or one new original work by Drake Merlin? Drake wasn't sure, then or ever. But two months after Ana had been placed in the cryowomb, he appeared in Bonvissuto's office one morning without warning. The teacher gave him one startled look, then turned his eyes away. "I know, I know," he said. "I'm terribly sorry."

It had been three years since the two last met, but Bonvissuto had followed the careers of all his former students. He took vast pride in them. Naturally, he knew about Ana.

"I didn't come here to talk about her," Drake said, "unless you want to, I mean. I came to ask your advice."

"Anything that I can do, I will. For you and little Ana, I will be happy . . ." Bonvissuto paused, swallowed, and turned away. The volatile Italian persona was not all fake.

"I have to make money." Drake spoke dispassionately to the other man's back. He needed advice, not emotional support. "A lot of money. I wondered if you could suggest a way."

"You! The least commercial of all my students. Oh!" Bonvissuto turned again, and Drake saw in his eyes a sudden understanding. "I know. I went through some of it myself, two years ago. The damned hospitals—the tests, and all the drugs, and prices you wouldn't believe —five dollars for an aspirin, two hundred dollars a day for a room, fifty dollars for a doctor who drops in on you for two minutes and doesn't even look at you—they bleed you dry."

Drake nodded. It was a mistaken assumption, but letting it stand saved lots of explanation. "I need to make as much money as I can. As quickly as I can. I don't know how."

"But I do." Bonvissuto went across to his piano. "Provided you are willing to lower your standards. Are you?"

"I don't know. What do you mean?"

"Don't worry. I am not about to suggest that you form a rock group. You compose well, and you compose fast. But your music is too difficult to be popular. This is what Drake Merlin is writing." Bonvissuto played a sequence of spare chords with no clear tonal center, and above them on the right hand a wandering angular melody.

"That's from my *Suite for Charon!*"

"It is indeed. I took the liberty of making a piano transcription." Bonvissuto sounded not at all apologetic. "It is very beautiful—to you, and me, and maybe a few thousand others. But if you want to appeal to a few *million,* you must be simpler, more accessible. Like this." Bonvissuto played a jaunty bass theme, accompanied by dazzling prestissimo downward runs on the right hand.

Drake frowned. "That's by Danny Elfman. It's film music."

"It is. Are you saying you are above such things?"

"Not at all. It's first-rate. But I can't walk into a film studio and say, let me score a movie. They'd throw me straight out."

"Of course." Bonvissuto shrugged. "It is obvious that you don't start there. Or rather, if you choose to start there, I can't help you. But a dozen paths can lead in that direction." He stood up, went to his old oak desk, and picked up a cheap black notebook with a spiral binder. "All the time, I hear of musical markets. I write them down. They are open to you, provided that you don't insist on writing compositions that break new ground. People are most comfortable with the familiar. They say they know what they like, but really they like what they know. See here."

He opened the book and ran down the list of entries with his long, thin index finger. "I include concerts and recitals on this list, but for you I strongly recommend composition. Are you willing to write a commemorative overture for the hundredth anniversary of the first heavier-than-air flight? That offers four thousand dollars, for eleven minutes. The time requirement is precise, no more, no less. The work will be played after the national anthem, after a *Star Wars* selection and before 'The Stars and Stripes Forever.' I would not recommend march tempo. Or how about this one, which came to me through private channels: a commission to ghost-write a violin concerto for a Cabinet member with musical delusions of grandeur."

"What would I do?"

"You would write the music, after listening for half an hour to Lamar Malory's vague and off-key humming of themes. Your name will not, of course, go on the finished work. His name will. The fee offered, for your music and your silence, is four hundred dollars per composed minute. It is not much, but the music does not have to be very good. In fact, it would be suspicious if it were."

Drake bit back the urge to ask why Bonvissuto did not take the commissions himself. "What are the deadlines?"

"How soon can you produce?"

"Faster than anyone else they can find. I'll take both of them. As many as I can get, in fact. I'll write around the clock if I have to."

"I'll see what I can do. I can't guarantee these or any other commissions, but I can make sure that you are on the short list. After that it's up to you. I warn you, you will be dealing with people who have no more music in them than a dog who howls at the moon." Bonvissuto shrugged. "I am sorry, but that is the price. Never mind. When you have the money that you need, you can return to normal life."

A normal life was not what Drake had in mind—not for a long time yet. But he could not discuss his plans. He thanked Bonvissuto and left.

It was the beginning of a long period of incessant work. Drake took commissions, wrote commemorative pieces, gave concerts, and made recordings. As his reputation for good, fast, and reliable work grew, he produced reams of music for good, bad, and indifferent shows and movies. If anyone compared his recent work with his earlier work, and thought that he was debasing his art, they were too polite to comment. His own attitude was simple: if it was lucrative, it was acceptable.

Once a month he visited Ana's cryowomb facility. He could not see her, but he could sit outside the room where she was housed. Knowledge of her presence produced in him a strange tranquillity. After a couple of hours with her, he could again face his work.

Sometimes that work was unpleasant, grinding toil. Since he agreed to tight deadlines, he was often forced to compose late at night when he was close to exhaustion. But sometimes the odd commercial challenges brought out the best in him. The finest melody of his life came to him as the theme music to a successful television show. And after four years he had an even bigger stroke of luck.

He had written a set of short pieces a couple of years after he and Ana first met, a kind of musical joke designed especially to appeal to her. They were baroque forms, with period harmonies, but he had added occasional modern harmonic twists, piquancy inserted where it would be most surprising and most appealing.

They had been quite successful, although only among a limited audience. Now, given a commission to provide the incidental music for a series of television dramas on life in eighteenth-century France, and facing another impossible delivery date, Drake returned to cannibalize, adapt, and simplify his own earlier work. The dramas turned out to be the hit of the decade. His music was credited as a big part of the reason for their success. Suddenly his minuets, bourrées, gavottes, sarabands, and rondeaux were everywhere. And as they flooded from the audio outlets, the royalties flooded in from every country around the globe.

Drake went on working as hard as ever. He established a foundation and trust fund. It guaranteed continued care for Ana's cryocorpse for many centuries, no matter what happened to Drake himself.

Freed from a need for money, his work changed direction. Instead of endless composition he became feverishly busy soaking up all that he could learn of the private and personal lives of his musical contemporaries. He interviewed, entertained, courted, and analyzed them, and he wrote about them extensively. But never quite in full. In every piece he was careful to leave a hanging tail, a hint that said, "There is much more to say and I know what it is; but for the moment I am deliberately leaving it unsaid."

What would the people of the future most want to know about their ancestors? Drake had his own answer. Their fascination would not be with the formal works, the official biographies, the text-book knowledge. They would have more than enough of those. What they would want would be the personal details, the chat, the gossip. They would want the equivalent of Boswell's journals and of Samuel Pepys' diaries. And if there was a way that they could have not only the written legacy, but the recorder himself, to talk to him and ask more questions . . .

It was not work that could be hurried. But finally, after nine long years, Drake was as ready as he would ever be. There was always the temptation to add one more interview, write one more article.

He resisted, and briefly worried a different question. How would he earn a living in the future? It might be only thirty years, but it might be eighty, two hundred, or a thousand. Could Beethoven, suddenly transported from 1810 to the year 2010, have earned a living as a musician?

More realistically, how would Spohr, or Hummel, or some other of Beethoven's less famous contemporaries have fared? Drake was betting that they, and he, could manage very well as soon as they had picked up the tricks of the time. Better, probably, than the far greater genius, the titan of Bonn. The others were more facile, more flexible, more politically astute.

And if he was wrong, and there was no way that he could make a living from music? Then he would do the twenty-third-century equivalent of washing dishes for a living. That was the least of his worries.

One day he stopped everything, put his affairs in order, and returned home. Without notice he headed for Tom Lambert's house. They had kept in touch, and he knew that Tom had married and was busy raising a family in the same house he had lived in all his life. But it was still a surprise to walk along that quiet tree-lined street, look over the same untidy privet hedge, and see Tom in the front yard playing baseball with a stranger, an eight-year-old boy who wore a flaming new version of Tom's graying red mop.

"Drake! My God, why didn't you call and tell me you were in town? How do you do it? You're as thin as ever." Tom had lost some of his hair but added a paunch to make up for it. He ushered Drake into the house and fussed over him like the Prodigal Son, leading the way into the familiar study. While his wife went into the kitchen to kill the fatted calf, he stood and beamed at Drake with pride and pleasure.

"We hear your music everywhere, you know," he said. "It's absolutely wonderful to know that your career is going so well."

Judged by Drake's own standards, it was not. He felt that he had done little first-rate composition in years. But Bonvissuto had been right: Tom, like most people, was comfortable musically with what he found familiar. From that point of view, and in terms of commercial success, Drake was riding high.

He itched to get down to business right away, but Tom's three young boys hovered around the study and the living room, curious to see the famous visitor. Then came a family dinner, and liqueurs after it watching the sunset. Drake sat in the guest-of-honor seat, with Tom and his wife, Mary-Jane, doing most of the talking.

At ten o'clock Mary-Jane disappeared to put the boys to bed. Drake was alone with Tom. *At last.* He took a deep breath, pulled out the application, and handed it to his friend without a word.

As Tom looked at it and realized what it was, the happiness faded from his face. He shook his head in disbelief.

"I thought you put all this behind you years ago. What started it going again?"

Drake stared at him without speaking, as though he had not understood the question.

"Or maybe it never stopped," Tom went on. "I should have guessed it hours ago. You used to be so full of life, so full of *fun.* Tonight I don't think I saw you smile once. When did you last take a vacation?"

"You gave me your word, Tom. Your promise."

Lambert studied the other man's thin face. "Never mind a vacation, when did you last take *any* sort of break from work? How long since you relaxed for an evening, or for an hour? Not tonight, that's for sure."

"I go out all the time. I go to concerts and to dinner parties."

"You do. And what do you do there? I bet you don't relax. You interview people, and you take notes, and you produce a stream of articles. You *work.* And you've been working, incessantly, year after year. How long since you've been with a woman?"

Drake shook his head but did not speak.

Tom sighed. "I'm sorry. Forget that I asked that. It was a dumb and insensitive thing to say. But you need to face a fact, Drake, and you shouldn't try to hide from it: She's dead. Do you hear me? *Ana is dead.* Work won't change that. Wishing won't change it. Nothing can bring her back to you. And you can't go on forever with your own emotions chained and harnessed."

"You promised me, Tom. You gave me your solemn word that you would help me."

"Drake!"

"Do you ever make promises to your children?"

"Of course I do."

"Do you keep them?"

"Drake, you can't use that argument, the situations are totally different. You act as though I made you some sort of solemn vow, but it wasn't like that at all."

"Then how was it? Don't bother to answer." Drake took the little recorder from his inside jacket pocket. "Listen. Listen to yourself."

The words were thin in tone but quite clear.

. . . if I come back to you, in, say, eight or ten years, and I ask you again, will you do it? Will you help me? I want you to give me an honest answer, and I want your word on it.

Ten years from now? Drake, if you come back to me in eight or ten years and ask me again, I'll admit I was completely wrong. And I promise you, I'll help you to do what you've asked.

An absolute promise? I don't want to hear some day that you changed your mind, or didn't mean what you said.

An absolute promise. Sure, I'll give you that . . . There was the sound of Tom's relieved laugh.

Drake turned off the recorder. "I said, eight to ten years. It has been nine."

"You recorded us, back then when Ana had just died? I can't believe you would do that."

"I had to, Tom. Even then, I was convinced that you would change your mind. But I knew that I wouldn't. You have to live up to your agreement. You promised."

"I promised to *help* you, to stop you from doing something crazy to yourself." Tom's face went ruddy with intolerable frustration. "For God's sake, Drake, I'm a *doctor*. You can't ask me to help you kill yourself."

"I'm not asking that."

"You might as well be. No one has ever been revived. Maybe no one ever will be. If they do learn how, Anastasia will be a candidate. She is in the best Second Chance womb, she had the best preparation money could buy. But you, you're different. You're not sick! Ana was dying before she was frozen, she had nothing to lose. You have *everything* to lose. You're healthy, you're productive, you're at the height of your career. And you are asking me to throw all that away, to help you take the chance that someday, God knows when, you might—just might—be revived. Don't you see, Drake, I can't help you."

"You gave me your promise."

"Stop saying that! I also have my oath as a physician: to do no harm. You want me to take you from perfect health to a high odds of final death."

"I have to do it, Tom. If you won't help me, I'll find someone who will. Probably someone less competent and reliable than you."

"*Why* do you have to do it? Give me one good reason."

"You know why, if you think about it." Drake spoke slowly, coaxingly. "For Ana's sake. Unless I go on ahead, they may never choose to wake her. She could be one of the last on their list. You and I know her for what she really is, a unique and marvelous woman. But what will the records show? A singer, still not as famous as she would have been, who died young of a devastating disease. I've had time to prepare, I'm sure that they will wake me. And it's an advantage that I'm in good health, because there will be no reason to delay my revival on medical grounds. As soon as I am sure that they have a cure for what killed Ana, I can wake her. We'll start over, the two of us."

Tom Lambert's cheeks had gone from fiery red to pale. "We have to talk about this some more, Drake. The whole idea is crazy. Did you really mean what you said, that if I won't help you will go to someone else?"

"Look at me, Tom. Tell me if you think that I mean it."

Lambert looked. He did not speak again; but his hands slowly came up to cover his eyes.

It took six days of solid argument, another seven to make final preparations. Drake Merlin and Tom Lambert drove together to Second Chance.

Drake took a long last look out of the window at the wind-blown trees and the cloudy sky, then climbed slowly into the thermal tank.

Tom injected the Asfanil.

Drake decided that the easy part was ending. That the hard part, if there was another part, was about to begin.

A few seconds later the long fall began, dropping him steadily down the longest descent that a human can ever make.

Down, down, down.

All the way down, to two degrees absolute; colder than the coldest hell ever conceived by Dante.

Chapter 5

Awakening

The great gamble had paid off, more successfully than he had dared to hope. Ana was alive, she was reanimated, she was healthy. But the technology of the future went far beyond health. It had made her, always beautiful, much more vigorous and desirable than she had ever been.

She was dancing, and as she danced she sang; not a serious work by her usual favorites, Mahler or Hugo Wolf or Brahms, but a frothy and light-hearted confection by Gilbert and Sullivan. "My object all sublime, I shall achieve in time," she caroled.

And then she was fading. Her body became as transparent as glass, her rich contralto a vanishing thread of sound. "To let the punishment fit the crime, The punishment fit the cri-i-i-me . . ."

She was gone.

Afterward, Drake could never be sure. Had he dreamed some superconducting dream, as he lay in the cryowomb twelve degrees colder than a block of solid hydrogen? Or had he only *dreamed* that he dreamed, as he came slowly back through the long thaw?

It made little difference. After the vision of Ana, all feelings of peace and certainty bled away. In their place came an eternity of twisted images, a procession of pale and terrifying lights moving against a pitch-dark background. They arrived ahead of consciousness, and they went on forever. He fought his way through them, through torment that went on and on with no promise that it would ever end.

It was daunting to learn later that he had been one of the lucky ones. In his case the freezing process had gone very smoothly. Some revivables awoke armless and legless, some shed their whole epidermis and had to be kept cocooned and motionless until it could regrow. He lost nothing during the thaw but an insignificant few square centimeters of skin.

But the pain of waking . . . that was something else. The final stages, from three degrees Celsius to normal body temperature, could not be rushed. They occupied a full thirty-six hours. For all that time Drake was pierced with an agony of waking tissues and returning circulation, unable to move or cry out. In the last stages, before full consciousness, hearing came before sight. He could hear speech around him. It was not in any tongue that he could recognize.

How long? How far had he traveled in time? Even before the pain faded, that question filled his mind.

The answer did not come at once. While he was still half-conscious he felt the sting of an injector spray. He blanked out again at once. After another infinite hiatus he came up all the way, opening his eyes to a quiet sunlit room not too different from the Second Chance facility where he had begun the descent.

A man and a woman in yellow uniforms were watching him, talking softly together. As soon as they saw that he was awake the man pressed a point on a segmented wall panel. The two went on with their work, lining up two complex and incomprehensible pieces of equipment. One sight of that told Drake that he had succeeded in at least one way. Nothing that he saw was familiar. He was in the future—but how far in the future?

The person who came in presently through the white sliding door was dark haired and oddly androgynous, with a face both clean shaven and also smooth and womanly. The clothing was equally uninformative, a loose-fitting suit of pale gray that concealed body shape. The newcomer stepped to the side of the bed and stood staring down at Drake with a pleased and proprietary air.

"How are you feeling?"

Drake knew then that it was a man. The language was English, oddly pronounced. That was reassuring. Drake had suffered two other worries as he slipped under. What if he were revived in just a few years' time, when nothing at all could be done to cure Ana? Or what if he surfaced after fifty thousand years, a living fossil, quite unable to communicate his needs to the men and women of the future?

"I feel all right." He had trouble speaking. His tongue felt swollen, and his mind was slow to produce the words that he needed. "But I feel very weak and confused." Drake thought of trying to sit up, and knew at once that he could not do it. "I can barely move."

"Naturally. But are you Drake Merlin?"

"I am."

The man had an open eager face, with furry eyebrows and a high forehead. He laughed aloud in delight and rubbed his hands together. "Excellent! My name is Par Leon. Can you understand me easily?"

"Perfectly easily." Drake's second worry returned. "Why do you ask that question? *When* am I?"

"I ask it because the old languages are not easy, even with augments and much study. For your second question, in your measure we are now in the year 2512 of the prophet Christ."

Five centuries! It was longer than Drake had expected and hoped. But better long than short. Before he was frozen he had entertained awful visions of diving down to the bottom of the Pit and clawing his agonized way back up to thawed life, not once but over and over.

"I have waited here through the whole warming and first treatment," Par Leon continued. "Soon I will leave you so you can have rest, more treatment, and first education. But I desired to speak with you at once when you became conscious. It is not rational, but I feared that there might have been a mistake in identity—that it might not be Drake Merlin, the Drake Merlin of my curiosity, who was awakened." Par Leon glanced at the equipment standing at the bedside and shook his head. "You are a strong man, Drake Merlin. Uniquely strong. The record shows that you did not once cry out or complain during all the thawing."

There had been more important things on Drake's mind. Could Ana be cured? Where was she now? Had she been kept safe, for however much time had passed? Was it possible that she had been awakened before him, even long before him? That would be a disaster.

He glanced across at the other two workers, who were still chatting together in an alien tongue. "Language must have changed completely. I can understand you easily, but I cannot understand them at all."

"You mean, understand the doctors?" The stranger Leon replied with a surprised expression on his lean face. "Of course you cannot. Neither can I. They are doctors. To each other they are naturally speaking Medicine."

Drake raised his eyebrows. The look must have survived with its meaning intact across the centuries, because Par Leon went on, "That is right, Medicine. I cannot help you. I myself am fluent in Music and History—and, of course, Universal. And I learned Old Anglic to be able to study your times and to speak with you. But I know little or no Medicine."

"Medicine is a *language*?" Drake felt that his mind had been slowed by the long sleep and thawing treatment.

"Of course. Like Music or Chemistry or Computing. But surely this was already true in your own time. Did you not have languages specific to each—what is the word you use?—discipline?"

"I suppose that we did; but we didn't realize it." Par Leon's question explained a great deal. No wonder that Drake had found psychologists, professional educators, social scientists, and physicists—to name but a few—incomprehensible. Even in his original time, the special jargon and odd acronyms had been signaling the arrival of new protolanguages, emerging forms as alien as Sanskrit or classical Greek. "How do you speak to the doctors?"

"For ordinary things? We employ Universal, which all understand. I do not attempt to speak actual Medicine. If I am in that subject-matter area, we keep a computer in the circuit to provide exact concept equivalents between language pairs."

It occurred to Drake that multidisciplinary programs must be hell. But not as bad as they had once been. Here at least there was an understanding that the problem *existed*. And what were computers like, after five more centuries of development? In his day they had been in their infancy. They ought to be able to do anything now, anything at all—like curing Ana. It was almost a surprise to see that there was still a place in the world for humans.

He was beginning to feel oddly and irrationally euphoric, a combination of drugs and the idea that he might succeed more easily than he had dreamed.

He made a more determined effort to sit up. His head lifted maybe five centimeters from the pillow, then fell back despite everything he could do to hold it up.

"Slowly. Rome—was not built—in a day." Par Leon glowed, clearly delighted at coming up with such a prize example of genuine Old Anglic. "It will be moons before you are fully strong. Two more things I will tell you, then I will allow your treatment to continue.

"First, it was I who arranged for you to be brought here and revived. I am a musicologist, interested in the twentieth and twenty-first centuries, and in particular your own time."

Drake's five-hundred-year-old bet had paid off. He wondered what modern music sounded like. Would he be able to listen to it with pleasure? To compose it?

"Under our laws," Par Leon went on, "you owe me for the cost of your revival and treatment. This amounts to six years of work from you. You are most fortunate that you were healthy and correctly frozen and maintained, or the time of service would have been much longer. However, I also believe that you will find your indenture with me both pleasant and interesting. I am proposing that you and I, together, write the definitive history of your own musical period."

So the question of earning a living was postponed for at least a few years. Par Leon would presumably have to feed Drake Merlin while he was paying off his debt.

"Second, I have good news for you." Par Leon was gazing at Drake expectantly. "When we examined you, our doctors found certain problems—*defects* is the word that you would use?—with your body and its glandular balance. They hope that they have cured the simpler body malfunctions, and they have provided standard stabilization of your chromosomal telomeres. You will still age, but slowly. You should live between two and three hundred years.

"However, the glandular imbalance represented a more subtle problem. It was likely to manifest itself as some form of madness, some uncontrollable compulsion. The doctors observed this as soon as you were thawed enough to respond to psychoprobes. They made small chemical changes and have, we hope, corrected the difficulty." Par Leon was watching Drake closely. "Please tell me now of your feelings toward your former wife, Anastasia Werlich."

Drake felt his heart racing. He could hear the blood pounding in his ears, and in his weakened condition it was as hard to breathe as if heavy weights had been dropped onto his chest. He closed his eyes for a long moment and thought about Ana. Gradually, he became calm again.

It was obvious what the other wanted to hear; and Ana was worth a million lies. Drake looked up at Par Leon and shook his head feebly. "I feel very little for her. No more than a faint sense that something was once there. I know that she was once very dear to me, but I am not sure how. It is like the scar of an old wound."

"Excellent!" The smile had kept its meaning. "That is most satisfying. The disease that killed the woman was eliminated from the human stock long ago, by careful mating choice—*eugenics,* as your language put it. We could certainly reanimate her, but according to our doctors it is still not clear that we would be able to cure her. However, we can see no reason to awaken her at all. Like most in the cryowombs, she is of little or no value to us. Most important of all, an involvement with her might interfere with your work for me."

"So her body is still stored?"

"Of course. We keep all the cryocorpses. Although most are of no present value, who knows what our future needs might be? The cryowombs are like a library of the past, to open whenever it will serve a purpose. Two hundred years from now someone may find a use for her, and her disease perhaps easily cured. Then she, too, may live and work again."

"Is Anastasia stored near here?"

"Of course not!" For the first time, Par Leon appeared to be shocked. "What a waste of space and energy that would imply. The cryowombs are maintained on Pluto, where space is cheap, cooling needs are small, and escape velocity is low."

That sentence, more than any other that Par Leon had spoken, wrenched Drake forward in time. What technology was it that could casually ship millions of bodies to the edge of the solar system rather than keep them in cold storage on Earth? If, that is, Pluto *was* the edge of the solar system. How many planets were known now? Even in his day, there was talk of many more bodies out in a region known as the Kuiper Belt. *Five centuries.* It was the time from Monteverdi to Shostakovich, from Copernicus to Einstein, from the Columbus discovery of America to the first landing on the Moon. He had come a long, long way.

Par Leon was still gazing at him, now a little suspiciously. "Again you ask about the woman, Anastasia Werlich. Why? Are you sure that you are in fact fully cured? If not, another course of treatment is easy to arrange."

Drake cursed his own stupidity and did his best to smile reassuringly. "I feel sure that will not be needed. Already her memory fades. As soon as I am strong enough, I am eager to begin my work with you."

"Wonderful." The smile was back, but Par Leon was wagging his finger in warning. "We will certainly work together, but only *after* you are fully recovered and have had some essential training. First, you must learn to speak Universal and Music and you must have enough background knowledge to live comfortably in this time. It will also be my responsibility to see that you are able to find suitable activity when your work with me is done, and for that you will need skills that today you lack.

"Rest now, Drake Merlin. I will return tomorrow, or

the next day. By that time you will already find yourself stronger. And you will be far more knowledgeable.''

As Par Leon left, the medical technicians carried forward a transparent helmet with silvered lines inscribed on its upper part. They lowered it carefully onto Drake's head.

He lost consciousness at once, too quickly to be aware of its cool touch.

Chapter 6

Brave New World

He awoke to the sound of two voices. One was an unfamiliar wordless chatter, a high-pitched and irritating tingle more in his brain than in his ear. The other voice he already knew. It was Par Leon, asking what seemed like an odd question after their previous conversation.

"Do you understand me, Drake Merlin?" There was a pause, then, more loudly: "Can you hear me? Do you understand me?"

"Of course I can. Of course I do." But Drake was having trouble controlling his own speech. He had to seek out each word. He opened his eyes. "We already . . . established that we can . . . understand each other."

Leon was standing in front of him, nodding in satisfaction. "We proved yesterday that we could communicate *in English*. But listen again to me . . . and listen to yourself."

The words were perfectly understandable—but they had been spoken in an alien tongue.

"What happened?" Drake asked. The sense of what he said was clear, but it sounded peculiar. With a deliberate effort, he repeated it in English, and the words came more easily. *"What happened?"*

"You learned, exactly as I hoped and expected." Leon replied in the same language. "But now"—Drake felt no decrease in his level of comprehension, yet he heard the change in the sounds—"now it is better if we both speak Universal."

"You said *yesterday.*" Drake's shift from one language to the other was labored and sluggish. "You taught me Universal . . . in a single day? How were you able to do that?"

"I am the wrong person to ask." Leon shrugged. "If I were to attempt an explanation, beyond saying that the helmet taught you, it would surely be inadequate. A suitable reply would be provided in Electronics or Medicine, possibly using dialects of the latter such as Neurology. I was taught something of those languages, long ago, but I found them uncongenial. If they are to your taste, you will have opportunity to learn them later. For the moment, relax. Go slowly. In two or three weeks, Universal will come easily to you. But now we have other priorities. Can you stand up?"

Rather than replying, Drake made the experiment. He pushed the helmet away from his head and rose to his feet. As he came upright there was one moment of unsteadiness, then he felt balanced and alert. Yesterday's weakness was gone completely.

"I feel fine," he said, and meant it.

"Splendid. Are you hungry?"

Drake had to pause and consider that question. The prospect of food produced no physical reaction. It was as though during five centuries of sleep his body had forgotten the need for sustenance.

Finally he shook his head. "I'm sorry. I just don't know."

Leon nodded sympathetically. "Let us then make the experiment. We will eat a meal at a restaurant. The world has changed much since your time, and there will be much that is different. But the need for nourishment has not changed. It will be reassuring for you to learn that some things are still the same."

Par Leon meant what he said; but to Drake, following him along a short corridor into a deserted white-walled room containing an array of cubicles, each equipped with a single chair and some kind of computer terminal, it seemed that nothing could be less familiar.

This was a restaurant? There were no waiters, no menus, no signs of food or drink. Each cubicle would hold only one person.

His bewilderment showed.

"Ah," Leon said. He seemed uncomfortable for the first time. "I am forgetting the customs of your era. Food today is normally taken alone. Only close associates and family eat in each other's presence." He pointed to a cubicle. "Sit down. The arrangement permits us to talk freely, even though we will be out of sight of each other."

Drake did as he was told, wondering what to do next. Was he supposed to indicate his preferences to the computer? Or would he somehow be fed automatically and ethereally, without the appearance of material foodstuffs? That was inconsistent with Par Leon's claim that food was a constant of the world, but five hundred years was a long time. Interpretations would surely have changed, even when the same words were used.

He looked more closely at the device before him. There was no screen or keyboard, only a flat rectangular box, and in front of that a level featureless surface like a small table.

Par Leon had vanished into a neighboring cubicle.

Drake waited through a long silence. Finally he said, not sure he would be heard, "I have a problem."

"Nothing is to your taste?" Leon's voice was clear, though no other sound had come through from the next room.

"I don't know. I haven't been offered any food."

"That is strange. What did you order?"

"Nothing. I don't know how."

"One moment." Then, after another and shorter silence, "This is my fault entirely. I assumed that general information had been provided to you along with your knowledge of Universal, but that is not so. It is scheduled for your next indoctrination period. The chef in front of you is simple enough to use, and tomorrow you will have no difficulty with it. This evening, however, with your permission I will order the meal for you."

"That's fine." It was Drake's first indication as to the time of day. The room where he had awakened lacked windows, and so did this place. Physically, he had no sense of night, morning, or any diurnal rhythm.

He waited and watched, until in a couple of minutes the box in front of him slid open where he had seen no seam, and delivered a steaming square container of food, a combined knife and fork utensil, and a transparent cylinder filled with red liquid.

The vegetables were colorful but unfamiliar. The meat—if it was meat—could have been flesh, fish, or fowl. But Drake had not been widely traveled in his own time. For all he knew the whole meal could have existed then, as part of the little-known cuisine of some foreign country. He leaned over and sniffed the sauce. A satisfying combination of odors filled his nostrils: cumin, sage, fennel, tarragon. He lifted the tall cylinder and tasted.

At last—thank God—something he recognized. He should have known. Wine had endured through five millennia before his time; it should be no surprise that it continued to cheer humans now, five hundred years later.

He raised his glass in a silent toast—*To us, Ana; we made it this far*—and took a first, deep draft.

Drake had no urge to talk while they were eating, but Par Leon was in a chatty mood. After promising that the world would be explained later while Drake slept, far better than he could do it during dinner and in much greater detail, Leon went ahead and explained anyhow.

It became clear in the next hour where his own interests lay. He had a good but superficial knowledge of Earth civilization and society, but he knew and cared little about the rest of the solar system.

The population of Earth, he said, was half a billion, less than one-tenth of what it had been in Drake's era. It was holding steady now. In the next two centuries it would undergo a planned rise to almost one billion, then decrease again to about its present level. He did not know the reason for the change. That sort of thing was in the hands of the resource management specialists.

And the population of other planets and moons? It was one of Drake's few questions. Par Leon replied with a verbal shrug. There were people living out there, certainly, but who cared how many? Other planets and moons had no long history, in particular no long musical history. Therefore, they were without interest. If Drake wanted to know such strange things, he could do so without taking the valuable time of a human. The machines and data banks were available. Even if Drake had to learn a new language, that also would be no problem. Vocabulary and grammatical rules could be instilled almost instantly using the feedback helmets. Use of language, particularly spoken language, came a little more slowly, because it required physical coordination and practice. A week, maybe, rather than a day.

"But now"—Leon had clearly spent as much time as he wanted to on such dull matters—"let's talk about music."

He did. Happily, and incomprehensibly. Drake did not tell him that he could not understand. He would do his duty and learn about modern music when the time came. For tonight, he was content to sit back, eat and drink, and build his resolve for whatever lay ahead.

A civilization consists of far more than facts, rules, and languages. After a couple of weeks of induced-knowledge nights, Drake began to wonder if some aspects of his new world would be forever beyond him, no matter how long he lived there.

Science was one of them. Twenty-sixth-century science, particularly the basic assumptions that lay beneath it, totally eluded him. It was no surprise that he would find the subject difficult. That had always been the case. In his own time his teachers had accused him of having talent but no interest, and of dreaming his days away with words and music.

Even so, the general ideas of science ought to be accessible. They were supposed to be no more than common sense, elevated to become a discipline. But he found himself struggling hopelessly—and he *was* struggling, hard, working to understand more than he had ever done as a young man. Ana's salvation, when it finally came, would derive from science, not from music.

Finally he sought help—not from Par Leon, who was itching for Drake's indoctrination to end so they could get to work, and who neither knew nor cared about science. Instead Drake dived into the data net, developed beyond anything dreamed of in his own time. He asked for someone who would be willing to translate for him from Science, which he could not speak or write, to Universal. In return he offered knowledge of his own times.

The woman who contacted him had no apparent interest in the early twenty-first century, or at least in the things that Drake might have to say about it. That confirmed the wisdom of his long-ago decision to provoke the curiosity of musical specialists. Cass Leemu was a specialist also, but her own field was one that Drake was unable to comprehend, even in general terms and even after hours of conversation and study. She said it was a form of physics. It seemed to be no more than pictures, that somehow yielded quantitative results.

Cass was a black woman whose age, like Par Leon's, was difficult to determine. She was a tall brunette with a slightly large and blocky head, no eyelashes or eyebrows, and a sumptuous body. Drake suspected minor genetic modifications. Her motive in meeting was either pure curiosity in a specimen of primitive humanity —Drake—or it was for a reason beyond his comprehension.

Her explanations were as clear as they could be, given Universal's limits for scientific explanation.

"It is the typical problem of a major paradigm shift." They were in her private quarters. Cass Leemu was almost naked, lolling back on a couch and scratching her bare belly thoughtfully as she spoke. In an earlier time, Drake reflected, her exposed body would have been a major obstacle to simple information transfer. It would also have been considered a clear invitation.

She went on, "Is the name of Isaac Newton familiar to you?"

"Of course. Gravity, and the laws of motion."

"Right. Familiar, and easy to comprehend. We agree on that. But did you know that most of his contemporaries found his work quite beyond them? He introduced notions of absolute space and time, which they found implausible. They argued, with justice, that only the *separation* between objects could have physical meaning. The idea of absolute coordinates, as opposed to relative distances, made no sense to them. Also, his work was most easily derived and understood employing the calculus, which to the scientists of the seventeenth century was shrouded in the paradoxes of infinitely small quantities. It took three generations to resolve the paradoxes, absorb the new world view, and work with it comfortably. The same thing happened two centuries later, when Maxwell elevated the concept of a *field* to central importance. Many of his contemporaries, to the end of their lives, tried to devise mechanical analogies that dispensed with the need for an electromagnetic field. And in the twentieth century, when uncertainty and undecidability assumed a dominant position in the prevailing world view, even the greatest scientist of his time—Einstein—had trouble accepting them."

"Are you telling me that the same thing happened again, after I entered the cryowomb?"

"Indeed it did." Cass Leemu smiled and stroked her right nipple. It was clear that she considered her action quite empty of erotic content. *Paradigm shift.* Drake was tempted to ask her to have a private meal with him, and see if and where she blushed.

"It has happened not once," she went on, "but three times. There have been three major viewpoint shifts. Our understanding of Nature differs more from the perspectives of your time, than yours differed from the Romans."

"So I am going to be like Newton's colleagues, unable to comprehend a new foundation."

"I am afraid so. Unless you can master the concept of . . ." She paused, then smiled again at Drake, this time apologetically. "I am sorry. The word for the idea that now underpins science lacks any adequate useful paraphrase in Universal. Even the general data banks are silent. But if you really wish to study science, and learn the Science language beginning with the absolute basics, I would be willing to help you."

"I can't do that. Not yet." Drake had already given up any notion of learning science for himself, but he was reluctant to say an outright no to Cass Leemu—he might need her later. "You see, Cass, I owe the next six years to Par Leon. He revived me."

"Of course. Six years only? He is being generous. A sponsor like Par Leon, who chooses an individual in whom no one else has an interest, can set his own terms with the Resurrect."

And there again was the paradigm shift. Cass was pointing out to Drake that the brave new world he now lived in contained other elements at least as hard to grasp as science.

After he had returned to his own spartan living quarters, he worried over the problem. Slavery did not exist. On the other hand, six years of absolute service to Par Leon was taken for granted. It was a form of slavery, but its ethical basis was never questioned. Drake could not understand that basis. He comforted himself with the thought that Henry VIII would have been appalled at wars that killed civilians, while accepting as natural a public hanging, drawing, and quartering.

As he placed his helmet over his head, he wondered what induced lesson he would receive tonight. He felt beyond surprise. Before he lost consciousness, it occurred to him that humanity was able to manage with very few absolutes. Why? Because people could live within—and apparently justify—any imaginable variation of ethics and morality.

Maybe that was why humans had survived.

Gradually, Drake became resigned to his own situation. He did not need to hurry. He had survived. Ana was safe in the Pluto cryowombs. Before he could do anything to change her status he would first have to earn his own freedom. He resolved to give Par Leon six good, solid years of effort toward the other man's great lifetime project: the analysis of musical trends in the late twentieth and early twenty-first centuries. In any case, as a Resurrect what other option did he have?

After the first few months, the shrewdness of Leon's act in reviving Drake was apparent. More important than any facts that he might provide were the perspectives that he could offer into the lifestyles of the late twentieth century. It was far more than just science and ethics that had changed.

Often, his information had Leon shaking his head. "It is truly astonishing. An insanity. Did man-woman relationships really play so large a part in *everything* in your society?"

"You know they did." Drake was learning his way around the data banks, with no help from Leon. "Your own records show it, the ones that we were examining just two days ago."

"Yes. They do show it, but believing it is difficult. Men and women actually appeared to hate each other in your era. Yet at the same time there was much random mating, mating on *impulse*. I do not mean mere sexual acts, that I can comprehend. But random mating that produced *offspring*, without benefit of genome maps or the most rudimentary genetic information on parents and grandparents . . ."

Drake started to explain, and quickly realized that it was hopeless. Here was another five-hundred-year gulf that could not be crossed. To Par Leon, mating was always dictated by the selection of desirable gene combinations. As he said, there was no other way to make sure that the children would be healthy. How could any other approach be justified? He reacted to the idea of reproduction between comparative strangers as Drake regarded public burning at the stake.

In any case, Drake was beginning to have problems of his own. There really was no case to be made for the

production of children, without thought for their future or for their physical and mental well-being. It was,
as Par Leon said, "the blind mating urge of the primeval slime, deified to become religious principle and
blind dogma."

Drake listened to those words and decided that he
was beginning to view his own epoch with a new perspective. He must control that tendency, or his main
value to Par Leon would disappear. For that reason,
and one other, he had to remain an outsider in this
century.

After six months, Drake realized that he was earning his
keep and more. Leon might be the century's foremost
expert on the music of Drake's period, but of some
events and forces he knew nothing. He was endlessly
fascinated by the smallest details.

"You say you *knew* him?" Par Leon leaned forward,
eyebrows raised on his high forehead. "You met Renselm in person?"

"A score of times. I was present at the first performance of Morani's *Concerto concertante,* written especially for Renselm, and I went backstage afterward.
Then we went to dinner, just the three of us. I thought
you already read about all this in one of my articles."

"Oh, yes." Par Leon made a dismissive gesture. "I
certainly *read* it. But this is different. Tell me about his
fingering, his posture at the keyboard, his strange reaction to applause. Tell me what he said to you about
Adele Winterberg—she was his mistress at the time, you
know." He laughed in delight. "Tell me, if you can
remember it, what you all ate for dinner."

Only once or twice did Par Leon express dissatisfac-
tion. And then it was because Drake had been frozen
just before some event that especially interested him.
"If you had only waited another three years . . ." he

would say; but he spoke philosophically and with good humor.

It was by no means a one-way transfer of information. From his vantage point five centuries ahead, Par Leon had insights into the musical life of an earlier era that left Drake gasping. For the first time he understood where certain contemporary musical currents had been heading in his own time. Krubak, in his much-ridiculed late works, had been feeling his way toward forms that would not mature until thirty years after Drake had been frozen.

The work went on, ten to twelve hours a day. If Leon ever wondered why Drake showed no curiosity at seeing firsthand the world as it had become in the twenty-sixth century, or in making other friends, or even in learning the twists and turns of human progress over the past five centuries, he never mentioned it.

For his part, Drake had no desire to be absorbed by or become part of the current society. Yet he had to know certain subjects in great detail, far more than Par Leon could tell him. Fortunately, the general data banks permitted near-infinite cross-checking and depth of inquiry.

Drake began to satisfy his own unique information needs.

The whole solar system had been explored and mapped in detail. Venus was in the first stages of terraforming, the acid witch's brew of its atmosphere creeping down in temperature and pressure. Mars had been colonized, not on the surface but within the extensive natural caverns beneath. There were permanent active stations—many of them "manned" by self-replicating computers and repair devices—on all the satellites of the major planets.

It was progress; yet to Drake it was less than expected. The projections made in his own time had seen the whole solar system crawling with humans and their intelligent machines. Sometime in the past five centuries, priorities had changed.

But what about Pluto?

Drake gave that little world his special attention. A small crew of scientists had a research station on Charon, the outsized satellite that made the Pluto-Charon system into a small planetary doublet. Pluto itself was uninhabited, unless one counted the dreaming serried ranks of the cryocorpses. The cryowombs were too cold for the comfortable permanent presence of animate humans. They hovered down at liquid helium temperature (Drake's earlier suspicion of liquid nitrogen storage had proved well founded). The vaults were tended, to the extent that they needed any sort of attention, by machines especially designed for extreme cold.

With the idea of money subsumed into some incomprehensible system of electronic credit, it was not clear to Drake when he would be able to afford to make the long trip out to Pluto. He forced himself to be patient, putting the question to one side until his time of service was closer to its end.

The work went on, hard but certainly not unrewarding. The text that they were producing grew steadily. By the beginning of the fourth year, Drake shared Par Leon's conviction that they were producing a classic. He listened to the suggestion that in fairness the two of them should be given equal credit, and shook his head.

"It was all your idea, Leon, not mine. You could have found someone else to do what I have done. But without you to revive me I could have done nothing . . ."

. . . *and if you shared credit with me, I would not be here long enough to take it. As soon as possible, I will be gone.*

That was the secret goal, thought about constantly but never mentioned.

And then, at the end of the fourth year, an event took place that changed all Drake's plans.

Chapter 7

"A wild call and a clear call that may not be denied"

$\mathscr{D}$rake was working. It was late or early, depending on the definition. The improvements to his body included a lessened need for sleep, and he did most of his private thinking and searching long after midnight. Tonight he had lost track of the hour as he strove to understand, for the hundredth time, the complex medical environment of Ana's disease. He could see why an ailment that had been bred out of the human race would attract little attention in the present day; but it seemed to him that treatments for other conditions might apply to this one.

He was toying with the daunting idea of learning Medicine—a multiyear commitment—when his outer portal reported a caller. He glanced up at the clock. Eight in the morning. He had time for a short nap, then he ought to call Par Leon and plan the rest of the day. They worked together flexibly and well, swapping opinions and thoughts and notes whenever either of them felt it useful; but they seldom met in person.

So who could be visiting, so early and uninvited? He lived in a tiny apartment. It was furnished with minimal facilities, and in four years he had never had a visitor.

The portal again reported a request for attention. He approved it, and stood up as the interlocking doors opened.

The caller was a woman. She did not wait for Drake's invitation before she entered. She walked in and swept her gaze over the interior of the apartment. She seemed to take everything in with a single glance from a pair of sapphire-blue eyes.

"You're Drake Merlin," she said firmly. "I'm Melissa Bierly."

She looked right at him, and he experienced for the first time the full force of her. Even long afterward, even when he knew the whole story, he was never able to explain the source of that peculiar power. She was striking looking, certainly, with a round, symmetrical face framed by straight black hair and wide eyes of pure deep blue; but a composer, especially one who had written music for movies, was exposed to many striking women. His first impression was that she was tall. Then she came closer and he realized that he was wrong. Her head scarcely came to his nose.

"Do I know you?" Drake said at last. He was sure that he did not. He had met hundreds of people since his awakening, usually through Par Leon and their mutual researches; but he would not have forgotten Melissa Bierly.

"Apparently not, though it would have been possible —just." She had switched to English. "We were around at the same time, but you were frozen when I was only one year old. I went to the cryowombs twenty-four years later, and this is the first resurrection for each of us."

Dead at twenty-five—younger even than Ana. Drake gestured to a chair, and she nodded and sat down. He sat on the low bed, facing her.

The sapphire eyes looked right inside him as she

went on, "I was revived two months ago. As soon as I could, I checked how many of us there are. Do you know that number?"

He shook his head, still without speaking. It was a question of no interest. At best it was irrelevant to his needs; at worst it would lead to an interaction with other Resurrects. That could waste time and distract him from his goals.

"There were fewer than fifty thousand placed in the cryowombs," Melissa went on. "Forty-eight thousand eight hundred and ninety-seven, to be exact. Most of them entered the cryowombs within fifty years after me. Apparently the idea went out of fashion when the revival success rate remained at zero for so long. Also, life expectancy had increased. Of the total frozen, only a hundred and thirty-two have been resurrected. How many of those have you met?"

"None."

"That's what I thought. As soon as I arrived, one of my first acts was to contact the other Resurrects. They form a closely knit group."

"I am not surprised to learn it." Drake was speaking in English, too, and he felt the shift in mental gears. It was his first use of the language in almost four years. It brought a surge of longing for the past, as strong and inexplicable as life returning with the spring.

He knew that his answer to Melissa Bierly had not been quite an honest one. He had examined the data base of Resurrects. He did not remember how many there were, but he recalled that they lived in a colony of their own and spent all their leisure time together.

"But you are unique," Melissa said. The eyes were boring into Drake. "You alone have had no contact with any of the others."

"Did they tell you to come and see me?" The presence of the woman was producing an effect on Drake, relaxing and unnerving him at the same time. Her gray dress was as concealing as Cass Leemu's scanty outfits were revealing, but with Melissa Bierly there was a crackling undercurrent of tension. He did not know if it was sexual or from some other cause. He had not generated it, and he did not want it. But it was there.

The dark head shook firmly, while the eyes never left his. "The others said nothing to me, except inviting me to join their group. I came to you precisely because of your aloofness. You see, I wish to undertake a project. I wish to see what the world has become, everywhere from pole to pole. I do not want to travel with a group. But I do want a companion."

Even before he replied, Drake felt the insidious lure of her suggestion. A knowledge of the world as it was now could only increase the chances of his own success. The data banks were vast beyond imagining, but surely they did not contain everything. Suppose that, in some far-off corner of the Earth, information existed that would allow Ana to be cured?

"Well?" Melissa had moved to stand in front of him, her hands on her hips.

He shook his head. "I'm afraid it's impossible. I'm busy on a long-term collaborative project."

"If it's long-term, why can't it wait a little while?" She moved closer and reached out to touch his hand. It was their first contact, and Drake felt the irrational spark of attraction.

"We wouldn't need to be gone long," she continued. She was smiling down at him. "Come on, come with me. Just for a few weeks. Surely you must have taken breaks in your work before."

"Never."

"How long have you been working on this project?"

"Four years."

She stared at him incredulously. "Without any time off at all? You *deserve* a vacation, and I'll bet you need one. Why not call your collaborator and see if he will agree to it?"

Drake felt no need of a vacation. He had resisted the

idea strongly, the half-dozen times that Par Leon suggested it. He had known Melissa Bierly for less than a quarter of an hour. But, beyond his comprehension, he found himself reaching out to call Par Leon.

Leon was sure to say no. There was no way, given the current status of the project, that he would agree. While the call was going through, Drake told himself to expect a refusal. And once Leon had said no, Drake would have something tangible to counterbalance his own irrational urge to say yes, and go off with Melissa to the ends of the Earth.

Then the screen was alive, Par Leon's open, dignified face was staring out at them, and Drake was making a half-coherent request to delay their work for a while.

And Leon was nodding, even before Drake had finished. "Of course you may go. I have plenty of work that I can manage very well in your absence. The project will not suffer. Go, and enjoy."

Even in Drake's dazed state of mind he felt that there was something wrong. Par Leon had no expression in his voice. It was as if the request had come to him as a follow-up on some earlier conversation. Also, Leon had not asked when Drake wanted to go, or where, or how long he might be away. And Drake had provided none of that information. Indeed, he did not know it himself.

But before he could speak again, Leon was gone; and Melissa had taken both his hands in hers and was lifting him easily to his feet.

"There," she said. "What did I tell you? Now that's done, we can sit down together and make plans and begin to get to know each other. You're very cramped in here. Why don't we go to my place? It's a lot more comfortable."

Drake thought for one moment of Ana. She lay secure in her frigid cryowomb, on far-off Pluto. But it was Melissa, warm and breathing and somehow compelling, who held his hands. It was her sparkling blue eyes, rather than Ana's gray ones, that smiled into his.

Unresisting, he allowed her to lead him to the door and out of his little apartment.

Drake was heading for the open air of Earth for the first time in five hundred years. Since the surface seemed to play no part in his plans after his resurrection, he had ignored its existence during his time working with Par Leon. And if he had been asked what he expected to find as the elevator carried him upward, he would have been hard put to provide a single answer. In any case, the answers he might have given were nothing like what he and Melissa found when the deep elevator finally reached the surface.

In the past few days she had taken charge of their lives. Although she had been thawed for less than seventy days, she seemed to know more than Drake about everything in their new world. After the first twenty-four hours he had surrendered his independence. She was like a force of nature. He did not attempt to argue with her or resist her. She knew where they were going, how they would get there, what they would do when they arrived.

Only occasionally, when they were waiting for something, did he notice a difference. The forceful, all-competent manner changed. The blue eyes became frenzied and crazy, and dark shadows crossed her face like demons.

It was happening now. They were at the surface, and the giant elevator doors were ready to release them to the outside air. Melissa should have been bubbling over with energy and excitement. Instead she was withdrawn, staring at the floor a few feet in front of them as if she saw all the devils of Hell in the pattern of tiles. It was Drake who was wide-eyed and curious, too absorbed to worry about the change in Melissa. Even the doors themselves aroused his interest. They had not opened, like normal doors, but seemed to dissolve to gray mist and then quietly vanish. Was this what the induced teaching meant, when it referred to "the transforming technology provided by a mastery of molecular bonds"?

He stared through the doors as they silently faded. Half a dozen possibilities filled his mind as to what he might see outside: a world completely paved over, with roads and vehicles everywhere? vast amounts of airborne traffic of strange and unfamiliar design, flying above his head? postnuclear devastation? gigantic buildings, arcologies in which half a million people could live? shimmering heat, as global warming ruled; or sheeted ice and visible breath, the precursors to some new Ice Age held at bay in his own time only by the widespread burning of fossil fuels? Or maybe the ozone layer was lost, and sunlight was now so fierce and strong in ultraviolet radiation that unshielded skin would turn purple black within minutes.

All these, and more, had been confidently predicted.

Drake looked. He saw an endless prairie, dotted in the distance with small clumps of trees. Of humans, and human influence, there was no sign. Melissa came to his side and took his hand. He glanced at her and saw that she was back once more to her usual confident self. She began to lead the way, walking toward that faroff blue-gray skyline.

As they went, Melissa explained. She had returned to her normal manner instantly, as soon as the doors were fully open and the surface beyond was visible.

"I could certainly see the signs in my time," she said, "and I'd be surprised if they weren't already visible in yours. If I was asked to provide a single word for what started the change, I'd give one that I've never seen quoted: glass. Before people had glass, there was a time when they didn't have buildings at all. They lived outside, in the middle of whatever was out there—animals of all sizes, from fleas to elephants. They might not have liked it, but they couldn't do a thing about it. As time went on people learned to make buildings and could live indoors. But if you wanted to see what you were doing, there had to be holes in the walls to let in light. You could make the holes small, so the elephants and wolves and bears couldn't get in. But there was no way of making the holes big enough to let light in, yet small enough to keep insects and spiders and wood lice and centipedes out. People still expected to live in the middle of bugs of all kinds. So they squashed them, or encouraged them—spiders will keep your house free of flies—or just put up with them.

"But then cheap, good-quality glass became available. You could make windows that let the light in and kept the bugs out. And that's when people started to think that spiders and cockroaches and ants were 'dirty,' and even 'unnatural.' I've known women who would scream if they found a decent-sized spider in their bathroom. And as for doing *this*—"

She reached down to the tall grass at their feet, and stood up again holding a big grasshopper gently in her cupped hands. "I knew people who wouldn't touch a harmless bug like this, not if you paid them. Don't you think it's peculiar, even the word *dirty* changed its meaning. We're walking on dirt. Dirt is everywhere. It's totally natural. The ground is made of dirt. But when you live in a totally artificial environment, shielded from the outside, you never see real earth. 'Dirty' things become completely *unnatural,* and you avoid them. The good news is, when people wanted less and less to go outside, because it was full of beetles and gnats and worms and earwigs and leeches, they were willing to let the surface become more like the way it used to be before humans took over." She bent down, released the grasshopper, and pointed away to their left. "Not just grasshoppers and bees and flies, either.

Go twenty to thirty kilometers that way, you'll find gazelles and wildebeest and cheetahs. Maybe lions, too.''

"Are we in the tropics? Or has the climate changed?'' One other confident prediction of Drake's own time had been that in another generation all the hoofed wildlife and the big predators would be gone.

"We're in what used to be Africa, about ten degrees north of the equator. It's what you would call Ethiopia. There has been some climate change, too. Think of this as just like Serengeti, even though it isn't.'' Melissa pointed again, this time upward toward the afternoon sun. "One reason it's not too hot, it's midwinter and we're fifteen hundred meters above sea level. Feel it in your lungs?'' And, as Drake drew in a deep breath of thin but warm and pollen-laden air, she added, "Come on. You've been stuck inside for four years, or maybe it's five hundred and four. Let's see what sort of job they did when they tuned up your body.''

She had given up the usual gray dress in favor of bright pink shorts and a red T-shirt. Her legs were shapely but well muscled. She began to run toward the nearest grove of trees, maybe a mile and a half away. After a moment Drake set out in pursuit. They were each carrying a backpack, which when Drake had put it on seemed to weigh next to nothing. Within the first quarter of a mile he changed his mind. He could feel it bouncing up and down on his back, the straps cutting into his shoulders. How could a meal weigh nothing when it was on the inside of you, and so much when you were carrying it on the outside?

He began to pant harder and felt in his calves and thighs the first pain of fatigue and oxygen starvation. The altitude made a tremendous difference, far more than he would have expected, and he had not taken regular exercise since he was thawed. His new body was supposed to make it unnecessary. He forced himself to run for another couple of minutes, then he had to stop. He had forgotten what it was like to be physically exhausted. He dropped heavily to the ground, and lay there panting on the dry, grassy soil.

All the time that he was running, Melissa had steadily increased her lead. She went all the way to the trees, circled them, and headed back at the same speed. She came to where he lay and stood by him with her legs wide apart and her hands on her hips.

Drake rolled on to his back and stared up at her. "What did they do with *your* body?"

"Not a thing. This is the original me." She squatted at his side. She wasn't even panting. "Now do you agree that it was a good idea to get you away from work for a while?"

"If it doesn't kill me when my heart gives out."

"It won't. Any problems like that would have been taken care of. Come on." She reached down and helped him rise to his feet. "We have to keep going if we want to get to a monitor lodge before darkness."

That sounded to Drake like an excellent idea. Lions might be twenty kilometers away. But how far were they likely to travel when they were hunting?

Melissa didn't seem worried, although fast and fit as she was she could not outspeed a hungry lion. On the other hand, it occurred to Drake that she didn't have to. All she had to do was run faster than him.

Drake's idea of Earth's future transportation system, if he had had one at all, was vague, busy, and grandiose— the chaotic vehicle mix of the late twentieth century, extrapolated to become faster, busier, and more tangled.

If the quiet open prairie had not set him right during the afternoon, Melissa did so that night. "The transportation system is all there," she said, "and according to the reports it's an excellent one. You can get anywhere in the world in just a few hours. We'll see it for ourselves when we use it tomorrow. But it's not heavily used. A few sightseers like us; and that's about it.''

They had settled into a comfortable lodge, empty except for service machines, and they were eating dinner. It was Drake's fourth meal with another human being since he had been resurrected. After three years of work together, Par Leon had shyly asked Drake if he would like to have dinner in person every three or four months. Drake took that for what it was, a sincere gesture of approval and friendship.

"So what happened?" he asked Melissa, as their empty plates vanished into the table. "I know that the population is down by a factor of ten from our time, but there still ought to be lots of traffic—people and goods. Why isn't there?"

She sighed, with the tolerance of a person with a full stomach. Although she was smaller than Drake, she had eaten at least twice as much. But there was no fat on her body. He put it down to her high burn rate and her endless energy.

"You really did tune out for four years, didn't you?" she said. "It must take a positive effort *not* to know what's going on in the world."

"I was planning to learn a lot about transportation systems, on this planet and off it. But not yet."

"There's less to learn than you might imagine. We could have guessed this, too, if we'd bothered to think. Why do people need transportation?"

"To carry goods from where they're made to where they're needed. To take people to work, and to let them meet each other."

"What you're describing is nowadays called a primitive industrial society. You and I lived at the end of that, though I don't think we knew it. Automated manufacturing and telework were just about to take off in our time. We are now in a postindustrial, machine-supported society. You don't need to carry goods when they can be made on the spot from simple raw materials. The manufacturing is all done by machines, smart enough so they don't need people to watch over them. People still work, but no one goes to work anymore. They don't need to. You must know that from your own project. You told me you don't actually *see* Par Leon more than once a month, and you could get by very well without that."

"So why is there a transportation system at all?"

"Because a few people want one and use one. Because it doesn't really cost anything to maintain it—the machines do all that, without a single human being involved. Same as this lodge. When we arrived, our meals were cooked and our beds prepared, and we didn't even have to request it. It's an odd thought, but if all the people were to die, the housekeeper here probably wouldn't notice. It would carry on as usual. I doubt if there's another person—I mean on the surface —within a hundred miles."

Drake went to the window and gazed out into the warm African night. It was bright moonlight, and fifty yards away he could see head-high grass swaying as some large invisible animal moved through it.

No other humans within a hundred miles of here. But there was a deeper question. What was *he* doing here?

He could not give an answer that made sense. Somehow, Melissa Bierly's requests carried the weight of absolute commands. He did not know how to refuse. If she told him to go outside and face hungry lions, he was sure that he would do it.

And there was another question. What was *she* doing here? Her desire to see the world made sense only if she was looking for something—or running from something.

He could not imagine what; but later, when they were lying side by side in the lodge's quiet bedroom, he heard her sighs. Melissa was moaning softly in her sleep. And every few minutes, until he finally fell asleep himself, he heard the sound of grinding teeth.

Morning restored Melissa's cheerfulness and drive. She announced that she had changed her mind. She wanted to head upward, to the top of the peak that loomed to the northeast, before they used the transportation system and flew to South America.

"Birhan?" Drake had called up a large-scale map and asked for an optimal route. Now he called up a topographic map. "Are you sure? It's a brute. According to this it rises above thirteen thousand feet. We won't be able to breathe."

"I'll breathe for both of us." Melissa was bursting with energy. "I'll help you, and we won't go all the way to the top. Just enough to get a view. Come on, let's go."

The housekeeper had anticipated their need for packaged food, just as it had provided breakfast and had a car ready. It knew which maps Drake had demanded, and it had decided that Birhan was not within a day's walk for a human.

The hovercar moved smoothly, about three feet above the surface, and made almost no noise. It handled all kinds of terrain with ease, water as well as land. When they drifted across the rocky near-dry course of a broad river, Drake looked up from the display that was tracing out their path.

"This is the Blue Nile. I wonder what happened to it."

"Diverted, four hundred years ago." As usual, Melissa knew everything. "It was once completely dry. It looks as though the old dams are breaking down. No one needs them anymore."

The ground was rising steadily, and the hovercar was following the upward slope effortlessly. So far as Drake was concerned he would have been happy to ride all the way to the snow-capped peak ahead. Melissa had other ideas.

"This will do." She stopped the car. "We're at eight thousand feet. Let's head for that, and eat when we get there. The car will stay here."

She was pointing, not at the mountain but at the display. It showed a small flattened area where the hillside leveled off about two thousand feet above them. It could be approached easily from one side, but the contour lines suggested that the other edge ended in a sheer thousand-foot drop.

Melissa jumped lightly down from the car. Drake did the same, less lightly. He flexed his shoulders. Already he was aware that his lungs were working harder.

They started up. Melissa seemed to have an instinct for the easiest route, and rather than competing, Drake stayed two paces behind and followed her lead. He was afraid that it would be worse than the day before, but Melissa held to a slow, steady pace that he could live with. They were both wearing heavier clothing. Melissa had on thick blue pants and a padded jacket that exactly matched the color of her eyes. Drake wondered how the lodge housekeeper had made or found the color—how it even *knew* the color.

Today, at this altitude, warm clothes were necessary. Drake felt the tingling in his ears. The breeze at his back was chilly, but it seemed to help by pushing him along.

Helped for a while, at least. He was still relieved when they breasted the final rise and emerged onto the little plateau. Melissa did not stop, but went walking over to the far side of it.

"There," she said. "That's why we're here. That's Africa."

She was pointing out to the west. Drake came to her side, then at once stepped back, appalled. The view was incredible. He could see what seemed like hundreds of miles across hills and plains. But they were standing at the very edge of a sheer cliff. It was so steep, it could not be natural. Someone, sometime, for some inexplicable reason, had sheered the whole mountain side to a rock face that dropped vertically without ledges or breaks to a boulder-strewn chasm a thousand feet below.

"Be careful, Melissa." He backed farther and sat down. There was a gusty wind blowing on the plateau, and to be anywhere near the edge was terrifying.

She turned and grinned at him. "You don't need to worry about me. Watch."

While he stared in horror she closed her eyes and walked along the very edge, so close that at each blind step only a part of her foot met the rock. When he was convinced that she must fall, she turned and sauntered over to him.

"All right, then. Lunch?"

"Lunch, dinner, anything you like—as long as you stay away from that edge."

"You worry too much, Drake." She sat down casually at his side. "Can't you see I could do this sort of thing all day, and never get hurt?"

He believed her, but to his relief she followed his lead and removed her backpack. He looked across to the other side of the plateau, with its easy descent. With any luck Melissa would feel they had done enough climbing for the day.

They began to eat. Even in midwinter, the sunlight at this latitude was intense. It picked out every detail of Melissa's face: the contented smile, the glow of perfect skin, and the dazzling blue eyes. Drake decided that he had never in his life seen a woman who looked healthier.

He was staring right at her when the change came. She had just crunched a crisp piece of celery. As she swallowed, the corners of her mouth turned down. Her face flushed darker, responding to a sudden rush of blood. The splendid eyes stared fixedly at nothing, then glared all around.

"It has to be," she said. "It has to be."

She stood up. While Drake sat frozen she walked back five steps. He was still trying to scramble to his feet when she ran forward and hurled herself over the sheer edge of the cliff.

"Melissa!" He forgot his own fears and ran to the edge.

She was falling, her arms held wide. She did not change her position, and she did not cry out. Drake stared in horror as her blue-clad figure diminished in size. Already she had dropped hundreds of feet. Her pose was a swan dive, perfectly balanced like a high diver in the first phase of descent. But instead of water, beneath her lay nothing but solid rock and sharp-sided boulders.

When nothing in the world could save her, the whole cliff face erupted suddenly from top to bottom. It threw off a cloud of dust atoms like a shaken carpet. Instead of falling or spreading, the particles converged to form a dense gray plume that coalesced further as it swooped after Melissa's plummeting body. When it was in the right position, it spread to form a gray blanket beneath her.

She must have seen it coming. She began to scream and flail, trying to avoid contact with the gray layer by changing the line of her fall. It was no good. The blanket reached her and folded itself about her. Drake saw her arms, protruding from the swaddling cover and beating at it desperately.

The downward plunge had been arrested. While he watched, the gray cylinder of blanket moved rapidly to the right, away from the main body of the mountain. In less than a minute it had vanished from his sight.

Drake stared down. Melissa was gone, but the rocky landscape at the foot of the cliff seemed to crawl and surge below him like an oily sea. His legs were too weak to support him. He cried out, and dropped to the rough surface of rock and gravel. He scrabbled at it with his fingers, trying to pull himself away from the edge.

He was still sitting, staring blindly into the fierce winter sunlight, when a wingless craft drifted down to his side.

"It's all right, Drake." Par Leon was inside the air-car. His voice was apologetic. A stony-faced woman was at his side. "Everything will be all right. We're going to take you home."

Chapter 8

Incomplete Superwoman

The woman's name was Rozi Tegger. Par Leon made it clear, more from his body language than his comments, that she was not a close friend. Both he and Tegger were handling Drake with great care, responding to his dazed questions as the aircar flew them home.

To Drake, only two questions really mattered: *Is she alive? Is she all right?*

"Melissa Bierly is certainly alive," Tegger replied. Leon yielded to her the first phase of explanation. "However, she is far from all right."

"She's hurt?"

"Not at all. Neither of you was in real danger, though we didn't want you to know it. You were monitored from the moment that you left the lodge."

"The hovercar?"

"That, and more than that. And far smaller. The automated safety service makes its own observing and protection units, and there were many billions of them in use all around you today. The ensemble that saved Melissa, after she threw herself off the cliff, is fairly typical. Each unit masses only a fraction of a gram. Each has sensors, flight capability, and real-time communication that allows all units to act in concert. Melissa tried to steer herself away from them and fall headfirst onto the rocks; but in reality she didn't have a chance.''

"I saw, but I don't understand. Melissa had everything to live for. Why would she try to kill herself?''

Par Leon and Rozi Tegger stared at each other. The tension in the car could not be missed.

"You have to tell him, you know,'' Leon said. "If you don't, I will. If you weren't prepared to do this, you never should have started.''

"I never thought it would turn out this way.''

"Nor did I; but it did.''

"I know, I know.'' Rozi Tegger sighed. "Very well, I'll do it.'' She turned to Drake. "How much did you learn from Melissa Bierly of her background?''

"I know that she was born one year before I entered the cryowombs. I know that she lived for twenty-four more years, then died and entered the cryowombs herself.''

"And that is all?''

"All I remember.''

"Very well.'' Rozi Tegger, like Par Leon, could have been any age. She had thick, chestnut-brown hair, and now she ran her fingers through it. "Let me begin at the real beginning, fifteen years before Melissa Bierly was born.

"The structure of DNA had been known for fifty years, and the first mapping of the human genome had just been completed. Molecular biologists were riding high. A few people were already worrying about the ethical problems involved in playing with human genetic structure, but none of the rules that we have now had been put in place. In fact, to our eyes your original time is most perplexing. Those who felt comfortable about gene manipulation to *cure* disease were often the same people who were strongly opposed to mandatory genetic selection to *avoid* disease. *Eugenics* was a socially unacceptable word.

"When technology flourishes and suitable laws are not in place to constrain its uses, there will surely be trouble.

"A group of scientists with strong social and political goals decided to employ the emerging technology to benefit the human race. They were well intentioned, we do not dispute that. They were also permitted to operate with a freedom unthinkable today. They saw ways to modify the human genome so as to create persons stronger, more intelligent, more long-lived, and more resistant to disease. That is what they did."

"Superman," Drake murmured. But he did so in English, and Rozi Tegger frowned at him in confusion.

"Superior men," Drake added, this time in Universal. "Supermen."

Tegger nodded. "And superior women. Do I have to say more? We did not change the body of Melissa Bierly upon resurrection, as yours was changed. We did not need to. You saw her, yet you were exposed to little of her full potential. She could run to the top of Birhan, or mountains far higher than that, without breathing equipment and without feeling fatigue. She could spend a winter night naked amid mountaintop snow and ice, and come down unharmed. She could hang from the cliff where we found you by one finger, hour after hour.

"But those are mere physical improvements, and we judge them trivial. Of far greater interest are the *mental* characteristics of Melissa Bierly and others like her. She has outstanding intellect. In two months she has come to understand more of this time, and what is in it, than most of us. She mastered access to the general data banks as though born to them. She became conversant with a dozen languages, from Economics to Astronautics, and made their cross-connections with ease.

"But these accomplishments are no better than those of many machines; although we can admire them, they are not the reason for Melissa's resurrection. My own field of study is . . ." She paused, then said three syllables in Universal that meant nothing to Drake. "I'm sorry, I know that the subject did not exist in your time. You can think of it as the study of all modes of influence. How does one individual persuade another? It is certainly not by words alone. By sound, yes, but also by body position and touch and pheromonal transfer and many other agents. This has been true through all of history. It may well predate the use of spoken language. What fascinated me about Melissa were the records of incredible persuasive force reported for her and her kin. I could not explain it, and I wanted to see for myself. Could it be real?"

"It's real." Drake saw in his mind the sparkling sapphire eyes. "It's more than what you say. She didn't *persuade* me. She made me *want* to do whatever she liked. If she had asked me to jump off the cliff with her, I think I would have done it. But you haven't explained what happened. *Why* did she jump?"

"She did not jump. She *dived*. The distinction is important." Rozi Tegger looked at Par Leon, who nodded grimly.

"Go on. I know this is especially painful for you, but Merlin has earned our explanation."

"Very well." Tegger turned unhappily to Drake. "You spent days with Melissa. Did you ever see changes of mood in her?"

"You couldn't miss it. Most of the time she was full of bounce and cheerfulness. But now and again she seemed angry or worried or desperate. It could switch in a second."

"But you never questioned her as to the way in which she died, before she entered the cryowombs?"

"We didn't talk about that."

"Or of her siblings and kinfolk?"

"It never came up."

"That is not surprising. There were sixteen children in that 'superior' experimental group, including Melissa herself. So far as I can tell, each of them enjoyed an equal degree of physical and mental advantage. However, it is impossible to prove this. No other was placed with Second Chance. And for good reason. All of them, except Melissa, died in such a way that the brain was destroyed. All of them committed suicide. So did Melissa, but she did it by slashing her throat. She thought that no one would find her body for hours, by which time her brain would be past recovery. But she was wrong. She was discovered by accident, very quickly, and prepared for the cryowomb by the scientists who had made her. They knew that they had created an incomplete superior form, one who for unknown reasons was driven to self-destruction. They left posterity to decide where they had gone wrong."

Rozi Tegger sighed. The aircar had entered a deep shaft and was descending. Their journey was almost over.

"And I," she went on, "I in my hubris believed that I could succeed where my ancestors had failed. I would resurrect the one remaining 'superwoman,' to borrow your word. I would make changes, very minor ones, not to her body but to her mind. And then my experiment could begin. Melissa would be allowed to go her way; and by observing her I would learn the nature of her unnatural power to persuade others.

"But in truth I learned only one thing: that the changes I made to Melissa were useless; that the death wish is as strong in her as ever."

"She didn't know about the safety service," Par Leon added, "any more than you did, Merlin. And she didn't just want to *die*."

"She wanted total self-destruction," Rozi Tegger

said. "You saw how she dived. She wanted to do what she had failed to do five centuries ago. She wanted her brain so completely pulped that there could be no thought of repair and resurrection."

Drake saw again in his mind that dwindling blue-clad doll figure, dropping forever down the stark cliff face. Melissa knew how to control her body attitude perfectly. She would have held the swan dive to the end. If the gray cloud of tiny rescue machines had not interfered, her head would have smashed and splattered against solid rock.

He felt sick: at the thought of what might have happened to Melissa, and also at the realization of the effortless power she had held over him. She had made him ignore his own vows in order to do her bidding.

"But Melissa is still alive. What will happen to her now?" He was almost afraid to hear the answer. If she were released, and came back to him. . . .

"That decision is not mine to make," Tegger said heavily. The car had come to a halt, and she was climbing down from it with the stiff-limbed action of an old, old woman. "It was decreed in advance, before permission could be given for my experiment. If I failed, Melissa Bierly would once more enter Second Chance. That is happening even as we speak. She will remain in the cryowombs until someone—some person much cleverer than I—can free her of that random and irresistible urge for self-immolation."

"Will you be all right?" Par Leon spoke anxiously, and he was addressing not Drake but Rozi Tegger. "Shouldn't you stay a while with us before you go home?"

"I can safely leave." Rozi Tegger gave Leon a grim smile. "I thank you for your consideration, but despite my depressed mood I do not propose to do away with myself. For I am, as I have proved to you so very clearly, far from being a superwoman."

•   •   •

Par Leon tried to pretend that the whole episode was over. Drake had to visit Leon and corner him, in person, the next day before they started work.

"There is something that was never explained to me," he said. "I did not ask you when Rozi Tegger was with us, but I think you owe me an answer now."

Par Leon was not good at dissembling. He craned his neck to one side and would not look at Drake. "Indeed?"

"Indeed. I can see very well why Rozi Tegger resurrected Melissa, because it related to her own field of study. But you never met Melissa, and you were never exposed to her power of persuasion. She could add nothing to the work that you and I have been doing, and she could detract from it by slowing our progress. So why did you allow me to go off with her to the surface? Why didn't you say no?"

Leon did not answer at once, and when he did his question astonished Drake. "Did you, uh," he said, "uh, did you . . . that is . . ." He paused. "Forgive me for asking, but did you and Melissa Bierly enter into a sexual relationship?"

It was Drake's turn to hesitate. "Yes," he said at last. "Yes, we did. When we were staying at the lodge."

It was a lie, and a possibly unsafe one. Drake knew that he and Melissa had been monitored from the time that they left the lodge. Wasn't it likely that the same automatic safety service had observed everything inside the lodge? And although sex would presumably not have triggered the rescue process, the records of the night at the lodge might be on file somewhere in the data banks.

But Par Leon was nodding and smiling. "I thought so. And that is why I agreed to your going, although I knew that we would sacrifice a little work time.

"I had been worried about you," he went on, before

Drake could express his perplexity. "I like to work hard, but you seemed to work incessantly. You did not —forgive me for my intrusiveness, but I thought it important, so I checked—you did not ever form a relationship with any man or woman, although your body modifications at resurrection permit and actually benefit from sexual activity. You had remained celibate for four years. And there was the matter of the woman in the cryowombs, your former wife. Several times, you alluded to her."

Had he? Drake did not recall doing so, but there was no reason for Leon to lie.

"I wondered," Leon continued. "Your obsession with the woman Anastasia was supposedly cured during resurrection. But was it possible that it had been done incorrectly? I wondered this, long before we learned yesterday of another case where changes made at resurrection were unsuccessful. So I was delighted when you called me, to request time to travel with Melissa Bierly. I knew little about her at the time, except the important thing: she was not Anastasia. I agreed, gladly. And as you see, although Rozi Tegger is disappointed by the outcome, I am not. You proved that you have indeed conquered your old obsession. There is no danger of a new obsession, with Melissa Bierly. My fears have been put to rest, and our work can go forward together with new confidence."

He beamed at Drake, who slowly nodded. "I have only one more question. Why did Melissa choose me, of all the Resurrects?"

"I can only pass along to you the conjecture of Rozi Tegger. You alone possess an independence of mind and spirit. The other Resurrects cluster together and follow each other. You pursue your own agenda, steadfastly. Melissa Bierly liked that. And also, she conceivably thought of it as a challenge to her own powers."

It had not been, not at all. Drake realized that. He

was dismayed by his own lack of resolve. From now on, he would keep his goal clearly in focus.

And one more thing, above all others: he must never again, under any circumstances, mention Ana's name to Par Leon.

Par Leon's great project continued, faster than expected. He and Drake worked together as a perfect team. By the middle of the sixth year they were approaching completion. They had also become close friends, or as close as Drake dared to permit; close enough, however, to sense that Par Leon, a good man by any moral compass that Drake would ever be able to comprehend, was beginning to worry about something else.

He said little to Drake, beyond hinting at other possible collaborations. Drake read the deeper concern. What would the future hold when the project ended? It had apparently not occurred to Par Leon six years ago, but a resurrection was not unlike a birth. And now, like a parent, Par Leon felt responsibility for the future of his "offspring."

Drake was soon able to reassure him, and in an unexpected way. While they were still putting the finishing touches to their mammoth study of the "ancient" music of the twentieth and early twenty-first centuries, he started to compose again. He had learned during the project that musical knowledge of the time before his birth had some big gaps in it, and facility in different musical idioms had always come easily to him. He could steal tricks from the giants of the past, dress them in a modern style, and pass it off as innovation.

In less than a year he had a burgeoning reputation, which he knew was undeserved, a group of imitators, largely untalented, and—most important—a growing financial credit.

At last he could delicately explore a long-postponed

question. He chose his moment carefully, when Par Leon was euphoric over a particular section on thematic influences that Drake had just completed.

"A couple of days more, and I will be finished." Drake did his best to sound casual. "How about you?"

He knew the answer. They had agreed that Leon would be responsible for the final overall review, to ensure uniformity of style.

"Four weeks, at least, from the time that I have all the pieces." Leon sounded apologetic. "I can't do the final assembly in any less time."

"You shouldn't rush. The last review is the most critical one." Drake stretched and yawned. "I could stay around and help you, you know. On the other hand, if you don't need me while you're working through the material, I thought maybe I would take a vacation."

"Do it. You've earned some time off—more than earned it." Leon sounded relieved. The last thing a successful project needed was two people trying to direct the final pen.

"I was thinking of having a look at some of the rest of the solar system. You know, in my time we'd seen pictures of all the planets, but only a handful of people had been as far as the Moon."

"Which is considerably farther than I have been—or choose to go!" Leon's furry eyebrows went up. "Why would you *want* to travel so far? You are not an astronomer, or a terraform designer, or an astronaut. There's absolutely nothing out in space for a musician."

"I think it might help me in composition. New visual experiences always stimulate my musical imagination."

"You mean, we might get new music from you? Then by all means, go, and enjoy yourself. Visit Venus, tour Titan, meet Mars. Produce something to match this." Par Leon began to rap on the desk in front of him the rhythm of the 'Mars, the Bringer of War' section of Gustav Holst's 'The Planets.' With their own work so close to its end, he was in high good humor.

"I'd like to go." Drake had to be careful what he said next. "I was just wondering if I'd be able to afford it."

The smile on Leon's face was replaced by a puzzled frown. "*Afford* it?"

"The cost of the fares. Mars is a long way away."

Par Leon frowned, as though he did not understand the relevance of the remark. "The cost? Who are you proposing to take with you?"

"No one. Just me."

"Then cost does not enter into it. The ship will fly itself."

"But who pays for the ship?"

"The question is meaningless. There are ships available, as many as you want. But they are manufactured automatically. Machines make them, and they also fly them. Machine use is free. There is no *human* cost to making and flying a ship. Cost becomes relevant only when you demand that human time be devoted to something. Like now." Par Leon laughed, his good humor restored. "I could charge you for this advice, you know. But I won't. Go on, Drake, take your holiday. You've certainly earned it."

"I will. In a few more days."

"But if you are crazy enough to go to space, don't ask me to go with you!"

Drake laughed, too. He did not mention the subject again to Par Leon, but in the next week he quietly took accelerated courses in astronautics, astronomy, and space systems, subjects that previously had never interested him at all. He was astonished by what he found. Par Leon had understated the situation. Ships were available in abundance, with drives that could take them close to light speed. It made Drake reevaluate all his own plans. He had been thinking that he would have to return to a frozen state. Now there might be other options.

He did not even try to understand the technique of

inertia shedding that bypassed what should have been a killing 4000g acceleration as the ship moved to and from the light-speed region. That understanding required a working knowledge of a Science language far beyond his capabilities. Instead, he thought of the changes in the world. If this capability had been around at the end of the twentieth century, it would have been used by millions. Now, few people seemed to care. Although the stars were within easy reach, humanity was not stretching out to enfold them. Civilization seemed stable, static, content to remain within the comfortable limits of the solar system. Was that progress, or was it regress?

After nine days Drake was ready. He had done all that he could. The night before he was scheduled to depart he invited Par Leon out for a ceremonial dinner. By this time it was assumed that they would eat and drink comfortably in each other's presence. Leon had hinted once or twice at a more intimate relationship, but he had not been offended when Drake declined.

They went to Leon's favorite eating place, ate his favorite foods, and drank his favorite wines. It was an unexpected bonus that by coincidence one of Drake's own new compositions was playing in the background.

"There." Par Leon jerked his head toward an invisible speaker. "That is real and deserved fame. Music good enough to eat to."

"But not to listen to." Drake shrugged off the compliment. "Table music is like table wine, usually nothing special. Telemann could compose it as fast as he could write it down."

"True. But do not undervalue yourself, my friend. Mozart's *divertimenti* are often both artful and memorable."

The conversation was on satisfying and familiar ground. Drake felt the glow that comes with good, compatible company. He was going to miss that.

The urge to tell the full truth became very great.

Surely, if he confided in Par Leon his commitment and the depth of his feelings, the other man would become a willing accomplice.

"Leon."

"Yes?"

"Oh, nothing. I'm just thinking about my trip."

He stifled the idea before it could develop further. His new plans were shaping up, and they were nothing as simple as controlled freezing and a return to the cryowombs. They might lead to danger and destruction. He would not want Par Leon to bear any guilt by association.

He also would not—could not, dare not—do anything at all that might endanger his chances of success.

Chapter 9

Escape to Nowhere

$\mathcal{D}$rake had decided to proceed with great caution. For at least the first part of his trip, he must look and sound like a genuine tourist. His resurrection helped. He could tell anyone he met that he had been recently thawed (he would not define *recently*). He would say he was still trying to get the hang of his new era. He would gape at anything he saw, like the original hick. He would be free to ask a million innocent questions.

Drake had delved into solar system geometry long before he left Earth. At first he had been worried. By an accident of timing, Pluto was almost exactly at aphelion, as far away from the Sun as it could get. But then he looked at the performance of the ships. They could accelerate so hard, and achieve huge speeds so quickly, that nowhere in the system was more than a few days away. Travel times became irrelevant.

Mars, first, then, just as he had told Par Leon upon his departure. Drake could imagine his friend and mentor checking the first phase of his travel, but he would lose interest once he was sure that Drake had arrived safely.

Mars was described in the Earthside databases as undergoing a "modest" terraforming effort; nothing, the sources said, compared with the major effort going on at Venus. The Mars project was designed only to increase the available surface water, and it did not interfere with life in the Martian interior.

Drake's ship took him to Mars in a day and a half. He landed; and found hell.

The planet was under ceaseless bombardment. Every twenty minutes a cometary fragment, a couple of hundred meters across, hit the surface. It had been directed in from the Kuiper Belt, nine billion kilometers from the Sun, and it struck Mars tangentially, precisely at dawn on the day-night terminator. Each impact came within twenty degrees of the equator. The Mars atmosphere was too thin to carry sound, but land waves shook the surface around the point of arrival.

Drake donned a suit and stepped out of the ship. He was well away from the impact zone. Even so, he felt the compacted rubble of the regolith tremble and shake beneath his boots.

He looked up. The sky was a dirty gray, streaked and filmed with white haze. Most of the added dust and water vapor in the air came not from comet fragments, but from the ejecta of vaporized surface rocks and permafrost, blown high into the Martian stratosphere. That permafrost was the main source of atmospheric water. It returned to the ground as a thin drizzle of ice particles. For the first time in a billion years, snow was falling on Mars.

As Drake watched, another ball of fire flamed across the dull southern sky. It moved from west to east, and vanished. One minute later a flash of crimson light lit the southeastern horizon. It was hard to believe that a rough-edged chunk of water ice, dirtied with smears of ammonia ice, silicate rock, and metallic ore, and no more than two hundred meters in diameter, could produce such violence. But a few million tons of mass, moving at forty kilometers a second, carries formidable amounts of kinetic energy. The energy release for each impact was around a thousand megatons. Each arrival had the force of a big volcanic explosion back on Earth. The thin atmosphere of Mars did little to dissipate it.

Drake watched the tumult for a couple of hours. Finally he decided that the open face of the planet, battered by hailstones bigger than the Great Pyramid, was more likely to stimulate nightmares than musical creation.

He went inside the ship and considered his next move. He had told Par Leon that he would visit the Mars deep caverns. Natural formations, kilometers across, they had been interlocked and fortified over the centuries by tunneling and construction moles. Now they stood second only to Earth as a center for human civilization.

Caution said he should visit the caves, as originally planned. After that, his original itinerary called for visits to Europa and Ganymede, the satellites of Jupiter, and to Neptune's big moon, Triton. But a new knowledge was burning inside him. The trip to Mars had changed his perspective on interplanetary travel. He knew that he was, if he chose, only a few days away from Ana. From Mars to Pluto, even without invoking emergency status and maximum accelerations, was just a thirty-six-hour run.

The temptation was too much. He ordered a message sent to Par Leon, back on Earth, announcing his safe arrival on Mars. Then he gave his command.

The ship rose from the surface and arrowed out, directly away from the Sun's warmth. It would bypass Jupiter and Saturn, bypass Uranus and Neptune. It would not stop until it reached Pluto, out at the frigid limit of the solar system; out where Sol was no more than a bright spark in the sky, and the cryocorpses slept their ancient, dreamless sleep beneath the silent stars.

A little knowledge could be almost too much. In six years of work on Earth, Drake had become used to the idea of robotic servants. They were of varying levels of intelligence, depending on their function, but they all had one thing in common: they accepted every command without question, provided that it was not dangerous and did not exceed their available resources of materials or knowledge.

He assumed that it would be equally true on Pluto, and it began that way. His ship landed without incident on the frozen surface. Machines attended his arrival. There were no humans, and he had expected none. The nearest people resided at the research station on Charon, seventeen thousand kilometers away. Pluto and Charon were more like a pair of little moons than a planet with a satellite—Pluto was smaller than Earth's moon, while Charon was half the size of its primary. The pair were tidally locked, always showing the same face to each other. Drake, standing on the surface of Pluto and looking up, saw Charon hanging pendant in the sky above him, like a giant dull ruby. The research station was not visible. From this distance, there was no evidence to be seen on Charon of any human activities.

Even though Charon was so close, the machines on Pluto were designed to operate without advice or assistance from there or anywhere else. Drake's command to be taken to the cryowombs was obeyed without question.

The surface of Pluto was one of the quietest places in the solar system. However, there would be occasional impacts from meteorites and cometary debris. The wombs, for additional safety, had been placed deep within the interior to protect against disturbance.

It had not occurred to Drake that he himself constituted such a disturbance, until he had been led at least a kilometer along a descending ramp. He and his attendant machine entered a large open chamber, where his suit was placed within another and larger one. The space between the suits was filled with liquid helium.

"Is this necessary?" He could imagine the second suit interfering with his mobility.

"It is necessary. There must be no energy release within the vaults to raise the ambient temperature. I myself cannot proceed beyond this point. I am too warm." The machine raised a spidery articulated arm and pointed at a hovering blue pyramid, half a meter on a side. "This is now your guide."

Ever since they left the surface it had become steadily darker. All light sources now disappeared as Drake followed the drifting blue pyramid out of the chamber and into the next level of the Pluto vault.

According to the first machine, the cryotanks were stored in regular rows within the main cryowomb. Drake strained his eyes into the darkness ahead. He could see nothing but the faint blue light in front of him. He was at the mercy of his robot guide, who must know the deep vault's geometry and contents through programmed memory.

Encased within his double suit, Drake followed the blue glimmer, on and on. Finally it halted. Drake moved closer, and by its feeble illumination he saw the outline of a cryotank. It was like a great coffin, two meters long and a meter wide and deep. Although the cryowomb was kept at a controlled temperature, for double security each tank also contained its own temperature control and source of refrigeration.

"This is the one?" He crouched low, seeking the identification.

He was not sure that the blue pyramid could hear him, understand him, or talk to him, until he heard the sibilant whisper in his helmet. "It is the one."

"I cannot see any identification. Are you sure it is the cryocorpse of Anastasia Werlich?"

"I am sure."

"Then lift it carefully, and bring it with you. Lead us back to the surface and to my ship."

He could see no way that the blue pyramid could exert force, but after a moment of hesitation the cryotank lifted in the low gravity. Two seconds more, and the blue gleam was moving again through the vault. It led the way steadily upward, to the first-level chamber where Drake's outer suit was removed. Twenty minutes more, and he was supervising the careful placement of Ana's cryotank in the aft storage compartment of his ship.

The machine attendants had gone and he was ready to tell the ship to lift from the surface of Pluto, when the communication panel lit with a busy constellation of red and yellow lights.

"The removal of a cryotank from the Pluto cryowomb, and its placement aboard this ship, is unauthorized," said a quiet voice. *"The cryotank must be returned at once."*

Drake cursed his own stupidity. The actions of the machines must be reported automatically to some central data bank. It was only his good luck that screening for anomalies apparently took a few minutes to perform.

Rather than replying, he locked the outside ports and gave the order for instant departure from the surface.

"The removal of any cryotank from the Pluto vaults is forbidden without proper authorization," repeated the voice. *"You do not have such authorization. Do not attempt to leave Pluto. It will not be permitted."*

Drake ignored the warning. He dropped into the pilot's seat. Why hadn't the ship taken off? When he left Earth and Mars, his commands had been executed immediately.

He could guess the answer: the ship's automatic piloting system was being overridden from outside. If he wanted to leave, he would have to assume manual control. He knew how to fly the ship in theory, from his crash courses in astronautics and space systems. In practice, he had never tried anything like it.

He hit the switches to turn off the ship's computer control, cursing the messages that came back to him:

"The requested action will remove the vessel from automated path guidance. Do you wish to proceed?"

"Yes."

"The requested action will inhibit the use of all trajectory planning functions. Do you wish to proceed?"

"Yes."

"The requested action will also disconnect this vessel from the solar system protective navigation system. Do you wish to proceed?"

"Yes, yes, yes!"

He was hitting the manual lift sequence, over and over, convinced that outside the ship more direct methods were being put in place to prevent takeoff.

Finally—at last—he saw that the ship was rising. Pluto's surface of rock and ice receded below them.

He set a simple outward course, directly away from the Sun. He did not care where he went, provided it was *away*.

It should have been easy. The Pluto approach corridor had been completely deserted on his arrival. Now it was buzzing with ships. His control board showed scores of them in the space ahead. Where had they all come from? Was it like the automated service that had caught Melissa, a whole invisible safety net of ships that sprang into action exactly when it was needed?

No time to worry about what or why. The ships ahead were converging, moving to intersect the course that he had set for the solar system perimeter. Somehow they knew his flight plan. It must be transmitted automatically, even when he was flying manual.

"DO NOT ATTEMPT TO PROCEED." The command was louder and more peremptory. *"RETURN AT ONCE TO PLUTO."*

Drake set the ship to maximum acceleration and kept going, driving toward the heart of the converging cluster of ships.

"TURN OFF YOUR DRIVE. YOU ARE MOVING IN EXCESS OF FORTY KILOMETERS PER SECOND, AND ACCELERATING. IMPACT AT SUCH SPEED CAN HAVE FATAL CONSEQUENCES."

It was a great understatement. Impact with another ship at forty kilometers a second would leave random bits of melted metal and vaporized plastic.

"YOU ARE ON A COLLISION COURSE."

A grating siren sounded in Drake's ear. The ship's own detection system was blaring its warning. Collision and destruction were no more than a split second away.

And then, at the last moment, the other ships sheered off. The center of the cluster became open. Drake flew on through.

He wondered what had saved him. Did the interceptors have their own prohibition against causing harm to a human? Or against permitting their own destruction?

He angled wide of another group of ships that had appeared far ahead. They moved toward him, but he was racing along too fast. He was soon past them. Still at maximum acceleration, he fled for the edge of the solar system.

As soon as the sky was clear ahead, he set a course for Canopus.

At last he was able to breathe. If he might have been judged a murderer in an earlier generation for what he and Tom Lambert had done to Ana, he was certainly considered a thief or worse in this one.

Who cared? He and Ana were together, that was all that mattered. Although pursuit was still possible, he could see no signs of it. And he would be hard to catch. The ship was still accelerating monstrously. Soon it would crowd light speed, moving just 125 meters per second slower than a traveling wave front. Even that was not the limit. If need be, he could reach within a meter a second of light speed.

But it should not be necessary. He examined the control board. Unless he saw signs of pursuit, their planned top speed would be just right. Relativistic time dilatation was going to be a powerful factor. Years would pass on Earth for every day of shipboard time. The trip out to Canopus and back would be a few months for him, but almost three hundred years back on Earth.

And for Ana?

She was still trapped outside of time, in her personal fermata, a temporal hiatus without end where duration and interval did not exist.

He felt a great urge to gaze upon her face within the sealed cryotank. Instead he moved forward to peer ahead to the distant star that he had chosen as their destination. Even from a hundred light-years away, by some miracle of the ship's imaging system Canopus was already revealed as a tiny bright disk.

He went to where the ship's computer was housed. Now that they were far beyond pursuit, he had returned to automatic control. He was curious to see what the computer looked like, the multipurpose processor that with equal ease planned trajectories, cooked meals, and maintained all the onboard life-support systems.

He lifted the plastic access panel to the main processor, and peered into a small dark cavity. He saw a lattice of red beads, each one no bigger than a pinhead. Tiny sparkles of violet light passed among them. A soft voice from the ship's address system said in mild rebuke, *"Exposure to external light sources is discouraged, since it causes the computer to operate with reduced speed and efficiency."*

Drake went back to the controls and turned his attention to the general functions of the ship. It could support him and his life-system needs, apparently indefinitely. Its speed and maneuverability never ceased to amaze him. And yet it was in many ways less surprising than the civilization that had made it. A civilization that could produce such a miracle of performance and potential—and then allow it to go unused; that was the most incomprehensible mystery of all.

Was it the temporal dislocation produced by time dilatation that was psychologically unacceptable to humans? Drake was depending on it. But did others hate to leave, and upon their return find their friends in the cryowombs, or perhaps dead? But as lifespans increased, that would be less and less a factor. If that were the main reason why the ships were not more widely used, the future should see more travel to the stars.

The ship was approaching its planned maximum speed. Drake noticed that the ship's external mass indicator showed more than 140,000 tons, up from a rest mass of 130 tons. To an outside observer, Drake himself would seem to mass eighty-eight tons, and be foreshortened to a length of less than two millimeters. The shields hid the view ahead of the ship, but he knew that the picture he was seeing on his screen had been subjected to extreme image motion compensation. An unshielded view would reveal the universal three-degree background radiation, Doppler-shifted up to visible wavelengths. Far behind, hard X-ray sources were faded to pale red stars.

The ship was nowhere close to its performance limits. If necessary, he and Ana could fly on forever, to the end of the universe. Except that he was confident that it would not be necessary. He closed his eyes and heard a broad, calm melody, the music of the stars themselves, stirring within his brain. He lay back and allowed music to fill his mind.

For the first time in five centuries, Drake was at peace.

Chapter 10

"Yet each man kills the thing he loves"

$\mathcal{I}$n the silence between the stars there were no distractions. Drake started to compose again, convinced that it would be his best work ever. It would distill all his emotions, for all the days since that ominous first morning when he had seen a red car in the drive where no car should have been; on through the darkest days, when nothing seemed possible; on all the way to the glad confident morning of the present.

The ship's flight was fully controlled by its tiny but vastly capable computer. In her cabin aft, Ana lay safe in the cryotank. Drake had all the time that he needed. As the days went by, he allowed the new composition to mature steadily within him. If ever he felt like a break, he would go to Ana's room, sit down by the cryotank, and reveal to her his thoughts and dreams.

He assured her that a few months of shipboard time would be enough. Almost three hundred years would speed away on Earth, before their return, and in those centuries Earth's physicians would surely have found a safe and certain cure. If they had not, he would simply head out again, and repeat the entire cycle.

And what if, after many tries, Earth finally fails us?

He imagined Ana's question in his mind, and he had an answer. They would go elsewhere, on beyond the stars in search of other solutions. The ship was completely self-sustaining. It had ample power and supplies for many subjective lifetimes of travel.

But Drake hoped that one trip would be enough. He told Ana that it was one of his smaller ambitions, on his return, to locate the cryocorpse of his friend Par Leon and return the favor. She would like Par Leon.

He was strangely, sublimely happy, as the ship approached Canopus. His original plan had been for a gravitational swing-by, a maneuver that would take the ship through a tight hyperbolic trajectory close to Canopus and then hurtle away again the way they had come.

But perhaps he had been enjoying himself too much to be in a hurry, or maybe he felt a simple curiosity to see what worlds might circle another sun. For whatever reason, he chose to decelerate during the last couple of weeks and put the ship into a bound orbit about four hundred million kilometers from Canopus.

He turned the ship's imaging devices to scan the stellar system. There were planets, as he had hoped, four gas-giants each the size of Jupiter. Closer in he located a round dozen of smaller worlds. But he had ignored or forgotten the infernal power of Canopus itself. It was a fearsome sight, more than a thousand times as luminous as the Sun and spouting green flares of gas millions of kilometers long. The inner planets were mere blackened cinders, airless and arid, charred by the furnace heat of the star. The outer gas-giants were all atmosphere, except for a small compressed solid core where the pressure was millions of Earth atmospheres. No life in any form that he would recognize could exist there.

But he stayed and looked. In two days of fascinated observation, his eyes turned again and again to the fusion fire of Canopus. He wondered. Had some other human been here, when ships like the one that he was flying were new? Had any *intelligence* been here before, human or nonhuman? Or were his the first sentient eyes to dwell on those dark twisted striations—not sunspots, but sun *scars*—that gouged the boiling surface of the star?

If others had been here, and they were anything like him, he pitied them. Canopus set up in his mind a resonance of terror beyond reason and beyond explanation.

At last Drake could stand it no longer. Like a lost soul flying from hell's gate he turned and ran. He needed the infinite silence of space, and beyond that the comforting shelter of the solar system. If another trip out were necessary with Ana, it would be to a smaller and less turbulent star.

As the ship began to accelerate he turned the imaging equipment for one last look at Canopus, knowing even as he did it that he was making a mistake. The lost souls were there. Unable to flee like him, they burned in dark torment within the stellar furnace. Smoky demons danced about them, in tongues of flame that gaped and gibbered in triumph. Drake shuddered, cringed, and looked away.

As the star receded to a blazing point of light, he tried to settle back into his shipboard routine. But all harmony, mental and musical, had been banished. What he saw, over and over, was that vision of the Pit. He was circling endlessly, in tight orbit around Canopus. Flaming gas prominences, bright jets of green and white and blue danced a witch's sabbat in his mind. He could not eat, drink, or sleep. The urge to see Ana, to seek peace in her face, grew within him.

Finally Drake went aft and sat by the cryotank. It was guaranteed to soothe all worries.

But not today. His mind churned.

"What's wrong with me, Ana? Am I going crazy?"

The usual imagined reply did not come. He stared at the cryotank. There she was, only a few feet away. If only he could see her, just for a second . . .

The outside of the cryotank was at room temperature. Inside, the cryocorpse was insulated by two more protective layers. Both of them were transparent. He could open the tank, take one look, and close it before there was a noticeable temperature change.

Slowly, he released the seals and lifted the tight outer cover.

She lay quiet in the tank, pale and peaceful as a Snow Goddess. He took one look at her pearly eyes and skin of milky crystal, afraid to open the cover more than a crack. An icy vapor, colder than innermost hell, breathed from within. While he watched, dew formed and froze on the inner layer. Ana's body faded and blurred, like an image placed behind frosted glass.

Rapidly, he closed and sealed the outer lid. That one moment had been enough. He was able to control himself again and think of other things.

He told himself, for the hundredth time, how fortunate he was. He had never dreamed of light-speed ships and time dilatation, when he had made his plans so long ago. At best he had envisioned a chancy succession of freezings and thawings, farther and farther off in time, until at last Ana could safely be revived and cured. He had imagined and dreaded the uncertainty of multiple awakenings, not sure where he was, not sure where Ana might be, not even sure if she still lay within a cryowomb.

Instead of such a dangerous quest, Ana was here with him. He could safeguard her himself and protect her from all risks.

The rest of the journey home was, if anything, more tranquil than the voyage out. During the final phases he scanned all the ship's communication channels, electromagnetic and neutrino, wondering what might await him back in the solar system. He found nothing but silence. The centuries must have changed technology again; he had been away long enough for some totally new communications system to have taken over. Three centuries were also—a frightening prospect—time enough for humanity itself to have changed; even, perhaps, for humans to have destroyed themselves.

He would proceed with great caution, until he knew the nature of the system to which he and Ana were returning. While still far from home he decelerated from their near light-speed race. Moving at a steadily diminishing velocity the ship coasted in toward Sol; past the barren and arid Dry Tortugas, the outermost limits of the Sun's gravitational domain; past the outer borders of the Oort Cloud; into and through the Kuiper Belt. There was no sign of human presence. The scouts who had been busy on the Outer System survey when Drake left were all gone.

By the time that they came to the frozen wastes of Pluto, the ship was drifting inward at only a few hundred kilometers a second. Drake was becoming worried. The imaging system, even at highest resolution, showed no evidence of activity on either Pluto or Charon. The research station had vanished.

Did Melissa Bierly lie in the Pluto cryowombs now? Or had a treatment been found, one that could relieve the torment of a flawed masterpiece of genetic science? Drake realized that he was afraid of Melissa's power over him. Rather than approaching the planetary doublet for a landing, as he had intended, he stepped up the ship's speed and headed for the inner planets. He had started from Earth; he would return there, and make his case to whomever or whatever he found.

The mode of his approach to the inner system was taken out of his hands as the ship passed the Asteroid Belt. As they floated high above the ecliptic, a navigation and guidance beam locked on to them, taking over the ship's internal controls. Drake attempted a manual override. It had succeeded once, but now his command was ignored. Powerless to affect his path, he watched the ship steered steadily in to a landing on the surface of the Moon.

The spaceport was new. Drake was dropping toward a flat plain of gleaming yellow, dotted with massive silver columns set in a regular triangular array. Ships, if they were ships, formed dark, windowless tetrahedra at the center of each triangle. Nothing remotely like Drake's ship was visible. Space flight, and perhaps everything else, had changed in three centuries.

A small wheeled guide met Drake at the ship's lock. Its body comprised a one-foot sphere, with a thin upright cylinder above it, and a whisk-broom of flexible metal fibers above that. The broom head dipped toward Drake in greeting. The machine rolled toward a head-high oval aperture at the base of a silver column. Drake followed, ducking his head, and passed through the opening. There was no sign of an airlock, but his suit monitor suddenly showed breathable air and a comfortable outside temperature. He removed the suit as his wheeled guide instructed and followed it along a short corridor to another interior chamber.

One man was waiting there, a dignified figure with the distant eyes of a prophet. Drake had expected more: a reception committee, perhaps, or maybe even a show of force. The man merely nodded and said quietly in Universal, "Welcome again to Earthspace, Drake Merlin."

Drake had been wrong. He had thought himself prepared for anything. What he had never expected was to be recognized, and *named*.

Even with that thought, he realized that he had no reason to be surprised. The ship would have revealed its identity back in the Asteroid Belt, during its first handshake with the navigation and guidance beam of the inner system. The data banks would have shown the

ship's history. Presumably they would also have recorded its sudden disappearance from the solar system.

Drake wondered what else the files might say about
the ship's run from Pluto. No matter what they said, he
would gain nothing by lying about his actions.

"Since you know my name," he said, while the other
man regarded him calmly and without expression,
"then perhaps you also know my history. If you do, you
will realize that I have returned to seek your help."

Drake found it hard to accept that he had been
greeted in a familiar language. Par Leon had been able
to speak to him on his resurrection, but only because of
long preparation for Drake's arrival, and extensive
studies of the right historical period.

Had language become static, totally fixed over the
centuries because it had become embedded within the
universal data banks? Or was the robed figure in front
of him simply giving a formal greeting, a single sentence that he had learned of Universal?

But the man was nodding and speaking again. "My
name is Trismon Sorel. I know something of your history as it has come down to us from long ago, although
a serious . . . event, almost a century ago, led to our
records being seriously incomplete and inconsistent. In
your case, there are two versions of events. One states
that three centuries ago you lost control of your ship,
and were carried off unwillingly to the far depths of
space. Another version suggests that your removal of a
cryocorpse from the Pluto cryowombs and the immediately subsequent departure of your ship were linked
events. It proposes that your disappearance at close to
light speed, however curious and bewildering, was intentional. I await your elucidation. However, we should
first proceed to another environment, where we will
find conversation easier."

There were small pauses in his speech, slight hesita-
tions in places where it was not natural to break the
pattern of words. As Drake was led out of the room and

down a spiral flight of metallic stairs, he decided that Universal must be a learned language for Trismon Sorel, just as Old Anglic had been for Par Leon. But to learn Universal so quickly and so well, in the day since the return of Drake's ship to the inner system, was beyond the powers of the learning inducers. It suggested that Trismon Sorel, in spite of his normal appearance, represented some huge advance in human mental powers.

They had entered a room that could have existed in Drake's own time. Only the light lunar gravity, one-sixth of Earth's, told Drake that he was far from home. Sorel gestured to two comfortable-looking chairs and settled into one of them. As the little wheeled servant moved forward with refreshments, he gazed at Drake with steady, knowing eyes.

"Speak, Drake Merlin. Tell your story."

Drake nodded and sat down opposite Trismon Sorel. He felt a rising tension. In a few minutes he would know if the long quest was finally over, and his life could begin again.

"My departure from the solar system was indeed intentional." It had become difficult to speak, and he had to swallow and pause before he could continue. "It was intentional, and done for a good reason. But I cannot begin there. I must begin long ago, more than eight hundred years ago. At that time, the cryocorpse who now lies safe within the ship that brought me here was my wife. After many happy years together, we learned that she was suffering from an incurable disease . . ."

As Drake told his story he was forced to relive scenes that he had suppressed for centuries. If Ana was to be helped, Trismon Sorel had to know everything: all Ana's symptoms, the progress of her illness, the manner of her death, the procedure in her freezing.

Sorel listened intently. He raised his hand to interrupt only when Drake spoke of the awful hours with Ana at the Second Chance cryonics facility.

"One moment. You say that the original medical records were stored with the cryocorpse. Are they there now?"

"They should be. Everything should be there, inside the cryotank."

"Then before we proceed further let me summon the necessary experts, in both antique Medicine and Languages. Let me say at once, we are able to cure all known diseases. That includes every past disease of which we have ever heard. However, we will need to examine the records and the cryocorpse itself." He sat, eyes distant, for three or four seconds.

Two waves of emotion swept through Drake. He felt a wild and terrible joy, like an agony of relief: Ana would be cured at last. But he also felt a superstitious awe. Trismon Sorel's advanced mental powers seemed to include telepathy. "You are speaking to other people directly, by transmitting your thoughts?"

Sorel looked puzzled, and again there was a brief pause before he smiled. "Not in the way that you are perhaps thinking. I can do no more than you yourself will be able to accomplish in a few days' time. You will share your thoughts with others. You will have instant access to all information in the data banks. You will calculate faster and better than the computer of the ship that brought you here. Look."

He turned his head and raised the hair above his temple. Drake saw a faint, thin discoloration, normally covered by the hairline.

"That marks where the implant sits," Sorel went on. "It is normally installed in early infancy, and can be changed at any time. It is tiny, smaller and thinner than a pin, and it serves multiple purposes: as a body function monitor, as a slave computer, and as a transmitter and receiver. Commands, requests, data, and programs can be sent or received. I can speak with data banks or with other individuals. I have requested via the Copernicus network that both medical and language experts go directly to your ship. And I am able to speak to you now, in real time, because although your language is new to me, I am employing the language translation modules within the Tycho network."

Some transfer of information was still directly from person to person. Sorel read Drake's misgivings from his facial expression. "Do not worry about this. In your case—as in all cryowomb revivals—the implant will be totally optional. Before you make a decision you will have ample opportunity to observe its use in others. But I can assure you that if you do proceed, you will find it hard within a few weeks to believe that you were ever able to function without such a service. You will possess total recall; you will be a calculator beyond the most powerful computers of your time; and you will have immediate access to every data bank within the solar system—although, naturally, access and transmission time to people and data banks on other planets is considerable. Do you have questions, Drake Merlin?"

"Only one. I want to know if Ana can be cured."

"I have asked the medical team that question. They are already on board your ship, and they are performing their assessment. I will inquire as to their progress. One moment."

The gray eyes widened. Their expression again became remote and preoccupied. This time the wait stretched on, to become one minute and then two.

As the silence continued, Drake felt a knife of tension twisting inside him. If communication was mind-to-mind, what was taking so long? He was afraid that something was going wrong, but what could it possibly be? He comforted himself with Trismon Sorel's assurance: this society was able to cure all diseases of humans, including every known past disease.

But it was taking too long. Finally he could stand to

remain silent no longer. "Are you talking to them? What do they say to you?"

Sorel's eyes focused again on Drake. "I am talking now to the medical specialists. It is somewhat . . . complicated. Give me one moment more."

The gray eyes were changing. They became gentler and more personal. At last Trismon Sorel nodded, as though confirming something that he already feared. He spoke to Drake more slowly, choosing his words with great care.

"They ask me to ask you certain questions. The woman in the cryotank, Anastasia. According to our records she had been constantly maintained in the Pluto cryowombs. Is that correct?"

Drake nodded.

"And when you found her, she was within a cryotank?"

Again, Drake nodded.

"You did not remove her, but you brought the whole cryotank with you on board the ship?"

"That's right." Drake's mind was filled with foreboding. "I had the tank carried from the cryowombs to the ship, exactly as I found it. It was done very carefully. The gravity on Pluto is low, and the machines had no trouble handling it."

Trismon Sorel was frowning. "Then it is difficult to see how there could be any problem. Unless—Drake Merlin, think hard. Did you open the tank, for any reason, after your ship left Pluto?"

Drake saw again before him Ana's peaceful face, her pearly eyes and milky skin. He felt a sickness like death. "I did open it. Just once. The outer case, for a few moments, after we left Canopus. The inner seals were unbroken. I looked for only a second or two. I was careful to seal the cryotank afterward . . ."

It was pointless to try to explain why he had done it, to say that he had been unable *not* to do it. Trismon

Sorel was regarding him sorrowfully, across an eight-hundred-year gulf. Somehow his face was Tom Lambert's, and also Par Leon's. The eyes spoke the same sad message.

"Drake Merlin, a Pluto cryotank is not designed for sealing and resealing. Closing calls for special equipment and special procedures, available only in the cryowombs. When a seal is broken, it is assumed that the person will at once be resurrected, or special resealing methods must be adopted. Do you understand what I am saying? With an imperfect seal, suitable conditions cannot be maintained within a cryotank."

"Then Ana . . ."

"One moment more. Again I must consult the specialists, and the data banks." The eyes once more became unblinking. The silence dragged on and on, longer than before. When Trismon Sorel at last focused on Drake, his face was beyond doubt.

"I have checked all our references. The medical team, at my request, did the same to provide independent confirmation. We have formed the same conclusion. The problem that faces us is quite different from that of curing a disease. The damage caused to a body, and particularly to a body's brain, when a cryotank is opened and resurrection is not performed at once . . . that damage is permanent. It cannot be repaired, and there can be no possible revival. Now, or ever.

"I am sorry, Drake Merlin. Anastasia is dead. Forever dead."

Forever dead. Ana is dead. Trismon Sorel's words echoed those of Tom Lambert, so long ago. But this time Drake heard the ring of complete certainty.

Yet each man kills the thing he loves. He, not disease, had killed Ana. Like Orpheus of the old myths, he had pursued his Eurydice through hell. In his case it had been a double hell of cryodeath and Canopus, but like Orpheus in Hades he had found his love and brought her back toward life. Like Orpheus he had looked at her; and in looking he had lost her.

With that thought age-old barriers came down inside his mind. For the first time he noticed a spicy fragrance in the air that he was breathing. He felt a steady dry breeze blowing past him, and far-off along the corridor he heard the faint concert pitch A-natural of vibrating metal. It was as though all his senses were opening, after long centuries of hibernation.

Trismon Sorel was speaking again. "One possibility remains. Anastasia, the woman that you knew, cannot be reanimated. That is quite impossible. However, many whole cells remain intact within her body. She could be cloned without difficulty. Her growth and education would begin anew. But it would, you must understand, be a *new* Anastasia. There is no hope of sufficient memory transfer from undamaged cells for any inkling of her former existence to pass to her new body. Your former relationship would of course be known to *you*, but it would be irrelevant to her. Should we proceed?"

The temptation was enormous. To see Ana once more standing before him, blooming and vibrant as he had once known her. . . .

That was the selfish answer. There was a better one: Ana had the *right* to a healthy new life in this world, eight hundred years beyond their own time. He could not deny it to her.

She would live again. And yet . . .

It would not be the Ana that he knew and loved. It would be a quite different person. Could he bear to look on her, a woman who was Ana and yet not Ana, a woman who would not feel for him the overwhelming love that he felt for her?

Except that he had no choice. Ana deserved resurrection, and a new life.

Sorel had been waiting sympathetically. Drake nodded at last. "Proceed. Make a clone of Ana."

Trismon Sorel also nodded, and smiled. Drake saw the relief on his face. Sorel knew, with the authority of eight hundred more years of science and technological progress, that the Ana whom Drake had known was gone forever.

But—

A tiny seed of doubt sprouted deep in Drake's mind. But what would science say in another three hundred years? in a thousand, or ten thousand, or a hundred thousand? Science had come so far. Surely no one, least of all a scientist, would say that it was now at an end and could go no further.

Trismon Sorel was talking to him again, trying to catch his attention. He forced himself to listen.

"Ana cannot be revived and cured," Sorel was saying, "not in the way that you hoped when you took her body from the cryowombs. But we can help *you*."

"Me?"

"Certainly. We can cure you. There is evidence that a cure was attempted three hundred years ago, but it clearly failed. We have superior techniques now. They can end your obsession with Anastasia. It would, of course, be done only with your consent."

"Do I have a choice?"

"You have an infinite number of choices. The right to self-determination—even self-destruction, if you wish it—is basic." Trismon Sorel leaned forward. "Now I would like to speak personally, for myself alone. I hope that you will agree to a cure, and enjoy your own new life. I have vast sympathy for you. I have searched the whole data bank as we have been speaking, and your suffering seems unique. No quest and sacrifice comparable to yours can be found, anywhere."

"I have not suffered." Drake had made up his mind. "I have not sacrificed. And I know what I would like."

"State it."

"I would like a cloned form for a new Ana, just as you offered."

"We have agreed, that will be done. But for yourself?"

"I want to remain here just long enough to be sure that Ana's cloning can proceed without problems. Then I wish to leave."

"Leave?" Trismon Sorel was bewildered. "Go from here? Go where? The universe is open to you, but we can offer you everything that your heart might desire."

"No, that is not true. You cannot offer me the Anastasia that I know and love. And that is what I want—all I want. Put me back into the cryowombs, with Ana's body at my side. Let us travel together to the future."

"But I told you, the real Ana, the Ana that you knew, is not in that body. Too many brain cells have been destroyed. Your Ana is gone."

"She is gone. But gone *where*?"

"Drake Merlin, that is a meaningless question. It is like asking where the wind goes when it is no longer blowing, or where is the odor of a flower after the flower dies."

"It seems a meaningless question today. But it may not always be meaningless. You told me that I have an infinite number of choices. My choice is simple, and I say it again: I want to be placed in the Pluto cryowombs. Do I have that right?"

"You do." Trismon Sorel could not conceal his dismay and disappointment. "We cannot deny it to you. But I beg you to reconsider. You can return to cryosleep for as long as you choose, but when will you be awakened? In a century? In five?"

"I do not know. I want to leave this instruction with my freezing: Awaken me when new evidence comes into the data banks that seems relevant to the re-creation of Anastasia's *original* personality. And not until then."

"It can be done. But I must be honest with you. I do not think such new evidence will ever appear. If you hope to sleep until your Ana can return, I believe that you will sleep forever."

You have everything to lose. You're healthy, you're productive, you're at the height of your career. And you are asking me to throw all that away, to help you take the chance that someday, God knows when, you might—just might—be revived. Don't you see, Drake, I can't help you. Across a gulf of eight centuries, Tom Lambert's words reverberated in Drake's mind.

"I've heard that logic before," Drake said, "and it proved wrong. I will take that risk. It is smaller than risks that I have taken in the past. Can we begin . . . now?"

"If you insist." Trismon Sorel held up his hand. Drake was already rising from his seat. "But there is one thing more. While we have been speaking, a group-mind meeting has been in progress involving every human within easy signal range. A conclusion has been reached. Your request will be granted, but with one condition: You do not go alone. You will have a companion for your travel into the future, just as each of us has a companion, to share our fortunes and to stand by our side through good and bad."

"I desire no woman in the cryowomb with me, other than my own Ana. And no man, either."

"We would condemn neither living man nor living woman to such an uncertain future. Your companion will not reside in the cryowombs. It will be a Servitor, designed for on-demand operation, exactly like my own Servitor." Trismon Sorel gestured to the little wheeled sphere with its metal whisk-broom head, waiting quietly at his side. "So long as you do not call upon its services, it will remain dormant and in communion with the data banks. When you need a companion or an assistant, it will be there to obey your commands."

Sorel stood up. "Come with me now. The preparations are already beginning for the cloning of Ana.

While that is proceeding, I will explain to you the end-less virtues of the Servitor class. And you can decide on the appearance and name of your own personal model, to travel with you into the undiscovered country of the future.''

Chapter 11

The Return of Ana

$\mathcal{D}$rake woke quickly and easily, rising at once to full consciousness. He felt rested and full of energy, without pain or weakness. His immediate thought was that something had gone badly wrong. He was supposed to have descended into cryosleep. Instead he was awakening, as the effects of the first cryonic tranquilizing drug wore off.

He opened his eyes, expecting to see the cryolab facility and Trismon Sorel's face. Instead he found himself lounging at ease in a deep armchair. A woman with the strong features, raven hair, and dark complexion of a gypsy sat opposite. She was watching him closely. When his eyes opened she nodded but did not speak.

"What happened?" His mouth was a little dry, but that was normal after sedation. "Why didn't I go into cryosleep?"

"And what makes you think you didn't?" She arched jet-black eyebrows at him. "Don't you believe in progress? The old barbarism of waking agony is long in the past. Today the thawing is no different from rising after a natural sleep.''

She spoke not in Universal but in perfect English, unaccented and without pauses.

He glanced around him. His last waking sight had been of the cryolab, deep within the sterile interior of the Moon. Now he was back on Earth, held to his chair by the familiar tug of a standard gravity. The room's long window faced out over a sandy beach and a restless ocean. It was windy outside. He could hear the gusts moaning around the outside of the building and see tiny sparks of sunlight reflecting from distant white-caps.

Suddenly, he knew exactly where he was. He and Ana, on one of their rare trips abroad, had worked together for a month in Italy. They had taken an extra two weeks of vacation after the assignment was over, and rented a small villa on the Sorrento Peninsula just south of Naples. He was there now. The restless sea that he was looking at was the Tyrrhenian Sea, part of the Mediterranean; the little island far to the west was Capri.

He even recognized the room and furniture of the villa.

Recognized it, after more than eight hundred years?

His moment of pleasure was swept away by fear. *"How long?"*

''I was hoping that we might postpone that question for at least a little while.'' The woman sighed. ''I should have known better. All your records display a remarkable focus of attention. To answer your question, it has been rather a long time—much longer than I suspect you hoped. In your notation, this is the year 32,072. It is more than twenty-nine thousand years since you last descended into cryosleep.''

Long enough, surely, for real progress in the reconstruction of his Ana.

But longer, also, than the whole of humanity's previous recorded history. Drake stared in disbelief. He had again tried to prepare his mind for anything, for any amount of change. And again he was surprised. The last thing that he expected was sameness. But the room he was sitting in was exactly as he remembered it. The scene outside was a pleasant day of late spring. The sun was high in the sky, and it must be close to noon. At any moment the villa's housekeeper would enter with an aperitif of *sambuca,* before serving lunch for him and Ana outside on the little paved terrace.

"It's not real, is it?" He gestured around him. "All this is an electronic simulation, designed for my benefit." A worse thought struck. "In fact, *I'm* not real, either. I've not been resurrected at all. I've been downloaded."

"Not true." The woman frowned reprovingly. "You have certainly been resurrected, and you are the real corporeal you, occupying your own revivified body. Although the capability exists to download a person to inorganic storage, this was not done in your case. It requires the consent of the individual, since once done it of course admits the possibility of multiple selves. However, you are right at least in part. The scene around you was synthesized from your own memories. It is being inserted for your comfort and convenience into your optic chiasma and other sensory afferent nerves—nonintrusively, I might add. The old indignities of body invasion disgust today's society."

"I don't find this either comforting or convenient. I want to know where I really am. I want my surroundings to be as they really are."

"Very well." She paused. "Are you quite sure? We judged this synthesis to be the best way of minimizing cross-cultural shock."

"You were wrong. Get rid of all of it." Drake waved his arm at the room, the easy chairs, and the blue sea and sky beyond the long window.

"Very well. However, there is one other thing that

you should know before you leave derived reality." The woman stared at Drake, her dark eyes troubled. "You are real flesh and blood. But I am not. I am a part of the synthesis, and I will disappear when it does."

She raised her hand in farewell.

"Wait a minute!" Drake found himself standing, on legs that shook with nervousness. "Don't go yet. I have to know. Has there been progress in resurrecting Ana?"

"I am afraid that there has not. It is still considered an impossible problem."

"But I was supposed to remain in the cryowomb until there was hope of a new approach. Why am I awake?"

"I hear the question." The dark head nodded. "However, it is best answered by another. Good-bye, Drake Merlin."

She was gone. With her went the sunlit room and its pleasant prospect of a windswept ocean. Drake found himself recumbent on an adjustable bed surrounded by an array of unfamiliar machinery. The room was small, drab, and oddly shaped. Its octagonal walls bulged up to a multifaceted convex ceiling, across which crawled faint patterns like blue clouds. Earth's gravity had disappeared. His body was close to weightless. He felt that with a tiny effort he would become airborne, floating up to rest on that pale sky-ceiling.

Where was he? And why had he been awakened?

Trismon Sorel had assured him that his Servitor would accompany him everywhere, through space and time, and would be required to approve his resurrection. Drake stared around the room, seeking the wheeled form of the Servitor. But then all questions of his location and condition vanished.

A woman waited in the narrow doorway.

It was Ana.

Ana, happy and blooming with health. She was standing exactly as he'd seen her a thousand times, head to one side and her mouth quirked into a question.

The moment of intense joy was blotted out by a terrible disappointment. This was another synthesis, more cruel than the last.

Drake tried to stand up, but instead he found himself rising straight into the air and turning end over end.

"Easy now." Ana was somehow at his side, steadying him. "I'm sorry, I ought to have waited until you had become accustomed to a low-gee environment."

"You are a synthesis—not real."

"That is not true."

"The dark-haired woman—the simulation of the woman—she said there had not been progress—"

"It spoke the truth." Ana had floated them back down, to sit side by side on the bed. "At least on that subject. There has been no progress in the problem that interests you."

"But you—you are here, you are alive." Again, the fear was there. Could a simulation be made to lie? "Aren't you?"

"I am indeed. But it is not the way you think it is." The gentle tone in Ana's voice was infinitely familiar. "Isn't it obvious to you who I am?"

"You are Ana."

"Yes. But I am not *your* Ana." She took him by the arm, and turned so that they were face-to-face. "Look at me. Can't you see the difference? I am the Ana to whom you gave life. I am the clone of your wife, the person grown from her cells by Trismon Sorel and his colleagues."

"But the other woman said it had been twenty-nine thousand years—have you been alive for so long?"

"Not continuously. That is not the custom." She laughed, and at the sound Drake felt his heart break. "Like most people, I choose short periods of wakefulness between long ones in hibernation—what you would call cryosleep. Almost everyone is curious to know the future, to meet the future.

"And for twenty-nine thousand years, I have been curious to meet *you*. Each time I woke, I checked your condition in the cryowomb. Each time, before I went again to hibernation, I asked to be awakened should you waken."

"But I ought not to be awake now," Drake protested. "I was supposed to remain in cryosleep until the restoration of Ana's personality became possible. I gave those explicit instructions to my Servitor when I entered the cryotank."

Entered the cryotank—twenty-nine thousand years ago. Long enough for steel to rust and stone to crumble. Long enough for even the concept of a Servitor to have been lost. Long enough for hopes and thoughts and wishes to have been forgotten. It was folly to expect anything to endure over thirty millennia.

Except that some things had endured. Drake's own emotions had survived unchanged. He realized that he was delighted to be awake. To be sitting two feet away from Ana, watching the old expressions of thought and concern run across her face—that was infinite bliss.

"I am sorry." The new Ana bowed her head. "Your Servitor is not at fault. Your awakening is my doing. I came to Pluto, and as a human, I overrode the instructions given by you to your Servitor." She frowned. "It says its name is Milton. An odd name for a Servitor."

"Not really." Drake felt a twinge of uneasiness at that comment, which he pushed aside. "Milton is the name that I gave it."

"In any case, I directed that you be reanimated."

"And I'm glad that you did." Drake reached out to embrace her, but she leaned away.

"No. I should have realized that this might happen. Let me try to explain." She stood up and drifted safely out of arm's reach. "You feel that you know me well, and more than well. But you do not actually know me at all; and I do not know you. Although I have gazed at your picture and listened to your voice a thousand times, you are a stranger to me. When I first reached consciousness you were already in the cryowombs. As I grew older I learned everything that I could about you and your life. What you did—and tried to do—seemed to me the noblest and bravest thing in the whole universe. I cannot say how much I longed to see you, to speak to you, to thank you for giving me life. But despite that longing, through all past years I respected what *you* wanted. And I knew that you did not want me."

"I have never wanted anyone but you."

"No. You want Ana—your Ana. I am Ana, yes, but I am a different person. I have my own memories, my own joys and sorrows, my own fears. You do not share them." She sighed. "Anyway, a few months ago I agreed to do something that I have been asked to do many times: to go away with friends on a long journey. We will fly out to the human colony on Rigel Calorans. I expect to be away for many thousands of Earth years. When I made that decision to leave the solar system for so long, I wondered: When I return, who knows where Drake Merlin might be? I could not bear the thought that I might never, ever, see you and know you. So I gave the command for resurrection." She gazed at Drake with those clear, gray eyes that he had known forever. "I did not think of what would come *after* that. I did not ask myself what pain I might cause you. I realize now that what I did was a selfish and an unforgivable act."

"You are wrong. It is forgiven already."

"It may be forgiven by you, but it was nonetheless unforgivable. It was my plan to leave Pluto after speaking with you, and proceed to the edge of the Oort Cloud where the members of the Rigel Calorans expedition will assemble. I can no longer do that, at least at this time. I must respect your feelings. How can I atone for waking you against your will?"

"Stay with me." Drake did not say it, but his mind added the word *forever*.

"I certainly owe that to you." Ana smiled, with that familiar rueful downturn of one side of her mouth. "And now, like the self-serving wretch that I am, I will try to justify my own action in resurrecting you. There is a level of temporal shock after any hibernation, even if it is no more than a few hundred years. I have felt it many times; a reaction to changes in the world, in areas where no change was imagined and anticipated. In your case it has been nearly thirty millennia, and you were not prepared for it as we are. So I will take it as my task to lessen the blow of twenty-nine thousand vanished years." She reached out her hand, and her touch made him shiver. "Come along, Drake Merlin. Your patient Servitor is waiting outside. It is most irritated that a mere irrational human would override your explicit instructions. Come along with me, and listen to my abject apologies."

Chapter 12

"These were never your true love's eyes,
Why do you feign that you love them?"

$\mathcal{A}$na's warning of temporal shock at first seemed greatly overstated. The evidence of human presence on Pluto was mostly the cryowombs. Drake could see little change in the wombs or the planet since his mad run from them, twenty-nine thousand years earlier.

"True enough." Ana had all her old calm and common sense. "On the other hand, this is Pluto. You can't do much without raising the temperature and disturbing the cryowombs, which no one wants to do. Almost everybody has ancestors stored here, even if they don't quite know who they are."

"How many have been resurrected?"

She grimaced. "I knew you would ask me that. The cryowombs still hold close to fifty thousand people. Fewer than five hundred of those have been revivified. None but you has been resurrected in the past twenty-five thousand years. You and Melissa Bierly are the only people to have entered the cryowombs twice, and been resurrected twice."

"Melissa. What happened to Melissa?" Drake saw again those sapphire eyes, blazing with madness.

"She was resurrected."

"Was she insane?"

"Once, she was. But she is cured."

"She's *alive*?"

"Very much alive. Still superhuman smart and healthy and intelligent, only now she's happy and no longer suicidal."

"You *met* Melissa?"

"Certainly." Ana smiled at Drake, with an expression that he read as totally loving. "You have your obsessions, Drake, you must permit me mine. I sought Melissa out originally, just because she knew you. We have talked about you, many times. She forms part of the expedition to Rigel Calorans. More than that—"

Drake interrupted: "But I thought that resurrection had become trivial, for anyone who was properly frozen. Why have so few been revived?"

"Resurrection is trivial. The problem isn't technological; it's emotional and ethical. If I revive a cryocorpse, what are my responsibilities toward that person? What are my emotional commitments? Although everyone recognizes that their ancestors are here, those are *remote* ancestors. Think of your own time. Would you, if you could, have resurrected Hammurabi, or Augustus Caesar—even if you were a distant descendant? They would have been lost in your world of telephones and automobiles and computers. Yet they were exceptional people, not like most of the cryocorpses. Do you know the prime criterion that decided who was preserved in the cryowombs?"

Drake nodded glumly. "I can guess, from what the people at Second Chance told me. Money."

"Exactly. It took money to be frozen, and much more to maintain the condition over the centuries. You are an anomaly, Drake. I read all I could find about you, and I know that money didn't interest you. You acquired plenty, but only so you could be frozen. What you did was very smart. You learned things that people of the future would want to know. What you had in your head was true wealth. But wealth as you knew it no longer exists.

"You have a powerful imagination, Drake. Imagine this. Imagine resurrecting somebody who proves to be a money-hungry fanatic—someone who was once very rich, expects to be rich now, and hopes to receive special treatment simply because of that. Such people almost surely know nothing of interest to us. How could they be anything but miserable today?"

"You're saying it's becoming less and less likely that someone will be resurrected. So why are the cryowombs maintained?"

"What else can we do with them?" Ana shook her head in frustration. "The people in the wombs are legally dead, but because they can be resurrected we cannot think of them as dead. So what do we do? We do nothing, and pass the problem to our descendants."

She was sitting in the pilot's seat of a two-person ship, and now she stabbed at the control panel. "Don't give us too much credit, Drake," she said, as they lifted from Pluto's craggy surface. "People haven't changed at all. When it comes to making tough decisions, we're no better now than we were in your time."

People haven't changed. Perhaps not, but other things certainly had. The evidence that Ana was both right and wrong began to appear as the ship cruised closer to the Sun. It was her idea to introduce Drake to the new solar system in a practical way, by visiting or passing close to every planet and major moon, then heading out for the remoter and less familiar region of the Oort Cloud. It had been Drake's idea to use the small two-person ship, and leave their Servitors behind on Pluto until they returned.

Ana had also preferred a leisurely tour, one that would give them time to talk and Drake time to adjust. On their two-day journey to Neptune he decided that he was going to need all of it. Ana had stated that people had not changed. But what were *people*?

He had called for information about Neptune, and now he was staring at the three-dimensional image in the ship's display. It showed a large silvery superspider, fourteen multijointed legs emerging from a smooth central ovoid. The object was described as an "inhabitant of Neptune."

"What does it mean, 'inhabitant'?" He turned for the fiftieth time to Ana for assistance. "That suggests I'm looking at something intelligent, something that lives on Neptune. I thought that was impossible."

After the first few hours, he had stopped puzzling over the mysteries of language. Another sea change in communications technology had occurred since Par Leon's and Trismon Morel's time. The old languages, filled with their magical resonances of old times and beauties, still existed; but a new language, pruned of ambiguities and redundancies, had been created.

It was much preferred for factual transfers of information, and he and Ana were using it now. Misunderstanding in the new language, according to Ana, was almost impossible.

Maybe. But Drake, approaching communication with a context that was thirty thousand years out of date, suspected that he was coming perilously close.

"That's a Neptune dweller all right." Ana did not share his misgivings or confusion. "Of course, it's not an organic form—we may have evolved organic forms by now that can survive on Neptune, but I don't know what they are. That's an inorganic form, and it operates deep enough in the Neptune atmosphere to be buoyant and mobile."

"But it says there, *male human*."

"Correct. That means it's a fully human male intelligence, downloaded to a brain of inorganic form. If it were anything different, it would say 'human-modified,' or 'human-augmented.' "

"How can you say a downloaded intelligence is human? That thing is nothing like a human."

"That argument ended a long time ago. Or let's just say, people gave up on it. Can you define a human? I know I can't. *It* says it's human, that Neptune dweller. That's good enough for me."

"But what happened to the original human being?"

"I don't know. I expect he's around somewhere close by—on the big moon, Triton, more than likely. Neptune has been developed in a very natural way. There are colonies of humans and machines on Triton, and even a few on Nereid, though that doesn't have much to offer. The planet hardly needs human intelligence at all. There are plenty of Von Neumanns." She laughed at the look on Drake's face. "No, I don't mean the downloaded person. He died before cryocorpses. Von Neumanns are just self-reproducing machines."

"How many of them are on Neptune?"

"Millions? Billions? I have no idea. I doubt if anyone does, since they're self-reproducing. They're mining volatiles and collecting the rare heavier elements, and they manage very well on their own. The human Neptunians are not there for supervision. They have other reasons: to satisfy their curiosity, to experiment with extreme forms, or to maintain some privacy."

Neptune has been developed in a very natural way. Drake, peering down through endless kilometers of hydrogen and helium atmosphere smudged with icy methane clouds, could see no evidence of development; but according to Ana and the ship's information service, Neptune beneath those cloud layers swarmed with the spin-offs of human activity, with machines capable of independent activity like humans, and with humans that seemed more like machines.

He would call it anything but natural development.

He changed his mind when the ship flew on to their next port of call. Compared with Uranus, Neptune's development *was* natural.

Something monstrous was happening to Uranus.

The major moons, except for little Miranda nearest to the planet, had gone. The ship swung into co-orbit with Miranda and circled Uranus for two full revolutions. The gas-giant world was marked with a pattern of bright spots, ninety-six of them evenly spaced around the flattened sphere of the planet.

"Nothing yet," Ana said in reply to Drake's question. "In another two thousand years or so, when the preparation work is all done, those will be the main nodes. The stimulated fusion program will begin. Uranus is too small to maintain its own fusion, so there will have to be continuous priming and pumping. They'll move Miranda farther out, and do the fusion pumping from there."

She spoke casually, as though the conversion of a major component of the solar system from planet to miniature star was a routine operation. And perhaps it was.

"What happened to all the other moons?" He could see fifteen listed in the ship's data set, from tiny Cordelia, barely more than an orbiting mountain that shepherded the Uranus Epsilon ring, out to Titania and Oberon, good-sized worlds half as big as Earth's Moon. Miranda was now the only survivor.

"Oh, they're all right. They'll be moved back eventually." Again, the astonishing thing about Ana's reply was her offhand manner. "Miranda couldn't be moved, because it was needed. But the others must have been in the way for this phase of the work."

Drake stared out of the ports and wondered. Uranus had not been a promising candidate for life to begin with. It would become an impossible one when hydrogen fusion turned the whole world to incandescence.

The thought nagged at him: Why do such a thing,

within the original home system of mankind? On those rare occasions in the old days when he thought about the far future, he had imagined Earth, together with all the other planets of the solar system, preserved as some kind of grand museum. Humanity might spread out across the Galaxy, but the home worlds would always be there. Preserved in pristine condition, they would remind people of their origins.

But what had made him believe that, when Earth itself had already provided such a different lesson? Humans had been changing Earth in a thousand ways for five thousand years: draining lakes, damming rivers, making deserts bloom, razing mountains, clearing forests. Why would they stop, simply because they had left Earth?

Drake wondered if it was all his own wishful thinking: a human urge to turn back the clock to a happy time of simplicity and certitude. He stole a glance at Ana, who was looking out of the port and humming to herself in that beloved rich contralto. A surge of happiness engulfed him. Humans could change, the solar system could change, the universe itself could change. It did not matter, as long as Ana was with him.

After Uranus, the happenings about Saturn seemed minor. Its biggest moon, Titan, was being developed. It was not, however, being terraformed by machines or downloaded humans. Instead, bioengineered human forms were colonizing the unmodified moon.

"It's another experiment, of course," Ana said. "Just to see how far the human biological limits can be pushed. There's no doubt that we could do here exactly what we're doing on Neptune, but where's the fun and challenge in that? As it is, what we have on Titan is quite an undertaking. It's not the low temperature. That's a hundred and eighty below water freezing point, but it can be handled easily—just a matter of insulation, when you get right down to it. The hard piece is the chemistry, ours and Titan's. Nitrogen, methane, ethane, and organic smog: how would you like the problem of adapting a human to breathe and drink those? Do you want to take a closer look?" And, after one look at Drake's face, "Right, then, I guess that's all for Titan and Saturn. Jupiter it is."

The activities they had seen back on Uranus made more sense to Drake after they had left Saturn and its horde of moons, approached Jupiter, and descended at last for a feathery landing on one of the Jovian satel-lites.

He remembered Europa from Par Leon's time as an ice world, the fifty-kilometer deeps of its continuous ocean plated over by a kilometer and more of icy plateaus and thick-ribbed pressure ridges. But it was that way no longer. Their little ship landed on a giant iceberg, floating in random currents along a broad river. With the sunlight striking in at a low angle, the long stretch of open water seemed mottled and tawny like the skin of a great snake. It wound its way to the horizon between palisades and battlements of blue crystal. As the berg carrying the ship moved sluggishly along, Drake saw open water leads running off in all directions. He shivered. He could imagine strange creatures, huge and misshapen, writhing along the icy horizon.

Europa in its tide-locked orbit turned steadily about Jupiter. The Sun slowly vanished from the black sky. The sounds of jostling floes became louder, carried to the ship through the water and ice of the dark surface. To Drake's musician's ear the bergs cried out to each other, sharp high-pitched whines and portamento moans in frightening counterpoint, against a background of deeper grumbles.

"This is why we need the Uranus fusion project," Ana said cheerfully. "Europa is warmed at the moment by individual fusion plants within the deep ocean, and that leads to patchy melting. It will be a lot better here when Jupiter produces a decent amount of heat.''

''You mean you'll do the same thing for Jupiter as you're doing for Uranus?''

''Not the same. But similar. Uranus is really more like a test case.''

''But if you're going to do it eventually, why wait?''

''Oh, the age-old problem. We still have ————.'' She said a word that Drake had never heard before. A soft voice from the ship's communications system at once added, in English: ''no exact equivalent; conservatives/Luddites is closest match.'' It was the first time Drake had realized that the ship's computer monitored every conversation, and had a program to provide near-equivalents for references it judged unfamiliar to Drake.

Ana didn't seem to realize how incongruous it was, that a project to transform Uranus beyond recognition could be judged as the ''conservative'' and old-fashioned approach. She went on, ''But the Jupiter transformation will be approved eventually. Give it a few thousand years, and it will all be finished and working. The ice will go. And we'll have another whole world for development.''

She had been setting out a meal for the two of them, and she obviously did not share Drake's increasing uneasiness. But she must have sensed it, because suddenly she stopped what she was doing and came across to his side.

''What's wrong?''

''I'm fine.'' It was preposterous to be anything other than fine. He was with Ana again, after an endless separation. But maybe it was *because* he was with her that he was allowed to admit to fears and doubts. In any case, try as he would he could not stop shivering.

''You don't look good.'' She placed her hand on his

forehead. "And you don't feel good. Damp and clammy. Let's take a look at you."

She walked over to the ship's controls, touched a panel, and studied a display.

"Hmm. It's nothing physical."

"How can you tell?"

"I can't. The ship can. It monitors the health of both of us continuously. It says you're all right. But it only deals with physical problems. So the rest is up to us."

Ana went across to the table where she had been working, returned to Drake's side, and handed him a drink. "Here. This should help for starters. I told you there would be temporal shock, and I was right. It just took a while to show up. You sip on that, while I order something as close as this crazy chef can manage to the foods you were raised on. And for tonight, I think we'll manage with a little less Europa. I'm going to dim the lights and close the ship screens. You can sit there and imagine you're safely back on good old Earth."

She could not have known it, but long ago, back in the happy days that Drake had not even allowed himself to think about, Ana had done just the same thing when he was upset. She took over. She was strong when he was weak, obligingly weak when he felt strong.

Drake did just as he was told. They ate a full, leisurely meal, with Ana doing almost all the talking. The chef provided a reasonable shot at the foods and even the wines of Old Earth. Finally, Drake could begin to relax and probe the cause of his problem. It was not rational, but he realized that it was the *sounds* of Europa. He could not rid his mind of them. Others might hear nothing but moving ice floes on a changing moon. He heard tormented groans, and the agonized death cries of ice demons.

"You have too much imagination," Ana said firmly, when he told her about it. "One day you will have your reward. All this will turn itself into music." She switched off the lights, lay down next to him, and cradled his head against her breast. He hid himself away in the perfumed night of her long hair.

It was natural, perhaps inevitable, that they would become lovers that evening. Neither of them realized that Drake, deep inside, thought of it as "lovers *again*."

Chapter 13

"And I was desolate and sick of an old passion."

Physical euphoria carried everything before it, all the way into the inner solar system. Lovemaking, as always with Ana, provided an epiphany for Drake. As an antidote to temporal shock it could not have been better. Immersed in the familiar touch and smell and taste of her soft body, he would have seen Earth and Sun destroyed with equanimity.

It was not quite that bad, although four thousand years earlier the Earth had come close.

"A disaster?" Drake looked around at the place where the ship had landed. They were on the winter edge of a diminished Antarctic ice cap. In his time, nothing had grown on this rocky shore. The only animal life in June and July had been the emperor penguins, huddled over their eggs to protect them from the fifty-below-zero polar blizzard.

Now a gentle rain was falling, and the air was filled with calling seabirds, skuas and petrels and albatrosses and terns. Rank grass and flowering plants flourished along the salty margin of the beach. Plovers and curlews were nesting there in enormous numbers.

"It doesn't *look* like a disaster," Drake added. He and Ana were strolling along the shore, bareheaded.

She paused and skipped a flat stone over the brackish waters of the estuary. "Believe me, it was."

"What caused it?"

"The usual: stupidity. We still have our share of that. The old assumption was that Earth's whole biosphere had strong homeostasis. Disturb it, no matter how, and forces would come into play to restore it to its original condition. So while everyone was looking the other way, not worrying about this planet and wondering what to do with Venus and Europa and Ganymede and Titan, Earth started an environmental runaway."

"Runaway how?"

"Temperature, mostly. The atmospheric composition was starting to change, too, but the biggest problem was greenhouse warming. It was caught before it could go too far. Turning it around was another matter. For a while, people were imagining a new homeostatic end point, with temperatures hot enough to boil water."

Drake stared out over the peaceful estuary. "Hubris," he said, in English.

"What?"

"Too much arrogance; the belief that you can do anything."

Ana stared at him. "Anything, no," she said at last. "A lot, yes. Recovery has been slow but steady. Mean equatorial temperatures are below forty degrees Celsius. The land animals are heading out of the temperate zone jungles, and they're traveling sunward. Don't worry, we've learned our lesson. This won't happen again—ever."

"I've learned not to trust *ever*." Drake looked north. "We used to live in a place called Spring Valley. If I tell you how to reach it, could we go there?"

"Were you living up in the mountains, or close to sea level?"

"Down right at the shore." Drake did not notice the change Ana had made, from "we" to "you."

"Then we could go there, but it would be a waste of time. I don't just mean the heat—suits would take care of that. But sea levels are up. Your old home will be under five to ten meters of water. Come back again in ten thousand years. The sea level should have dropped enough for you to pay a visit on dry land. But if you'd like to visit mountains, I have my favorites."

"You've been to Earth before?" It seemed like a ludicrous question—his Ana had been born and raised on Earth.

But she just nodded. "Five times. It's a backwater, but it's on every tourist list. The original home, the birthplace, the shrine of humanity. But if most people were honest, they'd admit that it's rather dull. It's not where the action is. Are there other things that you want to see?"

"My old mentor, Par Leon, lived deep beneath the African plateau. That was high above sea level. I know the location. If we could just fly over there . . ."

"Of course."

Ana agreed readily, although she must have suspected what they would find. Africa, at ten degrees north of the equator, was a seared world of dust and dead rock. The snows of Birhan were a memory, the peak a stark blackness jutting into a sky of fuming yellow. Drake looked at it and nodded to Ana. He had seen enough.

They took off for space and wandered to the innermost system. Venus terraforming, according to Ana, was right on schedule. The surface pressure was down from a stupefying ninety Earth atmospheres to less than twenty. Bespoke bacteria converted the sulfuric acid clouds to sulfur, water, and oxygen. The sulfur was delivered to the deep planetary interior. It would not emerge for hundreds of millions of years. Cyanobacteria, seeded into the upper atmosphere, went about their steady business, absorbing carbon dioxide, releasing oxygen, fixing nitrogen, and delivering a rain of organic detritus to start a planetary topsoil.

"Water is still the main problem," Ana said. "There's simply not as much as we would like. Venus will always be dry, unless we do an extensive Oort Cloud transfer, or combine the planet with one of the big Jovian water moons, like Callisto."

"Is that feasible?" The cure for temporal shock seemed to be working; Drake was starting to feel that anything was possible. But flying a satellite of Jupiter to coalesce with an inner planet? That still sounded ludicrous.

"It's not feasible *yet*," Ana said. "The impact would destroy Venus. But we're learning how to do a soft merge. For the moment, I don't recommend we make a Venus landing. It's too hot down there—hotter than Earth ever got, even at the height of the runaway. It would have to be suits all the time. Are you ready to go somewhere else?"

Drake nodded.

"Right." Ana paused at the control panel. "Lots of options. Unless you're really keen, I suggest that we skip Mercury completely. It has the research domes, but nothing really worth seeing."

The ship flew on, skimming the broad face of the Sun. Close up, that mottled surface was as raging and demonic as anything that Drake had encountered on his visit to Canopus. They passed through hydrogen prominences that roared and flamed with prodigal energy. Drake remained unperturbed. The ship's refrigeration held the interior temperature at a comfortable level; in any case, Ana was at his side.

The Sun fell rapidly behind, and the outward journey began. Drake did not care where he went. It was at Ana's insistence that they head for Mars.

"Just for fun," she said.

It did not sound like fun. Drake recalled the fury of the Mars bombardment, the cloud-streaked sky of dirty gray and the torn and quaking surface.

But . . .

Twenty-nine and a half millennia was a long time. Drake's memories were distant history. Their landing was in midmorning, on a calm world of thin, clear air and dark blue sky.

"A lot more atmosphere than there used to be," Ana said, as Drake gazed out at a green cover of plants, a thin carpet from which jutted hair-thin stems with fat blue lollipops at their ends. "But there's not nearly enough oxygen to breathe. Not for us, at least."

"Why did they stop halfway?" Drake was becoming blasé when it came to planetary transformation. "I'd have thought Mars would be easy."

"It would. You'll see why in a minute." Ana watched as Drake disappeared within his bulky symbiote. She tried to restrain herself, then began to giggle helplessly.

"I'm sorry. I know I'm going to be the same—but just look at you."

Drake did. In a mirror he saw a mournful marsupial, an overweight kangaroo with a wobbling paunch and a long camel's nose. The outsized ears stuck up to provide a constantly surprised expression. He stuck out his tongue. The face in the mirror extended a black appendage at least a foot long. He blinked. The dark liquid eyes blinked back at him, protected by an inner transparent membrane and outer lids with eyelashes long and thick enough to be the envy of any glamour queen.

Ana was allowing her own symbiote to envelop her. "*Now* we can go out," she said, as her new body seemed to inflate before Drake's eyes. "Follow me."

To hell, if you ask me to. But he had already done that. Drake heard the hiss as the ship's cabin pressure dropped. The hatch opened. He did nothing, but his great paunch began to move in and out with its own rhythm. He saw that Ana's belly was doing the same.

"If you decided to live here," she said, in a voice half an octave higher than usual, "you wouldn't have to make a decision whether to live on the surface, where there's not much oxygen, or in the deep caverns, where there is. You'd just let your symbsuit sort that out, and provide whatever you need. Mars surface dwellers never disengage from their symbsuits. They eat, drink, sleep, and die with them—even when they go to the caverns."

Drake could understand why, when they left the ship and began to wander the broken plain outside. It didn't feel anything like wearing a suit. The symbiote was his own body. It merely happened to be a new body that could endure extreme cold and make do on less than a quarter of a human's oxygen needs.

"Eat, drink, sleep, and die," he said. "Make love, too?"

"Can you imagine humans living for years in an environment where they *couldn't* make love? See that group?" Ana was pointing to the horizon. "Go and ask them."

Half a dozen people/symbiotes had appeared. They were moving in true kangaroo fashion, bounding along with fifteen-meter leaps in the low Mars gravity.

Drake watched them wave and point, inviting Ana and him over to an open structure beside a jumble of rocks.

"Fine," he said. "Let's go and chat."

He was curious to hear about life on the surface of Mars, but he didn't want to talk to them about lovemaking activities involving a symbsuit. He was quite capable of conducting his own experiments on that subject.

The change took place on the second day on Mars. Ana became suddenly withdrawn and remote. Drake didn't

know what it was—something he had said or done?—
and she did not want to talk.

That had never happened in the old days. It was not
that they had never argued. But they had a standard
rule. As Ana put it, "Never go to bed mad. Stay up and
fight."

When one's feelings were hurt, the other always
knew. They would sit and talk, argue as much as necessary, and get every nagging pain or upset out into the
open. Once the sore point was exposed, the other
could stroke it better.

But Ana refused to do it. She only said, "It's nothing." When clearly it wasn't.

The return flight to Pluto, cruising out to where
Drake's Servitor was patiently (or perhaps impatiently)
awaiting his return, was quiet and unsatisfying. According to Ana, the trip had been a complete success. If
there had been major temporal shock, it now lay in the
past.

But if it was a success, why was she so distant?

He found out on the final morning of the flight,
minutes before they were due to land at the station on
Charon. Ana had been a lot more cheerful during the
previous twenty-four hours. He assumed that the trouble, whatever it had been, was over. Because his guard
was down, the shock was so much harder to take.

"What do you mean, our last few days together?"
Drake had been watching the ship's automatic docking
on Charon when Ana's quiet statement jerked him to
attention.

Had he heard right? Had she really said, "I wish we
could have made more of our last few days together."

He said, "I thought we could stay here in the outer
system for as long as we like."

"You can." She moved to stand in front of him. "But
I can't. I made promises. The people heading for Rigel
Calorans are waiting for me, but they won't wait for-
ever. I have to head out and join them."

"But what about *us*?" And when Ana shook her head, he went on, "Look, if you already made promises to them, I completely understand. I wouldn't want you to go back on your word. But I have nothing to hold me close to Sol—nothing but you. I'll come with you, join your group."

"No, Drake, that isn't it at all." She took his hand in hers. "I like you a lot, and I will never forget that I owe my life to you. But you can't go with me. Let me put it more brutally: I don't *want* you to go with me. I do not love you as you love your Ana."

"I don't believe it. Everything we've said to each other, everything we've done—"

"Everything that *you* have said. We make fine, fond lovers, physically we fit together beautifully, I don't deny it."

"So what's the problem? Ana, we can talk this through, we always have."

"*That's* the problem, right there. I'm not Ana—not *your* Ana. I'm *me*. You and I have never talked through any problems together. Think about it, and you will realize that what I say is true." She released his hand and stepped away. "Drake, this is all my fault. I should never have revivified you. I see you looking at me, and I know you are seeing someone else."

"I don't want anyone else. I want you."

"No. You are blind. You want what you see, what you think I am. There's so much background that you and your Ana shared. I don't have that, but you don't even realize it's missing. Let me give you just one example. You assumed I would know why you call your Servitor *Milton*, so you've never bothered to explain it to me. But I don't know."

" 'They also serve who only stand and wait'; an ancient poet, John Milton, wrote that. It was just a sort of joke when I said it, because the Servitor—"

"Drake, I don't know and I don't *want* to know. I want to leave, right now."

"You can't leave. What will I do without you?"

"You will become what you were before I appeared to mess up your life: strong, dedicated, brave." She came toward him, hesitated, and then at last kissed him quickly on the lips as the airlock cycled open. "There's more to it than that, Drake. I thought you guessed, but apparently you didn't. I started to tell you once, but you cut me off as though you didn't want to discuss it."

Drake turned. Melissa Bierly was standing in the open doorway. The brilliant sapphire eyes smiled a welcome. There was a radiance and a calmness in her face that Drake had never seen before. Then Ana was rushing forward, and the two women embraced fiercely.

"Hello, Drake Merlin." Melissa spoke softly, almost shyly. "It's good to see you again."

"You? . . . and Ana . . ."

"We are companions. Life mates. We go as a team to Rigel Calorans." Melissa, still holding Ana by the hand, came toward him. "We owe you a lot."

"Everything," Ana added. "You are the reason that Melissa and I met. You were not here, Drake, but you brought us together. I sought her out because she had known you."

She turned to Melissa. Drake saw again that look in Ana's eyes, the totally loving look. He had seen it once before—when they were speaking of Melissa.

"But we were *lovers*," he whispered. And, when Ana merely nodded, "How could you do that with me, if you are bonded to *her*?"

Both woman stared at him in confusion. "For your comfort," Ana said slowly. "To cheer you, when you were frightened and upset. How could I have done anything else? Melissa would have done no less."

Melissa nodded. She placed her arms around Ana, resting her head on her shoulder. "I would, Drake, if you needed me. But Ana *did*. She soothes pain almost before it is there. That is one reason why I love her."

Drake stepped backward and slumped into the ship's

control chair. "And Ana loves you, and not me. I am going to lose her."

"Yes," said Ana. "You will lose me. But don't get it wrong. I told you, what you will lose is Ana, but it is not *your* Ana."

"I will be without you, again. What can I do? How will I live?"

Both women came forward and stooped to kiss him on both cheeks.

"Don't give up," Melissa said softly. "Keep your faith, Drake, and go on. We agree with you; somewhere, sometime, you will find Anastasia. Not *my* Ana. *Your* Ana."

Ana and Melissa stepped away. Hand in hand, they moved toward the airlock. Drake rose halfway out of his seat, as though he intended to follow them. Then he slumped back. The door of the airlock slid shut.

He was still sitting, staring blindly at the displays of the rugged surface of Charon, when the door opened again. The little Servitor, Milton, eased quietly into the room. It rolled forward to stand at Drake's side. As though sensing the human's mood, it did not say a word.

Milton had been on Charon when Melissa Bierly arrived, and it had listened in on the whole conversation. It knew what would happen next.

Chapter 14

"These our actors,
As I foretold you, were all spirits and
Are melted into air, into thin air."

There was the same pleasant room, the same outlook onto a broad bay and windswept ocean: the Bay of Naples, and farther off the timeless waters of the Tyrrhenian Sea. But this time the sea was slate gray, and to the north, ominous rain clouds stood above the ancient city; in place of the raven-haired gypsy woman, a long-haired person with handsome androgynous features was sitting in the easy chair opposite.

Drake turned his head back and forth. His neck was slightly stiff, as though he had been sitting for too long in the same position. The ludicrous nature of that thought hit him, as he said, "I'd rather you didn't bother with all this, you know. I much prefer the real thing."

"I think not." It was a man, judging from the voice. The English he spoke was perfect, accent-free. "There have been . . . changes."

"I expect changes. I *need* changes. Past eras could do

nothing to help Ana. Let's dispense with the simulations."

"That is, I am afraid, impossible."

"My body—"

"Is preserved. Your cryocorpse, together with Ana's original body, is still in the cryowomb. That womb is no longer held on Pluto, for reasons that will become obvious to you later. However, your body is unchanged. It could be revivified, although as you see we no longer find it necessary to reanimate you in order to converse. We are maintaining a direct superconducting link with your brain."

"Who are you?"

"That also calls for explanation." The man smiled, an easy and friendly grin that seemed impossible to simulate. "Let us say, I am 'such stuff as dreams are made on.' As you can see, after the misunderstanding of your last resurrection we have made an effort to be familiar with the writings of your times. Call me Ariel, if you must have a name familiar to you from that era. With your permission, I will now bring someone else to this meeting."

"Melissa, and Ana's clone . . ."

Drake had asked, as strongly as a man with no real power could ask, that he remain frozen until something could be done to restore to him the original Ana; but his last awakening had taught him that others had their own overriding needs.

Ariel shook his blond tresses. "Not Melissa Bierly, nor the clone of Anastasia."

"Are they alive?"

"I would say yes; but not in any form that would be recognizable to you. Patience, Drake Merlin. Much has happened, and much needs to be said and done. First, however . . ."

The man did not move, but at his side a familiar sphere topped by a metal whisk broom blinked into existence.

"With profound apologies." The Servitor nodded its eyeless head toward Drake. "Your instructions to me upon freezing were quite explicit: only when new information was available concerning Ana's condition were you to be resurrected. However, upon reflection I judged it necessary to interface with you before taking certain other required actions. I recognize that an argument could be made that you have not in fact been reanimated, and therefore that your instructions have not been disobeyed. However, I reject that as a form of special pleading on my own behalf."

"You are Milton? You don't sound at all as you used to."

"I am Milton, but in composition more than Milton. I appear in this form only for your convenience. Although much time has passed, I remain your Servitor and obey your commands."

"How much time?" Drake sat up straight, aware that his real body deep in cryosleep could not move a micrometer. What miracle of science gave him total control of this other body, in derived reality? What magic permitted his supercooled brain to think? "Don't offer me the same runaround as I had last time. How long has it been since I returned to the cryowomb?"

There was a perceptible hesitation before Milton answered. "There is no deception. By your standards, it has certainly been a long time; but there have also been changes in the perception and measurement of time. And there have been . . . discontinuities . . . in human history and development."

"You mean a collapse of human civilization? I worried about that, before I first went into cryosleep."

"There has been no collapse in the sense that you imply, with complete loss of technology. However, on three occasions human development has proceeded in other directions—what we now consider to have been false directions. During two of those periods, the idea of technology lacked meaning."

"You can tell me about that later. How long since I went to the cryowomb? Are you going to say, or aren't you? Forget the 'temporal shock' nonsense and tell me. You say that you obey my commands. That is a command."

"Even without reinforcement from the composite, I am obliged to reject any command you give me that is provably contrary to your ultimate well-being. However, I will answer. Your body has been within the cryowomb for a period which, in your most familiar units of Earth orbital revolutions, equates to fourteen million years." The Servitor paused. When Drake did not move or speak, it continued: "Fourteen million years. Which is to say, a period equal to—"

"I know what fourteen million years is." Drake laughed, a humorless bark of disbelief, while he tried to comprehend such a length of time. In his original innocence, he had imagined being frozen for up to a thousand years. He had thought of that as a huge interval.

It *was* a huge interval, a period long enough for civilizations to flourish and fall, for cities and dynasties to rise from the earth and return to it. Rome had endured and ruled for a thousand years. Once that had been regarded as a model of human stability. But while he slept, fourteen thousand Roman Empires could have appeared, one after another. A hundred thousand Caesars, enough to fill a football stadium, could have conquered, ruled, and been brought down. Fourteen thousand Gibbons could have chronicled their rise and bloody fall.

"Or maybe you're right," he said at last. "I don't know what fourteen million years means. And I guess I was wrong. I'm not immune to temporal shock. I'm *in* temporal shock. Give me a minute or two, Milton."

"As long as you need." The Servitor rolled backward a few feet, and the fair-haired man in the armchair continued, "We assume that you refer to subjective minutes. One advantage of a superconducting interface is speed. This meeting is taking place with subjective time rate equal to less than one thousandth real time—"

"I need to *know*," Drake interrupted. "I need to know what's happened to the solar system—why you woke me—if there has been progress with Ana's problem." He had a thrilling thought. "Is it possible to interface with *her* brain, the way you have with mine?"

"Unfortunately, it is not. We made contact with the residue, long ago. There are many intact brain cells, as you might imagine. But the connectivity, the whole that permits the concept of mind, has been destroyed."

"Let me try it for myself." Drake found that he was trembling with eagerness. "I know her better than anyone. Put me in touch with her, let me make my own evaluation."

"We judge that would be most unwise." Ariel's face was calm but compassionate. "Unwise for your sake. Just as it is unwise to expose you, immediately, to humankind as it exists today. There must be a period of adjustment. Your strength and mental resilience are extraordinary by any standards, but we do not wish to push it too far. We feared that you might retreat to insanity immediately after being contacted. You have not done so. But a meeting with the sad, muddied remnant of mind that sits now within Anastasia's body would try your sanity past bearing."

"Has there been other progress, though? If her original brain cannot be repaired—"

"We will come to the question of scientific progress in due course. For the moment, we judge it best for you to begin with something familiar. Your Servitor will show you around the solar system. Then it will be time for us to talk again."

"I don't want a stupid tour of the solar system. Last time, that made me feel worse. I'm interested in people, not planets. I want to know what changes in the past fourteen million years might affect Ana's return."

Drake leaned forward, ready to argue. He was given no chance to do so. With one final wave of his hand, Ariel vanished; in the same moment, Drake was on board a ship.

Although Drake's frozen body remained in the cry-owomb, the illusion that he had been reanimated was quite perfect. He and Milton seemed to be traveling together in a real ship, its motion and progress constrained by the laws of dynamics and solar system geometry. He experienced real hunger and fatigue. After eighteen or twenty hours of subjective wakefulness, he would begin to yawn and feel the need for sleep.

It was the new solar system that seemed to lack reality.

They had begun close to the Sun, where the familiar, steady beacon offered constancy and comfort. A few million years were nothing within the lifetime of a G-class star. It had looked down on Drake's birth, and it would probably look down unchanged on his final death, whenever that might be.

But unlike his birth, final death would not take place on Earth. Drake had stared from the ship's ports unmoved as they swept out past the hot cinder of Mercury and the garden world of Venus, with its blue-white atmosphere, placid seas, and sculpted continents. The transformation of the second planet might have been surprising and wonderful to those in Drake's own time, but it had been predicted since the era of Par Leon; the transformation had been well underway during his last resurrection.

His interest was focused on Earth long before they arrived there. The near-disastrous environmental runaway whose consequences he had seen on his last visit had lasted a few tens of thousands of years, but that was a mere blip on the long scroll of Earth's history. Ana had assured him that the correction was made. She had been sure that a similar mistake would never be allowed again.

So what would the home world have become, after so many millions of years of habitation and development?

As they drew closer, Drake looked and looked again. Something was wrong, but what was it?

The Earth-Moon doublet was growing in the ship's displays. The proportions were right, Earth's disk bulking more than ten times the area of its satellite; but the *colors* were peculiar. The smaller world was an angry red tinged with yellow smears. The larger one, instead of the familiar blue gray of Earth, gleamed a dull and mottled white that was naggingly suggestive and familiar.

He stared hard at that pale orb. The perspective shift took place within his mind.

"That big one's the *Moon*, the markings are changed but it has just the right color! But then where's Earth? Unless it was changed to look like the Moon, and the Moon. . . . Milton, I know this is a simulation. Does this represent reality, or are you playing tricks?"

The Servitor was at his side. It had spoken little since the journey began, but now the response was immediate. "It is not a simulation in the usual sense. It is a representation. By which I mean, although our whole journey is in derived reality, what you are seeing exactly matches the physical solar system, as it exists today."

"What happened to Earth?"

"It is easier to say *why* than *what*. As we told you, while you were in cryosleep another direction was three times taken by humanity. In two of those, technology was ignored. In the third, it took a leap that even now we do not understand. The center of that new technology was Earth. One day, without warning, Earth collapsed to a fraction of its old size. Its surface closed. Its mass remained unchanged."

"It collapsed while it was still inhabited?"

"Correct."

Drake gazed in horror on the shrunken red- and yellow-smeared orb. "So everyone and everything on Earth was killed?"

"We think not. We believe that in some form everything on Earth has survived. Space within has been folded, and we believe that on the interior there was no collapse. We have no direct proof of this, since even after a million Earth years, no one has managed to penetrate the sphere that you see. It emits its own radiation, but it remains impermeable to everything from outside. Sometimes we see changes, occasionally there are what look like planet-wide lightning storms. Our best theory is that the sphere is constantly maintained by a single entity within it, a supermind combination of organic and inorganic intelligence.

"Of perhaps greater consequence to the rest of the solar system, at the time of Earth's collapse and closure the planet was the central repository of all solar system data banks. Their loss had a profound effect on human development—even on human sanity. Everyone was suddenly deprived of a vital group memory and a species cohesive force. The process of reconstruction was begun, from partial databases elsewhere, but it was slow, uncertain, and imperfect. After Earth's closure, every person in the Pluto cryowombs was revivified. Their memories assisted in the re-creation of the oldest historical records."

In Drake, that information produced a feeling of bitter irony. He had been wrong, totally and hopelessly wrong. He had argued, back in the quiet suburban house while the children were noisy upstairs and Tom Lambert sat pale-faced before him, that his own sacrifice was necessary. Without his help, Ana would never be resurrected. In fact, every long shot placed in Second Chance had paid off; even the "useless" ones, whom he had thought no one would bother to revive.

Instead of freezing himself he should have followed Tom Lambert's advice, and lived out his life. Better yet, instead of fleeing from Pluto he should have placed himself with Ana in the cryowombs there. They would have been resurrected together, to live the rest of their lives with each other.

Instead . . .

"I said, everyone was revivified," the Servitor continued. "That was of course not quite true. You alone, because I was armed with your specific instructions on your resurrection, were exempt."

"I am conscious now, even if I am not resurrected."

"True. We will come to that question in due course. But now, do you wish to go closer to Earth, for sentimental reasons?" The Servitor's wiry broom of sensors turned toward Drake. "Even were we not in derived reality, it would be quite safe to go to Earth. There has never been interference with an approaching ship, not even ones that have landed upon the impenetrable outer surface. They are simply ignored."

"That isn't Earth, no matter what you call it." Drake turned his back on the displays. "Take me away. There's nothing for me here."

Nothing for him, perhaps, anywhere in the solar system. That thought grew stronger as they flew outward from the Sun. It was not a problem of physical changes, which were substantial: Jupiter, glowing dully like a dying ember, flooding its satellites with abundant infrared radiation; the rings of Saturn, gone; Uranus like a miniature second sun illuminating the outer system; Neptune, vanished; Pluto basking in new heat to the point where nitrogen was a liquid on its surface and the cryowomb containing Drake and Ana—and only Drake and Ana—had been moved far out to a cooler location.

More important than all those were the changes that could not be seen. When Drake heard the words "fourteen million years" he had not at first thought through the implications. The news that everyone else in the cryowombs had been resurrected brought the understanding that he had become what he had once most feared: a living fossil, a creature from the remote past. Nothing he knew or was could interest anyone in this far future. Even the cryowombs themselves were an anachronism. Drake owed his own and Ana's continued existence in cryosleep only to Milton's literal, persistent, and conscientious mind.

And it *was* a mind. Drake could no longer think of the Servitor as a type of mechanical aide. Considered alone, Milton possessed mental powers that rivaled those of any human from Drake's time; considered as part of some still-undefined composite, the Servitor far surpassed human intelligence.

The ship flew on, beyond the solar system known to Drake. The Sun dwindled to a point. The constellations that filled the sky formed new and anonymous patterns. Fourteen million years was long enough for the slow movement of the "fixed" stars to have changed the face of the heavens.

"The Oort Cloud," Milton said, "was at your previous time of awakening undergoing its first exploration. It has changed a great deal. It is now a coalescence of a hundred million worldlets and interlocking intelligences. We do not propose to spend time there, since in your present form it is beyond your comprehension. Of greater interest to you is this."

The Servitor did not give any noticeable signal, but suddenly the ship vanished. Drake was hanging in open space before a lopsided and flattened disk, composed of thousands of bright sparks of light.

"We are looking at human star space," Milton went on. "This is the part of the galaxy that humanity and machines, in all their composite and complementary forms, have reached, developed, and colonized. Sol lies roughly at the center. Although less than a millionth of our whole galaxy, human space includes eighty thousand suns. The perimeter grows continually, and asymmetrically, at a substantial fraction of light speed."

"Aliens?" The great disk seemed to be several hun-

dred light-years across. Surely humans must have encountered fellow travelers through space and time. But
the wire-broom head was shaking in dissent.

"Not yet. Life in abundance, yes. Even multicelled
animal life, with nucleotide-base pair genetics and reproduction. But intelligence, no." Milton was calm and
fatalistic. "The search continues. Someday the contact
will surely take place.

"However, this is the end of our own brief outward
journey. We must return now to the vicinity of your
cryotank; there we face a more immediate problem."

Chapter 15

Downloading

$\mathcal{D}$erived reality had at least one advantage over normal space and time: travel could be instantaneous. Milton might speak of "heading back" to the region of the cryotanks, but that was for Drake's convenience. There had been no physical travel. At one moment they were hovering far outside the solar system, contemplating the vast lopsided region of the spiral arm that was occupied by humans and their constructs; then they were again looking out over the Bay of Naples, where the dark clouds still hovered.

Ariel nodded to Drake, and began to speak.

"You have seen something of what humans and our inorganic companions can do and have done. Now it is time to talk of what we cannot do. Our limitations explain why we found it necessary to interact with you. The reason is simply stated: You cannot remain in the cryowomb for the indefinite future."

Drake had foreseen such a moment many millions of years ago, before he was ever frozen. Someday all his assets would become worthless. Who then would pay for the cost of continued cryotank operation?

He had hoped that the problem was solved when Par Leon informed him that activities involving the use of *human* time were the only ones with an implied cost. Now, apparently, the rules had changed again.

But he had learned not to accept negative answers. "Is there any way that I can be resurrected and earn credit? All that I know may be without value, but I would volunteer for any function that might allow Ana to remain in the cryowomb."

"You misunderstand. Maintenance of the cryowomb will shortly cease, but not because of any problems of maintenance. Each tank has its own long-lived power source, able to preserve a cryocorpse for an extremely long time without external support. Long enough, in fact, that we do not know its true lifetime, except that it would be measured in billions of years. The cryowomb with its cryotanks is already at the extreme edge of the Oort Cloud, and it is steadily drifting farther out to interstellar space. You and Ana have long been its only occupants. That, however, is not the reason why the cryowomb is increasingly irrelevant. The problem is far more basic. Look at this."

The window did not move, but the scene outside it changed. Drake found that he was staring through the glass at a naked body—*his* body, as it was stored in its cryotank.

"Again, we are in derived reality," Ariel said. "This time for a different reason. Watch closely."

Drake's cryocorpse did not move, but the flesh and bones gradually became translucent. Drake, staring uneasily at his own fading body, saw sparks of light appearing within it. They came randomly and infrequently, one every few seconds.

"One thing we cannot do," Ariel went on, "is control the probabilities that determine quantum processes. What you are seeing are changes to atoms or molecules within your own real body and brain, the result of quantum transitions. To minimize such events, we long ago dropped the temperature in the cryotanks from the original liquid helium ambience, all the way to a fraction of a microkelvin. As a result, changes of atomic and molecular states became far less frequent. They did not, however, cease totally. Nor will they, no matter how close to absolute zero we take the temperature. Vacuum fluctuations guarantee it. There is no way to prevent or control such quantum effects."

Drake saw two more sparks of light, one in his cryocorpse's belly and one at the base of his brain. "You're telling me that I'm changing, even in the cryotank; and there's no way to stop it."

"You are changing—but very slowly. We are showing you quantum events at a greatly accelerated rate. Fifty years passed in real time, for each second shown on this display. However, your general conclusion is valid. There is no way to stop the changes. Left in a cryotank, at no matter how low a temperature, your body must inevitably be altered. Quantum state transitions will eventually affect your memory and your mind."

The scene outside the window flickered gray, then returned to show Naples and the clouded bay. Milton had been waiting silent at Ariel's side. Now the Servitor rolled closer to Drake. "You will appreciate my dilemma. On the one hand, your direct order was to leave you unchanged in the cryotank until such time as there was new learning that might affect our ability to reanimate Ana, as she was in your time. On the other hand, it proves impossible to leave you *unchanged* in the cryotank, since your very presence there inevitably produces change. Therefore I, whether I followed action or inaction, was unable to obey your command. We decided to interact with your cryocorpse, as we are doing now, to explore another option."

"You have one?"

"Of course: downloading. The conversion of the complete contents of your brain to electronic storage."

"You mean, become some sort of computer program? Forget it."

"Listen a little longer, before you reject. If you are downloaded, and at some future time you wish to function again in fleshly form, that can easily be done. It calls only for the storage, along with your brain's contents, of somatic information. Such information is contained in the nucleus of every cell of your body. From your genetic blueprint, your new body can be grown. You would then be uploaded to the new brain from electronic storage."

"That can really be done?"

"Can be, and has been, a billion times. It is the standard procedure for establishing research teams on the planets of other stars."

"But isn't electronic storage just as subject to change as storage in my frozen brain? It's not immune to quantum processes. You just said there's no way to prevent or control quantum effects."

"Quite true; there is, however, a way to *compensate* for them. It is done through simple redundancy and comparison. After we perform an electronic download from a brain, we create three identical copies. Each of those copies, as you observed, is subject to statistical change because of quantum effects. Periodically, we therefore perform a complete bit-by-bit comparison of all three copies. Occasionally, one copy will show a difference from the other two. We attribute that change to a quantum fluctuation, and we correct the variant copy at that point to agree with the other two. It is, of course, mathematically possible for *two* quantum changes to take place in the stored brain map, on the same element of information and at the same time. That would produce three different versions, and there would be no way to decide which one was true to the original.

Fortunately, the probability of such an event is so small as to be of no concern."

"I assume you've done all this to somebody?"

"More than that." The Servitor lacked the means for a physical expression of embarrassment, but the voice slowed and changed. "For the past fourteen million years, I have been applying the technique to you. As soon as the technology permitted a complete download, I performed one of you. Since it was held in a totally dormant condition, and since you were still in the cryowomb, I felt that I had not violated your instructions."

"You mean I've been downloaded *already*, without ever being asked? You've got a nerve."

"What other option did I have? You ordered me to leave you *unchanged* in the cryotank, but leaving you there would itself change you. The only way to guarantee that you remained unaltered was to monitor changes in your frozen brain through triple redundancy checks on the downloaded versions, and then correct you appropriately in the cryotank. I can vouch for the effectiveness and reliability of the method, since it is close to the one that I employ on my own composite."

"How do you know that you don't change, Milton? You might be different than you were yesterday."

"And you may not be the Drake Merlin who went into cryosleep, or the same person who met with Trismon Sorel. No one can prove that they are what they were. I can say only this: uploading represents your only chance of remaining unchanged into the far future."

"What about my body?"

"Your original body?" Ariel answered the question. "It becomes of no interest. Its performance, without electronic update, must gradually degrade. We would propose to leave it in the cryowomb."

"My *body* is of no interest?"

"Certainly. You were disposing of your body, cell by

cell, every hour and minute that you were alive. Ask yourself, where is the body that you wore when you were five years old? Where is the body in which you first met your beloved Anastasia? They are gone, stranded far back upon the banks and shoals of time. It is only your mind, the essential spirit of Drake Merlin, that floats free toward the uncharted ocean of the future."

"Ariel, I don't know you at all; but if you were back in my own time I'd be worried. I once had a teacher who told me, 'Watch out when the talk gets *molto legato*' —very smooth. Too smooth, and too flowery. What are you leaving out?"

"You had a suspicious-minded teacher, Drake Merlin. Very well. There are several other things that should be said. The first concerns Ana. Her full genome is already in electronic storage, so future cloning would be trivial. But there is no 'complete Ana' available for electronic download. Her brain can yield no more than a random chaos of disconnected elements. Their transference would be pointless."

"If I move to electronic form, whatever remains of Ana must move with me."

"I suspected that would be your reply. But it is really quite illogical. If her personality could ever be restored, the existence of primitive brain residues will not be a factor."

"So you say—now. But I've heard too often that nothing can be done for Ana. Both of us get downloaded, or neither one."

"We hear you." Ariel nodded in resignation. "Milton?"

"It will be done."

The Servitor vanished. Ariel looked more pensive. "We have debated the wisdom of mentioning this next item," he said. "We do not wish to arouse in you hopeless and unrealizable expectations. In fact, had it not been necessary to contact you concerning your removal from the cryowomb, we would have remained silent.

But having gone so far, I will continue. Your goal, for fourteen million years, has been to restore Ana to the form that you knew—not merely her body, but her whole personality."

"And I've been told, over and over, that it's quite impossible. Are you telling me that it isn't?"

"It *is* impossible, today and for the known future. The question is, will it *always* be impossible? What I can tell you is this: whether Ana's restoration is feasible or infeasible, in principle, in the very long-term future, does not depend on your actions or on my actions. It depends on the overall nature of the universe itself. And it is because our perceptions of that future have been changing that I am willing to discuss it with you now."

"You've lost me. Totally."

"As I was afraid I might. It is not easy to explain in a way that you will understand, or to know where to start so as to maximize the probability of your comprehension. But let us begin with a question: Do you know the difference between an open universe and a closed universe?"

"I know what the terms used to mean, at the time that I was frozen."

"The notions have not changed, except possibly in minor details. The more distant galaxies recede from us, and more distant galaxies recede *faster*."

"Even in my time, most people knew *that.*"

"Then the definitions with which you are familiar still apply. In an *open* universe, the galaxies go on receding from each other, forever. In a *closed* universe, they one day reverse their motion and begin to approach each other. In a closed universe, the end point for that approach is a collapse to a point of infinite density, pressure, and temperature. Is that clear?"

"Clear, and totally irrelevant. I'm interested in restoring Ana, not in discussing cosmology."

"That is understood. But the two are not unrelated.

Permit me to proceed. Whether or not the universe is open or closed depends on only one thing: the overall density of matter within it. If that density is too low, the universe must be open. If the matter density is high enough, past a critical value, the universe must be closed. What I say next may seem very difficult to you, and the minds of my composite are not sure that you can ever understand it fully; but the possibility of restoring Ana—your original Ana—depends on whether the universe is open or closed. Hence it depends on the density of matter, or more strictly speaking on the mass-energy density of the universe."

"You are quite right, I don't understand you. But if I did, so what? Either the universe is open, or it is closed." Drake could not conceal his impatience. He realized that he did not fit well into the world of Ariel and Milton. He was too focused, too direct, too impetuous and emotional, a living fossil atavism in a gentler and easier society. He did not know what the changed physical form of humanity looked like, but his guess was that nails and teeth had long gone. He alone possessed residual claws and fangs.

"We must be patient." Ariel himself showed neither anger nor impatience. "If your original training had perhaps been in mathematics and physics, rather than in music, this would be simpler. But we will work with what we have." There was no implied criticism, as Ariel continued, "Certain other things become possible in a closed universe. Such a universe possesses, as I said, a single, final end point: an eschaton. At that eschaton, that ultimate stage of confluence of all things, the universe contracts to a singularity. Everything converges, everything meets. This was known to scientists and philosophers at the time of your own birth, who sometimes referred to it as the Omega Point.

"And now we come to the most significant point. Just before the eschaton is reached, all that has ever been known, all information past or present, becomes accessible. Every item of information about people who died a thousand years ago—or fourteen million years ago—becomes available. At the eschaton, every personality who ever existed could in principle be re-created, in perfect detail."

"Including Ana! I understand, I understand exactly."

But Drake was filled with rage, not exhilaration. "If this was known millions of years ago, why the devil was it never once mentioned to me?"

"Because it seemed totally irrelevant. The potential for such future action exists only if the universe is *closed*. In your time, the observations of mass-energy density provided too low a value, by a factor of ten to twenty. That indicated an open universe. Later, scientists decided on theoretical grounds that the universe ought to sit exactly on the boundary between an open and a closed universe. They sought experimental evidence for the missing matter, and they slowly found it. There was still uncertainty; however, they thought that the universe would expand forever, but more and more slowly. In such a case the Omega Point would never exist.

"But that has at last changed. For reasons that we still do not understand, recent measurements reveal a mass-energy density *higher* than the critical value. That points to a closed universe. The eschaton will exist. One day, many billions of years hence, it must be reached."

"And Ana can then return to me. When? When will it happen?"

"If it is ever possible, it will be in the far, far future. Our estimate is that the eschaton will be reached fifty billion years from now. That is a time so long that it makes the interval from your first moment of cryosleep to the present day seem less than the blink of an eye. The universe itself is only fifteen billion years old. I recommend that you do not let this conversation affect your subsequent actions. But your own wishes are important. I would like to know what you want."

"You're crazy!" Drake glared at Ariel in disbelief. "You know what I want. Why do you think I was frozen in the first place? I want to be with Ana. I'll wait forever if I have to. I don't care how long I have to stay in electronic storage."

"We feared such a response. We deem it irrational. However, we sense your resolution and the force of your will. There is still one more thing."

"There always is. Another problem?"

"Not at all. A recommendation. You will, I feel sure, want to understand as completely as possible the concept of a closed universe, and its implications for the Omega Point. That would become vastly easier were you to become part of a composite mind. You would have access to all that any knew, science and mathematics and language and philosophy."

It sounded tempting. Surely, the more that he knew relevant to Ana's ultimate resurrection, the better. But Drake had learned to be wary. Might there also be negatives, so well hidden that the composite represented by Ariel and Milton was not aware of them?

Drake could sense one, a subtlety that was hard to define precisely. There was a *softness* to this age, a kindness and a willingness to bend and compromise. That sounded like real progress for the human species (if that name still applied). But as part of a composite, Drake would surely find his own anachronistic claws and fangs vanishing, dissolved by the pacifism and gentle altruism of the group mind.

A change for the better? Not necessarily. What was good for today might prove fatal tomorrow. Might there be a new future when polish and diplomacy were useless, where what was needed to restore Ana was raw resolve and crude energy?

Merging into a group was a risk too big to take.

"I don't want to become part of a composite,"

Drake said at last. Ariel had been waiting patiently. "I am willing to be downloaded into the database. But I don't want to be *awake* in electronic storage. Let me sleep until I can *do* some thing."

"That can be done. There are, however, other and more pleasant options. It would be very easy to create for you a derived reality, one in which you and Ana are continuously together. Before the general use of the composites, many people lived their whole lives in such an environment."

"How could I be with Ana? She does not exist."

"We would provide a simulation. But, I guarantee, a highly plausible one."

"No." Drake did not tell of the zombie image that came into his head: Ana's dead body, somehow reanimated but possessed of no genuine life, took hold of him in clammy hands and pressed cold lips to his. "No, Ariel. That would be the worst thing I can imagine. Let me lie dormant. Activate me only if there is significant new information about the Omega Point relevant to Ana's restoration."

Ariel bowed his head. "I am sorry that you will not join us, and I am sorry that you refuse derived reality. I believe that we could have soothed your pain."

"Forget me and my pain. There are worse things in the world than pain. As soon as you are able, I want to become dormant."

Drake paused. He had said all that he needed to say, yet it felt incomplete. Something ought to be added of his own great personal debt: to this epoch, to his faithful Servitor, to Ariel, and to the people who had finally offered him a faint and far-distant hope that he might succeed. It was unlikely that he could ever repay Ariel and Milton and their descendants, but he must make the offer.

"Waken me in one other circumstance." Drake could feel his attention fading. Ariel was taking him at his word, and already moving him toward dormancy.

"Wake me if ever you have problems"—he had to struggle to think, struggle to finish what he wanted to say—"tough problems, ones where I might be able to help. Bring me from dormancy, and I will do my best for you.

"Don't hold out too much hope. I haven't had a single idea in fourteen million years, but who knows? Maybe in another fourteen million I'll get lucky and come up with one."

Love alters not with his brief hours and weeks,
But bears it out even to the edge of doom.

Interlude:
Dying

Aye, but to die, and go we know not where;
To lie in cold obstruction, and to rot;
This sensible warm motion to become
A kneaded clod, and the delighted spirit
To bathe in fiery floods or to reside
In thrilling regions of thick-ribbed ice;
To be imprisoned in the viewless winds,
And borne with restless violence round about
This pendent world.

There are worse things in the world than pain.

It was easy to say, hard to believe. Every fiber of every muscle was at full contraction. Tendons stretched, bones creaked and bent.

Something had gone wrong; terribly, terribly wrong. That knowledge filled Drake's mind as the agony continued without end. If this was the price of electronic downloading into a new body, he would take a thousand primitive thawings any day.

One thing, and one thing only, saved his sanity: if he was being resurrected, it must be because there was also some new hope of resurrecting Ana. For that promise, any pain could be endured.

The knotting of his muscles was finally easing. It was replaced by a great weariness and lassitude. He opened his eyes.

Too soon. He saw only darkness shot through with streaks of flickering white. He lay back and waited.

Now he could both hear and feel. A high-pitched

series of clicks sounded, very close. The skin of his chest and belly prickled and tickled, disturbing but not painful.

Vision was returning. He was lying on his back with his head turned to one side. In front of his eyes he saw a milky, translucent sheet, bowed down into a shallow depression under his weight. It felt cool and sticky on his cheek. He tried to lift his head and managed to do so even in his weakened condition. That success convinced him that he was not on Earth or in a simulated gravity close to that on Earth. He was *light*.

Pluto again? One of the asteroids, or a moon of one of the bigger planets? Or somewhere totally new, out in the Oort Cloud or beyond? Or perhaps he was in de-rived reality, where anything was possible. The real question, as always, was *when*. How long had he been downloaded and dormant before entering his new body?

Something had appeared in his field of vision. It was a black, shiny, convex surface, ribbed with spokes that radiated from a central boss like the spokes of an open umbrella. It was small, not much bigger than an out-stretched hand. And it was moving, inching its way down past his body.

He tried to speak, to ask a question in Universal. All that emerged was a gargling grunt. His throat felt filled with phlegm. He tried again, lifting his head and coughing out a single word: *When?*

No human was visible to answer him. Looking down the length of his naked body, he saw four more of the black umbrella objects crouched close by. He learned the source of the gentle prickling on his chest and belly. Dozens of tiny turquoise objects, hard-cased and articulated like small insects, were crawling busily over him. His movement and garbled attempt at speech aroused them to a frenzy of activity. They scurried down the sides of his body and vanished underneath the little arched umbrellas. He heard a louder sequence of excited hisses and clicks from the umbrellas themselves. They all lifted and began to walk on the ends of their spokes, away across the white, sticky membrane on which he was lying. The turquoise insects went with them, clinging to their undersides, or perhaps lodged inside the umbrella crawlers.

Drake realized that the whole surface on which he lay was only a few meters across. It was surrounded and covered by a hemispherical dome. The crawlers advanced to the dome's edge, pushed against it, and slid easily through.

Drake was alone. And he had never felt more alone.

He summoned all his strength and managed to sit up. His pains had not disappeared, but they had become more localized. His hands and feet burned, with the pain of returning circulation. He lifted his right hand close to his face and studied it. It was his own hand, he recognized the familiar pattern of lines on the palm. But the skin was wrinkled, as though he had been immersed in water for a long time. The fingertips were blue-white and dead looking. When he pinched his forefinger between the thumb and fingers of his left hand, there was no sensation. He had feeling only in his palms and wrists—and that feeling was pain.

He could not stand, but he could crawl. On hands and knees he made his way to the edge of the little hemispherical room. He found that he could push his hand into and through the wall. Presumably he could push the whole of him through just as easily.

And go where?

Weakness was sweeping over him again, and he lay down on his stomach on the sticky floor. An awful conviction filled his mind. Nothing that he had seen was in any way familiar. Perhaps the strangest thing about his previous resurrection, fourteen million years beyond the time of his original birth, was not that so much had changed. It was that so much had been the same, that humans had endured, that something remained recognizable. At the time of his first freezing, true humans had been less than three million years old. How many million years would the species continue, in any form? And after humans, what? Perhaps machines were the inheritors—but machines so different from any that he had ever seen that he would not even know what they were. Machines, like the ones that he had seen creeping over his body.

He felt like staying where he was, closing his eyes, and giving up. But Melissa Bierly's words, from long ago, would not permit that. "Keep your faith, Drake, and go on . . . somewhere, sometime, you will find Anastasia."

There was a dark side to those words, one that he had never appreciated before. Assume that he had been downloaded because there was now a way to resurrect his Ana. Into what kind of future world would he be bringing her? It would be supremely selfish to pull Ana from her fermata of endless sleep, if the universe that he had to offer was so alien that pleasure and happiness were impossible.

Well, it was his job to find out. And it would not do to be a pessimist. Since he had been downloaded, no matter how far in the future he had come, the human information network of an earlier time must still exist. Other humans, in flesh or in electronic form, would also exist. They, like he, could be placed in a cloned form of their original body, whose genetic blueprint was stored with the contents of their minds and memories. So his problem would be to contact those humans, in whatever form they endured.

Drake sat up, cursing his own physical weakness. His heart was pounding. That was probably the air. It smelled strange, and he had to breathe faster than usual. He started again toward the wall of the room, determined this time to force his way through and see what lay on the other side. His head was pushing against the wall when a dozen of the little umbrella crawlers came in from the other side of the membrane. Their hissing and clicking reached a new level of excitement when they saw what he was doing. They bunched up in front of him, pushing at his hands and forearms. At first he resisted, but a dozen reinforcements came through the wall and added their efforts to the others. Each one was carrying a narrow section of transparent flexible sheet. One of them waved a piece urgently at Drake.

They were trying to tell him something. And since they had resurrected him, they were probably not intending to do him harm. He allowed himself to be shepherded to the middle of the hemisphere, and laid out flat on his back. Hundreds of the blue-green insectile objects emerged from the crawlers. They seized the flexible sheets and began to place them in position around his body. Where the edges met, the sheets formed a tight and invisible seal.

Drake finally knew what the blue-green workers were doing when a sheet was placed in position over his face. He reached up to tear it free of his mouth and nose, then realized that it left a couple of inches of free space there.

"A suit!" he gargled. "You making me a suit?"

He did not expect an answer. Now he understood the reason for the excitement when he tried to push his way through the wall of the room where he had been lying. Whatever was out there, he could not handle it without special protection. The crawlers knew it. Either they were intelligent themselves, or they were under the control of an intelligence. That intelligence would eventually tell him where he was, and how far into the future he had traveled.

He began to cooperate more actively, lifting his arms and legs so that the sheets could be placed into position. The turquoise workers moved faster, scuttling all around him to make a complete sheath around his body. Each finger, each toe, each ear, was precisely and individually wrapped. He was nervous when the last big piece went into place, sealing off the back of his head and his access to the air in the room. The suit could hold only enough air for a few minutes. He told himself to relax. If they didn't want him alive, why would they have resurrected him?

He noticed no change at all in his breathing. As an experiment he spoke again, through clotted and phlegm-filled vocal cords. "All right, what's next?"

Apparently sound passed through his body sheath with no difficulty. The crawlers hummed and clicked in reply and retreated from him. The blue-green workers returned to them and disappeared through small apertures beneath the ends of the umbrella spokes. All the crawlers headed together for the wall of the room, and paused there.

Drake followed. This time there was no objection when he pushed against the sticky membrane. He forced his way through.

It was obvious now why his earlier effort had been prevented. He was emerging onto the surface of a moon or planet. It was a small one, with a horizon only a kilometer or so away. The hard and unvarying light of the stars above him suggested that if any atmosphere existed, it was far too thin to breathe.

Another mystery. The membrane wall had allowed him to push through easily, but it did not release its air. Nor did there seem to be a hole where he had passed through. Technology was still advancing.

Cautiously, he stood up. His feet felt pain at the ankles and were dead below. Balancing was not easy. He stared upward. The pattern of constellations had been unfamiliar on his earlier resurrection, so it was too much to hope that he would recognize them this time. One thing he was sure of: There were far too many stars, thousands after thousands of them. In such a crowded sky, it would be difficult for the mind to create the old imagined shapes of bears, dragons, swans, or crosses.

Where was he? Drake's conviction that he had traveled far in time and space became stronger. A sky should appear so crowded only close to the center of the Galaxy, thirty thousand light-years from Earth.

Or not even there. The stars above were thickly scattered, enough to make vision easy; but not so thick that other objects could not be seen beyond them. High to Drake's right, like a shadow behind the stars, he could make out a great misty spiral of light. He was looking at it from above and slightly away from its axis of rotation.

He had wondered where he was. Still he did not know, but now he could make a guess. His first thought had been that he was in the dense middle of his own galaxy, staring out at some other spiral. But there was no spiral galaxy nearly so close—the one he was looking at was bright and sprawled over a quarter of the sky. Unless he was in the unimaginably distant future, the object overhead must be *the* Galaxy, the one that formed the home of Earth and Sol. He was seeing it from a dense cluster of stars that in intergalactic terms was a close neighbor, one of the Magellanic Clouds— tight groups of billions of stars that were gravitationally tied to the Galaxy and a couple of hundred thousand light-years away from it.

And that gave a partial answer to his other question: When? Unless some method had been discovered to travel faster than light, he was at least hundreds of thousands of years beyond the time of his downloading. That, however, represented an absolute lower bound. His own feelings, irrationally combined with the sense of infinite age and weariness in his body, convinced him that he had moved many tens of millions of years into the future.

His companions, machines or bioengineered creatures, had waited patiently at his side. They were at ease in near or total vacuum. Maybe they were the "people" of the future, wearing superior physical forms. Unless he found a way to talk to them, he would never know.

They had no limbs, no eyes, no visible way of providing or receiving a message. Yet clearly they were able to communicate with each other. All their efforts to keep him inside the membrane until he had a suit had been tightly coordinated.

He stooped down and picked up one of the little umbrella crawlers. He hoped they would not misunderstand his motives.

The downward movement made his head swim. There was something awfully wrong with his resurrected body. Instead of becoming more at ease, he was experiencing greater pain and discomfort with every minute. He waited until his balance at last returned, then examined the crawler.

It had seven-fold symmetry. There were seven thin "ribs" that radiated from a central boss. At the very end of each rib, on the upper side, a small darker spot gleamed blackish green. It had the round structure of an eye, or a photoelectric cell. The crawlers could probably see him, and each other. It would simplify their acting in concert.

Beneath each rib was a small opening, no bigger than a fingernail. He could not examine the apertures easily in the position that he was holding the crawler, but it had been sitting motionless and unresisting in his grasp. He inverted it. It did not react. The bottom was seamless and uniform, the same deep black as the upper surface. At the middle he saw another and bigger hole, as wide as his thumb. That one was empty, but at the opening of each of the other holes he could make out a blue-green gleam. When he tilted the crawler to get a better look, he saw a stirring of movement. After a few seconds, one of the turquoise insect machines partially showed itself at the mouth of the hole.

He reached out and eased it clear. The move was almost one of desperation. He was sicker than he had

realized on first awakening. His fingers had no sensa-
tions, and the pain in his arms and legs seemed to
reach farther up his limbs. He also felt nauseated.
When he belched, a foul stench rose from his stomach
and filled his suit. It was the smell of decaying meat, the
stink of his own rotting insides.

He brought the little blue-green carapace close to
his face, but his eyes were failing as fast as the rest of
him. No matter how much he peered through the thin
layer of his suit, all he saw was an unfocused colored
blur of tiny legs and body. After a few seconds he gave
up. He reached down and carefully placed the insect
form on the rocky surface in front of him. He half
expected it to scuttle off and hide within one of the
other crawlers, but instead it ran aimlessly around in
circles for half a minute, then froze.

Did each little blue-green robot, if that's what they
were, report to its own home crawler? Drake bent
down, with swimming vision and swirling dizziness, and
placed the crawler a few feet from the motionless turquoise glint. A high-pitched clicking and humming
sounded at once. The lost beetle hurried back to the
crawler, and disappeared. It seemed as though the one
housed the other, at least most of the time; if they were
bioengineered forms, they must be symbiotic.

The crawlers were moving again, all together across
a smooth terrain. Drake followed. The surface was so
uniform and highly polished that he wondered if the
whole world was an artifact. The high curvature showed
that the object must be no more than a few tens of
kilometers across. Making such a thing would be trivial
to the technology that far earlier had been able to turn
Uranus into a new sun and change the whole face of
the solar system.

He sniffed and was aware again of the charnel-house
smell of his own body within his suit. The sniff was one
of self-disgust—and not only at his smell. He ought to
have learned over the centuries and millennia not to

make flying leaps of logic. What proof was there that the progress of technology had been uniform, always in the direction of advancing capabilities? He already knew of three eras in which the definition of "progress" had changed, and there had been time since then for a hundred or a thousand such transitions. Certainly, nothing that he had seen in this resurrection suggested an orderly progression of civilization from Ariel's time to this one. Other than basic astronomy, everything seemed beyond his knowledge and comprehension.

And where was Milton? Drake thought of his Servitor for the first time since his own resurrection. He could not imagine Milton deserting him, for as long as the Servitor possessed consciousness. It was more evidence of the passage of time while he had drowsed in electronic storage.

The crawlers had been heading steadily around the curve of the surface. The top of a building was appearing on the horizon. As he came closer Drake saw that it formed a squat truncated pyramid, its shiny gold walls jutting upward against the star-strewn sky. The crawlers led him toward an open door, about two feet square, sitting at the building's base. It was barely big enough, but Drake lay on his belly and inched forward, following the crawlers through and up a gently spiraling tunnel. Another translucent wall lay at the end. He pushed through that membrane and found himself in a dimly lit chamber about twenty feet square and six feet high. The floor was more of the sticky, milky sheet on which he had first awakened. The walls had foot-wide round apertures spaced along them, windows providing views of the smooth outside surface and the dazzling star field. The center of the chamber was occupied by a transparent column filled with pink bubbling liquid. Scores of the black umbrella crawlers littered the floor, while half a dozen were slotted into a set of narrow letter-box slits that rose vertically against one wall.

Drake stood up, his suited head touching the low

ceiling. It was not easy to balance on a surface that bowed beneath his feet like a great air balloon, and apparently standing was in any case the wrong thing to do. The crawlers immediately became noisy. Drake heard a frenzy of clicks and chirps and hisses. The nearest ones came across to him, swarmed up onto his body, and pushed at him with their thin spokes. It was enough to throw him off his uncertain balance, and he toppled lightly to the cushioned floor. The crawlers settled by his side, silent as long as he did not attempt to rise.

He wanted to explore the other parts of the building, and tackle the difficult problem of communicating with the crawlers. *If humans still exist, take me to them.* How could he tell them that, or anything else, as long as he lay useless? He had to find a common language of gestures. He was sitting up again, ignoring the protests of the crawlers, when the whole room started a gentle vibration.

He lay back on the floor, thinking that the pyramid might be some sort of ground transportation device. Was it trundling them to another part of the surface, where he would learn what was happening? He turned his head and stared out of the nearest wall aperture.

The outside surface was moving. They were traveling not along it, but away from it. He could see farther around the curve of the world, and more of the star field.

He had been close; not a method for ground transportation, yet still a transportation system. Drake lay silent, pressed to the soft floor. The squat pyramid accelerated harder away from the surface and headed for open space.

The ship was more proof, if proof were needed, of profound change that could hardly be described as progress. The technique of inertia shedding, which Drake had never understood, had been in use when he fled to Canopus more than fourteen million years ago. Now that secret was lost, or ignored. He felt in full each change in the ship's acceleration, by the change to his own apparent weight.

He still lay with his head to one side, facing the nearest porthole. In the first seconds of flight, the port had filled with an intolerable blue-white brightness that forced him to close his bleary and aching eyes. He realized after a few seconds what it must be. They had risen far enough from the surface to be exposed to the light of a nearby star.

Think positively. That could be good news. With stars came planets, and perhaps people. He waited patiently, until the glare of light swung away from him to illuminate the rest of the chamber. He studied its color. The star that produced such light must be hotter, brighter, and younger than Sol. Unfortunately, that told him nothing about his particular location—there must be a billion stars like this in the Galaxy and the Magellanic Clouds.

The ship's acceleration dropped dramatically. It was the signal for the crawlers to begin moving. About twenty of them moved to his side and disgorged hundreds of what Drake thought of as "workers." The little turquoise insects moved onto his body and systematically began to remove his suit. More good news. He was heading away from the near vacuum of the little planetoid, presumably to a place where there would be breathable air. That suggested a planet.

But there was bad news, too. Drake examined his naked body as the transparent shielding was stripped away by the workers. It was visible proof of what he already knew from the way that he was feeling. Instead of being resurrected in a body that was stronger, fitter, and more long-lived than his old one, he now resided in a failing wreck. He could see the blackish green of gangrene on his fingers and toes. There was no feeling there, and soft tissue was already sloughing away. The rest of his hands and feet were cold and blue tinged. His forearms and calves were red and they felt warm. They were in the preliminary stages of mortification.

The internal changes were worse. He had not seen anything like food since he was resurrected, but in any case he knew that he would not be able to eat. His teeth felt loose in his head. His belly churned with gas, and there was an unspeakable taste in his mouth. His lungs fought harder for air with every breath. His eyes saw less clearly, their vision spotted with random dark patches.

It was not difficult to reach an overall assessment. He had been embodied in a near corpse, and the necrosis was spreading throughout his whole body. If he was to survive, he had to reach a place where technicians could work on him the sort of medical miracles that had once been possible. And he had to do it *quickly*.

Drake lifted himself onto his hands and knees and moved over to the porthole. This time the crawlers did not object. Three of them crabbed their way along at his side as he placed his nose close to the window. The surface was sticky and smelled like acetone.

He looked out. The planetoid where he had been resurrected was invisible, far behind them. To his left, the blue-white star dominated the heavens, outshining all the scattered millions of the Cloud cluster. The star loomed in the sky, three times the size of Sol from Earth. They were too close. Habitable planets, if there were any, ought to be farther out.

He looked, but it was an impossible task. A planet would be one more spark of light among the millions. A computer, attached to a telescope and observing for many days, might distinguish a planet from the starry background by comparing images and noting the planet's motion over time relative to the slowly moving stars. But Drake did not have a computer; he did not have a telescope; and he was sure that he did not have many days.

Just as he concluded that finding a planet would be impossible, he saw a dark shape biting into the edge of the blue-white sun. He decided that he was indeed seeing a planet, then one second later realized that it could not be so. The shape was wrong—a sharp-edged oblong, rather than a circle—and it was growing in size far too fast. The ship could be no more than a few kilometers away from it. The object was far smaller than the planetoid that they had left a few minutes earlier. It was probably no more than a hundred meters along its longest side.

The ship drifted nearer, its drive powered down to provide a tiny final deceleration. As it came alongside the dark oblong, Drake could take a closer look. The surface was a roughened and pitted black, nothing like the shiny gold of the ship. It seemed perfectly flat and featureless, but presumably the crawlers knew better. Half a dozen of them had wandered across to the entry tunnel. They were hovering there as though waiting for him. There had been no attempt to provide him with another suit.

He wasn't sure how much physical effort he could manage, but he had no choice. He lay on the floor and inched his way painfully through the white membrane and on into the spiraling tunnel. He could feel the rotting skin of his naked chest sticking to the tunnel floor, then tearing free as he pushed forward. At one point he could go no farther until the crawlers, behind and beside and ahead of him, eased him along through a tight spot.

They emerged into a sounding, cavernous chamber. It was totally sealed, totally dark, and icily cold. Not even starlight penetrated. Drake, shivering and listening to the sound of his own labored breath, did not know what to do. At last the crawlers accompanying

him began to glow. A line of green light like a ghostly
bioluminescence showed along each of their seven ribs.
As their light brightened and Drake's eyes adjusted, he
was able to make out something of his surroundings.

The fittings of the great chamber showed that it had
once held scores or hundreds of identical objects, serried ranks of them running off into the distance. That
had been long, long ago. The objects had all gone.
Dust filled every marked furrow where something had
once rested. Dust in a deep layer covered everything.

Drake sagged with weakness and disappointment.
There was nothing for him here, no reason for the
crawlers to have brought him so far and with such effort. But they were once more moving forward, then
waiting as though expecting him to follow.

He could barely propel himself, even in such a negligible field. He dragged himself along for a few yards
with his arms through the thick dust; then he was
forced to pause and rest. The crawlers came to either
side, lifting his body and easing it along. They were
helping him, but why?

Where were they taking him? Why did they think he
might want to see it, whatever it was?

He was not resisting, but neither was he helping. He
simply allowed himself to be carried, eyes almost
closed, until at last the crawlers released their hold and
eased away from his body.

Your move, that said. But it was no move he could
imagine.

He forced his weary eyes to open. In front of his
face, no more than a few inches away, stood a vertical
wall of dark metal. He raised his head, and saw that it
ended two feet or so above his own recumbent eye
level. He made a supreme effort, reached up to the top
of the wall, and lifted himself. He peered over the edge.

It was not a wall. It was the side of a big tank. And
not just any storage tank. He recognized it, this was a

cryotank. The seals had been broken, the outer and inner lids removed.

He peered inside. It was empty. He stood, dazed and bewildered. A cryotank.

And, a few yards farther along, another. Just the two of them. He held on to the tank side for support, and clawed and scrabbled his way around toward the other tank.

It, too, stood with the seals broken. The outer and inner lids had been removed.

But it was not empty. Drake stared, eyes failing and mind reeling. There was a body inside. A dried and mummified body that he recognized.

It was Ana's body. He knew the color of the hair, the shape of the beloved skull that showed its bones beneath the taut and yellow skin. Ana's body.

He wanted to groan, but his throat was too agonizingly sore. Not really Ana, but the empty husk of what she had once been. It was the end of all hope, the end of everything.

Then the remnants of reason came back. He should not be here, standing by an ancient cryotank. He had been downloaded into electronic storage. His resurrection had been promised from that electronic storage into a new, cloned body. And Ana, too, had moved to electronic storage.

So what was this tank, and why was he here?

Even as he asked the question, he knew the answer. These were the *original* cryotanks, the ones that had held him and Ana.

"Each tank has its own long-lived power source, able to preserve a cryocorpse for an extremely long time without external support. . . . The cryowomb with its cryotanks is already at the extreme edge of the Oort Cloud, and it is steadily drifting farther out to interstellar space. You and Ana have long been its only occupants."

It had never occurred to Drake that those original cryotanks might be left to wander wherever the winds

of space chose to take them, but why not? It would not
have occurred to Ariel and his composite to destroy the
tank and the womb, since from their point of view
the only important versions of Drake and Ana were the
ones in electronic storage.

Drifting farther out to interstellar space—and farther yet.
How many millions, or more likely billions, of years had
it taken for the wandering flotsam of the cryowomb to
find its way beyond the Galaxy, all the way to the Magellanic Cloud? How many millions more before it was
found by the exploring crawlers?

No wonder that Drake had seen the discontinuity of
technology development everywhere. It was not discontinuity—it was an independent development. The
crawlers were aliens. There was no connection between
them and human civilization. Drake was probably their
first evidence of the existence of humans.

And no wonder, either, that the attempt at resurrection by the umbrella crawlers and the workers had produced such an ailing, sickly, and imperfect result.
Without prior knowledge of human physiology or the
correct thawing procedure, it was a miracle that the
umbrella crawlers had done as well as they did. Drake
had been revivified, even if only for a short time.

Or maybe they had succeeded as well as anything
ever could. Drake had been downloaded to electronic
storage precisely because cryotank storage was unreliable over long time periods. He had no idea how long
it had been since he joined Ana in the cryowomb.
Long enough for resurrection to be totally unreliable?
Long enough to make his present disintegration inevitable?

The great thing was, it didn't matter. This was not
the end of all hope, the end of everything. The hollow
shell beside him was not the only Ana, just as he was not
the only Drake. Somewhere he and Ana still existed in
electronic storage. Somewhere, at some time, they
might be reunited. No. They *would* be reunited.

Drake ignored his pain and weakness. He laughed aloud.

It was a mistake. The decaying fabric of his lungs ripped under the stress like wet paper. His throat filled with blood, and he died.

PART TWO
Iliad

Chapter 16

"By a knight of ghosts and shadows,
I summoned am to tourney."

There are worse things in the world than pain.

Pain can be channeled and concentrated, marshaled and molded, directed to draw some element of the world into bright particular focus. Harsher pain can force a tighter focus.

But panic, heart-stilling, gut-twisting panic, has no redeeming value. It dissipates instead of distilling. When blind panic roars and surges, all concentration is lost.

Drake awoke to that knowledge. Terror and horror howled at him from every direction. He had no idea of the cause. Worse, he did not know how to find out. He was blind to everything, deaf to all but the screaming of frightened minds. He tried to order the chaos around him and structure the questions that he wanted answered:

Where am I? When am I? How long was I dormant? How far in the future have I traveled this time? What progress has there been in restoring Ana?

It was hopeless. He could form the questions, but a hundred billion replies came raging in at once. They said everything and nothing, individual vectors combining to give a null resultant.

He tried different questions: *Why are you so afraid? What is the source of fear?*

A hundred billion answers came in unison. The force of the signal was too much to handle. Drake made a supreme effort. He ignored the torrent of inputs from those countless billions of accessible minds, and looked inward to create his own working environment.

A sunny room, windowed and comfortable. The familiar prospect beyond it of a windswept Bay of Naples.

And in the seat opposite, ready to answer his questions—

Drake recoiled. Instinctively he had thought of Ana, and she sat waiting. It was the worst possible choice. In Ana's presence, even with an Ana that he had himself created, he would not seek answers. Like the lotus-eaters, he would dream away the time.

Who?

People flickered into the armchair. Par Leon, Ariel, Melissa Bierly, Trismon Sorel, Milton, Cass Leemu . . .

None would hold. They appeared, and were as quickly gone.

Who?

Tom Lambert. Yes, yes, yes. Don't go!

The outline of the doctor had been faint and wavering. Now his figure stayed and steadied. He shook his head reprovingly. "Dumb, very dumb. I don't mean you, Drake. Us. Not your fault, but ours—the composite's. We should have known better."

"Better than what?" Drake saw that it was Tom at thirty, leaner than the paunchy and balding version of their last meeting.

"Than to expose you all at once to our situation." The man in the other chair was so real, so tangible, that it was impossible to think of him as some ghostly and evanescent swirl of electrons. "Heaven knows, we've talked enough about temporal shock. We have plenty of experience with it. You'd think we would have learned to believe in it."

"I'm not feeling temporal shock."

"You will. Do you insist on this form of interaction, by the way? It will severely limit the rate of information transfer."

"I can handle this. I couldn't take it the other way."

"Then I suppose we'll have to live with it. That *is* temporal shock, even if you don't want to use the term. You'll get used to the new reality after a while. I'd suggest we take this slowly, maybe have little practice sessions until you learn how to structure and sort inputs."

"I'm ready to sort some inputs now, Tom, without any practice at all. Tell me three things. Can Ana be brought back to me? When am I? And where am I? And *don't* tell me that I'll have trouble understanding or accepting whatever the truth is. I've heard that line of talk every time I've been resurrected, and every time I managed."

"I'll see what I can do." Tom leaned back, pipe and lighted match in hand. He was still in his tobacco-addiction days, shortly before acute sinus problems and the anomaly of a physician practicing the opposite of what he preached had forced him to give up smoking. "You know, Drake, some of the questions that you asked are pretty damned hard to answer."

"I thought they seemed very basic."

"Well, you asked about *time* again. I know what you mean: How many years has it been since your upload into the data banks? But you must understand that with people buzzing all over the Galaxy, or operating in electronic form, or sitting in strong gravitational fields, everyone's clock runs at a different rate. We use a completely different technique for describing time now. If I told you how it worked, it wouldn't mean a thing to you. I'll give you an answer, I promise. I'll find a way of showing you. But for the moment, why don't we just agree that however you measure it, it's been a very long time compared with your previous dormancies."

A very long time—compared with fourteen million years? Drake suspected he would not like Tom's answer, when it was stated in his old-fashioned terms.

"What about Ana?"

"Sorry. No real change since last time. We have confirmed the closed nature of the universe, so there is a possibility of ultimate resurrection close to the Omega Point, in the far, far future. Today, we can't do a thing for her."

"So why am I awake, instead of dormant in electronic storage? Have you forgotten what I requested?"

"Not at all. We have honored your wishes for a long time . . . perhaps too long. But we have our worries, too. Our own needs have finally reached a point of urgency that cannot be denied. More to the point, if we do not solve our problem, your own needs and requests will become academic. We have to save ourselves if we are to save you."

Tom Lambert was adding to Drake's perplexity. He could imagine that the composite might have problems; but the composite must also possess overwhelming capabilities and resources. Drake could not see how his own resurrection and involvement would change anything. If he had been a living fossil long ago, he was far more of one now.

"I don't understand what your problem has to do with me, Tom. And I don't see what I have to do with it. But I think you'd better tell me about it."

"I intend to. And believe me, it *is* a problem, the very devil of a problem, nothing to do with you or Ana. We have gone beyond desperation. I'll be honest, you are our last hope, and a long shot it is. A *damned* long shot. We need a new thought. Or maybe an old thought." Tom's mouth trembled, and the fingers holding his pipe writhed. On the fringes of Drake's mind he heard again the cry and yammer of countless terrified souls. He suppressed them ruthlessly, building a gate in his own consciousness that admitted only the calmest components.

"Thanks. That's a lot better." Tom took the pipe from his mouth and laid it down on the broad window-sill. He rummaged in his pocket for his tobacco pouch. Drake noted, with no surprise, that it was a black leather one given to him by Ana.

"Might be a good thing if I show you directly," Tom continued, as he filled and tamped his pipe. "Let you see for yourself, eh? You know the old advice that Professor Bonvissuto drilled into your head: Don't tell, show."

"Do it any way you like. I'll let you know soon enough if I can't take it."

"Fine. I'm going to begin with the solar system. It *is* relevant, even though you may think at first that it isn't. Hold on to your hat, Drake. And hey, presto." Tom clapped his hands. The inside lights turned off. The scene beyond the picture window changed. The Bay of Naples had gone. Suddenly it was dark outside, with no hint of sea or sky. The room hovered on the edge of a bleak and endless void, lit only by glittering stars.

As Drake stared, the scene began to move smoothly to the right, as though the whole room was turning in space. A huge globe came into view. It was bloated and orange red, its glowing surface mottled with darker spots.

"The Sun," Tom Lambert said simply.

Drake stared at the dull and gigantic orb. "You mean, the Sun as it is *today*?"

"That's right. Real time presentation. Of course, we're not as close as it looks. That's as seen through an imaging system. But you're looking at Sol, the genuine article, with realistic colors and surface features."

Sol transformed—by nature, or human activities?

"Did you make it that way?"

"Not at all." Tom was lighting his pipe again, and his presence was revealed only by a dull red glow that waxed and waned. "We could have done it, but we didn't. Natural stellar evolution made the change."

Sol had been transformed by time, from the warm star that Drake had known into a brooding stranger. He had learned enough over the millennia to understand some of the implications. Tom Lambert had answered one of Drake's questions without saying a word. The change of the Sun from the G-2 dwarf star of their own day to a red giant required five billion years or more of stellar evolution. Sol had now depleted most of its store of hydrogen, and was relying for energy on the fusion of helium and heavier elements.

"What happened to the planets? I don't see them at all."

"Not enough natural reflected light. But I can highlight them for you." The field of view changed as Tom spoke, backing off from the Sun. Brighter flashes of light appeared on each side of the glowing ball of orange. "That's Jupiter." One light began to blink more urgently. "And that's Saturn, and Uranus, and Neptune."

"Uranus used to have its own fusion reaction. Jupiter, too."

The glowing pipe bowl moved in the darkness, as Tom shook his head. "Long gone. Those couldn't be more than short-term fixes, given the limited fusion materials."

"What about the inner planets? What about Earth? Can you show me them?"

"No. Sol's red giant phase is a hundred times its old radius, two thousand times the old luminosity. If Earth had remained in its original orbit it would have been incinerated, just like Venus. Mercury was swallowed up completely. Don't worry about Earth, though, it still exists. The singularity sphere has been removed, and it is more like the Earth that you knew of old. But it was moved far away, along with Mars. There's no point in looking for it"—Drake had unconsciously been turning his head to scan the sky—"you'll never see it from our present location. If you like I can show you the Moon. We left that behind."

Far away. How far away? What would a human (if there were still such a thing as a living, flesh-and-blood human) see today, looking upward from the surface of that distant Earth?

" 'I had a dream which was not all a dream.' " Drake muttered the words as they welled up in his mind. " 'The bright sun was extinguished, and the stars did wander darkling in the eternal space, rayless, and pathless, and the icy earth swung blind and blackening in the moonless air.' "

"Sorry?" Tom's voice was puzzled. "I don't quite grasp what you're getting at."

"Not my thoughts. Those of a writer dead before we were born. Don't worry about me, Tom, I'm not losing it. Let's keep going."

"Are you sure? I don't want to overload you again. Remember, this is only our first session."

"I can take it. Go ahead."

"If you say so. I wanted to start close to home, give you the local perspective, so to speak, then move us out bit by bit. So here we go again."

Sol began to shrink. The room that Drake was sitting in backed away into space and lifted high above the ecliptic. Sol became a tiny disk. The highlighted flicker of the outer planets moved in to merge with it and become a single point.

The apparent distance to Sol was increasing. In another half minute the inner region of the diffuse globe of the Oort Cloud was visible. Billions of separate and faint points of light were smeared by distance to a glowing haze. "Every one has been highlighted for the display," Tom said casually. "Have to do it that way, or you wouldn't see a thing. Not much sunlight so far out. And of course we've been showing just the inhabited bodies. What you might call the 'old' solar system colonies, before the spread outward really began. Wanted you to see that, but now if you don't mind, I'm going to pick up the pace a bit. Don't want to take all day."

The outward movement accelerated, accompanied by Tom Lambert's apparently offhand commentary (Drake realized that the composite speaking through Tom was actually anything but casual; it was his own needs, structuring the form of the input). The whole Oort Cloud was seen briefly, then in turn it shrank rapidly with distance from huge globe to small disk to tiny point of light. Other stars with inhabited planets, or planet-sized free space habitats, appeared as fiery sparks of blue-white and magenta.

At last the whole galactic spiral arm came into view. It was filled with the flashing lights of occupied worlds. The interarm gaps showed no more than a sparse scattering of points, but across those gulfs the Sagittarius and Perseus arms were as densely populated as the local Orion arm. Finally the whole disk of the Galaxy was visible. The colored flecks of light were everywhere, from the dense galactic center to its wispy outer fringes. Humans and their creations spanned the Galaxy.

The display froze at last.

"In all our forms," Tom said, "we endured. More than endured: prospered. That's the way things stood, just one-tenth of a galactic revolution ago—twenty-five million years, in the old terms of time. Development, by organic, inorganic, and composite forms, had been steady and peaceful through thirty full revolutions of the Sun about the galactic center. Pretty impressive, eh?"

Very impressive. Drake recalled that one galactic revolution took about two hundred million years. Humans had survived and prospered for more than six billion years.

"But it's not like that anymore," Tom added. "I'm going to show you a recent time evolution—in terms familiar to you, I will display what has been happening in the past few tens of millions of Earth years."

Again there was a tremor in his voice, a hint of uncounted minds quivering beyond the gate and walls imposed by Drake. The static view outside the picture window began to change.

At first it was no more than a hint of asymmetry in the great pattern of spirals, one side of the Galaxy showing a shade less full than the other. After a few moments the differences became more pronounced and more specific. A dark sector was appearing on one side of the disk. On the outermost spiral arm, far across the Galaxy from Sol, the bright points of light were snuffed out one by one. Drake thought at first of an eclipse, as though some unimaginably big and dark sphere was occulting the whole galactic plane. Then he realized that the analogy was no good. The blackness at the edge of the Galaxy was not of constant diameter. It was increasing in size. Some outside influence was moving in to invade the galactic disk, and growing constantly as it did so.

"And now you see it as it is today," Tom said quietly. The lights had come on again within the room, dimming the display outside. Drake did not know if that was under his control or Tom's, as Tom continued, "Except, of course, that it has not ended. The change continues, faster than ever."

A crescent wedge had been carved from the Galaxy, cutting out a substantial fraction of the whole disk.

"Colonies vanish. Without a signal, without a sign." Tom sounded bewildered. "If we assume that all the composites in the vanished zone have been destroyed, as the silence would suggest, then billions of sentient beings are dying from moment to moment even while we are speaking."

It was a tragedy beyond all tragedies. Drake had become used to the tours of a changing solar system, provided on each resurrection until overstimulation led to numbness; but death was different.

He had been touched by death just five times in his own life: his parents, Ana's parents, and the death of Ana herself. Those single incidents loomed enormous, but they sat within a century of larger disasters—of war and famine and disease. Thirty million had been killed in two world wars, twenty million dead of influenza in a single year, twenty million starved to death by the deliberate act of one powerful man.

Those were huge, unthinkable numbers, but still they were *millions,* not billions. They were nothing, compared with what he was facing now.

Tom said softly, "Our galaxy is being invaded by something from outside. We are being destroyed, faster than we can escape."

Drake knew that. He also knew he did not want to face it. "Your problem is terrible, but it has nothing to do with me. More than that, there is nothing that I can do about it."

"You do not know, unless you try."

"Try what? You are being ridiculous."

"If we knew *what* to try, we would long since have tried it. Drake, we did not rouse you from dormancy on a whim, or without prior thought. You are from an earlier age, more familiar with aggression. If anyone can suggest a way to protect us, you can do so."

"Why me? There were fifty thousand others in the cryotanks, all from my era. They were resurrected, every one of them. I assume that some at least are still conscious entities."

"Most are. But they no longer exist as isolated intelligences. All, except you, form part of composites. The result lacks—please do not misunderstand me—your primitive drive and aggression."

"You need me because I'm a *barbarian*!"

"Exactly."

"To try and do what you refuse to do."

"No. What we are *unable* to do. As I said, you are our last hope, and it is a desperate hope indeed. Drake, let me suggest that you have no choice. If you want Ana to return to you, *ever*, you must help us."

"Blackmail."

"Not at all. Consider. If you fail to help, and if human civilization falls, so too do the electronic data banks. You will then cease to exist, and so will any possibility of resurrecting Ana. This is not, in the language of game theory, a two-person zero-sum game between you and the rest of humanity. Only if humanity wins can you possibly win. In order for that maximum benefit to be reached, by you *and* by humanity, it is necessary for you yourself to suffer a period of great effort, with no guarantee of return on that effort. No guarantee, indeed, that your effort is even needed. It is conceivable that, without you, we might come up with an answer to our problem tomorrow. But I do not think so. We have tried everything that we know. Well, Drake?"

Drake shook his head and stared out at the mutilated disk of the Galaxy. "You sure don't sound much like Tom Lambert. Tom couldn't have talked about zero-sum games to save his own life."

"This was your chosen medium of interaction, not ours. The composite that is addressing you is purely electronic. And talk of zero-sum games may be needed to save all our lives."

The scene beyond the window changed. Again it was the seacoast villa, looking across a bay tossed now by whitecaps beneath racing storm clouds.

"You see," Tom said. "You make my point. That is *your* vision, not ours. But we do not dispute its accuracy, as a possible harbinger of things to come."

Drake turned moodily to face the south, where a single sailboat was running for shelter. A squall struck as he watched, catching the little vessel and leaning its pink sails far over to starboard.

"I think we ought to start over," he said at last. "Tell me and show me everything, right from the beginning. Then I have a thousand questions."

Chapter 17

Star Wars

"I know more than Apollo,
For oft when he lies sleeping
I see the stars at bloody wars
In the wounded welkin weeping."

Drake could have anticipated the problem. Composites came in all sizes and types, remote and nearby, wise and foolish, planetary and free-space, organic and inorganic. Their constant interactions blurred the lines of identity, until it was not clear which elements were speaking or which were in control. Since he saw that problem in others, he had to assume that the same thing might happen to him when he worked with them. Yet he must, at all costs, maintain his individual character and agenda.

He decided that he had to create a private record of his own thoughts and actions. It seemed not a luxury or a personal indulgence, but a necessity.

The irony of the whole situation was not lost on him. He had been a lifelong and dedicated pacifist, hating all things military—so much so that until Ana went into the cryowomb and he was desperate for money, he would not consider military music commissions, no matter how much they offered. Now, so far in the future that he did not like to think about it, he was an aggression consultant to the whole Galaxy.

His private thought: the incompetent and the ignorant are now leading the innocent; but he did not offer that comment to anyone else.

"What have you tried?" Drake was in working session with Tom Lambert. He was sure that he couldn't really help, but he was also sure that the composites wouldn't accept a negative answer. More than that, for Ana's sake *he* could not accept it. He had to pretend, to himself more than anyone, that he knew what he was doing.

"Drake, we have tried many things. We sent S-wave signals to that sector of the Galaxy. There was never any reply—"

"Back up, Tom. *S-wave* signals?"

"Fast signals. Superluminal signals, that employ an S-wave carrier to advance at high multiples of light speed."

"You can travel faster than light? I thought that was impossible."

"It is, for material objects. We have superluminal capability for signals only. Just as well that we do, because we really need it. How else could a composite with widespread components operate as a unit? Anyway, we sent fast signals to the silent region, but no reply was ever received. We wondered if the problem might be that the other entities could not detect superluminal messages. So we sent subluminal signals and inorganic probes. We waited for millions of years, knowing that all the time more of our stellar systems were becoming mute. Nothing returned. We sent ships bearing organic units, and ships carrying full composites. Nothing has ever come back."

"Were your ships . . . armed?" Drake had to hunt the data banks for that final word, but apparently it gave Tom even more trouble. There was a long silence.

"Armed?" Tom said at last. He sounded perplexed.

"Equipped with *weapons*." Drake wondered. Had aggressive impulses been stamped out completely, as an impediment to steady progress and the colonization of the Galaxy? When Tom didn't answer, he added, "*Weapons* are things able to inflict damage. Weapons would permit a ship to defend itself if it were to be attacked."

Tom Lambert didn't like that, either. His image flickered and wavered, as though whatever was communicating had suffered a temporary breakdown. Confusion bled in from the clamoring host of minds in the background.

"They had no 'weapons.'" Tom was steadying again. "There are no 'weapons.' The details of the concept have been relegated to remote third-level storage, and it is poorly defined even there. What are you suggesting?"

"Something very simple. This galaxy is being—" Now Drake had to pause. He wanted to say 'invaded,' but that word had apparently vanished from the language.

"Something outside the Galaxy is moving into it," he said at last. "Do you agree?"

"So it would appear."

"And that something is displacing human civilization."

"Yes. That is our fear, although we have no direct proof. But what could be doing this?"

"I have no idea. That's something we're going to find out. You've been making too many assumptions, Tom. One is that you are seeing something *intelligent* at work; something with a developed technology."

"We made no such assumptions."

"Of course you did. Not explicitly, but you did it. You say you sent signals and you received no reply—but even to *expect* a reply presumes that something out there is able to detect a signal, comprehend a signal, and reply to a signal. Suppose that the entity moving into our Galaxy has no intelligence at all?''

"Then we will never be able to communicate with it. We are doomed.''

"Why?'' Drake, in spite of his own reservations about his ability to help, was becoming annoyed with the composites. They were such a spineless lot, ready to lie down and die before they were even touched. "Why are you doomed? You don't need to *communicate*, you know. You just need to stop the—the—'' Again, the need for a word that did not exist. The composites had not named the problem. "The blight,'' he said at last. "The marauder, the Shiva, the destroyer, the whatever we choose to call it. I don't know if it's intelligent or nonintelligent, but it's changing the Galaxy in a way that's deadly to humans. Even if the Shiva don't *mean* to kill, they are silencing stellar systems by the billion. Never mind *understanding* what's happening. That would be nice, but the main thing is, we have to defend ourselves against the effects.''

"But we have no idea how to do that.''

"I'm going to tell you how.'' The amazing thing was that he was starting to believe his own words. It was a chilling reflection on the humans of earlier times. No one, no matter how much the pacifist, could in his own era go from child to adult without becoming steeped in the vocabulary, ideas, and procedures of war. Even games were a form of combat, using the language of conflict. Drake knew more than he realized about the theory and practice of warfare.

"We have to do a few things for ourselves,'' he went on, "before we can consider external action. First, we have to create and become familiar with a new language. You must learn to speak *War*.'' Drake said the last word in English. "You need to be able to *think* war, and before you can think it you have to be able to speak it. I will provide the concepts, you will deal with the mechanics of language creation. All right?''

Silence from Tom. Drake took it as reluctant assent, and went on. "Second, we must form something called a *chain of command*. You were right when you told me that this form of communication between us limits the rate of information transfer. We have to change the system. I'm sure I can't deal directly with billions of composites, so we need a new structure. I will deal with no more than—how many? Let's say six—I'll work with half a dozen composites like you. Then each of you will work with six more, and so on to successive tiers. How many levels will be necessary to fit every composite into such a framework?"

"Nineteen levels will be enough."

Tom's reply was instantaneous. Drake tried to do the inverse calculation, and failed. Six to the nineteenth. How many billions, how many trillions? Let's just say, a mind-boggling number.

And he was supposed to direct the actions of every one of them. How? He had no idea. Composers were not expected to run things. Had any musician in history ever managed a group bigger than an orchestra? The only one he could think of was the pianist Paderewski, who early in the twentieth century interrupted his performing career to become prime minister of Poland. Great pianist, average politician.

He pressed on, before worries and irrelevant thoughts like that could take over.

"Third, I must learn your science and technology. I don't mean I have to *understand* it, because I'm quite sure I can't. But I have to know what the technology can *do*. In return, I'll tell you what weapons are, and you must learn what weapons do, and how to make them. I'll warn you, you won't like what you hear—any more than I'll enjoy telling you."

"We'll learn." Tom was calm now. He even shrugged his shoulders and ran his hands through his mop of red hair. "When we asked for help, you know, we didn't assume that we'd be sitting around doing nothing. And we didn't assume we'd enjoy our part of it."

"I'll go further. You won't. Let's begin by defining the first level of the chain of command. As I said, I can't interface with you all the time, and I certainly can't interface directly with umpteen billion composites."

"Six hundred trillion."

"Thanks." Six hundred *trillion*. It was worse than Drake had thought. "So we set up the chain of command, then we'll talk about *self-defense*. You ought to send that information immediately to the section of the Galaxy likely to be the next one threatened. It might help, and it can't hurt."

He would prove disastrously wrong on that last point, but he didn't know it.

"Self-defense?" Tom said.

"Don't worry about it. You won't have to harm anything that doesn't try to harm you. You'll find self-defense easy. But after that it may start to get nasty."

Just how could a planet or a space colony defend itself from outside attack? How could humans counterattack or make a preemptive defensive strike? How did one fight something unknown? Drake rummaged for long-buried ideas, things he had read when he was young and never expected to use or need. His mind was disturbingly well-stocked with them. So much for his pacifist self-image.

Until Ana went to the cryowomb and he was scrambling for money, he had resisted the idea of producing any form of professional description. He had been pretty snooty about it. What could words possibly say, he said to himself and to anyone else who would listen, about the ability to write interesting music?

Times changed. Now he could produce an intriguing résumé: Drake Merlin; composer; performer; would-be pacifist; and Supreme Commander of Combined Galactic Forces.

• • •

The easiest part seemed to be the creation of a chain of command. He needed to worry about just the first level. Even so, he learned within minutes that he could only interface with a composite if it simulated an individual with whom he was familiar and comfortable. That narrowed the options enormously; especially since any kind of Ana simulation was out of the question.

First, though, he had to select a command headquarters. That wasn't hard; he had returned to consciousness so often through the ages in the little villa overlooking the Bay of Naples and Tyrrhenian Sea, it was starting to feel like home. He fixed it in his mind, furnished for his own comfort.

Then it was time to define his principal assistants. Tom Lambert assured him that all he had to do was think of the person, and the composites would handle the rest. Tom didn't say how, and Drake didn't ask. He just set to work.

Tom, of course. And Milton. The Servitor had abandoned the original wheeled sphere and whisk broom of many billions of years ago, but it was the form most familiar to Drake. Milton might as well stay in that shape. Cass Leemu, who had tried to teach him science so long ago—and failed—would be his chief scientific adviser. And Melissa Bierly. He wondered about that choice, until she appeared at the table. She was not the woman he had last met, sane and contented and the lover and companion of the cloned Ana, but the mercurial and mad Melissa as she had been at her first creation. War was a form of insanity. Drake needed an element of madness. He could see it now, in those brilliant sapphire eyes.

Trismon Sorel and Ariel appeared briefly, but they would not hold their shapes. It was Drake's own mind, rejecting them for its own reasons: either he did not know them well enough, or they did not fit his present needs.

He was not happy with the two who completed the half dozen. Par Leon had appeared first, as unwarlike as a human could be. Maybe that meant he was close in temperament to Drake, who needed him for that reason. But then there had to be a balance.

Drake called on someone he hated. Mel Bradley had been the scourge of his childhood; short, hyperactive, hotheaded, ready to fight over nothing. He had sneered at Drake, calling him a girl and a soft-head sissy who liked stupid poetry. In their one confrontation as eleven-year-olds, he had given Drake a black eye. After that Drake went out of his way to avoid him, without ever quite admitting that he was scared. Now Mel, adult and wary, glowered at Drake from the other end of the room.

Six assistants. He looked along the polished table and considered the result of his efforts. How much reality was there in any of this? The others had been created out of his own stored consciousness, plus the combined contents of the data banks. All of them (including Drake himself!) consisted of nothing more than a random movement of electrons. But hadn't that always been true of thoughts in every brain, whether organic or inorganic, wetware or hardware?

And if Drake was not fully satisfied with his chosen assistants, hadn't that always been true of all leaders? He remembered what the Duke of Wellington said, after he reviewed his own poorly trained and ill-equipped troops and before they went into battle: "I don't know what effect these men will have upon the enemy, but by God they terrify me."

Drake never expected to see the rest of his own "troops." All instructions would go out, and all reports come in, through the chosen six. That might be a problem. Old wars had been plagued by officers who restricted access to their generals and told them only what they wanted to hear: "The fort is impregnable. . . ." "The morale of the men remains excellent. . . ." "Strategic bombing will weaken the enemy to the point where their resistance is impossible. . . ." "The adversary's losses far exceed our own. . . ." "One more increase in troop strength will turn the tide in our favor."

And the slaughter had rolled on.

Well, with luck, the composites would have forgotten how to lie. They should have no interest in telling Drake only what they thought might please him.

But in fact, none of this could ever please him. He told himself, over and over, why he was doing this: only in order that, someday, he and Ana could be together again.

The next task was to divide up the workload among his chosen helpers.

"You, Cass." Drake wondered how long it would be before giving orders came easily to him. At the moment he hated it. "I want you to produce the science and technology summary for me. I have to know what's available now, because that's going to be the basis for our weapons development. Milton, you will be the expert on alien life-forms, anywhere in the Galaxy. Par Leon, I want you to learn exactly which stars have been affected by the Shiva, and tell me which ones are now in most danger. Mel, you are in charge of *offense.* That means you'll be planning counterattacks. You ought to love that. Melissa, you'll be my expert on the Shiva themselves—everything that humans know, I want to know. Tom, as my general support, you are to remain flexible, ready to tackle anything that comes up.

"Any questions?"

"Yes." It was Melissa. Her reply stopped Drake cold. It seemed to him he had been perfectly clear and he wasn't expecting questions. He frowned at her. "What's the problem?"

"I'm confused. It seems to me that my task is already finished."

"You have a report on the Shiva?" Even with the uncanny computing speed of the composites, that seemed impossible.

"In a manner of speaking. And so do you. We know all there is to be known."

She didn't sound confused. She sounded sure of herself, the confident, competent, all-seeing Melissa that Drake had known of old. He groaned inwardly. They had hardly begun, and already he sensed trouble.

Melissa was right. Her briefing took many minutes, but the main conclusion could be summarized in seconds.

One stellar system, far out beyond the main galactic rim, had ceased to communicate with all other humans thirty-three million years earlier. That was the first. The change had been noted, but it drew no attention. Composites and civilizations often chose to go their own ways, even as Earth had gone its own way and withdrawn from the solar system back in what was now considered the dawn of history.

Over the next several thousand years, half a dozen more systems fell silent. They were in the same remote galactic region as the first one. Still, no one was worried. They were presumed to be part of the same social experiment.

A hundred, a thousand, ten thousand; not until a hundred thousand colonies were silent did humanity sit up and take notice. Before any action was taken, the number had grown to over a million.

Even then, the superluminal S-wave queries suggested more curiosity than worry. They were polite requests for a reply: *"Are you all right? Is there anything that we can do for you?"*

To that question, and to every other direct and indirect form of approach, the colonies sent the same reply: nothing. Humans, composites, ships, sub- and superluminal signals: whatever was sent did not return. A multimillion-year silence had begun its spread across the Galaxy.

Melissa was detailing that spread, system by system, millennium by millennium, when Drake interrupted her.

"All right, I agree with you. The role that I assigned you makes no sense. So let's change it to this: Since we don't know anything about the Shiva, you and I will make it our job to find out."

He knew that he was on the right track. By some means or other, by skill or subterfuge or treachery or outright murder, they had to collect information about the Shiva. He was glad that Melissa spared him the obvious question: How?

Drake no longer had organic components. His consciousness had no need for food or rest. There was no reason he could not work around the clock, every second of every day. So was it only his own stubbornness that imposed a circadian rhythm on his actions, including "day," "night," "sleep," and "meals"?

He thought not. He had a logic for his behavior: since this era had failed to solve the problem of the Shiva, his own value, if any, must lie in the fact that he was a savage throwback to the earliest human times; the more that he could retain of those archaic traits, the more likely he was to offer something new (or old) and different.

He set up his own working regime. He held "breakfast briefings," "working lunches," "strategic planning sessions" each "afternoon," and "end-of the-day wrap-ups." His preference was for small groups, not more than two or three present at a time. He insisted on taking breaks from everyone, when he could be alone to think things over.

The huge mass of composites, nineteen layers deep, did not like that approach. He could feel their impatience as an invisible pressure transmitted through his chosen six. He sent back his own message: *I do things my way, or not at all.*

It took nerve to stick to that, after his first meeting with Par Leon and Cass Leemu.

"It's thirty-three million years since we had the first evidence of the Shiva," Leon said. "The current total of known colonies that have become silent is between ninety-seven and ninety-eight billion. I do not include in this the colonies in parts of the Galaxy far from the troubled region, which have withdrawn from interaction presumably for other reasons. If you would like the numbers exactly . . ." And, at Drake's impatient shake of the head, he continued, "They suggest the extinction, or at least the silencing, of almost three thousand colonies a year. But that number is highly misleading. The process began slowly and has been growing exponentially. In the past year, as you like to measure time, contact has been lost with almost seventy-five thousand colonies. Two hundred a day, one every seven minutes.

"Here are their locations." The great spiral of the Galaxy glowed in the air before them. A curved bite had been taken from it. On the edge of that dark sector, thousands of dots flashed orange. They highlighted a thin boundary between light and dark.

"And now look here." The orange dots vanished, to be replaced by another set a tiny step closer to the galactic center. "These, according to our best estimates, are the colonies where the Shiva may be expected to appear next."

It seemed a minute change. Measured against the whole Galaxy, it was; but Drake was not misled. Seventy-five hundred stellar systems or free-space colonies, lost from all human contact.

"What are the composites doing about it?"

He didn't expect a useful reply, and he didn't get one.

Par Leon just rubbed his chin and looked unhappy. "Doing? What can we do?"

"Well, at the very least, you can *warn* the colonies."

"But they already know. They have known for hundreds or even thousands of years."

"And they're just sitting there, doing nothing?"

"Not at all. Many have moved, closer to the galactic center."

"Fine. So you keep moving—until a few million years from now, when the Shiva occupy the whole Galaxy. Where will you go then?"

Drake turned to Cass Leemu. "I know it's going to take a while to inventory all of human technology, but we can't wait. We have to do something *now*. Take the list you have so far and pick out the ten devices with the highest energy density. I'll want to look at the whole list, but don't wait for me. Get with Mel Bradley and send superluminal S-wave messages to the colonies that are next on Leon's list. Tell them to make sure those top ten devices get built as soon as possible and are ready for use. Tell them we'll be sending another S-wave message very soon, showing how to make the devices operate as defensive weapons against an invasion from space."

Cass didn't hesitate. "The list is on the table in front of you." It was suddenly there. "It's ready for your review, in interactive nested form. You can ask for more detail about any part of it."

She and Par Leon vanished. Had Drake ordered them to do that? It didn't matter. When dealing with the composites he was never sure who was doing what.

He turned to Cass's first cut at a list of useful technology. He had given her a few ground rules that might sort devices into an order of probable value: anything that involved huge amounts of energy, of any form; anything that performed a large-scale manipulation of time and space; anything that could be used to act as a shield to divert objects or radiation; anything able to perform planetary or stellar modification. Finally—he realized that his own ignorance might make him miss the most important defenses of all—he had asked Cass to include anything that she thought would be totally incomprehensible to Drake.

There seemed to be more of that last category than of any other. Humans, in composite form and working with or without their inorganic helpers, had become superhuman by the measures of earlier times. There seemed nothing that they could not do. They had ways to turn off and on the light of stars. They could create black holes in open space, or use existing ones for energy sources. They could build free-space colonies the size of the whole solar system. They could send message-bearing accelerated wave fronts a hundred thousand light-years, clear from one side of the Galaxy to the other, in hours. They could shield an object against any attack, from fusion bombs to neutrino beams.

Any attack. Why couldn't they shield against the attack of the Shiva? Surely, in all those millions of years since the arrival of the Shiva in the Galaxy, some colony of the endless billions that had fallen silent would have tried the shield as a natural protective move. And it must have failed. Drake worried again about the nature of his unseen adversary.

Most mysterious technology of all, humans had found a way to create a type of space-time singularity never found in nature. There was no word for them that Drake recognized, but they were translated to him as caesuras. They were described as cuts in a Riemann sheet of order four, but that told him very little. He visualized them as slits, mailboxes in smooth space-time, capable of admitting material objects. In fact, they had been developed in an attempt to bypass the light-

speed limit for solid matter. From that point of view
they were a "failed" technology. They did not achieve
their objective in a controlled way. One time in a million (once in 969,119 attempts, to be precise) they
would send an object instantaneously to the desired
destination, even if it was in the most remote regions of
the Galaxy. There was another theoretical possibility,
even less likely, that the object would be hurled to some
unknown destination much farther off in space and
time; in all other cases the caesura would throw the
object out of the universe completely.

"Do you mean out of the Galaxy?" Drake wondered
if he was misunderstanding what he was seeing and
hearing.

"No. Out of the universe." The interactive list replied in Drake's own voice.

"Throw them out of the universe to *where*?"

"That remains unresolved. Most probably, to a universe like our own, perhaps to one with different constants of nature. These conjectures are based on
theoretical analyses only. Many probes have been sent
through a caesura, but none has ever returned."

"Is it possible that the Shiva are sending our colonies through a caesura?"

"It is quite impossible. We know from numerous observations that the suns and planets in the silent zone
remain exactly where they were before. They merely
refuse to respond to us in any way. When we send a
probe to them, it remains active and returns signals all
the way. After its arrival at the planet, it falls silent."

Drake fell silent, too. He was persuaded; the Shiva
were not making use of the caesuras. But as for the
caesuras themselves . . .

He did not understand them, but he could not get
them out of his mind. He called for Mel Bradley. In the
short term, the colonies would have to be protected
with whatever was to hand. He was not optimistic about

that, when the shields had not worked. What could penetrate a total shield?

He would ponder that question. And in the meantime—which might be a very long time—he and Mel would work on another option.

Chapter 18

"Lord of our far-flung battle line"

Waiting.

Drake considered himself an expert on waiting. What else had he been doing for the past six billion years but waiting and hoping?

This time, though, it was different. This time he could not drift dormant through the ages; this time he must remain conscious, day after day, waiting and watching and wondering.

Cass Leemu and Mel Bradley, with Drake's guidance and close direction, had taken existing technology and adapted it to provide planetary defenses. Superluminal signals had been sent out to the colonies; not only to the ones that according to Par Leon were in the most immediate danger, but to the next line back.

The main focus was going to be on that second line. Drake had made the decision and kept it to himself, knowing that he dare not discuss it with the others. His action was going to doom billions of thinking beings to extinction. The composites would not be able to handle such an idea. Drake, however, had no choice. If he were right, this was going to be a war of long duration. Before he could produce a long-term strategy, he needed to see exactly what happened when the Shiva became active in a region; then he needed time to build a wall of defense, observation posts, and lines of communication. Except as information sources, he had to write off planets that would probably fall in the next year or two.

The outgoing messages to the colonies gave precise instructions on fabricating and installing the defense systems. Within a few months, the superluminal S-wave messages came flowing back. Defenses had been built and tested on thousands of worlds. Shields were in place. Fusion, fission, cavitation, and particle beams sat prepared for instant use. The colonies were nervous, but they claimed to be ready for anything.

That worried Drake more than it heartened him. In every resurrection he had believed himself ready for anything; each time, he had been astonished by events.

What else could he do while he was waiting? The little villa had become a headquarters for galactic action. He prowled it, night and day. The living room was now a War Room for the whole Galaxy, where reports from a billion suns were sifted, analyzed, and summarized by the multiple working layers of composites. The placid view of the Bay of Naples had long since gone. In its place was an ever-changing display of the "battle front." Drake thought of it that way, although there was still no sign of conflict; only reports from the colonies and regular messages from the probes that were observing them from a safe distance. A copy of Par Leon was on each of those probes, transmitted as S-wave signals and downloaded to permanent storage as part of the resident composite.

Everything was ready. Ready for anything? Drake watched and wondered.

And then the silence began. One of the front line planets stopped transmitting.

It was almost too much for that copy of Par Leon. The returning messages from the probe took on a hysterical overtone. "We can see the planet, it looks just the same as it always has. There's no sign of damage or change. But they don't reply! We keep sending, and they won't reply!"

Underneath Par Leon's words, like a carrier wave, was the suppressed terror of a billion more voices. Drake itched to be part of the probe composite, to see things at firsthand. But that would break one of his prime rules: he had to remain separate and aloof, a primitive throwback to earlier times uncontaminated by the gentler present. Otherwise he would be no more useful than a hundred trillion others.

"It's all right, Leon. Keep calm. How far from the planet are you?"

"Two and a half light-hours."

Drake called for a conversion to a measure more familiar to him: nearly three billion kilometers. "You're probably safe. Is that the best image you can send us?" The War Room display showed a grainy and fluctuating picture of a gray-green blob.

"The best we can do from this distance. We're observing at our highest magnification."

"It's not good enough. I can't see any detail at all. You have to take the probe closer. But don't take risks. Turn around and run if you sense any kind of trouble."

"Trouble? Do you think it's safe to go closer? We sent hundreds of messages to them, and they don't reply anymore."

"You said yourself, the planet looks just the way it did before it went quiet."

It sounded like an answer to Par Leon's question, but it wasn't. If Drake had to guess, he would say that any probe approaching a silent planet was not safe at all. It was in terrible danger. But he could not mention that to anyone. If he was to save trillions, he might have to sacrifice billions. He had to have *information*.

He told himself that he was not sending anyone to a real death. The composite represented by Par Leon would still exist here, even if every probe copy was annihilated. And yet he recognized that as a bogus logic. The death of a clone was a real death—to the clone.

Drake asked to be informed when the probe came within ten light-minutes of its planetary goal, and turned his attention elsewhere. Other messages were streaming in from other places. It was more of the same bad news: planets and their colonies, unaffected in appearance, were vanishing from the universe of communication. They were becoming part of a great and spreading silence.

He measured the total time for fifty more cases of signal loss: a little less than six hours. Allowing for statistical error, Par Leon's estimate of two hundred lost worlds a day was spot on.

Drake did not try to examine each situation in detail. Melissa and Tom would be doing that, and they would provide their analyses later. He turned his attention back to the first world. The probe was within ten light-minutes. While it flew closer, Drake called for backup planetary data.

This was one world in a triple dwarf-star system of over a hundred. And it was the only one that was even remotely habitable, with native life-forms and an oxygen atmosphere. That gave it a certain distinction: planetary orbits in multiple systems were normally too variable for life to develop, sometimes sweeping in searingly close to one of the stars, then wandering off for cold years in the outer darkness. This world had been lucky—its name translated to Drake as "Felicity." It had hovered in the middle region, not too close and not too far, for the billion years that life needed.

That's where its claim to distinction ended. The native life had not progressed beyond cyanobacteria, a coating of blue, green, and sickly yellow that covered the surface of the single ocean and most of the land. For humans interested in planetary transformation, though, Felicity with its surface water and thin oxygen atmosphere was 99 percent of the way there. All that had to be done was a stabilization of the orbit, a boost to the gravitational field, a buildup of the atmosphere, and the introduction of multiple-celled organisms. Trivial. The work had been completed half a billion years ago. Felicity had become a typical member of the teeming galactic family of inhabited worlds.

And now?

The image from the probe was providing better definition as the distance decreased. Drake half expected to see a yellow-streaked globe of sullen red, like Earth when it collapsed to one-tenth of its old size and isolated itself from the rest of the solar system. But he could see surface detail on Felicity. The outline of a single ocean, shaped like a blunt horse's head and low lit by the glancing light of the triple suns, matched the shape shown in the data bank. He saw the softening of texture that indicated the presence of an atmosphere, and occasional high clouds that confirmed it.

"It looks exactly the same." That was Par Leon, muttering his surprise. "Nothing at all seems to have happened to it. This was one of the worlds that installed our defense systems. Just a month ago, it told us that they were completed and working. So why doesn't it reply to us now?"

Drake could suggest a fistful of answers:

- A shield around the planet was inhibiting all outgoing signals or materials; but that clearly could not be the case. Visible wavelength radiation was being reflected from the surface, since the probe could see it. If necessary, anyone down on the surface could use the same wavelengths to send an outgoing signal.

- A shield was stopping all *ingoing* signals or materials;

but that was even worse. The world below the shield would be in total darkness. Clearly it was not, because sunlight was getting through. In any case, other worlds and colonies affected long ago by such a shield would soon have noticed that they were not receiving messages, and either come or call to ask what was going on.

- Something, a deadly ray or a toxic cloud of gas, had wiped out all life on Felicity. The planet would not at once change its appearance if that happened.

- Something had wiped out all *intelligent* life. It did not have to be fatal; if humans and their inorganic complements had been reduced to the thinking level of a smart dog, no piece of communications equipment —or any other technology—would mean anything.

(Ana, after leaving the home of a couple who swore that their pet was as smart as any human, had said: "No dog, no matter how well bred or well intentioned, can tell you that it came from poor but honest parents."

He missed her in a thousand ways, but most of all he missed her humor and her refusal to substitute sentiment for sense.)

Drake jerked his thoughts back to the task at hand:

- The population, for its own reasons, had chosen a policy of total isolationism. If just one world had been affected, that would be wholly plausible. It must have happened a million times. When thousands of neighboring worlds went the same way, though, plausibility became impossibility.

Unless the policy was contagious, an isolationist meme that spread from world to world as a message of irresistible power? But then why hadn't it traveled at superluminal speed and long ago converted the whole Galaxy? And why had the first world affected been far out on the galactic rim? That suggested an influence borne into humanity's domain from far, far away.

Well, they would know soon enough. Felicity was looming right ahead.

"Still no response." Par Leon was losing his nervousness. Drake couldn't understand why. Didn't Leon realize that this scenario must have been played out a million or a billion times, when a ship by an accident of timing had approached a world that had just become silent?

"We propose to land," Leon said. "Do you have any objection?" The probe was swinging into a descent orbit around Felicity's equator. The nightside view showed a scattering of lights. Cities, and a working power system. The planet still showed the signs of an intact civilization.

"None. Carry on with your landing." *And good luck, Leon.*

Something had to happen, and soon. No ship had ever returned a signal from one of the silent worlds. Either it had never reached the surface, or after it did so it could no longer send a message.

On the other hand, no world had ever to Drake's knowledge possessed its own powerful defenses. Was it as simple as that? Had the defense system done the trick? Was the battle for the Galaxy won already?

He didn't believe it. Too easy, and it would leave a huge mystery. Who and what were the aggressors?

"We still have no descent problems," Leon said. "But there is no navigation signal from the surface. We are going into the final entry phase."

Drake stared at the scene from the probe's imager. No vanished planet. No mysterious shields. Everything as normal could be.

While the thought was still forming, a bright spark of violet glowed ahead on the line of the equator. It grew as he watched, widening from a point to a soft-edged plume of glaring blue.

In the final moment before the fire reached up to envelop the probe, and the S-wave message stream to headquarters ceased, Drake understood several things at once.

First, he was going to learn nothing more about present conditions on the surface of Felicity; because the probe, along with Par Leon and the onboard composite, was doomed. They were about to be destroyed by a flame as hot as the center of a star.

Worse than that, humanity was going to learn nothing about the reason why billions of worlds had been silenced. Whatever had happened to them, it was different from what was happening now on Felicity.

Because the agent for this probe's destruction was not some alien and unknown force. It was part of a human defensive system; a system that had been designed and defined and described to the inhabitants of Felicity by Cass Leemu, Mel Bradley, and Drake Merlin.

This was no time for meeting in ones and twos. Drake could feel the pressure again, the countless terrified minds clamoring at the gates of the villa. They had been calm when the defenses were going into place, blindly hoping that the problem was solved. Was he the only one who had *expected* the next sector of the Galaxy to fall?—although even he had been shocked when the observing probes were destroyed by the defenses that he had installed.

All of his team were assembled in the War Room. They were stunned to silence. The scene that Drake had followed in detail for one probe had been repeated over and over, in a thousand variations. The planets remained apparently untouched and unchanged; but no probe had been able to land.

Par Leon was in the worst shape. It confirmed Drake's idea, that the death of a clone was perfectly real—and not only to the clone. Leon was shattered.

He had seen himself annihilated, time after time. Not one of his copies had tried to do anything about it. Each had gone fatalistically to his doom. It had been a mistake to send Leon, and Drake would not do it again.

He deliberately changed the War Room wall from its overview of newly silenced worlds to the old, white-capped seascape.

"We learned a lot from that experience." He was brisk and businesslike. "Of course, we'll do a full analysis of every case, but I only want Tom involved in that. The rest of you will have other assignments. Milton, we've been treating this as a problem just for humanity. It isn't. Every life-form on a silenced world must be affected. I want to meet with you and review every alien life-form in the Galaxy. We may learn something about the Shiva."

"But it was our understanding that the Shiva originated *outside* the Galaxy."

The Servitor was as deferential as ever—and as steadfast. Drake realized that Milton would be a better choice than Par Leon to send on future probes. But even Milton would not be ideal. What was needed was someone who would play a long shot, someone to take a wild risk when it was justified.

Who?

Drake postponed the question.

"I think the Shiva did originate from outside the Galaxy," he said. "But even if we don't find out anything about the Shiva from alien life-forms, the forms themselves may prove useful. Leon, I want you to work with Milton on this.

"Melissa, we know that what we tried last time didn't work. If we're going to stop the Shiva spread, we have to know more about how they do it. Can their influence move through open space, or does it need planets to do it efficiently? You are going to help us answer that question. You will have the job of creating a *firebreak*." Drake was forced to use the English word. "Do you know what that is? It's an empty region across the whole Galaxy, surrounding the segment affected by the Shiva. If they need planets, a void should slow and hinder their spread.''

Melissa's eyes opened wide, and she shook her head dubiously. "I'll do my best. But do you realize how big a job that will be?"

"It will be enormous. I want a quarantine zone, at least twenty light-years wide, between the edge of the affected sector and the nearest colonized world."

"You mean you want the colonies moved."

"I want more than that. I want the colonies moved to a safer location. But then I want space *completely empty* in that region. No planets, no stars. Not even dust clouds, if we can do it. I want hard vacuum and nothing else."

"That's impossible."

"I don't think so." Drake turned to Mel Bradley. "You and Cass have been evaluating the caesuras as possible attack weapons. Do you have an idea how big an object they can handle?"

"In principle, there is no limit." Mel had been the last addition to the team, but he was a great choice. While the others cringed at the very idea of violence, he reveled in it. "The caesuras seem to feed on their own activity," he went on. "The more you put into them, the bigger they get."

"Could you put a whole planet into one?"

"No!" But the hot, angry eyes were gleaming with curiosity. "Not yet, at any rate. We're orders of magnitude away from that. Right now I can put a small asteroid into a caesura. Do you *want* to put a planet in? Maybe, if we keep going . . ."

"Work on it."

"And you said *stars*, too?"

"One step at a time. When you get to the point where a caesura can handle a planet, I want to see a demonstration."

"Mobility is going to be the other problem. We either have to create a caesura where we need it or move one around. That's not going to be easy."

"Nothing is going to be easy. Get Cass to help you." Drake looked around the table. "All right, I think we've covered everything. Everyone has plenty to do. Let's go do it."

Except, of course, that they had not covered everything. Drake knew it, even if no one else did. He had ducked the most important question of all: Who was going to replace Par Leon as the on-site observer and principal actor in the next interaction with the Shiva?

He knew there would be another interaction. More than that, he expected a countless number of them, over many millennia and even many aeons, before the problem was resolved (one way or another; it might end with the Shiva taking over every world in the Galaxy. That was a resolution of sorts).

Par Leon would not do. He might learn someday to observe dispassionately, but in an emergency he would never know how to take action without direction.

The trouble was, Drake already knew the answer to his own question. It was obvious, as soon as he stated the issues clearly: Who would be willing to use weapons? Who could take a wild risk when it was justified? Who had the most to lose? Who had a motivation to survive, stronger than any of the composites?

The others were terrified when a planet became silent, but any planetary consciousness was likely to form part of a larger composite, with multiple components elsewhere. The disappearance of a planet from the communications web, or even its total annihilation, was not a total death for them. It was more like an amputation, the loss of fingers and toes—highly unpleasant and traumatic, but not fatal.

So. It had to be Drake himself. He would have to

agree to something that he had so far resisted, and allow multiple copies of himself to be downloaded, shipped off anywhere that they were needed, and used in either organic or inorganic form. And he had to remain an *individual,* not joined to form part of a composite. He had to be aware of and afraid of death, focused on his own survival, willing to use any weapon that would allow him to live. Multiple duplication sounded like a guarantee of immortality; he recognized it as a promise of multiple deaths.

He would probably die, over and over, in many places across the Galaxy. Was there any other alternative? If there was, he was not smart enough to see it.

So it had to be Drake. He didn't want to do it, but he would.

He would do it for the sake of Ana, and for their future together.

Chapter 19

Snark Hunt

$\mathcal{D}$rake had never felt better; fit, strong, and confident. He narrowed his nostrils against the dusty wind and nodded to Milton. "Ready when you are."

The Servitor was standing by his side. It wore the familiar shape of the wheeled sphere, topped by a whisk broom of motile wires. The wires wriggled and twisted as Milton said, "Are you sure? Do you not need more time to adapt?"

"I am adapted. Perfectly."

"You see, it was easy for me to take on my original form. But in your case . . ."

Drake knew what the Servitor was getting at. If he thought hard about it, he could recognize that the Sun was a peculiar and brilliant green, two sizes too small in the sky. The landscape of the planet, Graybill, glittered in prismatic silvers and blues. At the limit of vision, the land curved *upward* to a hazy horizon. He seemed to be standing in a giant bowl that quaked and shivered beneath his feet, like a tough skin stretched tight over viscous jelly.

No problem. Graybill orbited far from a K-type star whose photosphere was peculiarly high in metals. The bowl effect was a result of vastly higher atmospheric pressure. In fact, if he thought about it, he could explain all the things he saw and felt—just as he knew that he inhabited a thick-legged, shorter body, and that other versions of him, thousands or millions of them, existed far, far away.

None of these things mattered. So far as he was concerned, he was *the* Drake Merlin, the one and only. He suited this body and this world exactly.

"In your case," Milton continued. "I could not employ an exact clone. Your body would not have survived here without modification. It was necessary to download your somatic DNA, perform certain changes to it, then download your acquired database only after body growth was complete. So, even though I suspect that you would have preferred your own original body, as it was on Earth—"

"You can stop apologizing." Drake felt euphoric—dangerously so. Was it possible that Milton had slightly misjudged his body's required gaseous balance? He scratched at his scaly side. "Let's get down to business. Where's the alien?"

"Aliens. Many of them. Far from here. We landed in the equatorial region, and they reside on an isolated continent near the south pole. I wanted to be sure that you were fully operational and adjusted before you were exposed to danger."

"That bad?"

"Or good. It is a matter of definition. Let me say this: I have examined more than fourteen thousand other alien life-forms that fulfill some or all of the qualifications for sentience. Never, however, have I encountered one so feral and vicious."

"And intelligent?"

"Not in technological terms. The Snarks use no tools. They have not mastered fire. They modify their environment only in the simplest ways. They seem to possess no language."

"But you still say they are dangerous?"

"I know that they are." Milton led the way from the main ship to a smaller, wingless vehicle that rested on the glittering and shaking surface. "This is your third embodiment on this planet."

"What happened to the other two?"

It was a stupid question, and one that Milton was not supposed to answer. It was a rule that Drake himself had set up: each of his encounters with an alien would be judged on its own merits. Milton would be fully aware of the prior failed experiences, but Drake would not. It had been the same with the fourteen thousand cases. Drake—or one of his embodiments—must have met each of them, but apart from generalities all he knew was that none was useful against the Shiva.

Now the Servitor said only, "This time we are taking special precautions. They included landing far from the polar continent and all Snarks, until I was sure that you were totally at home with your embodiment."

No more information; except that a knowledge of two prior failures was itself information. On the twenty-minute suborbital flight toward Graybill's pole, Drake sat and wondered. What had he done the previous times to get himself killed? Would he be killed again? If so, it would be no less painful, merely because it had happened before.

The ship landed on a coastline that crawled with warm-blooded and active plants. Drake could feel a sharp drop in temperature, but his body remained quite comfortable. He merely felt a tightening in his outer layers as improved thermal insulation went into action. He walked to the waterline, knowing that it was not actually water. Any water was in solid form, lying on the bottom. This was some mix of alcohols and hydrocarbons, heptane and ether and propanol, all lighter than water ice.

He bent and scooped up a handful to his tendril-fringed mouth. It tasted fine.

"That way." Milton was pointing as Drake straightened up. "About seven kilometers inland you will find the first Snark nests. Do you wish me to accompany you?"

Milton's voice was hopeful. Drake shook his scaled and snouted head. The Servitor was smart, but some things it would never learn. There was no way that Milton could remain quiet if Drake was moving into danger. Not only that, no matter how much Drake discouraged it, the Servitor could not help giving hints designed to keep Drake out of danger. It was not Milton's fault. The Servitor was designed to protect and safeguard Drake Merlin. Its present role of bystander was more than it could stand.

Drake reinforced his gesture with words. "You stay right here until I come back. Don't leave the flier."

The wiry whisk broom contorted and turned uneasily. "That is what you said on the last occasion we were here."

More information that Drake was not supposed to have. "So I'm saying it again. If I am not back by dark, you can come looking for me."

"That will be a very long time. We are in the polar regions, and this is summer."

"One quarter of a planetary revolution period, then. If I'm not back in that time, come and pick up the pieces. But *not before*. I don't want you around when I'm at the nests. Remember, they also serve who only stand and wait." Drake headed inland. Milton was tireless and careful and conscientious, but sometimes the Servitor could be a real pain.

Seven kilometers: it sounded like a reasonable safety margin; except that he had no idea what senses were available to the Snarks. Vision by short wavelength light was the most commonly used sense in the Galaxy, evidence of the fact that the average main sequence star emits peak energy at a wavelength between one-half and one micron. However, a dozen other senses were in general use wherever there was an atmosphere: hearing, thermal infrared detection, direct monitoring of magnetic and electric fields, echo location, smell—the Snarks might use any or all of these. Back on ancient Earth, a polar bear could sniff a dead whale thirty kilometers away. A mating moth could identify its distant partner from a single molecule of pheromone. The Snarks might already be aware of Drake.

The ground was becoming increasingly rock strewn and broken, large boulders separated by stretches of flat gravel covered with slow-moving blue ferns. Drake reduced his pace at the two-kilometer mark and again as he caught his first glimpse of what must be the nests. They were well separated, each one long and thin and hollow, like a section of wide clay pipe laid on its side. He could see no sign of life there, but he stopped, crouched down onto his thick haunches, and waited. As soon as he was stationary, the warm-blooded vegetation crawled doggedly to his feet and around them. Tendrils like gentle blue fingers reached up, touched his legs, and apparently decided that he had no potential as a nutrient source. The warm fingers dropped back. The plants crept away.

At last, Drake could see something moving near the clay pipes. Would he have been so patient, without Milton's warning of earlier problems? Surely not. He would have kept going, because the things that he could see ahead moved not much faster than the plants.

There were scores of them. The Snarks were fat white segmented cylinders, supported by scores of slender white pseudopods. The bodies were about five feet long and a foot and a half wide. The head end, as judged from the direction that they moved, lacked all distinguishing marks. A curving tail of darker creamy-white arched up over the back to direct its sharp tip forward. The pointed end moved slowly from side to side. Did it, rather than the "head," house the sense organs? Perhaps that was the head, and a Snark walked backward.

The Snarks seemed to take no notice of each other or of their surroundings, but as he watched, four of them reared up slowly from their horizontal positions. Each blind head curved back until it met the tail and formed a complete loop. The tail stopped its slow oscillation. They held this position like statues for several minutes, then unwound to lie once more on the soggy ground. After that they did not move at all. The brief effort to defy gravity seemed to have exhausted them.

Drake drifted closer. He could see that each of the long brown cylinders of the nests curved down at one end to become a tunnel into the spongy surface. Tall stacks of uprooted plants stood next to each pipe. The top plants of the heap were still wriggling feebly, trying to find their way back to ground level.

Nesting materials or food? If the Snarks were herbivores, the source of possible danger to Drake became harder to explain. One of the Snarks had just ripped a plant out of the gritty surface with a pair of its front pseudopods. It was facing right toward Drake, and at last he could see a narrow horizontal slit like a dark gash across the whole lower edge of the face.

Drake moved closer yet. He itched to see just what the Snark was doing with that wriggling fern. It was not eating it. The pseudopods seemed to be peeling off an outer layer, but they were not moving it to the face slit. They were passing it *backward,* to other pairs of stubby feet. Again he wondered, Had he confused front and back? The curved tail was slowly swinging back and forth, like a lazy radar antenna.

He had been concentrating hard on the one Snark, ignoring the plants at his feet. His attention was brought back to them only when warm fingers reached up his legs.

It was because he had not been moving. He glanced down and scuffled his feet, encouraging the tendrils to fall away.

"Shoo!" he hissed under his breath. The plants were warm-blooded, regulating their own temperature. They were mobile. Was there a chance that they would some-day achieve sentience? Spaceflight? He shook his foot. "Go on, there's nothing for you. Get out of here!"

When they finally gave up and dropped away, he looked up again at the nests. Everything was the same as before. The Snark was still fiddling lethargically with its fern.

Then he realized that no other Snark was visible. While he had been watching one, all the rest had qui-etly vanished.

They must have crept into the nests, to the pipes and then maybe underground. He could go closer, or move around so that he could look into the open end of one of the pipes.

As other versions of Drake had done twice before? And never made it back to where Milton was waiting.

Drake decided that he had seen enough for one day. He could always return tomorrow. He turned and started back across the boulder-strewn landscape. The bright green sun was just as high in the sky, but he felt a colder breeze at his back. It encouraged him to hurry. By the time that he was halfway to the shore, he was loping along as fast as his stocky legs would carry him.

It seemed like gross overreaction—until he came to a place where a rock-free stretch of graveled surface made it safe to quickly turn his head.

The rocky surface behind him was clear. But to each side, converging on his path, he saw a dozen pale shapes. They were arranged in a fan-shaped pattern with him as its center. The closest Snarks were at the edge of the fan. They must have been setting up a wide circle, all the time that he was observing the nests. He had been lucky enough to leave when the encircling operation was only half-done.

He had time for no more than a quick look, then he had to turn his attention back to the boulder-strewn ground across which he was running. That one glance was enough to force him to seek more speed. The Snarks, slow as snails when he had first encountered them, were transformed. The pseudopods moved too fast to be seen, except as a pale blur beneath the segmented bodies. The Snarks themselves had become longer and thinner. The curved tail no longer swung from side to side but was flattened along the back.

The worst news was that they were gaining. He was sure of it, even though he dared not look around again. He took more risks, hurdling midsized boulders instead of going around them. He cursed his stumpy and heavyset body. He was low to the ground. That made it harder to see what lay on the other side. If he landed on a rock and fell over, or broke a leg . . .

The flier was visible ahead. Less than a kilometer. Where were the Snarks? He had to know.

Don't do it. Remember the runner who loses a race because he turns his head to see how big a lead he has.

It didn't matter. He *had* to know. He turned and saw two Snarks no more than twenty steps behind him.

He looked straight ahead and made a desperate final effort. He knew he wasn't going to make it. Only another couple of hundred meters, but he would need at least a second when he reached the flier. It would take time to jump in and slam the door closed. That's when the Snarks would get him. They would catch him and bring him down in the moment when he stopped to open the flier door.

"Milton!" He screamed the name, expecting nothing. He had told the Servitor to stay with the flier. Even if Milton heard him, the response would come too late.

But the little wheeled sphere was suddenly where it

was not supposed to be—right in front of him. It made a quick sideways zigzag out of Drake's path, then veered in behind him. He heard the thump of a solid collision.

The flier was a dozen steps away, door open and waiting. Drake jumped and in the same movement grabbed the handle, swung inside, and dropped the latch into position. There was a loud *splat* as something large and rubbery and moving at high speed hit the outside of the door.

The sound came again, and then again. Drake looked out of the flier window. A dozen Snarks were hurling themselves in mad succession against the closed door. The car was rocking with their impacts.

Beyond them, twenty meters away, another Snark reared high on its hindmost pseudopods. It had gone through a dramatic change of size and shape. It was about seven feet tall, swollen at the lower end like a giant pear. The white skin was stretched tight. As Drake watched, the skin undulated and bulged and squirmed. There was no sign of Milton.

Drake knew now what his own fate would have been. If the Servitor had not intercepted the Snarks and drawn their attention, he would be that great bulge. He might be wriggling, but not for long.

After another thirty seconds the bloated Snark toppled from its upright position. The slit on the blind face remained closed, but that dark gash stretched longer and longer. The Snark was changing shape again. Its broadest section was moving from one end to the other, traveling like a wave of obesity from tail to head.

The white skin dimpled and swelled and thrust out every few seconds at isolated points, randomly and erratically. The other Snarks one by one abandoned their attack on the flier and eased forward to form a circle around their bloated nestmate.

The featureless face could show no expression, but the squirming and wriggling suggested that the Snark was not enjoying itself. More waves of muscular contraction were running from front to back. Finally, slowly, reluctantly, the slit of a mouth began to alter in shape. It went from a single line to a narrow ellipse, then steadily expanded until it was a round hole three feet across. There was one final heave of peristalsis. Milton suddenly popped out, whisk broom first.

The Servitor was coated with dark-green slime. Milton started to roll upright, but before the move was complete another Snark had dived in. Pseudopods gripped the whisk-broom head and drew it toward a mouth that leered wider and wider.

Milton offered no resistance. Within a minute the Servitor was ingested, while the body of the Snark stretched to accommodate something wider than its usual dimension.

This time Drake was able to watch the whole process. It took about four minutes, from Milton's disappearance to his rebirth. The Snarks did not give up easily. Five more of them had a go at Milton. Five more times the Servitor was swallowed and regurgitated, before finally rolling unimpeded out of the waiting circle.

The little wheeled form moved to the aircar, and the wired head stared up at Drake. *Let me in.* The message did not need words. But Drake in the past half hour had acquired lots of respect for the Snarks.

"Just a minute."

He extended a cargo flap from the base of the car and waited as Milton rolled onto it. Once the Servitor was in position, Drake raised them a hundred feet into the air. That should be more than enough to foil the Snarks, leaping alone or working in concert. Even so, he moved the car sideways, out over the brooding blue sea, before he finally opened the door and allowed Milton to climb inside.

The Servitor was covered thicker than ever with slime. Milton looked disgusting and smelled worse. Drake didn't wait to learn what the Snarks were doing now but told the flier to return them at once to the main ship.

"I assume that we are done with the Snarks," Milton said. It was the closest that the Servitor would ever come to asking, "Can we go home now?"

Drake was inclined to say yes. Humans needed all the help they could get in combating the Shiva, but blind ferocity was not enough. It must be matched with intelligence. The Snarks had cunning and murderous intent, but having seen them throwing themselves one after another against the flier, Drake felt sure that they operated mainly at the level of instinct. They knew how to hunt in packs, even to set impressive traps for their prey. But a hundred Earth species had done that, and never been credited with intelligence.

On the other hand, if that huge Snark aggressiveness *had* been coupled with high intelligence . . .

Drake sat in the flier and stared down at his own heavily built body. "I want to try one more thing."

"Very well." Milton did not sigh. Servitors did not sigh.

"You took my somatic DNA and incorporated changes to give me a body suited to this planet. Where did you get those changes from?"

"From the genetic codes of certain life-forms native to this world—not, of course, from the Snarks."

"So it ought to be easy to perform a small variation to the procedure. Use my genetic material. We have a complete record of that. In particular, use the elements in me that code for intelligence. Merge them with Snark genetic material—and produce a smart Snark."

Milton received that suggestion with all the enthusiasm of a being who has been swallowed and disgorged half a dozen times in the past half hour. After a few seconds, the Servitor said, "I do not think that is possible."

"Why not? The technology sounds quite routine. No harder than what you did to put me in this body."

"The technology, perhaps. But we do not know the Snark genetic code."

"Not yet. But we'll find out all about it."

"How?"

"That's the easiest part." Drake snapped the fingers of his scaly paw. "Tomorrow we'll come back to the nests and kidnap one."

Chapter 20

*"When half-gods go,
The gods arrive."*

The syncarpal synthesis was a surprise to Drake. A merger of human and Snark genetic materials suggested many possible outcomes: a four-limbed sting-tailed caterpillar that stood upright; a faceless segmented cylinder with hair and hands; or maybe a bright-eyed human worm, using dozens of scaly protolimbs to grasp, to lift, and to walk.

The creature in the imager resembled none of these. The syncarpal synthesis—shortened to the carp, or usually just Carp, by Drake and Milton, could have walked among a crowd of humans and passed unnoticed. Drake, looking hard, could observe a few minor differences. The temples bulged too much, only partly concealed by long brown hair. There was something odd about the hips, as though the socket for the upper end of the thigh bone lay outside the pelvis. The bare skin was coarse and rough, protected by a dense layer of gray bristles (but Drake had seen hairier humans). Suitable clothing would hide all this, just as it would cover the unusual genitals. Those were hidden, withdrawn into the pelvic cavity, making sex determination impossible by observation. Drake thought of the carp as "him," but that probably reflected his own sense of identification with the naked being on the surface.

"And you, of course, are looking for differences," Milton said. Drake was seeing Carp in action for the first time, and the Servitor sounded defensive. Most of this was Milton's work, and no one else's. "In any case, outward appearance is of less importance than the modified inner features. And those are invisible to you."

The Servitor was not present in person. Drake, embodied in the scaled form designed for use on Graybill, had insisted on three levels of separation. He knew what he had asked for: extreme aggression combined with great intelligence; but neither he nor anyone else yet knew what they had.

So Drake and the only ship that could carry them to orbit sat in one location, close to the Graybill equator. Milton and an aircar were in another, on a long peninsula of the south polar continent; and Carp had been set free and remotely animated in a third place, on the shore close to the nests where Drake himself had narrowly escaped the Snarks.

Carp was independently monitored by both Drake and Milton. Drake zoomed in for a close-up of the face as Carp walked steadily toward the nests. The heavy features wore a placid and relaxed expression. The broad mouth was humming softly and tunelessly, and the eyes glanced from side to side, like a walker on a pleasant summer stroll.

Maybe that was the way Carp felt. Graybill's polar summer was ending in a lingering twilight, and already the temperature on the island of the Snarks was falling fast. The dusting of snow on the boulders and gravel was made of solid carbon dioxide. Carp's physical structure, however, had been optimized to its local conditions. In spite of his naked skin he probably felt right at home.

If only Drake could read the dark eyes hidden beneath bony and prominent brow ridges! What did Carp know? What did he *feel?* In many ways, Carp was Drake himself; all the human genetic material had come from him. In biological terms, this was his child.

His only child, in so many billion years. Yet how far from their dreams, when they bought the old brick Colonial with its four bedrooms and shady fenced yard, and made their happy plans. One moment in annihilation's waste. One moment of the well of life to taste. *But one moment* together. *Now he walked through eternity alone. Oh, Ana. . . .*

Carp was heading confidently inland, toward the location of the Snark nests. Going home. The Snark from which Milton extracted the nonhuman part of Carp's genetic material had been taken from this very set of nests. When that Snark had been released and returned, unharmed and apparently unchanged, the others had torn it to pieces. Maybe, like a migrating bird, Carp carried the homing instinct in every cell of his body; maybe that would prove fatal when he arrived home.

They would know soon enough. Carp was walking steadily across blue-green vegetation that soaked up a last dribble of sunlight before digging down belowground and hibernating until spring. The nest was in view, with its broad pipes. As before, dozens of Snarks were creeping around them, stacking piles of plant life against their sides.

Carp walked right into their midst. They did not turn or attack or crawl away. They went on exactly as before, taking no more notice of him than they did of each other. He squatted down by one of the heaps of dead plants, and did not move for many minutes.

"There is no sign that the others are stalking him," Milton said at last. "In your own case, they by this time had you close to surrounded. And had you approached the nests themselves, as you did in one previous embodiment, you would have been attacked. It seems that in spite of his appearance, they accept Carp as one of their own. What now?"

It was a good question. Drake was seeking evidence that Carp was a prototype for the fighting machine that humanity needed so desperately. Everything that he had tried against the Shiva had led to failure; every day the Silent Zone grew like a cancer, eating its way in a growing arc across the Galaxy.

The Snarks themselves had seemed like a good first test. The action would take place in a remote location, far from interference or assistance from Milton. If Carp so much as survived, he would be doing a lot better than Drake. In fact, he had already done better.

Drake zoomed in closer, studying Carp's face. It was thoughtful, as thoughtful as Drake himself. And quite unreadable.

"Milton, do you know how the Snarks decide what they'll attack, and what they'll leave alone?"

"Not from observation. However, if they are like most animals who form nesting colonies, the principal sense and signal is olfactory. It seems probable that Carp *smells* right to them."

Just as Drake had smelled wrong. He still had no answer to his old question: From what distance could a Snark detect a strange animal from its scent? But even if Carp smelled right to the Snarks, he certainly looked wrong. And Milton, who presumably smelled nothing at all like anything organic, had been attacked and swallowed mindlessly. Why hadn't the Snarks given Carp at least a test swallow?

For the same reason that they were not constantly swallowing each other. Maybe the test hadn't failed after all. Maybe Carp had taken it—and passed, by changing his smell to one acceptable to the Snarks.

And what was he doing now? He was still squatting by the heap of leaves, apparently lost in thought.

Drake noticed that the Snarks had begun a common activity. They were removing plants from the piles and dragging them across to make a master heap. In the first sign of peaceful cooperation that he had seen, four of them were using their many pseudopods to shape the heap. The sickle-shaped tails patted and smoothed the edges to round them off and provide a compact, flat-topped structure.

It only became obvious what they were doing when they were finished, and Carp moved across to lie down on the heap.

"Milton! They've made him a damned *bed.*"

"So it would appear."

"But how did he tell them what to do? You said that the Snarks have no language."

"Apparently I was wrong. Do you wish me to—abandon the experiment?"

The Servitor, like other composites, could not handle certain notions. What Milton meant was, Do you wish me to destroy Carp?

"Of course not. He found an answer that's a lot more effective than aggression: he has the Snarks working for him. I want you to go ahead with the next test. Pick him up—as soon as he's had some sleep."

If Carp was indeed proposing to sleep. He was stretched out comfortably on his back on the bed of plants, arms raised to cushion his head on his open hands. The dark, expressionless eyes were open, gazing up into a gentle downward drift of CO_2 snow.

He was awake, Drake realized. And thinking . . . what?

The Snarks were Graybill's most feral and dangerous species, but they were not the planet's only predator. The soundbugs were big gray invertebrates with formidable exoskeletons. They ruled the "tropics," where

Graybill's sun could, at zenith, sometimes melt mercury.

The soundbugs were solitary hunters. "They do not resemble the Snarks in appearance, form, or habits," Milton assured Drake. "Also, they hunt at night, and they use primarily sound and echo-location, like the bats of your own home world. It seems unlikely that smell will play any part in Carp's survival."

"If he survives." Drake had seen a close-up of a soundbug, and he shriveled inside at the idea of fighting one. The animal was like a hard-shelled scorpion, about two meters long and supported by a dozen strong and leathery legs. It weighed three or four hundred pounds, most of that the thick shield of dense armor on its back and belly. Like the Snarks, it swallowed its food whole; unlike them, it could not expand its body and mouth because the massive exoskeleton was of fixed width. Instead, two constriction rings at the front of the maw crushed the prey, living or dead, to a size where it could be engulfed.

"It is my opinion that our Carp will do more than survive. He will triumph." Milton had initially been dubious about the prospects of any combination of Snark and human. The idea that such a creature might be of value in the battle with the Shiva had seemed preposterous. Now the Servitor's position was changing. Milton had become a supporter, rooting for their creation and ready to believe that it could do anything.

The Servitor was ready to order Carp's release. At Drake's insistence, all activities would still be carried out using remote handling equipment. As an extra precaution, the pilotless flier that had taken Carp from the Snark colony to the equator contained no sentient components. Milton and Drake were directing operations from a station several hundreds of kilometers away and monitoring everything with ground-based, airborne, and spaceborne observing systems.

Graybill's long twilight was beginning when the door

of the aircar automatically opened, and Carp was free to step out onto the crumbling, orange-gray surface.

The planet's atmosphere was too thick for most stars to shine brightly through. Night observations had to rely on thermal and microwave signatures, and those pictures tended to be grainy and monochrome. Milton was already complaining of their poor quality and augmenting the results with sonic imaging. Drake worried that those high-frequency sound beams might interfere with the soundbug's own sonic pulses.

Milton reassured him. "It is a different frequency regime. The worst that can happen is occasional signal aliasing, and the soundbug's interpretation system has enough redundancy to compensate for that. Do not worry. The soundbug will be able to see Carp."

There was a problem with Milton's assessment. Unless Carp came out, no one would see him at all; and at the moment, nothing moved in the clearing where the flier stood.

"What's he doing in there?" Drake asked at last.

"I am sorry, but I am unable to answer your question. The flier's imaging systems are directed toward observation outside the car. Maybe we should change that in the future. But it is all right. Here he comes."

A shadowy figure was emerging from the flier's open door. Carp paused just a few feet from the flier, turning his head slowly from side to side.

"He won't see clearly for much longer. And when it is fully dark, he will lack our night sensors." Milton increased the image intensity. The scene became brighter, but no less grainy. "What can he be doing?"

The figure on the screen was bending low, touching the ground.

"He's digging," Drake said. "I have no idea why, but I'm sure that he does. Don't forget that his memories are derived from experiences on the surface of Graybill. He also has instincts, things going for him that we know nothing about. He recognizes a dangerous environment without being told. He knows about soundbugs and maybe he has a way to deal with them."

But a big part of Carp also derived from Drake Merlin. What would Drake do, himself, if he were outside and alone in the darkness?

Drake had information that Carp lacked. He knew that a soundbug, as big as any on Graybill, had its den a couple of kilometers to the west, across a narrow but deep hydrocarbon stream that ran to within thirty meters of the clearing. Worse than that, the soundbug's nightly hunting path took it across the stream and through the clearing. They had picked this particular site to make sure that there would be an encounter.

Drake decided he could answer his own question: If he were outside as dark approached, he would climb back into the flier, lock the door, and wait through the long fourteen hours until dawn. Strangely, that seemed to be what Carp was doing. He had raised from his stooped position and moved back inside the aircar. But the door of the car remained open.

Now Drake could see the result of Carp's digging with his hands. The soil of the clearing was soft and crumbling for only the first few inches, then it turned to a hard tangle of roots and rocks.

"He's coming out again," Milton said softly.

Drake could see that for himself. Carp had emerged from the car. He ignored his digging and headed west, toward the stream. He seemed to be following faint marks on the ground. When he reached the stream he stood on its bank for a few seconds, looking first up and then downstream. Graybill's plant life had never developed woody trunks, and it was limited in height to a couple of feet. Carp had a clear view of both directions. Upstream, to the north, the ground sloped rapidly higher, and at its narrowest point the stream became a series of fast-moving rapids. Downstream the flood slowed and widened to a series of pools and shallows.

Carp stepped into midstream and waded north. The

turbulent flow pushed against him, rising past his knees. At one point the stream became narrower and deeper, and he was in almost to his waist. After standing at that deepest point for a few moments, he turned and allowed the liquid flow to push him back downstream. He waded past his point of entry, on to where the flow was slower. There were calm, deep pools here, and the whole stream was much wider.

"But what is he *doing*?" Milton said.

Drake did not reply. Although the actions were mysterious, the Snark-human synthesis carried a sense of definite purpose in every movement.

Carp emerged from the stream and headed back to the flier. Once more he entered, and once more there was a long and frustrating wait. When he came out he carried a big bundle of soft material.

"He has been stripping the front cabin," Drake said quietly. "Those are seat materials and seat covers from the control chair. Are you sure there is no way that he can control the flier itself?"

"Quite sure." Milton displayed a confidence that Drake did not share. "He would need to change microchip settings from remote to manual, and that requires microtools and a knowledge of circuit designs. He has neither. But he has made sure that *we* cannot do anything with the flier, either. The cables he is carrying are the ones that control attitude and power levels. Do you think he merely seeks to hold the car as a place where he can hide?"

"No. He could do that without stripping the seats."

But Drake did not have a better suggestion. He watched as Carp, in near darkness now, retraced his steps toward the stream. The synthesis chose his site carefully, and on the stream bank formed a rough cylinder from the material that he was carrying. A long loop of cable went around it and back to his hands. Carp ran another noose on the soft ground, a full meter away from the cylinder in each direction, and held on to the free end of that line also. In the last glimmer of light he paid out both wire cables and stepped down into the water. Heading upstream, he came to the deepest point of the fast-running rapids. There he crouched down until only his head was visible.

"I think I get it," Drake said. "He saw the soundbug tracks, and he must have an idea what made them. He tried digging as a way to become invisible, but only the first few inches of ground are soft. So instead he's trying to use water to hide him."

"Water?"

"Sorry. I mean liquid hydrocarbons." Yet to Drake, in his present body, they seemed like water. What else should you call a clear, cold liquid that ran in pure streams, that evaporated from surface pools, that you could drink whenever you felt thirsty? He and Carp had a lot in common, even if Drake could not follow the other's thought processes. But it was the *difference* in thought patterns that provided the whole reason for Carp's existence.

That existence was now threatened. Milton grunted, and drew Drake's attention to another display. It was dark enough for the soundbug to waken from its daytime torpor, and it was on the move. It had emerged from its den and was making its way downhill. No sound signal accompanied the display, but the easy liquid movement across the uneven surface gave an impression of silent, ghostly progress.

That was confirmed when the soundbug came on its first prey of the night. The animal was a short, fat version of a polar Snark. It was scrabbling busily in the dirt, tail high in the air. The soundbug seized it before it realized it was in danger. The soundbug's leathery legs moved the victim to the front constricting rings and compression began. Blood spurted from the blind head end into the waiting maw of the soundbug, but the fat Snark did not die at once. It went on struggling, until the last wriggling tip of the tail was swallowed.

Drake did not look at Milton. He had no trouble imagining the Servitor's reaction, because he shared it. The original idea had sounded clean and simple: combine Snark ferocity with human cunning, to produce an organism more effective than either in combatting the Shiva. What had been left unmentioned was the question of testing the result.

In retrospect it was obvious: he and Milton would have to expose Carp to more and more dangerous situations, until one of them proved fatal. It was a particularly vicious form of torture, with no escape but death.

Drake made his decision. He might be willing to sacrifice himself to save the Galaxy from the Shiva, but he could not bear to create thinking beings merely in order to kill them. If Carp somehow survived through the night, that would be the end of the experiment. The Snark-human synthesis would live out his days in peace on Graybill. That sounded like a cruel enough punishment, forcing a sentient being to exist without others of its kind, but Drake could change that. It would be easy to develop a dozen copies of Carp in the off-world lab and transport them down for release on the surface of the planet.

More than likely, however, that would not be necessary. Every action of the soundbug seemed to emphasize its invulnerability. Nothing in the flier could penetrate that massive armor. Nothing could sever those tough limbs. Unless Drake flew to the distant site at once and rescued Carp, the chance of the synthesis being alive at dawn seemed close to zero.

Drake glanced from one screen to the other. The fat Snark had apparently been no more than an appetizer for the soundbug's main meal. It was on the move again, quartering the ground. Long antennas had unfurled above the armored back, to receive returning sound signals and interpret them as images.

The soundbug was closing on the stream. Very soon the pictures on the two display screens would merge and show the same scene. To Drake, who knew exactly where to look, Carp's head was easy to pick out. It was a lighter gray against the darker turbulent flow. The question was, would the soundbug recognize that feature of the stream as new and different, when natural rocks both upstream and downstream rose above the surface to interrupt the flow?

Very soon, they would know. Thirty meters more, and the soundbug was at the far bank. It had come to the narrowest point of the stream, and it hesitated there. The flier was over in the middle of the clearing. That would be new to the soundbug; but also new, and much closer, a fat cylinder lay on the other bank. As the soundbug paused, the cylinder twitched and jerked a couple of feet along the ground.

The soundbug crossed the stream and pounced in a single movement. As it grabbed the stuffed roll of seat covers, Carp stood upright in the middle of the stream. He pulled hard on the second wire, drawing a noose around the soundbug's legs and carapace.

The predator felt the pressure at once and reached its head down to grip the cable. The maw snapped shut on the closed loop.

The wire had an outer insulating layer, but its core had been designed to resist both shear and stretching. It would not break, nor could it be cut through. While the soundbug had all its attention on the confining cable, Carp hauled backward and dragged the struggling creature over the edge of the bank into the fast-flowing stream. Weighed down by its dense carapace, the soundbug plunged to the streambed, where it stood with the current swirling about its broad back.

Drake expected that Carp would now try to pull the soundbug upstream, and would fail. The drag of the current in the other direction was too great. But instead, the Snark-human synthesis began to wade forward and allowed the cable to slacken. With the noose still tight around its legs and hindering its movements, the soundbug scrabbled and splashed and was swept farther downstream.

Carp followed. Still holding the wire, he came dangerously close to the predator. Except that it was no longer quite so dangerous. The antennas, thoroughly soaked, lay flat along the back. When Carp pushed at the edge of the carapace, adding his weight for a moment to the force of the current, and then rapidly jumped away, Drake realized that the soundbug was blind. Its sound-emitting equipment was below the surface, and its wet receiving equipment had no signal to receive.

But the animal could still kill anything within reach. The multiple legs were grasping madly in all directions, while the constricting rings in a reflex of violence were dilating and snapping tight every couple of seconds.

Then the upper part of the leathery legs was no longer visible. The dome of the carapace showed less high above the surface. The current had carried the soundbug downstream to one of the deep pools.

Once the thick shield of the exoskeleton had vanished completely beneath the surface, Carp tightened the cable to prevent the sunken body from moving to shallower parts. Then he stood and waited.

Waves on the surface revealed the desperate activity beneath. Four times the soundbug reared up, and the edge of the carapace became visible. Before the head could appear, Carp pulled the body off-balance. The fourth time, the soundbug flipped over onto its back before it disappeared again. There was one last burst of furious splashing, which gradually subsided. Finally not a ripple showed on the surface of the pool.

Carp waited for another minute or two, before finally wading to the bank and hauling himself out. He sat for a while, hunched over and with his legs in the stream. He was still holding the cable that had trapped the soundbug in its noose.

He looked exhausted. It was not surprising. He had fought a creature that Drake had judged invulnerable; he had fought in a place that was not of his own choosing; and he had fought without weapons.

That was when Drake realized the most astonishing thing of all. He and Milton had watched the fight with the aid of microwave and high-frequency imaging sensors. They could see everything. The soundbug, until the stream drowned its sense organs, had also seen perfectly; but Carp could have seen nothing. It was too dark.

He had fought the soundbug totally blind. And still he had won. It was tempting to ask, what were the limits of Carp's abilities as a fighter? How far could he be pushed, before he lost?

That was an immoral question. Drake had made his decision earlier, before the fight began. He would not change it now.

"It's over." He spoke to Milton, who was staring at the display where Carp had at last roused himself and was hauling the dead body of the soundbug onto the bank of the stream. "We wait for dawn. Then first thing in the morning, we go and get the flier."

"And Carp?"

"He goes free. Don't you think he's earned it?"

"More than earned it. But what about the Shiva?"

"We'll have to find another way." Drake took a last look at Carp, who now had the soundbug on its back and was prying open the lower shell casing. There was every sign that the soundbug's final meal would be as a course and not as a diner. What senses was Carp using to guide him? It could only be touch and smell. If it was anything else, some sense undreamed of by humans, Drake would never find out what it was. Just as he would never know what thoughts were carried inside that long-haired skull.

"First thing in the morning," he repeated. "Then it's good-bye to Carp. Some means can never be justified, no matter what the ends."

It seemed natural that Drake would feel a form of bond with Carp, given the latter's genetic roots. What was more surprising was that Milton had similar feelings.

And yet, why not? Milton had done the genetic design work, plus the tricky splicing of human and Snark nucleotide coding. Milton had also grown Carp's body and downloaded into his brain a body of data that went beyond basic survival instincts. If Drake was the father and one of the Snarks was Carp's mother, then the Servitor could certainly claim to be the midwife.

Milton discussed none of this with Drake. The Servitor merely, and uncharacteristically, volunteered to go back to the clearing and collect the flier. Milton had confirmed that the car would no longer work by remote control, and suggested that it might be informative to learn what had been done to it.

"You can go, with two conditions." Drake was busy with his own work. He had vowed that Carp would have a group of his own kind as companions, as soon as possible. With Carp's template to work from, the task would be short and routine. The seed of the necessary lab had been dropped from orbit, the lab itself had been grown, and the lab's manufacturing line was already up and running.

"First," Drake continued, "you must handle everything with a heavy lift vehicle that stays continuously airborne. You hoist the flier with that, and you don't land anything at all on the surface—including you. Second, you make sure that Carp is nowhere around when you do it. Scan the flier, inside and out. If you see a sign of Carp, abandon the pickup operation at once and return to base."

"Which is precisely what I would have done, without

instructions." The Servitor was touchy on only a few subjects, but reliability and sound judgment were two of them. Milton rolled away, leaving Drake to continue the development of the Carp duplicates. The original cells were in a continuous-flow nutrient bath and had a constant doubling time of 820 seconds. Growth from primal cell to full-sized organism, ready to step out onto the surface of Graybill, was a twelve-hour operation. There were fewer than four hours to go.

Drake divided his attention three ways while the growth process proceeded. His main focus was on the development of the Carp clones, but at the same time he was making plans to wrap up operations on Graybill. The orbiting mother craft had already received instructions. It was prepared to send Drake and Milton back to headquarters by S-wave link, as soon as they were uploaded to it.

Every few minutes Drake made a spot check of Milton's progress. Like the downed flier, the heavy-lift air vehicle had been grown on Graybill. Both craft would be left behind on the planet after Drake and Milton were uploaded to orbit. The vehicles would not last long. With a planned decay time of less than a month, they would crumble to dust as intermolecular forces weakened.

The vehicles had also been built with an eye to rugged simplicity, rather than the ultimate in performance. That became clear during operations. The heavy-lift cargo car could hover, but it had a slight tendency to drift forward. Drake watched until, on the second sweep, the lifter's magnetic grapples secured the flier and hoisted it clear of the surface; then Drake returned to his other tasks. He had seen no signs of Carp on the ground, and he confirmed that Milton's observations had discovered no trace of him. The body of the soundbug had been opened and partly eaten. Without landing for a close inspection, it was hard to say how much of a hand Carp had had in that operation. Plenty of other native life-forms had probably been willing to enjoy breakfast at the soundbug's expense.

Drake checked the status of each biotank. By design, each copy of Carp had been given a slightly different development plan, and the results would all be a little different from each other. Drake spent the next hour monitoring and approving the progress of each variation.

Finally, he looked up and wondered what was delaying the heavy lifter. The vehicle had not been designed for speed, but the three-hundred-kilometer return trip should take no more than an hour. It must be slowed by the presence of the flier beneath it, and by the resistance of Graybill's dense atmosphere. There could be no major problem, otherwise the lifter's emergency beacon would have gone into operation.

Drake turned back to the biotank displays. Almost immediately he was interrupted. The heavy lift vehicle had finally arrived. It lowered the crippled aircar and released it onto the station pad, then made its own landing. Drake, watching at the window, saw the door of the heavy lifter open. Milton rolled out and headed for the aircar. The whisk-broom head turned toward the station. Drake waved and was answered by a nod of tangled wires.

Drake confirmed that the orbiting ship had registered the arrival of the lifter and was ready to upload him and Milton. He made a final check of the biotanks. Everything was proceeding on schedule. In another couple of hours, the biological growth operations within the tanks would be complete. Before the tanks opened, Drake and Milton would leave the planet. Each copy of Carp would awaken in a biotank that was already dissolving around it. Each copy contained genetic information that would guide it to Carp's location, together with general data about Graybill. After Drake and Merlin had been transferred to headquarters, the mother vessel would remain high above the surface to monitor activity on the planet below for the indefinite future.

Drake heard a sound at the open door of the station. If Milton were finished already, there was no reason they should not leave at once. He knew that his own wish, to stay long enough to make sure that the copies were delivered safely from the tanks, was unnecessary and even dangerous. As soon as they could go, they must leave.

He stood up. As he did so, Carp entered. Drake had no sense of rapid movement, but suddenly he was back in his chair and Carp was leaning over him. A bristly forearm across his throat held him in position, barely allowing him to breathe.

Dark eyes stared into his. They were all pupil, round and black and infinitely deep. Drake saw in them his own folly and stupidity, level after level of it. He had been crazy to think he could play God, devising a superior warrior that would help to battle the Shiva. If he failed, he failed, and the attempt was simply futile. But success was far worse. Why would such a being wait to fight the Shiva, when humans were so close to hand? What madness had led Drake to believe that such a creature, once brought into existence, could be controlled and confined?

A hundred stories, as old as history, told what happened when a man summoned forces he could not master.

And, the final folly. Why had he allowed Milton to go alone to retrieve the flier? If anyone went alone, it should have been Drake himself. He did not know what Carp had done to persuade or trick Milton, or even if Milton still existed. It did not matter.

"I'm sorry." The pressure on his throat was great, and he could barely utter the words. Carp's hands changed their position on his neck and began to twist.

Drake knew that he was going to die, and it would not be of strangulation.

"I'm sorry," he whispered again, as the turning force increased. *Sorry that I did this to you, bringing you into such a life, with such a purpose.*

There was a different look in Carp's eyes. Surprise, that a being who was about to be killed did not resist? Surprise at Drake's words, which surely Carp did not understand? Or a puzzled wonderment, as Carp, like Drake, stared into another's eyes and recognized part of himself?

But another presence lay within Carp; a cold, remorseless agent that could admit neither reason nor mercy. Like the Snarks, Carp killed because he had no choice. He killed because he had to kill.

Sorry. No words could come from Drake's throat. His neck was wrenched around to a point where the cervical vertebrae were ready to splinter and snap. *Sorry for what I did to you. And for what I must now do to you.*

Drake had been foolish, but he had not been finally and terminally foolish. The orbiting spacecraft was monitoring everything that happened to him. Certain safeguards were still in position.

Drake felt the bones of his neck breaking. His last moment of darkened vision showed Carp's face, puzzled and alert. Carp was aware that something new was happening, something beyond his control. Drake's final sensation was the onset of dissolution. The hands that gripped his throat, like Drake himself, seemed to weaken and crumble.

Drake's death provided the signal. Within him, within Carp's body, within the station, within all the biotanks, within the fliers, within every human presence or artifact on Graybill, the changes began. Molecular bonds lost their hold.

In the final moments, Carp released Drake's broken body and dropped it to the ground. He stood upright and motionless, feeling within himself the chaos of death. His final howl, the first sound that he had ever uttered, was a cry of anger. As he fell, he raged at the injustice of a universe that created a perfect fighting machine, then destroyed it before it had a chance to fulfill its destiny.

Chapter 21

"Out there, we've walked quite friendly up to Death."

Drake hung in open space, six light-hours from the nearest star. Mel Bradley was at his side. While Drake would have been quite willing to receive a report and a display in the War Room, Mel insisted that he see this at firsthand.

Drake knew exactly where he was: out on the far side of the Galaxy, a safe distance from the spreading Silent Zone controlled (or destroyed) by the Shiva. The nearest star of the Zone was about sixty light-years away.

He was less sure of *what* he was. He had been transmitted here at superluminal speed, but not to any recognizable form of embodiment. He could maneuver in space and look in any direction, but he was unaware of the nature of his body.

"You'd have to ask Cass Leemu about that," Mel said. He seemed unconcerned, his attention elsewhere. "It's something she dreamed up."

"Are we made of plasma?" Drake turned his own attention inward and saw nothing.

"Not the usual sort. We're an assembly of Bose-Einstein Condensates. Cass says a BEC assembly has two great advantages. When we're done we'll be transmitted back without modification."

"What's the second advantage?"

Mel had no way to grin, but he radiated a wolfish sense of glee. "If something goes wrong, Cass assured me that dissolution from a BEC form is painless. Of course, she's never tried it. Makes you think of the old preachers, talking about the delights of heaven or the torments of hell after you die. I always wanted to ask them, Did you die? How do you know what happens if you haven't tried it for yourself?"

Drake was listening, but with only half an ear. He was looking outward again. Mel had said that something was ready to begin. Drake had very little idea as to what would happen next.

Partly that was Mel's doing. He was perfect as the person to develop new offensive weapons, but he was also as awkward and cross-minded and independent as ever, wanting to do things in his own way. And partly it was Drake's doing. He had been learning over the millennia that either you learned to delegate or you drowned in details. Worse than that, if you were involved in the process, you lost the power to be objective about the outcome. It was Drake's job to review what Mel had done, then either approve or veto the next step.

But it was *hard*. The urge to meddle was deep-rooted in humans.

The nearby star was a white F0 type, like the blazing giant Canopus that had troubled Drake so many aeons ago. From this distance it showed a definite disk, slightly smaller and whiter than the Sun as seen from Earth. Drake could see a slight asymmetry. A straight line had been ruled across the left-hand limb. Beyond that line, but within the star's imagined circle, he could detect faint and scattered points of light. They were other stars.

"The caesura?"

Mel said, "You're looking at it. It's started." Even he seemed subdued. The star they were watching might seem small from this distance, but it was thirty million miles across.

And it was being eaten. The dividing line was moving steadily to the right. Drake stared hard at the remaining portion of the star. It seemed unaffected, untouched.

"Are you sure it's really happening, Mel? If the caesura is sending part of the star to another universe, why isn't the rest of it in turmoil? Unless somehow the gravitational effect is left behind. . . ."

"According to Cass, it's not. The whole thing goes—mass, matter, gravitational and magnetic fields, everything. We verified that on the small tests of asteroids and planets. I see no reason to think she's wrong this time."

"So why isn't there total chaos around the star?"

"Cheshire Cat effect. Cass doesn't call it that—she uses a string of Science gibberish. But there's a time lag before the field stresses disappear from our universe. It's long enough to keep the star intact as it moves into the caesura. If there were colonies on the planets around the star—there aren't, of course, they were moved long ago—and if the caesura hadn't swallowed them, the colonies would see the star vanish but measure its residual gravitational field. That fades smoothly away over an eight-hour period."

"Suppose the caesura moves *slowly*, and takes more than eight hours?"

"Then the part of the star that hasn't been absorbed will collapse. If half of it is left behind, you'll get an explosion with as much energy as a supernova. The nice thing is that this can be done with any type of star, and you can do it when you choose. *And* by picking the right caesura geometry you can beam the emitted energy in a particular direction. You can keep the beam collimated, so it doesn't spread much over interstellar distances. Intergalactic, either, if you take extra care. And there's your weapon."

A weapon, indeed. The ultimate weapon. Drake stared at the doomed star, reduced now to a mere sliver of brilliance. Only a thin sector of the right-hand side remained. Then he turned to look outward, toward the galactic edge. The stars blazed there, undiminished, but they were silent. Uncommunicating, controlled by the Shiva.

He knew now the power that lay within his hands. His own idea had been to use the caesuras to create a no-man's-land, an empty zone on the edge of Shiva territory. Even if the Shiva could cross that firebreak, the time it took would tell humans something more about the manner and speed of Shiva movement.

Now Mel was pointing out that they could do much more.

Pick a target star in the Silent Zone. Choose any planetless and expendable star in this region, or any other convenient place in the Galaxy. Create a caesura of the right dimensions and geometry.

Now if you moved the caesura to engulf your chosen star at the right speed, a tongue of energy from the stellar collapse would be thrown out into space. It would travel at a substantial fraction of the speed of light. When it reached the target star, any planets orbiting that star would become burned and lifeless cinders. The star's outer layers on one side would be stripped off. There was a chance that the star itself would explode.

There were more than enough available stars in the human sector of the Galaxy for a one-on-one matching with stars in the Silent Zone. The Shiva, whatever they were, could be destroyed.

Whatever they were. That was the trouble. It was easy to

examine the pattern by which the Shiva had entered
and spread through the Galaxy from outside, and conclude from the long silence of the old human colonies
that the Shiva were ruthless destroyers, inimical to anything other than their own kind.

And hence to propose the old human solution,
stated by Rome but surely far older: *Shiva delenda est;*
"the Shiva must be destroyed."

Conclusion was not the same as proof. Suppose that
the colonies throughout the Silent Zone still survived?
Suppose there was some other reason for their failure
to speak? The existence of the Shiva and the silence of
the colonies were not the elements of a syllogism. They
did not add up to a proof that the colonies no longer
existed.

Drake wondered just what it would take to persuade
him of that. Was he proving that the composites were
wrong, when they called him back to consciousness?
Maybe he was like them, lacking the resolve to do what
had to be done.

He looked again at the sky, which now showed nothing at all where star and caesura had been. He turned
to Mel Bradley.

"What happens to the caesura when it has done its
work?"

"It just sits there, a permanent feature of space-time
with zero associated mass-energy. It will never decay or
go away. Don't worry, though. I asked Cass Leemu the
same question. Unless it's activated in the right way it
won't absorb anything else. There's no danger that the
caesuras will keep going and swallow up the universe."

"That wasn't what I was thinking. I was wondering if
a caesura could go on and eat up another star."

"Any number. So far as we can tell there's no limit
to how much matter or energy you can put into a caesura and kick right out of the universe. But rather than
move one caesura all over the place, it's easier to make
another one. Cass and I have the technique down cold.

We can make one for each star in the Galaxy—if you want us to."

There was an implied suggestion behind Mel's words. *Which means we could make one for each star in the* Silent Zone, *if you wanted us to, and have plenty of the Galaxy left afterward.*

It was a solution, but one that Drake could not use. Not yet. Someday, maybe, when he had exhausted every other hope, or when absolute proof was produced to show that the Shiva were the destroyers that they seemed to be. But for the moment . . .

"Stay here. Make as many of the caesuras as you need for the firebreak. As soon as all the colonies are relocated to a safe region, remove the stars and get the break in position."

"Very good." Mel sounded disappointed. "And how should I use the caesuras, fast or slow?"

"Fast enough to avoid the problem of stellar collapse."

"If you say so. And the Silent Zone?"

"Stays silent, and untouched." Drake looked one last time toward the outer edge of the Galaxy, knowing that colonies were disappearing from the human community as he watched. He felt Mel Bradley's disapproval, weighted by the thoughts of hundreds of trillions of other composites across space.

"I intend to do something else about the Silent Zone," Drake continued. "You can start the return transmission any time. As soon as I'm back at headquarters I'm going to try a new approach."

It was one of the rare occasions when the thought of his own dissolution was preferable to the idea of what he had to do next. Dying once was not so bad. Everybody did it eventually, and it was part of your personal future even if you didn't know how or when.

Dying a billion times was less appealing.

•   •   •

The location of every lost world was well known. Drake had chosen one of the most recently silenced, vanished from the human community since the time of his own involvement.

He and Tom Lambert were on board a probe ship, downloaded to an inorganic form that shared the ship's eyes, ears, and communications unit.

Tom had taken charge of the ship's drive. "According to the records for other similar places," he said, "we're approaching the danger zone. That's the planet ahead."

They stared in silence at the image of a peaceful world. It was a look-alike for another planet about three hundred light-years away: same K-type primary; mass, size, orbital parameters and axial tilt within a few percent; atmosphere modified very slightly, if at all, to an Earth analog. Both worlds had been colonized by a human association of organic and inorganic forms within two million years of each other. Here were sister planets, celestial twins with one difference: this world, Argentil, after billions of years of active presence in the human community, had dropped all contact and refused to respond to any signals.

Tom finally broke the silence. "Do you want to hold our distance?"

"Everything we see is being sent back to headquarters?"

"Everything."

"Let's hold our position for one full Argentil day, and make sure we've seen everything that's down there. Then we'll go closer."

Drake suspected they had already seen all they were going to. Whatever the Shiva had done to this planet, they had not destroyed it or made it uninhabitable for humans. Changes had taken place in Argentil, particularly an increase in atmospheric carbon dioxide and water vapor, but those could be the result of natural long-term climatic changes. They could just as well be the work of humans. Either way, the planet was still comfortably habitable.

They were hovering far off on the sunward side. As the world turned slowly beneath the ship, Drake suddenly imagined himself with Ana, restored to human body form, strolling unsuited and bareheaded among the dark-green forest lands of Argentil.

The thought came as a shock. Ana had been absent from his mind for a long time. Once he would have sworn that could not happen, that no hour could pass in which he did not think about her.

"All right, Tom." Drake had to act. His mind felt oddly unbalanced. Maybe he had watched Argentil for too long. "Let's go. Take us closer. Take us all the way down to a landing."

How could he *not* be thinking constantly about Ana, when she was the whole reason that he was wandering here on the outer rim of the Galaxy?

He heard Tom screaming, but his own mind was far away. He was not seeing Argentil as the ship closed in for its final approach pattern. When the fusion fires rose from the surface to vaporize the descending ship, he saw only Ana. She was standing before him, telling him not to worry: they would still enjoy the future together, when all these events were nothing but a remote blip on the distant horizon of time.

The ship's communications unit was not controlled by Drake's wandering consciousness. A brief final message, triggered by the attack, went as an S-wave signal back to headquarters: it said that this ship, like so many others, was being destroyed—by a system sent to Argentil to defend the planet from the Shiva.

One more attempt. After how many?

Drake had lost count.

He studied the screens. It was information of a sort, even though it only confirmed what he already knew.

Where a giant artificial colony had once floated in free space, the sensors now showed nothing at all. However, the outer layers of the nearest star, only four light-minutes away, revealed subtle changes in its spectrum. There were more metal absorption lines than had been shown in the old records. And a nearby planet, which had once supported a human colony, was silent but apparently untouched.

It seemed as though the Shiva destroyed free-space colonies, while leaving the planets that they conquered able to support life. Drake pondered that fact as his lead ship turned cautiously toward the planet. Instead of Tom Lambert accompanying him, Drake had been downloaded to both ships. His two electronic versions had decided on a strategy on the way out from headquarters. Ship combinations had been sent out before, without success. After a million failed attempts he no longer hoped for definitive answers. He would settle for some small additional scrap of information.

When the first ship was within a few light-seconds of the planet, the second one released a tiny pod. It lacked a propulsion system, but it contained miniature sensors, an uploaded copy of Drake, and a low-data-rate transmitter.

The pod hung silent and motionless in space, while Drake on board it watched the approach of the two main ships to the planet. The first one vanished in a haze of high-energy particles and radiation. The second turned to flee, but a rolling torus of fire arrowed to it from the place where the other ship had been destroyed.

Drake reached a conclusion: the transmission link was an Achilles' heel. The second ship should have been at a safe distance, but after the Shiva had killed the first ship they had been able to follow the tiny pulses of communication between the two.

It was another crumb of information about the Shiva. It told him that he had to be ultracautious in his own transmission. He began to send data out, warily and slowly, varying the strength and direction of the signal. Thousands of receiving stations, all over the Galaxy, would each receive a disconnected nugget of information. When he was finished, headquarters would face the task of time-ordering the sequence of weak signals, allowing for travel times, and collating everything to a single message.

Drake sent the pulses out a thousand times, varying the order of the signal destinations. By the time that he was finished, twelve thousand years had passed and he had drifted far from the star where the ships had died.

He had no propulsion system. Even now, he dared not risk a rescue signal.

They also serve who only stand and wait.

He waited. For another one hundred and forty thousand interminable years, he waited. The pod contained minimal computing facilities and no other distractions. There was nothing for him to do.

At last he gave the internal command to turn off all systems within the pod.

"All systems?" The pod's intelligence was limited, but sufficient to follow the implications of the command.

"That is my instruction."

"I am sorry, but I am unable to perform that command."

"I see. Very well. Give me override."

"That is permitted."

Final authority for pod operations was turned over to Drake.

He switched off all systems; was erased; became nothing.

Chapter 22

"Her lips were red, her looks were free,
Her locks were yellow as gold;
Her skin was white as leprosy,
The nightmare Life-in-Death was she,
Who thicks man's blood with cold."

It wasn't working. Drake decided that a smarter man than he would have realized the truth long ago. With all their efforts, they had learned very little.

The most tangible piece of information had been provided by Mel Bradley: the rate of spread of the Shiva zone of influence was between one-half and three kilometers a second. In other words, the Shiva domain expanded across one light-year of space in between one hundred thousand and six hundred thousand Earth years. That had its own implications. The firebreak that Mel had made with the help of the caesuras was forty light-years thick. It had taken four million years before a world was lost on the "safe" side of it; twenty-five million years later, every world along the whole great arc of the firebreak was gone.

The other thing, pointed out by Cass Leemu, was more peculiar: the Shiva apparently spread *faster* through regions where humans had colonies. Logic said it ought to be the other way round, that the resistance of a colony ought to slow the Shiva. Instead, it speeded them up. A policy of flight, leaving a world before the Shiva were predicted to arrive, had proved the best defense for other colonies.

And that was it; the sum total of what they had learned, in fifty million years of effort and millions of star systems lost. The good news, if that was the word for it, was that it would take a few billion more years before the entire galaxy became part of the Silent Zone.

Drake wondered what to suggest next to the composites. That humanity, in all its forms, should flee to another galaxy?

Universal flight didn't seem feasible, even if it was psychologically acceptable.

He turned his total attention to a single question: Was there anything, anything at all, that they had not tried? He could think of just one thing. They had sent specially trained colonies to worlds that in the next centuries or millennia were candidates to fall to the Shiva. It had been done with single organic entities, with inorganics, and with composites, and always with the same results: the colonies reported that everything was all right, that they were doing fine, no problems. Then one day they fell silent.

But here was the oddity: *distant* worlds were not affected. The Shiva influence was a local effect. If there was a way to be close enough to observe a world as it was lost, yet somehow far enough away that the observer would not be swallowed up in silence, then humanity might learn something new.

That prompted another thought: Could it be that they were not going *early enough* to the endangered worlds? Suppose there were long-term changes, subtle warnings of the coming of the Shiva, that Drake's observers did not catch because they had not lived long enough on the planet.

What sort of indicators were plausible? He couldn't

say. Ice ages, variation in length of seasons, movement
of polar caps, polarity reversal of magnetic fields, earth-
quakes, modified physiology of individuals at the cell
level, homeostatic shift—it could be any or all of them.
Despite all his studies, he was not, and would never be,
a scientist.

But he could think of a way to test his idea. Embody
someone in a long-lived form. Make thousands of copies of him, organic or inorganic. Send a copy to each
world, long before the Shiva were expected there. Ask
each one to wait, observe, and prepare. Tell him to be
patient. Tell him to report back any anomaly, no matter
how small.

Drake reached one more conclusion. He had been
thinking "him," and it was not hard to see why. How
could he ask anyone else to endure an interminable
wait, especially one likely to end with final extinction?

It was not some indefinite "him." It was *Drake*.

It could be Drake and only Drake. He had to be the
one. He would prepare, and he would send copies of
himself. He would also be at headquarters and monitor
every incoming message. And one day, before the
whole galaxy was silenced, perhaps the Drake-that-goes
and the Drake-that-stays would learn something useful.

And one other thing must be done. A certain crucial
piece of information must be withheld from any copy
of Drake who descended to each planet.

He would consult Cass to find out just how to do
that.

Drake splayed his feet on the marshy surface and stared
up for a last sight of the spacecraft. It was difficult, not
only because the ship was dwindling in apparent size,
but because as it rose higher the rate of motion across
the sky decreased. Drake was embodied in a native
form known as a mander. Its eyes were like a frog's

eyes, good at seeing rapidly moving objects, less effective on anything that stayed in one position.

One final glimpse, and then the ship was gone. Human vision might follow it still, but Drake could not. It did not matter. He knew where it was and where it would remain, far beyond the atmosphere in a polar observation orbit.

He looked around. This planet, Lukoris, was his new home. He had better get used to it, because he was going to be here for a long time. Half a million years did not sound like much—if you said it fast. From three to five hundred thousand years were likely to elapse before the Shiva arrived. Half a million years of waiting, before this world became part of the expanding Silent Zone.

The first thing was to understand and feel at home in his own body. He had been animated less than ten minutes ago, as the ship was preparing to leave. Drake examined the mander's physiology with a fair amount of curiosity. He was supposed to live like this, awake or dormant, for a thousand human lifetimes. According to the composites this body would never age or wear out. Even if he were to remain continuously conscious, which was not his plan, the mander would be as healthy and limber in a million years as it was that day.

How could that be? But perhaps a better question was, why not? Why did organisms age at all?

The answer had been discovered, long, long ago, and soon followed by the longevity protocols. Death by aging was a far-off anachronism. But none of that explained, in a way that Drake could understand, *why* a being aged, or how current science could hold off old age indefinitely.

It was like much of science: important, useful, and totally mysterious.

Drake returned to the inspection of his body. This was, according to alien specialist Milton, the closest form to human on the whole planet. It was hard to believe.

Drake examined the mander's feet. They were large and webbed. The legs above them were long and powerfully muscled, ideal for long balanced leaps. If it swims like a frog, and jumps like a frog, and sees like a frog . . .

He stuck out one of his two tongues. It was short and not sticky or club ended. He had already known that, intellectually, but he wanted reassurance.

In other respects the mander body was not at all froglike. His skin was dry and soft to the touch, covered with material like feathery mole fur. His two mouths were not in his head, where the sense organs were clustered, but one on each side of the torso beneath the breathing apertures. His brain was centered between them, deep in the interior of his chest and protected by rings of bony plates. Nothing could reach it that would not kill him first.

His embodiment was not, according to Milton, the most intelligent life-form on the planet Lukoris. That position was claimed by a monstrous flying predator known as a sphexbat, a creature that bordered on self-awareness and rode the permanent thermals around Lukoris's crags and vertical precipices, landing neither to feed nor breed. The sphexbat's young developed within the body cavity of the parent until one day they were ejected, to fly or to fall to their deaths. Lukoris's mutation rate was high. The survival odds for infant sphexbats were no better than 30 percent.

Drake was interested in the animals mainly because they were interested in him—manders formed one of the sphexbat's preferred forms of food. An immortal body was immortal only against aging. It could still be killed. He, of course, could be reembodied, but death by sphexbat sounded unusually unpleasant. The sphexbats did not swoop down on their prey and carry it off, like the Earth raptors. First they made a low-level run across the surface, blowing a fine cloud of neuro-toxic vapor from glands at the base of their wings. Vegetation cover was not enough protection. Any mander inhaling the fog did not die, but it felt the urge to crawl into the open and there became paralyzed. The sphexbat returning at the end of the day for its second run found the prey alive and conscious but unable to move. The victim was scooped up from the surface and consumed at leisure. The sphexbats maintained live larders on high rock ledges, and a mander—or Drake—might wait there awake and immobilized for many days.

Danger from sphexbat attack was a potential problem on the surface, but that's not where Drake intended to spend most of his time. No one could live alone and conscious for a million years, in his own body or any other, and remain sane. Drake would mostly be at the bottom of the swamp with the other manders, ten meters down, dormant and safe from attack. His species estivated regularly.

Events on the surface would not be ignored. A network of instruments would record data until Drake's return to the surface. That information supplemented the observations of the orbiting ship.

Drake expected to return to the surface for Lukoris's winter, but not every time. Once every hundred or thousand years he would be above ground for a few months, to check the instruments and to conduct a planetary survey. Changes that occurred too slowly to be noticed in real time might jump out at him if he saw the planet as a series of snapshots, glimpses caught at widely separated intervals.

First, though, he needed a baseline from which to measure change. He must understand Lukoris in all its parts. He would travel around the world and observe as he had never observed before.

Drake sighed, and said to himself, *Why bother? Why am I doing this?*

But he knew the answer to that. He set to work.

• • •

Prior to Drake's arrival, Lukoris had been the home of a thriving colony for hundreds of millions of Earth years. When the great amalgam of panic-stricken humans, computers, composites, and all their trappings fled the path of the Shiva, they did not take everything. Drake was the inheritor of a whole planet and of the former colony's technology.

That technology was useful in Drake's own survey of Lukoris. The planetwide data net showed a divided world of extreme horizontals and verticals, of sluggish seas and swamps encircling near-vertical mountain ranges. The mander body could not survive the rarefied air of the highest peaks without equipment, but Drake had to know what was going on there. Who could say where and in what form the Shiva might choose to appear?

He spent the first long winter roaming the planet. In person and vicariously with the help of miniature remote sensing units, he traveled the three-thousand mile ice river in the south, visited the tropics where summer water boiled to steam and only sulfur-loving bacteria could survive, and surveyed the northern badlands where the sphexbats were evolving their first primitive art, drawing stylized animals in blood on sheer rock faces. The sphexbats circled about his equipment. They were cautious and they did not attack at once, but they called to each other constantly in what was clearly a developing language.

Drake stored every image and sound and smell in his body's augmented memory. He omitted nothing, and he did not hurry. There was plenty of time. If he missed something this winter, there would be a thousand more chances to pick it up.

Finally it was time for the first estivation.

His body started the process automatically, exuding a transparent liquid that hardened into a tough semipermeable membrane. Small amounts of oxygen and water could be imported, and waste products expelled. As the shell solidified, Drake's body began to dig. Beyond his conscious control it dived and tunneled its way through a thick green ooze that thickened steadily with depth.

The process was natural to the mander, but not to the consciousness trapped within it. Drake felt that he was drowning in total darkness, surrounded by viscous fluid that thwarted any effort to save himself.

When it finally became clear that he was not drowning, that the body he inhabited could take prolonged immersion in its stride, he was not much comforted. This was not the way he had imagined his future: trapped in a swamp, in an alien body, the single human intelligence within many light-years with nothing to look forward to but solitude. And he must go through this many thousands of times.

His body was beginning to turn off, powering down for the long night. Drake fought against it, trying to dictate the course of his dreams. He didn't want to be here. He wanted to fight his way back to the surface, to signal the watching ship to pick him up. He wanted to go home to Earth. He wanted time turned back, to the happy days of youth and love and music.

He wanted Ana . . .

But that, of course, was why he was here. That was why it was *right* for him to be here. He was on Lukoris so that he could, someday, be with Ana again.

Someday I will be with Ana again.

As his body cut back the oxygen supply to the brain, Drake clung to that thought. He curled into a ball and went contentedly to sleep.

The pulse of Lukoris's seasons was slower than Earth's. With little tilt to the axis of rotation, summer and winter were dictated only by the planet's movement along its twenty-year eccentric elliptic orbit.

Drake's modified body had been programmed to sleep through fifty of those long cycles. Awakening at last one early winter, he crawled from the depths and waited for his shell to crack. When it had crumbled enough to give him freedom of movement, he tried to begin his inspection. His mander body would not let him do it. It insisted that he eat and drink, ravenously, breaking an eight-hundred-year fast. Only after that was he allowed to turn his attention to Lukoris.

At once he thought that he saw changes. The instruments assured him that it was illusion. The variations he seemed to observe were purely psychological. He was adapting to the mander body, and as he did so Lukoris's bottle-green swamps and flame-colored precipices became beautiful to him.

It confirmed the wisdom of coming here long before any Shiva influence might be expected. The adaptation was a transient effect, something that would settle down after the first few estivations.

He continued his careful monitoring and recording of plant and animal populations, diurnal temperature variations, surface and subsurface geology, solar radiation levels, and ten thousand other variables. All measurements went up to the orbiting ship. From there they were transmitted by S-wave data link to headquarters, half a galaxy away.

What was important? Drake did not know. Maybe everything, maybe nothing.

There was one unplanned and unpleasant incident, when he became too interested in a threadlike plant that wove great mats on the swampy surface and lured big animals there. When the threads broke, apparently by intention and all at once, the animal sank into the ooze to die and provided nutrients. Drake was not heavy enough to be at risk; but he was far from any

cover when the sphexbat came sweeping on its first run
of the day.

It saw him and changed course. A cloud of white
vapor came drifting toward him as it passed overhead.
The only possible escape route was downward. Drake
plunged headfirst into the ooze with his mouths and
eyes tightly closed, wondering if this was merely a different way of dying. It was still midwinter, much too early
in the year for the mander to estivate.

The slime of the swamp was cool on his skin. After a
few minutes Drake realized that he was not suffocating.
His body could absorb enough oxygen through its epidermis to keep him alive, provided that he did not
move much.

He waited for seven hours, almost half a Lukoris day.
The neurotoxin cloud must be given enough time to be
absorbed into the swamp, or to dissociate chemically in
the presence of sunlight.

When he wriggled back to the surface through the
sucking ooze, the sphexbat was right in the middle of
its collection run and only a couple of kilometers away.
It swooped noiselessly toward Drake on twenty-meter
pinions, the capture scoop already open for pickup. It
was within thirty meters when it saw that Drake was
upright and moving, rather than lying immobile on the
mat of the swamp. Twin maws hooted a two-tone call of
surprise and rage. The sphexbat banked and veered
away.

Ten seconds later, at a higher altitude, it returned to
pass immediately overhead. A pair of black eyes ahead
of the scoop stared right down at Drake.

What would it tell its fellows on its return to the high
cliffs? That some variant mander had arisen, with a new
technique for self-defense?

Maybe, in Lukoris's far future, oral history around a
sphexbat tribal fire would tell of a time when a strange
creature had appeared on the surface, invulnerable to

the paralyzing neurotoxin on which all hunting depended.

Drake told himself that he was fantasizing. Lukoris did not have a far future that was continuous with the past and the present. The arrival of the Shiva would be a singular point on the time line, a moment when future and past were discontinuously connected.

He returned to his careful survey of Lukoris in all its aspects.

On and on.

Winters continued, one after another after another, until Drake no longer saw them in his mind as unique events but as a long continuum of insignificant change. If summers seemed more memorable, it was only because he remained awake more rarely. They formed unpleasant data points, when most of Lukoris experienced conditions of heat and dryness that the mander body could scarcely tolerate. Drake felt that he had to supplement the recording instruments on the surface and in orbit by ground surveys in summer as well as winter, but it was not easy. The changes made to the mander body could keep it awake, but at some level it knew a deeper truth. As temperatures rose, every cell of his body longed to be ten meters belowground, at rest in the cool and quiet dark.

On and on.

Year after long year, winter after winter, summer after summer. The possible arrival of the Shiva took on the overtones of ancient myth. In his mind the final confrontation became Armageddon, Ragnarok, Dies Irae, the Fimbulwinter, the Last Trumpet. It would never happen. They would never come.

Until, suddenly, they did.

Drake rose from his dark hiding place one morning, as he had emerged five hundred or a thousand times before. The rains had ended and the air was pleasantly cool. Even before his protective shell was gone, he knew there was a difference.

Not just a single, minor change, but changes everywhere.

He looked up. The late-summer sky of Lukoris was usually a smudged yellow. Today it was pristine blue, barred with a delicate herring-bone pattern of pink and white clouds. The air was clear, and in the near distance Drake could see hills. They were not vertiginous heights that rose sheer from the encircling plain, but gentle slopes dappled with light green vegetation and small copses of rough-barked trees.

There had never been trees on Lukoris. Only low-growing plants covered the endless swamp and formed dense mats on dark watery flats.

Swamp.

Then where was the feel of cool ooze?

Drake looked down. He should be seeing algal cover and swamp pads, not the short, springy grass and clumps of blue wildflowers that stretched in front of his feet. And those feet should be wide and gray and webbed, not pink and five toed.

Drake breathed deep. He smelled lavender and thyme and roses.

He looked up and saw someone walking to him across the springy carpet of grass. Her hair shone gold in the sunlight, and she moved with the old familiar grace of perfect health. She did not speak, but her red lips smiled a greeting. When she moved to embrace him he knew just where he was.

His long search was over. He was in Paradise, and the only person that he had ever needed or wanted was here with him to share it.

The mander body had been modified in ways deliberately withheld from Drake. During all his days and years on Lukoris, a continuous report of his condition and actions had been beamed without his knowledge from the augmented memory module of his mander brain, up to the orbiting ship and thence to far-off headquarters.

When the anomalous behavior began on the surface, the copy of Drake that existed in electronic form on the ship did not pause for analysis or explanations. He did not try to send out a superluminal signal, which had failed so often with the Shiva in the past. Instead, he activated the caesura.

It had stood near the ship, prepared and waiting for this moment, for more than half a million years. Into the caesura, one after another, went ten million separate copies of every observation ever made of Lukoris, right up to the final second.

The whole ship and its copy of Drake would go into the caesura also. It was almost unbearably tempting to wait and try to learn what had happened—Drake seemed to be down there on the surface of Lukoris with Ana, miraculously returned to him.

But waiting was too dangerous. Drake in orbit had to assume that the Shiva would soon know about and be able to use anything that was left behind, just as they had used other planetary defenses against humanity. He and the ship must follow the data packets. Immediately after that the caesura itself would close.

In the milliseconds before the ship entered the caesura, Drake had an idea as to what the Shiva might be and do. There was no time to attempt another message. All he could hope was that Drake Merlin back at headquarters would draw the same conclusion.

Ten million packets of data had left the ship—moving not into space, where they might be intercepted, but out of space completely. Not even the Shiva should be able to track something through a caesura or prevent its passage.

Drake knew the odds. They had been calculated by the composites billions of years ago. There was one chance in 969,119 that any single data packet would reach its destination at headquarters. There was the same small chance that the ship and Drake himself would arrive there. In all other cases, close to certainty, Drake would vanish completely from the universe and experience death in some unpredictable way.

But *ten million* independent packages of information about events on Lukoris had been sent into the caesura. That changed the overall odds completely. The chance that one or more of them would reach headquarters was good: in fact, there was only a chance of one in thirty thousand that *no data packet at all* would make it home.

Those were acceptable odds. Certainty would have been nicer; but certainties in the universe were rare.

Drake waited, calm and surprisingly content, for the caesura to swallow up the ship and send him with it into oblivion.

Chapter 23

"There's trouble in the wind, my boys,
There's trouble in the wind.
Oh, it's please to walk in front, sir,
When there's trouble in the wind."

At last.

After hundreds of millions of years and a hundred billion tries, Drake and his team had something to work with.

Of course, the something made little sense. The group in the War Room was puzzling over eight copies of data records, all identical, that had been delivered through the caesura.

"It's perfectly consistent with the statistics," Cass Leemu pointed out. "There was a ten percent chance that we'd get exactly eight copies, but anywhere between six and fourteen is high probability. I'm afraid there's no sign of the ship that was orbiting Lukoris."

She did not need to say "the ship with Drake on board."

"The statistics may make sense." Tom Lambert was studying one of the displays. "But nothing else does. Look at this."

The record of the final minutes on Lukoris existed

in two forms. One of them showed events as seen by the sensors scattered around the surface. The other was Drake's own perception as received through the mander embodiment.

According to the surface sensors, Lukoris was much the same as it had been in the previous year; or, for that matter, the past half million. Swamps, broken by clumps of scrubby plant life, stretched away flat and dull to the horizon, where mile-high scarps of rock loomed skyward. The sky above them was the unchanging sulfurous yellow of late summer.

But Drake's view . . .

"What is he *seeing*?" Milton said. "And what does he think he's *doing*?"

They were looking through the mander's eyes as it walked forward across a sward of healthy turf and spring flowers. Milton, who had never seen old Earth, was justifiably puzzled. But Drake, seated in the headquarters' War Room, knew where he was. He was having trouble answering Milton, because he also guessed what was coming next.

The mander embodiment had become human in form. It was walking barefoot on the Sussex Downs, one of Drake and Ana's favorite vacation spots. She had been standing by a hedgerow, admiring a thrush's nest. Now she turned at Drake's approach and smiled a greeting. Spontaneously, without a word, they embraced.

In that first ecstatic moment, Drake in the War Room forced himself to look across to the other display. The sensors showed the mander, unchanged in form, standing motionless before a foot-high bulbous plant with spiky silver leaves.

"Freeze!" Drake said urgently. And then, to the others, "You know the earlier records. Is that"—he indicated the little plant—"new to Lukoris, or to this region? I don't think I've ever seen it before."

"It appears to be new." The others, using the power

of their composites, could answer almost at once and simultaneously.

"But what is the significance?" Par Leon asked. "It is nothing but a plant."

"I'm not sure. Look for more of them."

That analysis was also finished almost before the command was given. All of the Galaxy's computing power was available when Drake asked for it. With such resources the problem was trivial. Using the spiky-leaved plant as a template for a matching algorithm, the global database of Lukoris was scanned and analyzed, every day of every year since observations first began.

"They're all over the place," Cass said. "This size or smaller. But ten years ago there were none. They've all sprung up in the past few years. Do you think they are real?"

"I'm sure they are. It's the *other* scene that's a false reality." Drake hated to say that. He wanted what he had seen to be true, and he found it almost impossible to keep his eyes away from the image of Ana. "I think the plant is able to create an illusion in the mind of an intelligent being."

"Why intelligent?" Par Leon asked.

"Imagination needs intelligence." Drake gestured again to the first display. The mander stood motionless before the plant, while other animals wandering the swampy surface apparently took no notice. "There must be a certain minimum awareness, a level of intelligence before a mind can be made to imagine something other than what it receives through its senses."

"Like hypnotism," Melissa said. "The subject sees what she is told is there."

Mel Bradley scowled. "Hypnotized by a *plant*?"

"Do you have a better explanation?" Drake zoomed in on the mander. "Look at me. Cass can probably suggest a thousand ways in which an electromagnetic signal, or a scent containing the right chemicals, could affect the functioning of the brain. Remember, the plant doesn't change Lukoris. It just persuades the subject to see an alternate reality."

"But *what* reality?" Milton sounded confused. "It surely can't impose its own reality on someone."

"No." It did not surprise Drake that he knew what was happening when the others did not. His understanding was exactly proportional to his pain.

"Not *its* reality," he went on. "*Your* reality. It allows you to see, and to imagine that you live in, the reality that you desire beyond any other."

He, more than anyone else in the universe, understood the seductive power of that vision. He would give anything to be that other Drake, kissing Ana in the quiet countryside. It was the siren call of the Shiva: *Stay with me, and receive your heart's desire.*

Drake tried to explain that to the others, but after a while he realized it was not working. They could not know the mind of the other Drake, and it was impossible for any of them to feel what he was feeling. They were merely asking more questions.

"How does it reach the planet in the first place?" Tom Lambert said.

"I don't know."

"Is that *it*, the whole thing?" said Mel Bradley. "You think the Shiva are nothing but little plants?"

"I don't know."

"And the planetary defense systems failing . . ."

"And their spreading between the stars, between the *galaxies.* . . . How?"

"And moving more slowly where we *didn't* have colonies. . . ."

"And the failure of the lost colonies to send any sort of message. . . ."

"I don't know." Drake was longing to terminate this meeting, so that he could enjoy the vicarious pleasure of Ana embracing his other self—even if it was nothing but illusion, he wanted it.

"You're missing the point," he continued. "This doesn't prove that some spiky little silver plant is all there is to the Shiva. It doesn't tell us how the Shiva spread, or why. It doesn't say what happens to a world after they reach it. It tells us little about the Shiva themselves. But we still have a reason to celebrate. *We've had a breakthrough.* For the first time ever, we've been present on a planet when the Shiva took over. We've sent back information about what happened.

"We don't have an end. We barely have a beginning. Here's what we must do next. We must install organic copies of me on every planet along the front of the Shiva's spread."

Drake paused, realizing what he had just said. Those copies were going to disappear, every one of them. *He* was going to vanish, a million times over. But now there was a hope that some of the embodiments would not die. He might be transported to a personal Paradise—a dream life, but a perfect dream from which the copies might never waken.

"We also," he went on at last, "have to put arrays of independent sensors on every planet. We must install caesuras on or near each planet, ready to operate whenever a reality shift signals that the Shiva have appeared. We must install on a ship near the caesura the equipment to produce millions of identical copies of all data, with the equipment to feed those copies into the caesura at the first sign of trouble."

Equipment. That was one way to describe it. But the equipment would include copies of himself—and these copies, unlike the ones down on the planetary surface, were surely doomed.

"And when we've done all that"—Drake's gaze, beyond his control, was drawn back to the display; it showed his other self, still holding Ana in his arms—"when we've done all that, and we have recorded the information from a thousand or a million or ten million worlds, maybe we'll get what we need. Maybe we'll find a way to fight back."

Breakthrough.

Drake had called it that, but it was the wrong word. No torrent of information flooded in from other worlds on the path of the Shiva expansion. No sudden insight explained everything.

What came was a slow dribble of isolated bits and pieces, an image here, a paradox there; confirmation of a hypothesis, a measurement of sizes and rates and masses, calculations of galactic geometry, the cross-correlation of events from a million worlds as they were absorbed into the Silent Zone.

Drake could not perform that analysis. It was far beyond him, calling for the combined analytical power of a trillion composites. All he could do was sit at headquarters and record the disappearance of each copy of his own self. There was always the possibility that a caesura would deliver a copy of Drake back to headquarters, along with the packets of acquired data; but it never happened.

Data collection and analysis continued; the arc of the Silent Zone spread its darkness farther across the face of the Galaxy; nothing seemed to change. But one day, a day that Drake saw as no different from any of the billion that preceded it, his assistants appeared unsummoned in the villa headquarters.

"Drake, we must talk." Milton had been appointed as the spokesman. The Servitor's physical form was the usual one, but now Drake detected a weariness and a discomfort, a gray translucency to the presence. The tangle of wires on the whisk broom were in constant agitation.

"I'm listening." Drake looked them over, Cass and Milton and Tom, Melissa and Par Leon and Mel Bradley. They all displayed that same uneasiness. "Bad news?"

"Yes," Milton said. "But not what you might be thinking. Every composite in the Galaxy has been in full superluminal connection for the past few days. We finally have an integrated picture of Shiva activities. It is an inference derived from many trillions of pieces of data, but we are convinced that it is a correct one."

"That doesn't sound like bad news. Quite the opposite."

"In many ways you are right; but it introduces . . . complications. First, let me summarize for you our understanding of the nature and actions of the Shiva. Much of this you may already know or have guessed. Some of your original conclusions were, if I may suggest it, wrong."

Milton paused, and Drake laughed.

"Don't worry about hurting my feelings. I've been wrong more often than you can imagine."

"But right more often than any other being in the Galaxy. Let me continue. The Shiva are living organisms, unlike any encountered before. They have four distinct phases to their life cycle. Two of those phases are capable of two different forms of reproduction. The first phase, which we will call the adult Shiva, is immobile and enormous—one full-grown specimen can measure two hundred kilometers across its base, and stretches high enough for its top to extend beyond the atmosphere of most planets. The adult is invulnerable to normal predator attack, because of its size, and also because it is protected by a second form. We will call this second form the *warrior*, although it acts aggressively only in defense of the adult. The warriors are one form of offspring of the adults.

"It is important to note that the adult, in spite of its size, can survive only in certain environments. Atmospheric oxygen and water vapor must lie within tight limits. Most worlds of the Galaxy do not come close to satisfying that requirement. We will come back to this question later.

"And one other point, perhaps an obvious one: an adult, because of its size, grows, lives, and dies on a single planet. No Shiva adult can ever travel to another world.

"But when they achieve full size, the adults can send another form of offspring out into space. There is a mystery here—the propagation mechanism is not something as simple as dehiscence, an explosive projection of seeds. However, let us use the analogy and call this phase a Shiva *seed*. The seed is tiny and light, nothing like the warrior, and once in space its movement is assisted by two factors: radiation pressure, pushing it away from the planet's primary, and the galactic magnetic field. Originally, the seeds may have propagated only to other parts of the home world; but billions of years ago they became an interplanetary and an interstellar traveler; eventually, an intergalactic one. We do not know where the Shiva originated, but it was not in our galaxy.

"The Shiva seed is enormously tough and durable, able to survive extreme environments and a multimillion-year passage through space. There is another mystery which still waits an explanation: the seed motion is not mere random drift. Movement is preferentially toward other stellar systems. In the final stages, that implies movement *against* radiation pressure.

"Most Shiva seeds must end their lives on barren planets, or burn up as they fall into stars; but there are enormous numbers of them. Some small fraction will meet a world and drift down through the atmosphere to a surface on which they can transform to the next stage of the life cycle.

"This stage we will call the *worker*, though analogy with Earth's social insects must not be carried too far. It would be just as good to call it a *changer* or a *preparer*. The worker, like the adult, is a sessile form incapable of movement. It is the plantlike entity that we saw long ago on Lukoris. Like the seeds, it is tough and robust. Workers thrive on worlds that would quickly kill an adult. They also propagate like plants, and they do so very fast.

"We have debated whether the worker or the adult should be considered the mature form of the Shiva, and decided that the question is meaningless. As in cryptogams, the ferns of Earth, two forms are alternating mature phases of a complex life cycle.

"Much more important, from the human point of view, is the worker's other function. It is able, through a combination of generated fields and chemical diffusion, to affect the behavior of native animals on a planet. You have argued that only intelligent beings could be affected by the Shiva, since they alone are able to consider an alternate reality. It was then natural to conclude that the worker form of the Shiva must be intelligent.

"We now believe that those deductions are false. In our own galaxy, before the spread of humans, life developed on a billion worlds. Only five of that great multitude of forms achieved self-awareness. A life-form that *relied* on the presence of intelligence on every planet that it reached would surely fail. Moreover, the worker is not itself intelligent, and thus can have no concept of intelligence. Unable to move, it must somehow achieve its objective while remaining in one place. The objective is simple: the planet must be changed from its initial state to one in which an adult Shiva can thrive. Then, and only then, will the worker advance to its second form of breeding and produce not more workers, but *new adults*. Those will in turn grow, mature, and allow the Shiva to reach new worlds.

"The workers employ the native life-forms on a world as the unwitting agents for planetary change. Their breeding, their numbers, and their patterns of behavior alter under the workers' control, to make the

world suitable for adult Shiva habitation. Some native
species will become extinct. Some will thrive, some will
evolve to other forms. When the planet is ready, the
adults begin their growth. The workers disappear. The
life cycle begins again.''

Milton fell silent. The wiry head began to writhe
more furiously than ever.

"That's wonderful." Drake wondered what was not
being said. "Once you understand something, it's
much easier to stop it. The Shiva are vulnerable. We
can destroy their seeds as they reach a planet, or kill the
workers as soon as the plants appear. If I hear you right,
humans don't suffer their changed perception of reality until the workers begin to operate."

"That is correct."

"So let's get going. There's plenty of work to do."

Milton sat silent, and at last Tom Lambert said, "A
ton of work. But there are a few more things that we
have to talk about. First, we've been thinking all the
time of the Shiva as *evil*—as deliberate, calculating destroyers. That just isn't true. There was no malice involved, no plan to achieve destruction. Changing
human perceptions, even making the colonies use the
defenses that we installed against us, was an accident.
We believe that the adult form of the Shiva possesses
some kind of intelligence and self-awareness, but the
workers do not. They were simply doing what all life-
forms do, trying to ensure their own survival and
propagation. In the case of humans, Shiva propagation
required the acceptance of a false reality that justified
human actions."

"And, sooner or later, led to the human's death."

"True. But now that we know what's going on, we
may find many ways to stop the Shiva. Peaceful ways.
There will be no more wholesale destruction of our
planets or theirs; no more firebreaks, devastating whole
arcs of the Galaxy; no more use of the caesuras, casting
ships and intelligences and worlds beyond the bounds

of space and time. And there will be no need for certain other things."

And Drake, at last, saw what they were unwilling to tell him directly. "You mean, there will be no more need for *me*."

"Yes. The service that you have performed for us is too great ever to be measured. We are eternally in your debt. When we thought that the Shiva were malicious and deliberately trying to destroy us, your presence and courage and mode of thinking were absolutely essential. Now, they are not. Of course, we would not suggest that you, or we, do anything at once. Many, many unknowns and potential difficulties remain. We hope that you will assist in their solution. But ultimately we see you as a hindrance to *peaceful* answers. You are too steeped in war, too much in favor of the crudities of combat." Tom Lambert ducked his head. "I'm sorry, Drake."

"That's all right." There was no point in explaining that he was not aggressive, that his instincts had always been toward peace. They would not understand. He had operated as commander in chief for many hundreds of millions of years. So far as the composites were concerned, a militant Drake had been summoned from electronic darkness to fight a battle, to rid the universe of the threat of the Shiva. And when that threat passed, Drake would be useless. Worse than useless—he would be an embarrassment, a source of violence, a reminder of the ancient and cruel ancestry of humanity.

"You don't need me now that the problem is solved and the war is ending, right? I understand, Tom. It's all happened before."

"It has?" Tom looked and sounded bewildered. "You have encountered a similar situation in the past?"

"Not me personally. But it's as old as human history. Remember the Pied Piper, and Tommy Atkins?"

They did not, and he didn't expect them to. There were blank looks on every face. Drake could imagine countless invisible composites, delving into fourth- and fifth-level storage, trying to make sense of his reference. Maybe they would find it; or maybe he alone held that particle of early human folklore. Either way, it didn't matter. His own next step was clear.

"You say that you're in my debt. I agree. So do something for me. Return me to electronic storage and let me remain dormant. Keep looking for new ways in which Ana might be restored to me. And wake me again only when you make progress."

Drake anticipated no problem with his request. But again, he saw hesitation and embarrassment in the other's eyes.

"What's wrong this time? Come on, Tom, spit it out."

"There is one more difficulty. You have always refused to become part of any composite."

"I still do. You know why. I didn't survive for eight billion years, just to lose focus now. I can't afford to become part of a shared consciousness. I want to stay me. Think what shape you would be in if I'd chosen differently."

"We appreciate that. We know that we cannot change your obsession. But what you ask is impossible. You already exist in multiple forms. As the spread of the Shiva is halted, many of those forms will survive. Someday, they will return."

And of course, Tom was right. Drake had become accustomed to the idea that billion after billion copies of his personality had been created and sent as S-wave signals across the Galaxy. He knew that they had been embodied in native forms on a hundred million planets, and set to watch and listen on a billion ships along the Shiva frontier. Those innumerable versions of himself would be changing, absorbing new experiences, becoming quite different from the Drake Merlin who remained at headquarters.

He had learned to live with the idea that he was

dying, daily, in endless different ways. What he had never considered was the time when an understanding of the Shiva was reached, and all the scattered copies were no longer doomed. As ways were discovered to deal with the Shiva, they would survive in increasing numbers.

"I get it. You can't handle one of me. How do you hope to deal with a billion?"

"We fear that we cannot. We want to ask your help—again. Many of the returning minds will be changed, many will be seriously damaged. You are the only being in the whole universe who can understand and help them. We will promise you unlimited resources from us, anything that we have, in performing your task. We ask only that you should avoid contact with our composites."

"You mean you want to lock me up, me and every version of me?"

"No. There would be no restriction of your freedom. You would travel as you choose, and act as you choose. The only condition that we ask is that there be a separation between us and you. You may find this ridiculous, but we fear your intensity—what is, quite literally, your single-mindedness in our universe of composites. If you agree, we promise in return continued research on the subject that most interests you: the return of Ana."

"Has there been progress?" Drake had hardly thought to ask that question in a hundred million years.

"Nothing of immediate value. It should be possible to re-create Ana at the eschaton, when the universe approaches final convergence. But that is far off. We promise to continue working on other possibilities, if you in turn will help us. What is your answer? Will you deal with the copies of Drake Merlin, returning in their broken billions from the Shiva frontier?"

What option was there? How could a man turn his

back on his own self—especially on a damaged and troubled self?

"Give me your tired, your poor, your huddled masses yearning to breathe free, the wretched refuse of your teeming shore, send these, the homeless, tempest-tos't to me."

He spoke more to himself than to the others, and their baffled faces showed that again they didn't understand. Drake turned away. The composites were digging into the historical data banks, seeking a reference, wondering what he had just said.

He knew, even if they did not. He had agreed to do what they asked. The war with the Shiva might soon be ending, but his own most difficult task lay ahead.

Chapter 24

E pluribus unum

$\mathcal{T}$rillions of bits, billions of pages; now it was all unnecessary. Drake surveyed the mass of storage that represented his private journal and reflected on a curious irony: The prospect of victory rendered his work irrelevant, as danger and defeat could not.

He had no cause to complain. He had known what was coming, the moment he said yes to Tom and the others in the War Room.

For all the years since first resurrection, he had kept strictly to himself. Originally it was because no one else understood his need or shared his quest for Ana. His solitude had seemed even more crucial when the Shiva appeared on the scene. His was the only consciousness in the Galaxy left over from humanity's early days, and he dared not become close to any composite—certainly, he could not consider a merger with the webs. He had even refused to share the contents of their data banks.

His obstinacy had caused trouble, a billion times

over, but he had felt that he had no choice. Inefficient as it was to rely on others for most of his information, he must do it that way. He had to remain aloof. Someone must make the hard decisions. Someone had to be willing to sacrifice humans and composites and whole planets. No one but Drake would do that, and he dared not risk any dilution of his own will.

Drake glanced again over the long record of events. The composites must think that he had no heart and no soul; certainly, they believed he had no imagination. They could not see how else he was able to send out countless versions of *himself*, to face an uncertain end on the dark borders of the Galaxy.

They knew nothing of the effort that it had taken. And why should they? He had not said anything to them. He had done it, and that was the important thing.

When the Shiva were ascendant, it had been a one-way process. Copies of him had gone out and never come back. But no longer. One week ago, the first copy had returned. *He* had returned.

The composites urged him to study that copy well before he attempted contact with it. They were worried because his returning self had been through what they felt was a "traumatic experience." There were also, they warned, a hundred billion more like it on the way.

A traumatic experience? You might say so.

Drake had checked the background, and this case was probably typical. Downloaded and shipped out eight hundred thousand years ago, as a superluminal signal to a ship in permanent orbit about a planet of a faint star on the other side of the Galaxy. Taken down to the surface of that world and embodied in an enhanced alien life-form of increased life expectancy. Left there to survive, endure, observe, and await the arrival of the Shiva.

Except that this one had been retrieved, without

warning. The Shiva seeds were to land soon on its world. The composites were making special preparations there, as on a hundred million other planets, and they did not want an uncontrolled element disturbing their plans. They feared that this being, like the others that would be retrieved, might have "major instabilities."

"Traumatic experience," "study it well," "major instabilities." Bland, aseptic words.

Didn't they understand that anyone left alone for a million years *must* have instabilities? Didn't they realize that Drake had no need to study the returning copy, that he understood it perfectly already? That whatever came back from the other side of the Galaxy was not *it*. What came back was *him*, Drake Merlin.

A different him, certainly. That must be so, because the revenant had unique experiences. But it was Drake, nonetheless. And the composites were right about one thing: the returning Drake needed help.

He had stood apart from all others for so long, it was an ingrained habit. But how could he hold apart from himself?

He could not.

So, at last, Drake Merlin would become part of a composite. This, however, was going to be a unique composite—every element of it would also be Drake.

He had no idea how it would work out. The returning selves had been scattered far off through space and time. He had long ago lost count of their number. Some would be maimed or incomplete versions of a whole Drake Merlin; some would surely be totally deranged. Perhaps they would unbalance the whole.

No matter what happened in the long run, at first it was going to be total chaos. Each one of him, without exception, was going to be *different*. Time and events produce changes in form, in perspective, even in self-image.

It would be his job to understand, to assimilate, and ultimately—if he could—to integrate every part to a single being.

How? He had no idea.

He called on Ana to give him strength.

Chapter 25

*"Let me not to the marriage of true minds
Admit impediments."*

The first one is the most difficult.

As Drake repeated this to himself he tried to believe it. His revenant self had been dormant when it was retrieved from eight-hundred-thousand-year isolation. It still wore the snakelike organic form considered best for the surface of the planet Greenmantle.

Drake faced his first decision: Should he transfer the mind of his other self to electronic storage, before the interaction began? The technique to do it was routine, and information transfer would surely be easier and faster if they were both electronic. But would the change offer an additional shock that made the revenant's awakening harder to bear?

It was better to do it the other way around, at least for the first meeting. Electronic downloading and merger could come later. Drake arranged for his own transfer to the same snaky form. When he awoke he occupied the body of a legless animal with vestigial wings on its sides and a triplet of prehensile tentacles on the blunt head.

He gave the signal to awaken the other, and wondered: *What am I going to call him, whenever in my own mind I must distinguish us?*

Again, the answer was obvious. *If he is to suffer minimal shock, he has to be Drake Merlin. If anyone changes his name, I must do it.*

Slitted green eyes opened and stared at him.

"Hello." His own greeting came out as a complex waving of the three flexible proboscises.

The other Drake regarded him warily but said nothing. He felt sure he knew why. Drake Two was thinking, *Has the planet fallen to the Shiva? Is this some manifestation of them, designed to trick me and destroy me?*

"Drake, don't go by appearances. You are among humans again. You were retrieved before the Shiva reached your planet."

There was a long, thoughtful pause. The response, when it came, was not quite what he would have provided. The revenant's isolation had produced changes.

"Who are you?"

"I am you. Another version of you."

"Prove it. Tell me something that no one else in the universe knows. Something about me that no one but me could possibly know."

That no one else could possibly know. It took a few seconds, then he had it.

"Our teacher was Professor Bonvissuto."

"Known to me, and also to all the data banks."

"Surely. In our second year with him, he entered us in a statewide contest. We won, mainly because a big part of the competition was to improvise on a given theme."

"Also recorded, I suspect, in the same data banks." Drake Two must suspect where this was heading, but the snaky tentacles gave nothing away.

"But we weren't really improvising at all. When we

had breakfast in a hotel near the concert hall the morning before the competition, we were given a table that hadn't yet been cleared. The previous diner had scribbled a series of notes on a napkin, then crossed them out. We noticed the last one, because it had the same three ascending G-minor notes that start the third movement of Mozart's Fortieth Symphony, and also the third movement of Schubert's Fifth Symphony. We started to wonder what you could do with the theme, and we doodled around with it off and on for the rest of the day.

"When the judge offered the theme on which we were to improvise, we realized who had been sitting at the table before us. Naturally, we did a spectacular job and astonished everyone. We felt like cheats, but we didn't say anything to anybody—not even to Ana."

Drake Two was gesturing agreement. "I am persuaded. So what now? Why was I returned?" And then, with a wave of comical puzzlement that Drake understood exactly, "I am Drake—but what do I call you?"

"Call me Walter, if you have to. You know how much we hated our given name. I must give you an update on events. There have been great changes; mostly for the good, but we have bad news too."

He outlined the progress in understanding the Shiva, and the effect that would have on society's need for Drake Merlin. At the end of the explanation, his other self gave the gesture of grim assent.

"If you are no longer needed, I am in the same position. So are all the other versions of us. We are dangerous atavisms—until the next time that the galaxy needs us."

"Which may be never." He regarded his companion self. Given his experiences, he was comfortingly normal. He had known that already, since the responses were close to his own responses. Which suggested another step. "There will be countless billions like us, returning from service beyond the stars. They will not all be as balanced as you. Even so, they must be welcomed, provided with explanations, and restored so far as possible to normal function. Will you help?"

If Drake was truly Drake, the answer could not be in doubt.

"Tell me what I must do."

"Some of our returning selves are likely to be hugely unstable. I am not sure if I—or you—could suffer such an interaction alone and retain our own sanity. We need to reinforce each other. We need to combine our strength. We need—"

"—to merge. I understand."

"But not in this form. I am not sure that is even possible. It must be accomplished when we are in electronic storage."

"Of course. Proceed."

No need to explain, no need to persuade. Of course not. Not unless a man had to persuade himself.

Already his vision had begun to blur. Uploading and merger became simpler when the mind was fully quiescent. As his consciousness began to fade, he wondered.

What would he be like—*they* be like—when the merger was complete? Was he a caterpillar, ready to change to a chrysalis before transforming to a butterfly? It would not be like that. In the caterpillar's metamorphosis there was no combining of materials. Two gametes, then, joining to form a single zygote in the fertilized egg? That was closer, except that his parts were—or had once been—absolutely identical.

As he drifted off into limbo, he hit another simile: he was like identical twins; born together, parted for a long, long time, and at last reunited.

Drake awoke and recognized at once that his groping comparisons were worthless. He had no sense of a merger. He would never believe that he had once been two separate individuals, except that his memories beyond a certain point in the past were duplicates. He had been eeling his way through the swamps of Greenmantle and at the same time directing operations in the War Room. In his mind's eye he looked to the heavens and recalled two starscapes of vastly different skies.

But he had also been right. His mental strength, stability, and resilience had never been so great. For the first time, he understood why humanity chose to exist as elements of a composite. If the merger of two felt like this, what would a multitude be like? Omnipotent and omniscient?

He was about to find out. A thousand returned copies were waiting for his attention. Millions more were on the way.

But even when those were all merged to a single Drake Merlin, it would be no more than a beginning.

The first one is the most difficult.

Drake recalled that optimistic assessment and wished that it were true. This was not the first, nor even the hundred and first. But he was fighting for his sanity and his own existence.

There had been no warning. An organic revenant, seemingly no different from ten thousand others, had agreed to merge into shared consciousness. The upload to electronic form had been routine. The merger began. And Drake felt within him the white-hot flame of insanity.

Alone, he would have had no chance. It was his extended self, protected by the finite transmission times of even S-wave communication, that provided an opportunity for defense.

An opportunity, but not a guarantee. The force of madness was strong beyond belief. A single command was repeated over and over. It ordered every part of Drake to forget the external world, to sink with it into an autism that knew nothing beyond self.

But one part of Drake, farthest off in space, was able to resist. It offered its urgent warning: *If we move inward upon ourselves, we will never return. Remember doomed Narcissus, who fell in love with his own reflection. Look outward. Turn outward.*

The struggle continued. Drake became oblivious to external time and place. That was exactly what the insane component wanted. Only a continuing, intrusive, distant voice—*look outward, turn outward*—provided the lifeline that returned Drake to external reality.

At one point he thought he saw an opportunity to destroy the component, erasing it completely from all stored memory forms. At the last moment he realized that was a trap. He was the copy, and the copy was Drake. By accepting its annihilation, he would be endorsing the idea of self-annihilation, and ultimately he would guarantee his own dissolution.

Look outward, turn outward. He continued the fight. At last, little by little, his dispersed self found a purchase on the lost mind. He turned it, screaming and struggling, to face the united force of ten thousand components, each delivering the same message.

It was hopeless. The revenant was obdurate, irrational, impenetrable. And at the moment when he came to that conclusion, a critical stage was reached. Without warning, the phase change took place. All resistance ended and the madness dissolved. The mad mind, broken and bewildered by past insanity, could not explain what had happened.

Drake soothed it and welcomed another self to the expanding society of the composite. At the same time, he made a solemn vow: Never, no matter how many components were added to his composite self, would he again assume that adding the next one would be easier.

• • •

It ought to be a moment for rejoicing. Drake had kept strict accounting, and this was the millionth component to return for rehabilitation. He was getting there, slowly but surely.

It was a pity that the millionth had to be such a case, one that made any idea of celebration impossible. Perhaps it was the gods of ancient times, punishing hubris in their own way. Drake had felt his power growing as the number of his components grew, and he had exulted in it. He spanned a million stars, and there was nothing he could not do.

Except this.

He examined the profile of the new revenant. This Drake had suffered a unique and terrible fate. A hundred million years ago, he had assumed a local organic form and been landed on a world where the Shiva were expected. He had remained there for half a million years, and at last been rescued and returned for possible rehabilitation.

Sometime during that half-million years, a parasite had entered Drake's body without his knowledge. For native life-forms, the organism was actually a symbiote that improved its host's chances of survival. No native life-form was intelligent, so it was not important that as an accidental by-product, brain tissue atrophied in the presence of the parasite. The infected animal was still able to breed. Its life expectancy and reproductive capacity were somewhat improved.

Drake's intelligence had been housed in the brain of the native animal, with a slight organic memory augment. The decline had been too slow to notice, and at some point there was no intellect—or anything else—left to worry about.

The mind and memory of the returned copy had been downloaded to electronic storage, so that Drake's composite could examine it bit by bit. There was still something, the vaguest feeble glimmer of self-awareness. By no rational standard could it be called intelligent. And by no emotional standard could it be destroyed.

Drake initiated the merger with himself. The poor, damaged relic of the revenant had done its duty. It deserved the best that the composite could offer. Even if nothing at all was contributed to the intellectual power of the extended group mind, perhaps the millionth merger would add its iota of emotion and compassion.

And maybe the million and first revenant, or the billionth one, would experience the benefit.

Brooding over the abyss, Drake contemplated his growing self. He stretched across a million galaxies, adding to his numbers every day and every year. The threat of the Shiva to humanity was ancient history. Nowhere was there danger, nowhere was there conflict. The potential for his own growth was endless. He might one day occupy the whole universe.

And yet . . .

Yet there was a feeling that something was missing.

How could that be? His task was complete. Every one of the components that he had sent out, on every planet once threatened by the Shiva, was fully accounted for. Every one that had not been destroyed in the battle had returned. Over long aeons they had added to his extended composite. There was no way that he could have missed one.

So it was an illusion. Nothing was going wrong. Nothing was lost or forgotten, nothing could be.

Drake felt himself, for the first time that he could remember, at peace. At last he could relax.

PART THREE
Odyssey

Chapter 26

"From out our bourne of Time and Place
The flood may bear me far."

Drake's memory of the final minute was clear and vivid. He had been standing at the ship's port, gazing down on a world below. It was almost one full day since he had been embodied, and now he was ready to board a lander and begin the descent.

He already knew the planet and the local skyscape. A wealth of information about both had been loaded into him during embodiment. But that was abstract knowledge. Now he desired the real thing: the feel of alien soil or sand beneath his clawed feet, the first breath of whatever passed for air, the sight of sun and moons and starry constellations diffused through haze and cloud and nighttime mist.

He took a last look down. The world was close to Earth type, and his embodiment reflected that: arms and legs and neckless head; three-fingered hands; a body able to walk upright rather than crawl or burrow or scuttle across a rocky seabed.

He turned to enter the lander, and in that moment

the ship's control system spoke: *"Shiva presence detected. Landing aborted. Caesura activated. Final entry commences in five seconds."*

So soon? The ship's message had just told him that he was going to die. He had expected a long and lonely vigil on the surface, with only memories of Ana to sustain him, and at the end of it the arrival of a Shiva influence and an unknown destiny. Instead he would find oblivion within the next few seconds.

Since there was not one thing he could do about it, Drake stood perfectly still, watched, and listened. The caesura had already appeared. He could see a roiling spiral of darkness with a blacker eye at the center. A caesura was a slit in space-time, but this seemed more like a bottomless funnel, a conical swirl of ink and dark oil.

The ship was poised on the brink. Drake, knowing that his final moment of consciousness had arrived, thought of Ana. Now he would never see her again.

He squeezed his eyes shut. . . .

. . . and opened them. There had been a violent moment of disorientation in which his fractionated body twisted and spun in a hundred directions at once. But when that ended, he was still alive. All was calm. The port beside him showed no chaos, no blazing glare or stygian dark, nothing but peaceful stars.

Had the Shiva prevented the caesura from operating?

"What went wrong? Why didn't it work?"

Before he could struggle for his own answers to those questions, the ship was replying: *"Nothing is wrong. Everything has proceeded exactly consistent with theory."*

"Do you know what happened?" Of all improbabilities, this was the greatest: that Drake and the ship had been flung to another universe looking exactly like their own. He stared again out of the port. The sky showed stars, gas clouds, and the faint misty patches of spiral nebulae. But the stars were in unfamiliar patterns, and the planet had vanished entirely. "Where are we?"

"Specifically? I do not know."

"The caesura was supposed to annihilate us—to throw us into another universe. This looks like *our* universe."

"It is our universe. I have estimated the local physical constants, and they are the same within the limits of measurement. The probability of this occurring in another universe is vanishingly small. I am now in the process of measuring the global universe parameters."

"Do you know what has happened to us?"

"I have no proof, but on the basis of deductive logic I can make a strong inference. The operation of the caesuras follows an unpredictable statistical pattern, thus the outcome of any specific use cannot be predicted. But the probabilities have long been known. In almost every case, the caesura serves to eject an object that enters it into another universe. Once in a million uses, the caesura serves as an instantaneous transportation device to a chosen location. And sometimes, so rarely that we had assumed it would never happen in practice, the caesura may transport an object to an unknown place and time within our own universe. The evidence indicates that has happened to us. According to the records, this possible outcome was explained to you long ago."

Drake remembered it—vaguely. It had been mentioned when the idea of using caesuras first came up; then he had ignored it, thinking of the caesuras only as weapons. But the Bose-Einstein Condensate that formed the ship's cooled brain forgot nothing, and its atomic lattice memory held millions of times as much information as all of Earth's old storage systems combined. The ship probably knew everything that Drake had ever been told, as a tiny subset of its database.

He regarded the stars outside with a new eye. "We

are still in our own universe, but far away from where we started. Is it possible for you to take me back to headquarters?"

"It may be possible, eventually. It cannot be done quickly, for several reasons. First, this vessel is able to travel only at subluminal velocities. Extended travel must necessarily be slow. Second, the caesura can cause translation through both time and space. We are now within a galaxy older than the one that we left. That also suggests the passage of considerable time."

"What do you mean, considerable?"

"I have not yet determined that. It could be many billions of years. I will know better when I have completed my estimate of the universe's global constants. Third, I have already sought to detect evidence of superluminal signals. I find nothing above threshold. Therefore, we cannot be anywhere within our original galaxy, or else S-wave communication has been replaced by something else. Finally, I do not recognize any galactic spatial patterns, as I would if we were somewhere within the local galactic supergroup. We have traveled, at a minimum, hundreds of millions of light-years. The problem of discovering the location of our galaxy is formidable. Even if that were solved, the problem of reaching it would remain."

A ship's brain was designed to be free of emotional circuits, including any trace of humor or fear. Now Drake wished it were otherwise. He could use support at the moment from Tom Lambert or Par Leon. But the ship's design was his own doing. He had not wanted others to be forced to face their own extinction, and perhaps to flinch. He was less lucky. He had emotion aplenty and enough intelligence to understand the implications of what he had just been told.

He stared down at his body, never used for its original purpose and now useless. It had been enhanced for what seemed a more than adequate life expectancy, at least a million years. For any point within his own galaxy that would have been more than enough. He could have endured until contact was established with other humanity or until an S-wave signal facility was reached.

Movement to the galactic scale changed everything. The home galaxy contained about a hundred billion stars, all packed within a flat disk a hundred thousand light-years across. The whole universe contained a hundred billion similar galaxies. The tiny misty patches he could see outside the ship faded to invisibility across more than twelve billion light-years. Each was an island of suns, from the densely packed galactic center to the fading edge of the outermost spiral rim.

Somewhere, far out there, his own galaxy endured. The desperate struggle to contain the Shiva continued. The suffering and terror of trillions of sentient beings were reduced by distance to a silent and ethereal dust mote of light. He wondered what was happening now. Were other copies of him, in other ships, at last making progress against the Shiva? Were the Shiva sweeping on, unstoppable, across the whole galactic disk? He would never find out. Even if he knew his destination and could head for home at once, his body would wear out and die before he had traveled a tiny fraction of the journey.

And if the search for the home galaxy had to proceed at random? Then a searcher would still be wandering through space thirty or forty billion years in the future, when the universe collapsed toward its inexorable endpoint of infinite pressure and temperature. That searcher could not be Drake or this ship. Long before the end, in less than an eye blink on the cosmic scale, they would be dust.

It was a moment for despair. The logical thing was to end it now, before continued existence brought more grief and longing. He was looking down at his new, flawless, smooth-skinned body, wondering how it could most easily be given a peaceful end, when the ship spoke again:

"My defined actions did not extend beyond the point of

entry into the caesura. I require new instructions. Can you tell me the nature of our future, and what activities you plan?"

A moment for despair. That much was permitted. Now it must be over. Someone depended on him—even if it was only a ship. He could not give up.

"You know the main criteria for stellar type and planetary orbits that encourage the development of life. Do you have instruments to determine the nearest and most promising stars that satisfy those criteria?"

"Certainly."

"What about the development of intelligent life?"

"Essentially unpredictable. I can make crude estimates, but with little confidence in the results. The ascent of a native intelligence depends on too many random events in the evolutionary process."

"That's what I was afraid you'd say. All right, I want a systematic survey and catalog of all stars in this galaxy likely to have developed life. Throw in your best guesses for the development of intelligence. Give each one a probability, and place them in order of our distance from them."

"That can be done."

"Another question: What is the programmed lifetime of this ship?"

"Given raw materials, it is indefinite. I contain instructions for repair, for maintenance, and if necessary for self-replication. My memory has quadruple redundancy to allow for quantum changes. As any component ages, it can be renewed."

"How about me? I know there's a lab on board that can build a body to specification and download a person into it, because that's what you did to make me as I am. Is the lab still working?"

"It is working now. Since it is a part of me, it should continue to do so for the indefinite future."

"What about the other way around?" Drake, despite his determination to think positive, felt a tension he could not ignore. This was the key question. "Could you take me as I am now, and *upload* me from this body into electronic storage? And if you did that, could you download me later into another body, either the same or a different one? And could you do the same thing over and over?"

The pause seemed long, though it was probably no more than a second.

"What you ask was not in the original mission plan, but it seems completely feasible. The body for future download would need to be specified. Also, I could not go beyond two hundred embodiments without replenishment. If more were necessary I would require a planetary visit for the acquisition of more raw materials."

"I'm planning on planetary visits. In fact, I'm depending on them." Drake went again to the ship's port and stared out. The nearby stars were the brightest things he saw, but they were like cells in a human body, tiny subcomponents of a larger whole. The power was in the galaxies, stretching out into space forever. "What's the average distance between galaxies, and how far away is the nearest one?"

"Galaxies average a little more than 4,300,000 light-years apart. Of course, they are not homogeneously distributed."

"Of course." The ship did not catch irony, but maybe it could be taught. Certainly, they would have time enough.

"And the nearest galaxy to this one is about seven million light-years."

Seven lifetimes for this body. But long before that he would go crazy. The only way to survive was to spend the time between stellar encounters dormant, in electronic storage. And the next time around he would insist on his familiar human form.

"There is another factor that I should mention. When you asked me the mean distance between galaxies, I gave you an answer that applies today."

"That's what I expected."

"But if, as your other questions would suggest, you plan on

*searching for our galaxy of origin, another factor must be con-
sidered. The universe is expanding. The distance between the
galaxies constantly increases. If our target world lies many
billions of light-years away, then the rate at which it flies from
us will be a substantial fraction of light speed. Our effective
rate of travel toward it would be diminished. Perhaps greatly
diminished."*

"I see the problem; the Red Queen's race." Drake
was feeling dangerously unstable. "All right. What can't
be cured must be endured. How long before you can
pick a preferred stellar target?"

"That has already been done."

"With life, or with intelligent life?"

*"Both tables have been prepared. As I said earlier, little
confidence can be given for anything involving the development of intelligence."*

"We'll have to take that chance. Consider only systems with a better than ninety-five percent chance of
having life, and a better than ten percent chance of
having intelligent life. How many are there?"

"Between 120 and 250. It is hard to be more precise."

"How far to the nearest candidate?"

"Six thousand light-years."

"Take us there. And one other thing. You said you
could not detect any sign of S-wave signals. Is that because they travel only a finite distance?"

*"No. In principle, they have infinite range. In practice they
follow an inverse square law between source and receiver. With
the ship's on-board detection equipment, the signals become
indistinguishable from background at no more than a few tens
of thousands of light-years. That is adequate for signaling
within a galaxy but not outside it. However, even the strongest
and most tightly focused S-wave beam would be lost to our
limited equipment within a hundred million light-years. That
is why I am confident that we are nowhere within our original
local supergroup."*

"But you could do better with a better receiver. Do
you know how to make one?"

"I have the specifications for much larger receivers—for receivers of almost unlimited size, that would be able to pick up superluminal signals from the far depths of space. However, their fabrication could not be done on board. It would call for a free-space facility, and much assistance."

"Don't worry about that for the moment."

Six thousand light-years to the nearest prospect. Seven million light-years to the next galaxy. *One step at a time.* There were endless billions of years ahead of them, time enough for anything.

"I now have other information, and it amplifies my earlier statements. I have completed my estimate of global universe parameters. In particular, I have measured the galactic red shift. The result of that is surprising: There is no longer any red shift of distant galaxies."

The ship paused. Drake was learning how its analytical processes operated. He waited.

"Assuming that we are still in the same universe, which I continue to believe, the vanishing of the red shift is highly significant. It means that the universe is halfway through its total lifetime, and the blue shift phase is beginning. Within the limits of observational error, my best estimates of current epoch show that the initial singularity preceding the expansion occurred thirty-three billion years ago. The final singularity, the eschaton itself, lies thirty-two billion years in the future."

Not endless billions of years ahead, then, but thirty-two billion. At that final point lay the Omega Point, the ultimate last hope for Ana's resurrection. Except that Drake did not want to wait that long. And he was busy with his own calculation.

"We've jumped ahead eight billion years!"

"It is closer to nine billion."

Eight billion, nine billion, thirty-two billion—Drake found the numbers too big to have any meaning. *One step at a time.* "You asked about the nature of our future activities. I can tell you them. After we have finished speaking, I am to be uploaded to electronic storage—painlessly, please, if there's a way to do it. You will proceed to the chosen star system. Upon arrival there, you will make observations of life-bearing planets. If one of them offers evidence of an intelligent life-form with a working technology base, resurrect me. If not, select the next promising stellar target and continue the journey. Carry out the same procedures when you arrive there. If there is no intelligence or intelligence without technology, keep looking. Awaken me only for discovery of technological intelligence, or for an emergency that you are unable to deal with. Is all that clear?"

"You have left one important point unspecified. You order me to resurrect you when we reach a world that satisfies your criteria, but you have not specified a form for your embodiment."

"True." Drake abandoned, reluctantly, his plan to spend the rest of the future in his old human form. "Give me a body that can survive on the planet. Better still, make it the same body shape as that of the intelligent life-form."

"What if there should happen to be more than one?"

"Give me the form of the one that seems closest to human." Drake regarded his body, so soon assumed and so soon to be abandoned. Was there a reason to remain in it any longer? Not that he could think of. It would be another six thousand years—at an absolute minimum—before he had any reason to be conscious. He must not dwell on that. Think of it as a natural sleep/wake cycle, not as a time comprising the whole of written history before his own birth. "I'm ready to be uploaded. If you can't make up your mind which form to use when you get there, because they're not anything like human, don't worry about it. Just pick one."

"With what criteria?"

"I don't mind. Use a virtual coin if you have to—but don't wake me up to call the toss."

Chapter 27

Postindustrial

Drake awoke slowly and easily. As soon as he was able to think, he knew that something had gone badly awry.

His body did not feel wrong—it felt too *right*. His blood ran like ichor through his veins, and his mood was giddily euphoric. He knew of only one way that such a thing could happen.

He opened his eyes, lifted his head, and looked down at his naked body. As he had suspected; he was in his own human form, a new and blemish-free version of himself. He was also aboard the ship.

"What happened?" The vocal cords had never been used before, but they were in perfect working order. He tried an experimental laugh. Whatever else might be wrong, the embodiment lab was in fine shape. And so was he. "Are you telling me that you found a planet full of humans who look just like me in another galaxy?"

"No. I believe that we have encountered an intelligent form, but it is certainly not human."

"So why did you put me in this body?"

"It was a default option."

The ship sounded as frustrated as Drake felt exhilarated. He needed to be careful. The brain transients produced by new-body residence had not yet damped themselves out. He could feel the wild mood swings. How long had he been dormant?

"What do you mean, a 'default option'? Tell me what's going on."

"Your instructions were followed to the letter. We flew to our first target star. One of its planets bore life, but it had not progressed beyond single-celled prokaryotes. There is no possibility that intelligence will develop there for several billion years. I therefore proceeded to the second target, twelve thousand light-years away. I could determine, from a distance of half a light-year, that the nature of the atmosphere of all the planets in the system was such that no life in any form that we know it could survive. Nonetheless, I continued and found on closer approach that life had actually come and gone on one world. It had never achieved intelligence, and it had died out as temperatures rose during the normal brightening and expansion of its main sequence primary.

"On the third world, fifteen thousand light-years away, there were large artifacts and all the signs of sometime intelligence. But the creators had been destroyed, apparently by their own actions. No other life-form had the potential for near-term self-awareness.

"On the fourth world—"

"Wait a minute. How many targets have we visited?"

"This is the one hundred and twenty-fourth. I saw no point in resurrecting you on any earlier occasion. You are not interested in extinct intelligence, nor in possible future intelligence, but in present intelligence. We have never before found evidence of that."

"And now you have?"

"I believe so."

"And how long since the search began?"

"We have been traveling for slightly more than two million years."

"Fine." Drake decided that he had become blasé. Two million years no longer impressed him. To get his attention now, you had to talk billions. "So what's the problem?"

"When we were approaching the current target star, I examined it from far orbit and concluded that one of the planets was remarkably Earth-like. Its atmosphere told of the presence of oxygen-breathing life, and as we came closer I observed several characteristic markers of intelligence: long linear and rectangular surface features, modified river courses, patterns of nighttime lights, and cluster patterns supporting little or no plant life."

"That sounds right. Roads and dams and power and cities. Did you make detail scans?"

"I did so as we approached closer, images to the meter level of detail and beyond."

"So you know the shape of whoever was doing all the work. Why didn't you put me into *that* form?"

"Had I been able to find such a form, I would have done so. As it is, I found it necessary to invoke the default option of your original shape for the embodiment." The wall in front of Drake became a display screen. *"Observe. We are first looking from far away, on our approach orbit."*

The scene was the whole planet, seen from space. The ball glowed a mottled red and pink, from its banded midsection up to the small circles of white around the poles.

"Are those water-ice polar caps?" Drake had the irrelevant thought that he was looking at a gigantic Christmas tree ornament. He was bubbling over with excess energy, and his mind was ready to accept strange images.

"Correct. The mean temperature is that of Earth during one of your planet's warmer periods."

"I can't see much from this distance."

"Have patience. The images that you will soon see derive from lower orbit."

The pink sphere on the display was growing. It was possible to imagine dark lines on its surface, scattered close to the equator. Drake waited. He knew the tendency of the human eye to play "connect the dots" and discern linear patterns where there were none. His thoughts spun away to the far-off past. Who was it, long before his own time, who had been fooled by that built-in physiological quirk of the human brain and had drawn maps of nonexistent Martian "canals"?

Except that this was no optical illusion. The linear features were real, growing in clarity every minute. As the ship drew closer to the planet, the display could no longer hold the full image of the world. The focus moved to a line, dark and straight, at center screen. It was bordered by colored rectangles and triangles. To Drake's eye and imagination the line was a road across a Kansas flatland. The broad fields were different shades of red, a child's quilt with bright patches that ranged from light pink to deepest crimson. The yellow brick road had turned dark brown, but it ran through farmlands of fairy-tale color.

The scale that accompanied the display gave the lie to the illusion. The "road" was a kilometer wide. The quilt was monstrous, each of its patches the size of a county of old Earth. Scattered darker dots within the patches were big enough to be towns.

The field of view zoomed in toward a narrower black thread at the center of the broad swath of road. Drake could see that the edges of the patchwork quilt were not regular. They were broken and random, the boundaries intruding on each other. The pink had spread in places onto the darker swath, like crabgrass invading an untended lawn.

The black thread must surely be water. Unlike on Mars, these canals were real. The line of banks ran ruler straight across the surface. Close to the water's edge, every few kilometers, a five-sided open tower of girders stretched toward the sky. The display closed in on one.

"This is too tall to be built on this planet with natural materials. Carbon composites are essential for its building and continued stability, which implies a reasonably advanced technology. Technology implies intelligence. But where is that intelligence?"

Drake recalled his "firebreak," the millions of human worlds sacrificed and emptied to escape the Shiva. Had other galaxies been invaded? Were alien species trying the same delaying tactic, abandoning this world to slow an enemy's advance? Who was the Roman general famous for his scorched-earth policy and refusal to fight the Carthaginians directly?

"One might conclude that the intelligence is here."

The display homed in on a lighter-colored area by the canal. It was a clearing, a couple of hundred meters across, and it stood in the shadow of one of the great pentagonal structures. Drake was at last able to pick out surface life-forms.

The flat semicircle was bordered on its straight edge by water, and on its curved perimeter by a skimpy fence. A group of thirty or forty objects like oversized pink snails clustered against the boundary. They were creeping steadily along the fence. A dozen others, slightly smaller and faster moving, surrounded them.

A group of twenty other beings crouched close to the water's edge. They were dark red, with many legs, and they surrounded a dark, shallow pit in the surface. On closer inspection Drake could see that they came in three types. The ones on the very edge of the pit were the biggest, four times the size of the outermost group members.

"This depressed area"—a bright point of green, vivid against the pinks and browns, appeared on the display in the middle of the pit—*"is revealed by infrared imaging to be well above ambient temperature. I assume that it is a*

breeding pit, kept warm by rotting vegetation. It is not hot enough to be a cooking pit."

Drake thought that was an odd thing for the ship to say—the presence of the vast pentagonal towers spoke of a mastery of technology far beyond the use of fire. But he could see (or imagine) a consistent picture in what was going on in the clearing: herd animals, grazing, held by the fence and protected and chivied along by the equivalent of sheepdogs. The red creatures might be the breeding phase of either of the other types.

But where was the intelligence that had made the great towers? A primitive breeding/grazing society as he knew it could never produce such a technological tour de force.

"This settlement seems typical." The display scanned along the canal to show numerous colonies, each one close to a tower. *"The pattern is repeated in hundreds of places. Each time, the same organisms are seen. But now—observe."*

One of the towers had toppled over. It sprawled the skeleton of its length across the canal and far beyond, into the patchwork of open fields. It seemed intact after its collapse, vouching for the strength of the materials used to make it.

"There is no colony here. Every other tower has one. And see this."

The scene on the display was moving again, swinging away from the canal to a spider's web of converging roads. At the web center stood buildings, some low and dark roofed, others reaching for heaven like the pentagonal towers. Plants like long vines grew over the low roofs or wound around the towers' bottom girders. There was no sign of life anywhere.

"Buildings. Roads. Power stations. Lighted cities. Communications, unless the towers serve some other uses. There is civilization. But where are the beings who did all this? I would welcome your interpretation, before I offer mine."

"I can't even make a guess. Did you see signs of life or artifacts on any other planet of this system?"

"None."

"So they don't have spaceflight. Their development must have been enormously different from ours. What do you think is happening?"

"I have one piece of evidence that you have not yet seen. This is an image taken at night."

The bright cities stood out like clusters of jewels. The roads that joined them were invisible, but as Drake watched, lines of bright blue intermittently flashed along their lengths.

"I have enhanced the pulse in duration and lowered its apparent speed to a level where human eyes can follow. What you are seeing is a burst of information carried by optical laser. Given the absence of intelligent organic life, it suggests a simple explanation: This civilization has passed the industrial phase. It is now wholly concerned with information transfer among its separate elements. Physical transfer of material is no longer necessary."

"What about the beings who did the original development?"

"I assume that they went to inorganic form and were downloaded into a planetary network."

"One that takes no notice of us?"

"If they never discovered spaceflight, they may deny even the possibility of off-world existence. The question is, What do we do now? We need a working force to build an S-wave signal detector, but the intelligence of this planet has never worked in space. Also, like my own intelligence, it may be unable to appear in corporeal form. How can we determine if that is so?"

"Since they don't respond to our signals, I'll have to go down and take a look. Chances are there's nothing useful, but if this is the best you've seen in a hundred and twenty-four tries, we have to make sure."

"Not the best one. The only one."

"How many more hours of daylight?"

"Unless we elect to change longitude, there will be six hours before darkness."

Drake glanced at the sun, uncannily close in color to Sol. "I might be back by then. If not, I'll spend the night in the lander. Is it ready for use?"

"It is waiting."

"How much will you have to change me, before I can survive on the surface?"

"Some slight changes were made during your embodiment. This world is close to being an Earth look-alike. I would recommend, however, that you proceed with caution in ingesting native substances."

"Don't eat the food and don't drink the water. Sure. What else?"

"I believe no other changes are essential."

"You knew what I was going to decide, didn't you?"

"I had suspicions."

Drake wondered what the ship had been doing during the two million years in which he was dormant. Studying him, more than likely. Was there any way that a ship's brain could become smarter, or at least more *cunning*, over time? If experience worked for people, might it work for inorganic brains?

"You know what to do if I don't return, and the signals from me stop?"

"Regrettably, if you do not return I will be able to do nothing to help you. If you do not send instructions, I will wait for one year in orbit around this planet. Then the ship will go on to the next target star and continue the search. I will seek to recover the lander, if that is in any way possible."

Drake nodded. Nothing about recovering his body. There was only one lander. Whereas he . . .

He was completely expendable. If he came back, the Drake Merlin held in the ship's storage would be updated to reflect his experiences. On his next embodiment he would feel full continuity of consciousness.

If he *didn't* come back, a copy of him would still exist on board the ship. His next embodiment, at some new target world, would feel exactly as he felt: like the one and only real Drake Merlin. He would experience continuity of consciousness, although he would have no memory of a visit to this system.

Drake had a stranger thought yet. Another copy of him, or a hundred others, could be made at any time. Right now, he could ask for duplicates. Why not go down there with someone he could totally rely on—himself?

He sighed. He had too much adrenaline in his system. The sooner that he worked it off, the better.

"All right. I'm ready for the lander."

Drake had in his augmented memory a working knowledge of all known languages, visual, aural, tactile, and pheromonal.

How useful were they likely to be? He was not optimistic as the pinnace completed its braking phase and floated toward a landing a few kilometers west of one of the settlements. It was easy to be fooled by a planet superficially like Earth, but he might be ten billion light-years away. Every life-form in his native galaxy could be a close cousin compared with this.

He put the lander down on an open field at the edge of one of the deserted "towns." There was life here, but the forms were small and they scurried away before he could take a good look at them. Drake estimated that the biggest of the leggy red animals that they had observed by the canal was maybe a quarter of his size. He was the planet's giant.

He stepped down from the lander. A faint breeze on his face carried a scent that made him wrinkle his nose. It reminded him of pickled onions, and that in turn suggested concert recitals in Germany, followed by dark beer and laughter and late-night suppers. How long since anything had summoned up those memories?

He moved onto the road and knelt down to examine the surface.

"Are you getting all this?" Whatever he registered with his senses or his instruments should be automatically sent to the ship, hovering in stationary orbit.

"Everything. Continue."

"Just testing."

Drake probed the surface. The road was a fine glasslike gravel set in a tough bituminous matrix. It was tough and durable, but fine threads of bright red vegetation had taken a toehold at the edge. A narrow strip along the middle of the road was brighter than the rest, as though something continuously scoured it clean.

"This hasn't been used as a road for a long time. I think you may have it exactly right. They've advanced to pure electronic form and left material things behind. They didn't restore the fallen tower, because they no longer need it." Drake glanced at the sun. It was lower in the sky, and barred clouds were moving in across it. "If there's any sign of them, it ought to be in the towns."

"Two hours to sunset." The ship had noticed and interpreted his action. *"The town that you are about to enter did not show up on our orbital survey as one with nighttime lighting. There are rainclouds approaching from the west. I may lose the ability to monitor your environment visually. If you intend a detailed exploration, you should stay in the lander and wait for morning."*

"It's only a few minutes' walk. I'll take a quick look, and then come back to the lander for the night."

The two towers in the middle of the town were no more than a small fraction of the height of their counterparts by the canal, but as the sun went down they cast long shadows in Drake's direction. They were taller than he had thought, a hundred meters and more. The bigger one was in the exact center of the town. Drake walked toward it across a skeletal pattern of girder shadows on the dark road.

"I'm at the first building. Plants are growing around the walls, but they don't stop there. I can see vines entering through that break."

He pointed to a gap in the building wall. The semicircular arch was six feet tall and came down to within a foot or so of ground level. It ended in a flat ledge about four feet wide. He could easily enter if he were willing to step on the vines.

"What are the chances that touching the plants will hurt me?"

"Possible, but unlikely unless they are motion sensitive. They are chemically different enough that they will not respond to you as a living form. Warning: Within the next ten minutes there will be enough cloud cover to inhibit my visual oversight of you."

Drake poked his head through the opening. It took a few moments for his eyes to adjust to the gloom. He was looking into a small room, with another semicircular aperture at the far side. Dusky pink plant life covered everything like a carpet. Beyond the other opening he could see a downward ramp and, beside it, the faint outline of what looked like a piece of gray machinery.

He lifted his feet to avoid touching the plants and steadied himself with his hand on the side of the opening. A surface layer of wall material, about a quarter of an inch thick, crumbled to white powder at his touch. The dust made him sneeze. The wall behind was revealed as a solid metallic plate.

At the same moment his communications unit produced a staccato rattle. A diminished ship's voice said urgently but faintly, *"Your signal is weakening."*

Drake pulled back. "Is it active interference?"

"I think not. It is a natural fading. There must be some shield or insulation in the building walls and roof. I am predicting rain where you are located within the next quarter of an hour."

Drake looked again along the road that led to the

tower. Nothing moved. Even the faint breeze, with its odd smell, had died away to nothing. The setting sun was hidden behind a cloud bank.

"I'm going to take a quick look inside. Do you know what the roof is like?"

It is no longer visible because of the clouds, but our earlier survey showed two large round openings. Nothing could be seen within them. If the room that you looked into is of typical height, the building has three floors above ground level.

"The ramp that I saw goes down, not up. I'll see if there's any way to reach the upper floors."

Drake moved forward and stepped high across the ledge. He could not avoid treading on the plants at the other side. They gave beneath his weight, with a squeaking sound of crushed rubbery tendrils.

"Are we still in contact?"

The communications unit remained silent. Drake hurried across the room and into the next one. It contained gray machinery, solid, alien, and uninformative. He saw a tubby upright cylinder about three feet high that could have been anything from a spacewarp to a dishwasher. He ran his hand across the upper surface. His fingers came away covered with grime. Everything was coated with a thick, uniform layer of dust.

The ramp was steep by human standards, tilted at thirty degrees. He moved carefully downward, pushing his way through sheets of sticky material, thin as gossamer, that broke easily under his hands. Suddenly it was much darker. There was no opening to the outside at this level, and the sunlight that bled in from above was less and less. In another five minutes he would have to turn back. He wished that he had brought a light from the pinnace. Any exploration of lower levels would have to wait until morning.

He had reached the bottom of the ramp. His shoe hit something that rolled away in front of him. He moved toward it and bent low to see what he had kicked.

After one look he froze in his stooped position. He could not see colors in the gloom, but his foot had struck an object of a familiar size and shape. It was like one of the pink snails that crawled around the fence by the canal. This one was dead.

Drake picked it up. It was surprisingly light. The outer surface was smooth and rubbery, which allowed it to retain its original cylindrical shape, but the insides had been scooped out through a long slit at one end. He wondered for a moment if it were some kind of mummified form. His nose told him differently. It had been dead just long enough for the corpse to become putrid.

He could see half a dozen other remains on the floor ahead. One of them was bigger than the rest, a giant white version of the red multilegged creature that he had observed in the canal enclosure. Stretched upright, this one would loom over him. But it would never stretch over anything. It had been cut almost in two at its midsection.

He retreated, heading up the ramp a lot faster than he had descended. Sticky cobwebs clung to him, and he held up his arm to shield his eyes. He did not feel at ease until he had retraced his path, scrambled over the ledge, and was standing in gloomy twilight.

"Do we have contact?"

"I am receiving your signal clearly. I do not have visual monitoring."

The ship's voice was infinitely reassuring. Drake looked up into a heavy overcast, shielding his eyes against a rain that was gradually becoming stronger.

"I'm done for the day. I'm heading for the pinnace. I don't think we'll find any manufacturing capability here, but I want to take another look inside the buildings tomorrow."

As Drake spoke he was moving rapidly along the road, head ducked to keep cold drops of rain out of his eyes. He lifted his head for a moment to peer through the downpour and halted abruptly. The lander should have been by the side of the road, fifty or sixty meters from the buildings. The field ahead stretched far away. It was empty.

Had he turned himself around and headed out of town in a different direction?

That was impossible. He had left the building by the same opening and moved directly away from the tall central tower. He could see a flattened place in the field where the lander had been.

"Did you do something with the pinnace?"

"Certainly not. Has it been interfered with?"

"Worse than that—it's gone."

He hurried forward. Soon he was close enough to see other marks in the soaked vegetation. There was a distinct trail running off toward the town. The lander was equipped with a hover and forward motion capability, but that had not been used. Something had dragged it along the ground.

"I can see where it went. I'm going to follow."

Not just dragged, but hauled without caring whether or not the lander was damaged. As Drake followed the broad furrow, he came across a strip of metal and a torn-off bar from one of the lander's ground legs. He picked the bar up and held it close to his face. In addition to muddy streaks, it bore smudges as though something had picked it up, held it, and discarded it.

The trail led not to the nearest building, but to a bigger one on the left. The wall had a great black emblem marked in its middle. As Drake went closer he realized that the dark area was a gap in the wall itself. The furrow he was following led toward it, then faded to nothing as the surface changed from soft soil to hard impermeable material.

"I think the lander has been taken inside a building."

"What are you proposing to do?"

"I don't have a choice. I have to recover the lander. Without it, there's no way to get back to orbit."

"You could wait until morning."

"I daren't. It may have been accidental, but there has been damage."

As Drake spoke he was moving toward the building. He went carefully and quietly, the bar from the pinnace's landing gear held close to his chest. Everything was silent except for the slowing patter of raindrops.

At the wall he halted. The opening was big enough to take the whole lander. Was it just inside, where he might fly it right out again? Or had it been dragged down a ramp to some deeper level?

He took two cautious steps inside. Immediately he felt a violent blow on his ribs, just below the left nipple. He swung the bar without thinking. It crunched into something that screamed, so loudly and at so high a pitch that it hurt his ears. He felt a blow on his left hip, then another on his right arm. Two invisible objects brushed past him. He turned and followed. He was in time to see two tall white shapes vanishing into the twilight.

The rain had slowed to a few random drops. A ghostly flicker of light showed, far off across the field. Then another.

A creaking sound came from behind him. He quickly spun around to face it.

No tall white shape was leaping out of the dark doorway to attack him, but suddenly there was another flicker of light from inside the building. It provided enough illumination for him to see the lander. It had been hauled into the middle of the room and tilted onto its side. Unless it could be righted, it would not fly.

"Are you hurt?" The ship could not see him, but it was receiving a record of his rapid movements.

"I'm all right. But the lander is damaged."

"Can it be fixed?"

"I don't know." Again there was light inside the building, this time a ruddy glare that varied in brightness like a sputtering flame. "I have to go in again."

The ship said something in reply, but he did not hear it. His attention was focused on the wall beyond the opening. It reflected light from sources farther inside. Torches burned there, orange red and erratic.

Drake moved forward, the rough-edged metal bar over his shoulder. He thought he was ready, but the speed and violence of the attack surprised him.

Half a dozen of them came out of the darkness like white ghosts. They had crouched waiting at the side of the room. Sharp pincers sank into his left arm. His reflexive jerk backward at the sudden pain saved him. The crude machete that slashed at his middle cut through his clothing but made only a long and shallow skin wound.

He turned and smashed at the pincered head. It shattered and splashed cold liquid over his face and neck. He continued his turn, flailing away at anything within reach. The ghost with the machete whistled and screeched as the metal bar caught it solidly in the middle. It fell away, taking another with it. Then Drake was running for the opening. The torchlight behind him was brighter.

He ran thirty yards from the building before he turned to look behind. Everything was quiet. No white shapes sprang through the hole in the wall. No orange torches flared from inside. For the moment he was safe.

"Are you receiving me clearly?"

"Perfectly clearly. I project clearing skies and visual oversight in another two hours."

"That will be too long. Listen carefully and place this into the permanent record." The admonition was unnecessary, but Drake had to be sure. "Your suggestion that this planet has gone beyond the postindustrial phase was correct, but the principal intelligence has not moved to a more advanced form. It has regressed to primitivism. We did not observe the dominant intelligence earlier, because it is nocturnal and spends the days underground in these buildings. Based on what I have seen, there is no chance that this planet will provide the space-borne technology that we need. Many of the old systems are still running, but I'd guess that the present inhabitants have little idea how they work. It's just as likely that they worship them now.

"Here are your instructions. Continue the search for a space-faring civilization throughout this galaxy. If you are successful, resurrect a copy of me and enlist the aid of whatever beings you find. If you search this whole galaxy and find nothing useful, do not continue to the next nearest one. The quest for our home galaxy without a signal to guide us could take to the end of time. Instead, begin a survey of this galaxy with a different objective. Look for a stellar system where raw materials are available in easily accessible form. You know what is needed for the creation of an S-wave signal detector. When you reach the right stellar system, resurrect copies of me, as many as will be needed to perform the space construction work. Build the signal detector, and use it. Do you understand these instructions?"

"I understand their meaning, but not your reason for giving them. What of you? Do you not propose to seek the lander and return to orbit?"

"I wish I could do that."

"Then why do you give me instructions that omit discussion of your own future actions?"

"Because I don't think my actions here are going to have much bearing on what you must do." Drake could see the flicker of torches within the building. "I think the Morlocks are getting ready to try again."

"I do not understand the term 'Morlocks.'"

"That's all right. I didn't expect you to." The torches inside the building were brighter. Drake backed up a few steps. He could smell his own blood, a strong and characteristic scent that he had known only once before in his life. He rubbed at his wounded left arm, then at the cut on his right side. It was strange how little he felt the pain. How would they attack, singly or in groups? Would he be better off in the open, or with his back against one of the walls?

"I suggest that you proceed with patience. It is not necessary for you to return to orbit in the immediate future. The local food substances are not suitable for you, but I can transmit information for their processing that will allow you to consume them. The life expectancy of your body is many centuries. In that time the situation on the surface may change."

"It will change all right." Drake turned, wondering if he might find a hiding place along the road or out in the fields. He saw lights, far off but steadily nearing. He would do better to head for the nearest building and make his stand there.

"In any case." The ship spoke while he was sprinting across sodden vines. *"I cannot desert you. I must stay here as long as you survive. That may be centuries."*

"It may. It would be nice to think that it will be." Drake was panting, his back to the building wall. He clutched his metal bar, all that he had to hold on to. The torches were nearing, crowding in to make a dense ring through which he saw no way to break. "Stay until I die, then go."

They were closer. Long bodies gleamed pale orange in the smoky light of torches held in spidery forelimbs. He could see the razor-sharp pincers. They gaped wide enough to grasp his head. He lifted the metal bar, weighing it in his hands.

"Wish me luck." He took a deep breath through his mouth. "It won't be long now."

Interlude: Dutchman

The monitor ships had been designed by Cass Leemu and Mel Bradley with great care and ingenuity. They must be able to survive without external services or maintenance for up to a million years in orbit, all the while performing continuous observation and analysis. They must be entirely self-sufficient, able to take energy as necessary from any source. They must contain enough stored information to answer any question that a copy of Drake Merlin, embodied on the surface of a planet and awaiting the arrival of the Shiva, might ask.

The composites represented by Cass and Mel had been careful and ingenious in their work, but not wasteful. They did not include features that could not under any reasonable scenario be needed.

So no plan had been made for a ship to survive passage through a caesura. No ship had been designed to operate in galaxies far from human control and influence. No capability had been included for the on-board production of self-replicating machines. The design guaranteed that a ship be *able to operate for millions of years, but not for unspecified billions.*

Cass and Mel, at Drake's insistence, had gone beyond reasonable and foreseeable needs in just one area. The first humans, long ago, had emerged from the caves of Pleistocene Earth with brains already large enough to write sonnets, invent and play chess, compose fugues, and solve partial differential equations. They had not really needed such abilities in a world where hunting, gathering food, breeding, and nurturing seemed the only fixed constants. But a bigger-than-necessary brain had proved an advantage. It might be necessary again. Drake wanted each ship to be created not only self-aware, but intelligent enough to review the probable consequences of its instructions and of its own actions.

This ship had received unusual and specific instructions: Seek a civilization that was already space-faring. Then rouse Drake from dormancy to interact with whatever—if anything —was found. Should no space-faring intelligence be located within this galaxy, build a superluminal signal detector. Drake would have to be roused from dormancy and embodied to help with that, because the ship lacked the general-purpose robots needed for large space construction.

The instructions implied several other imperatives. First, the ship must survive. It must do whatever was needed to ensure its continued operation. It must also be patient.

The ship wandered alone across the sea of stars. There was no way that it could ever land on a body bigger than a small asteroid. Its own weight would destroy its fragile structure. A copy of Drake Merlin, far more robust, could be downloaded into an organic body while the ship was in orbit around a planet and landed there, but it was impossible for a large S-wave detector to be constructed on a planetary surface.

Remaining in operating condition would not be difficult for the ship itself. Material resources for self-renewal were plentiful around many stars and in the dust clouds scattered through the spiral arms.

In any case, that was not going to be the problem.

The ship found an open lane of the galaxy and drifted

along it, far from the disturbing effects of suns and singularities and dust clouds. It performed its careful analysis: eighty-eight billion stars in this galaxy; a mere two hundred targets as sources of potential intelligence—five-eighths of them already eliminated by direct inspection. It would be a straightforward if lengthy task to look at the rest. The ship could certainly handle that.

But now, assume that the search was unsuccessful, *that no space-going intelligent life was found, that it was necessary to take the next step. Then the time scale for action expanded enormously. Years increased from millions to billions. To build an S-wave detector—one large enough to see into the deepest reaches of space—was a monstrous task. Drake Merlin, in his final orders from the clouded surface of the planet, could not have known what he was demanding.*

But the ship knew.

It also knew that it had no choice. Unlike a human, a ship's brain could not elect the annihilation of self.

As the ship computed the trajectory for the next target star, it mapped out the mandated sequence of its future actions if the current search failed to produce the right kind of intelligent life.

Find the right type of dust cloud, one close enough to a recent supernova to be rich in the necessary heavy elements. Embody Drake Merlin—not once, but in a hundred or a thousand or a million copies. (And never consider their eventual fate.) Use the Merlins, singly and working in unison, as laborers. In the absence of intelligent robots, Merlins must mine the dust cloud, build the space production facility, shape the strands of the antennas and stretch them across space in the precise configuration demanded for signal detection of S-wave sources.

It could be done. The ship saw practical obstacles—it must husband its limited drive, coasting without power for thousands of years between target stars, taking advantage of every natural force field and particle wind of the galaxy; but there was nothing impossible.

Except, perhaps, for the time that all this would take.

The ship made the calculation and regarded the result. It could not sigh or wince, but it wished that it was possible to go back to Drake Merlin in the last moments before the horde of white ghosts had swarmed over him, and ask if this was what he really wanted.

It knew the answer to that question. The on-board information base made it clear: Drake Merlin did not want any of this. He wanted his lost wife. The odds against that made everything in the ship's calculations seem like certainty by comparison.

The next target star was known, the most economical flight path computed and ready. There was no further reason for delay.

The ship set out on its multibillion-year journey, sailing the endless trade winds of an indifferent galaxy.

Chapter 28

*"From far, from eve and morning
And yon twelve-winded sky"*

*W*ho would ever have thought that it could take so long?

Drake drifted through space, his suited body slowly turning. He had left the ship in order to inspect the overall condition of the structure. How many times had he been downloaded to do this, he or some other of the multiple copies of himself? How many times had everything been found to be in working order, and how many times had he returned to electronic storage?

A thousand, ten thousand, a million. It made no difference. The S-wave detector was all around, a construct whose nodes and gossamer filaments stretched away past the point where his eyes could trace their presence against the stars. The great array was supposed to be able to detect evidence of superluminal message activity out to the red shift limit. It had been set up to operate automatically and indefinitely, if necessary without human or ship supervision. One by one, galaxies would be looked at until the whole universe had been surveyed. The process would stop only when a signal was detected. So far the instrument had reported nothing but a steady hiss of background noise.

If the array was working to specification, was something wrong with the basic theory? In principle a superluminal signal would traverse the universe in hours; but confirmation of the theory had been made only in the home galaxy, over distances a millionth as far as current needs.

His attention moved beyond the detector array to the far-off glow of stars and galaxies. His eyes could not see the change, but he knew that it was there.

Not the end yet, but the subtle beginning of the end. Already the great dust clouds had been consumed, the blazing blue supergiant stars long ago exploded to supernovas or collapsed to black holes. Every main sequence star was far along in its lifetime, reduced from a bloated red giant to a white dwarf hardly bigger than the original Earth. Only the slow-burning low-mass stars remained, doling out miserly dribbles of radiation; their energy supply would be sufficient for another hundred billion years.

Except that such a period was not available. The cosmos itself was evolving, changing. The ship reported to Drake that the universe was far past its critical point. The remote galaxies displayed a strong blue shift, a displacement of the light toward shorter wavelengths. The microwave background radiation, diluted and cooled during the earlier expansion of the universe, now revealed an increase in its black body temperature.

The universe was warming up. The Great Expansion was far in the past. The collapse, toward the final singularity and the end of time, was under way.

But thought's the slave of life, and life time's fool; and time, that takes survey of all the world, must have a stop.

Drake halted his drift through space but permitted the slow rotation of his suited figure. He, like time, was taking survey of all the world. It seemed his task must have no stop—until the universe itself put an end to it.

The current inspection was complete. He might as well head back to the ship. On the other hand, there was no hurry. When he returned he would be uploaded again to electronic storage. His new sleep might be for a million or a billion years, but he could expect little change when he awoke. The march from here to the end of the universe would be slow and stately, a multibillion-year progression. Only the final months and days would be spectacular. To anyone around to watch them, they would display unimaginable violence.

The ship was a tiny gleam of gold at the center of the black web of the S-wave detection system. Drake headed toward it, glancing from time to time to his left. The dust cloud that had provided the materials for the detector still hung there, glowing faintly by its internal light. It was too small to collapse under its own gravitational attraction. That, and the constraining field placed in position by the ship, had been the key to its continued survival.

Drake, occupied with his thoughts, had turned off the suit unit linking him with the ship. There was no danger in doing so. Communications could be activated in an emergency by the ship's brain, although the many billions of years since entering the caesura had never produced a single override.

He switched the communicator on when he was just a few kilometers from the ship, and was shocked to hear a brief repeated message.

"Superluminal signal activity has been detected. Analysis is under way. Superluminal—"

"What! Why didn't you call and tell me?"

"That seemed . . . premature." The ship was oddly hesitant. *"There are anomalies that require explanation."*

"Then you'd better tell me about them." Drake was sliding through the molecular interstitial lock at record speed. He felt a sense of exultation at his special good fortune. He had been the one embodied when the signal came! Then he felt stupid. Since every embodiment was one version of him, there was no way that he could *not* be the one embodied when an S-wave message was detected.

"Where does the signal come from?"

"It is multiple signals, from a galaxy about eight hundred million light-years away. In cosmic terms, that is rather close. It lies on the far side of one of the great gulfs, but in a supercluster that is still one of our neighbors."

"What do the messages say?"

"That is where the anomaly begins. First, the signals lack standard header records, identifying their source and destination."

"Maybe they were broadcast."

"That cannot be the case. An S-wave signal is like any other, it must be tightly beamed to be read at more than a few hundred light-years. But even if the signals had been broadcast, they would carry a source identification. That, however, is not the most disturbing feature. The real problem is that the signals are unintelligible. *We are not dealing with a single detected signal, where the problem might be one of resolving ambiguities. We are picking up millions of bit streams, an abundance of test data. Although we carry with us every known communication protocol, these superluminal signals conform to none of them."*

"Maybe it's a new protocol, something that came into use after we passed through the caesura. We've been gone for so long, changes are inevitable."

"True. But the signals are totally *unrecognizable. Change is more than likely, it is even necessary to reflect new needs and new technology. However, just as the human body carries within it elements of your own most archaic history, from fingernails to body hair to embryonic gill slits, so any superluminal signal ought to carry at least some semblance of the old communication protocols. These do not. They are wholly unfamiliar."*

"Are you still working to crack them?"

"Naturally. However, I am not optimistic. Already I have employed eighty percent of the analytical tools available to me, with no success. The most probable explanation is also the least satisfying."

Drake didn't need to ask what it was. The possibility had been discussed with the ship's brain during each of his embodiments.

"Assume that it is an independent civilization, aliens who have never encountered humans but are advanced enough to use S-wave signaling. How would it affect our ability to send a signal to them?"

"To send a signal? That would be very easy. Our S-wave detector can transmit as accurately and rapidly as it receives. That would not seem to be the issue here. The question is, What will happen to our signal when it is received in the other galaxy?"

"That's going to be my problem, isn't it?" Drake saw no point in talking generalities any longer. "Once I'm back in electronic storage, how long will it take to transmit me superluminally?"

"A few hours at the most."

"Then let's do it. You said eight hundred million light-years?"

"Eight hundred and eighteen million, to be more precise."

"How much travel time is that for you—allowing for fuel and maintenance and everything else?"

"Most would have to be in coast phase, since between the galaxies there are no ready sources of materials or energy. Necessarily, that would imply long periods of low or zero acceleration. The travel time would be a billion years or more."

"You can survive that?"

"Of course. Already we have endured tens of times that interval. However, I must mention two other anomalous features of the received signals. First, although there are many signals, million after million of them, they clearly fall into two different types."

"How do you know that, if you can't understand what they say?"

"By statistical analysis of the bit streams. That analysis clearly reveals two distinct types, although the content of either type remains unknown. And that is the second anomaly. In principle, my analytical tools should permit the interpretation of any possible signal whatsoever. It makes no difference if the sender is human or nonhuman, organic or inorganic, familiar or utterly alien. If the laws of logic, which we have always believed to be universal, are being followed, the signal should be intelligible."

"But these are not? Very curious. Chances are it will be easier to sort out what's going on when we're there to see it." But Drake was expressing a confidence that he did not feel. He sensed old memories stirring within him. Two kinds of signal that clearly were signals, but neither of which could be interpreted. Why did that sound familiar?

"First, switch me back to electronic storage. Then send me on my way. After I'm gone, you can take the slow road and join me." *Signals that could not be understood. Algorithms that should be able to interpret anything, but failed to do so.* He postponed the question. He would have time to consider it when he reached the signal source. "Let's get me to electronic form, so I can go to work. Assuming that things work out all right, I'll beam myself back here and tell you what's going on."

Assuming that things work out all right.

It occurred to Drake, rising to consciousness, that nothing had gone right for aeons. They had certainly not gone right this time. Rather than waking in some other galaxy, delivered as an S-wave and reconstructed to consciousness, he was still on board the ship. And although he was awake, he was certainly not embodied. Instead he was in electronic form, sharing sensors and processors with the ship. He was also aware of the hundred or more other versions of himself, dormant around him.

"All right. It didn't work. What's happening now?"

Part of the answer came to him even before the ship spoke. The visible light sensors revealed face-on the disk of a barred galaxy. From the way that it filled the sky ahead, they were within a few tens of thousands of light-years—touching distance, in intergalactic terms.

Also, it was *the* galaxy. The ship's signal-receiving equipment showed the spiral arms filled with the glittering sparks of S-wave transmissions. The galaxy flamed with them, bright flickering points of blue and crimson. They had been color coded by the ship into type 1 and type 2—statistically different from each other, but equally mysterious.

If the ship was here, so close to the source of the signals, then a billion years or more must have passed since he was last conscious.

Why wasn't the ship answering his question? And then Drake realized that the ship *had* answered. A new block of information had been transferred, and his electronic consciousness was already processing it, thousands or millions of times faster than his old organic one. He knew, without being told . . .

The ship had remained for centuries at the focal point of the giant array. It had transmitted Drake as a superluminal signal—not once but a hundred times and more. It had waited patiently for a return signal. Nothing came into the array but the same endless stream of unintelligible communications.

At last the ship had to make a difficult choice. If it left the array, all chance of receiving an intergalactic signal from Drake was lost. The ship would be forced to rely again on the simple S-wave detection system that it carried on board. On the other hand, to remain in one place and wait for a signal from Drake might take until the end of the universe.

Finally the ship abandoned the array and set out on its lonely billion-year journey across the intergalactic gulf. In doing so, it lost the ability to pick up superluminal signals from its destination until the target galaxy was close enough for the on-board system to operate.

How close?

This close. Close enough for the ship to employ a synthetic aperture optical system, able to produce visible wavelength pictures of surface detail on planets the size of Earth.

And now a new problem arose. It was baffling enough for the ship to know that it needed help. It had brought Drake to consciousness.

And because he would need direct access to all sensor inputs, and because in any case there was no planet within twenty thousand light-years where an embodied organic form might prove useful, the ship employed a different procedure. It did not embody the aroused intelligence, but resurrected it in electronic form.

Drake examined one of the planetary images as the ship drifted steadily on through space. The world was superficially Earth-like, sufficiently massive and far enough from its primary to hold an atmosphere. It should have had air of some kind, nitrogen or methane or carbon dioxide or, if it bore life, oxygen and water vapor. No trace of any showed up in the gas spectral analysis. The surface, unobscured by clouds or a shroud of air, was black rock. It looked like volcanic basalt that had flowed under high temperature before pooling and hardening to grotesque formations. There was no sign of surface water, no sign of life or surface artifacts. Orbiting the world like a swarm of lightning bugs were hundreds of objects too small to be seen with the imagers. However, from time to time a flash from one of them showed that it was transmitting, and the ship was receiving, an outgoing S-wave signal.

What was there to talk about in facilities that orbited long-dead worlds?

Drake tracked the destinations of the outgoing data bursts, and the ship offered their images at his command: world after world, scene after scene of charred devastation. Every planet was in ruins. Each was clearly lifeless.

"I have performed as complete a survey as possible

from this distance." The ship's messages were clear and easy now that Drake knew how to listen to them. "The pattern repeats from one side of the galaxy to the other, from the outer rim to the central disk. Those worlds have in common what I have termed a type one superluminal message capability. Compare them with the type two worlds."

Another sequence of planets was offered for Drake's inspection. From the ship's point of view, there were large differences. From a human point of view, one similarity overwhelmed every other factor: organic life was absent.

Drake examined a thousand type 2 planets where everything that humans had learned of physics, planetology, and biology suggested that life should have developed. The sun was an appropriate spectral type, surface temperature was in the right range, the planet had a low-eccentricity orbit, there was plenty of surface water, and a thick atmosphere of hydrogen, carbon dioxide, and nitrogen.

Life should have developed—*must* have developed. And it *had* developed. The proof was in the swarm of active devices around each world, emitting and receiving their bursts of S-wave signals. No one would install such a system without a purpose. Life had once been on all these worlds. And somehow life had been destroyed, not as spectacularly as on the type 1 worlds, but just as finally.

"The problem is one that we never anticipated." Was that the ship speaking, or Drake's own thoughts? The dividing line became blurred when they shared common storage and processing power. "We had always assumed that superluminal signal capability would be accompanied by a working technology. Now we find abundant S-wave capacity and nothing else. Do we wish to visit a galaxy that seems dead of organic life?"

"Is it *safe* to do so?"

The last thought was surely Drake's alone. His

thoughts were moving again to old memories and offering an uneasy synthesis.

In an infinite universe, anything that can happen will happen.

He had been talking to himself, but his thoughts were no longer private.

"The universe is not infinite," the ship said. "It is finite in time both past and future, and it is finite but unbounded in space."

"All right. Change that to things that you never expected to happen, when you were long ago on a world far away, can happen if you wait long enough and go far enough."

He not only hadn't expected to see this—when he was young he had hardly taken notice of it. His interests revolved around music and Ana, and anything as dull as military policy or political strategy tended to be ignored. It was Ana, the social activist, who had educated him. He remembered one lazy October afternoon when they lay side by side in his little one-room apartment, with the Venetian blinds partly drawn and late sunlight casting elongated and distorted leaf shadows on the wall. Drake lay flat on his back. He didn't want to talk or think about anything and would have quite liked a nap. He found it easier to say nothing and pretend to listen, but he had got away with that for only a few minutes.

"You don't care, do you?" Ana punched him on the left shoulder and propped herself up on her elbow so that she could see his face and make sure that he wasn't going to sleep. "I'm telling you, it could happen again."

"Nah. Mutual Assured Destruction is a dead idea. And a dumb idea, too."

"It's worse than dumb, but I'm not sure it's dead. Brains and resources were wasted on it for two generations. Do you want to know why?"

Not really. But Drake said only, "Uh-huh."

"It kept on going because it was a big fat money tree, where corruption could thrive and contractors could get very rich. And because no matter what you do, for paranoid people more is never enough. If *they* build more weapons, or even if you just think that they might, *you* have to build more. They're as crazy as you are, so they have to build more, too; so you have to build more, so they have to build more, so you have to build more, so they have to build more, so you have to build more. . . ."

She paused, rather to Drake's disappointment. The cadence of the repeated phrase was relaxing, and he would happily have nodded off listening to it. Instead he said, "I don't know why you're still worrying about all this. It's ancient history. MAD went away over twenty years ago, along with the Soviet Union."

She snuggled up against him and put her hand flat on his bare belly. "That proves how little you understand the military. I drank this stuff in with my mother's milk. Four of my uncles and five of my cousins are regular army or air force. You should hear the talk at family reunions. You did me a big favor. They can't stand your politics."

"I don't have any."

"That's almost worse. But they don't want you around, and that gives me an excuse to stay away. I'll never be able to thank you enough."

"You can thank me by letting me rest. Anyway, you shouldn't be thanking me. Thank Professor Bonvissuto. He got you the scholarship."

"I'll thank both of you. You know what Uncle Dan said? He's the air force colonel, the one from Baltimore who told you that the finest vocal group in the world was the Singing Sergeants, and that Wagner was a boring old weirdo."

"I remember him. Rossini said much the same— about Wagner, I mean, not the Singing Sergeants. He said Wagner had beautiful moments, but awful quarter hours. He also said that he couldn't judge Wagner's *Lohengrin* from a single hearing, and he certainly didn't intend hearing it a second time."

"Ideas in the military don't go away, ever, Uncle Dan says." Ana wasn't going to let Drake distract her with musical anecdotes. "Old ideas get put on the shelf, and when the right funding cycle comes around they're dusted off and proposed again as new. I don't believe a lot of what he tells me, but I believe that. Balance of terror didn't start with Mutual Assured Destruction. And it won't end with it. Bad ideas are still sitting there on the shelf."

And sometimes they sit on that shelf for an awfully long time before they finally achieve their potential.

"I do not think that I am following you," the ship said.

It was hardly surprising—Drake's private thoughts had not been intended for anyone else. They had hopped randomly between past and present, and they included personal references that were surely not in any general database.

Drake addressed his remarks directly to the ship's interface. "Mutual Assured Destruction is a very simple idea: I build huge weapons systems. So do you. Then you daren't attack me, because if you do, I'll attack you in return and you'll die, too." (He had killed Ana, and he had died, too. He had thought of his actions as Mutual Assured Survival. Did that make him any different from the Mutual Assured Destruction lunatics?) "So neither one of us dares to attack the other. It sounds as though it might work, but MAD has one fatal flaw. It produces an equilibrium between two groups, but it's an *unstable* equilibrium. One accident, or even a misunderstanding, and both sides will use their weapons. They have to hit as hard as they can immediately, to neutralize as much of the other's firepower as they can. Just as bad, a third group with very few weapons can *force* a misunderstanding and make the two big powers fight each other, by faking an attack of one on the other. I think we are looking at the results when MAD is applied on a huge scale. I think it killed that whole galaxy."

"That cannot be true. Even now, I am detecting new superluminal messages. I cannot understand them, but it proves that intelligence continues to operate there."

"Intelligence of a sort. Sometimes if an idea is old enough, it can seem brand new. I ought to have known what was going on ages ago, as soon as you told me that there were two distinct types of signals coming from this galaxy, and that you were unable to interpret either of them. You said that any signal at all should be intelligible to you. But suppose it was *designed* not to be understood by anyone without a suitable key? Suppose both sides were employing ciphers, codes that the other could not break."

"Intentional obscurity. That is certainly possible. But what makes you so sure that the galaxy is dead? How can that be true, and the technology still be working?"

Drake realized that he could explain even that. His mind had thrown at him an image of a long-ago performance of Haydn's Farewell Symphony, of a conductor facing a group of players. In front of each stood a lighted candle. One by one, each musician finished his or her own orchestral part, snuffed out the candle, and left the stage. Finally the whole orchestra was gone. The conductor stood alone in darkness.

The ship was unlikely to benefit much from that thought. "Let me tell you what happened on Earth," Drake said, "in the years just after I was born. Two great powers had been busy building up their nuclear weapons. The chance of all-out war seemed very high. That war, if it happened, would be short. A couple of hours and it would be all over. Missiles over the pole could be launched to reach any target within thirty minutes. The military on one side—our side, people would say, though I never thought of it as *my* side—

decided that they must keep some kind of communications system working, even after the main war was over. They imagined a space-based command post, a whole constellation of special satellites in orbit around the Earth. The spacecraft would be completely operated by computers, and they would form a kind of central nervous system for all fighting, no matter when it happened. The system was called MILSTAR, for Military Strategic, Tactical, and Relay system, and it was supposed to be able to function even after the main spasm of war was over. The military planners didn't intend for MILSTAR to help with civilian reconstruction. That wasn't its job. They wanted it to handle *military* communications—and to be able to support fighting again, if necessary, months or years later. They wanted MILSTAR ready to fight another war. It was designed to function even if all the surface command structures had been obliterated. It was supposed to be able to call on robot weaponry, whether or not there were humans around.''

The image came again. The conductor stood facing a full complement of players. As the military powers on land, sea, and air were snuffed out by enemy action, MILSTAR continued, organizing and optimizing resources that became smaller every second. Finally, the stage held nothing but orchestral desks and empty instrument cases. The conductor waved his baton over a vanished army of players. MILSTAR floated serenely on through space, its communications system in full working order and ready to shape a second symphony of Armageddon.

''The MILSTAR satellites had to be very sophisticated. They needed a long operating lifetime. They had to be mobile, to avoid direct missile attack; durable, to operate for years without a single human mind to direct them; robust, to survive electromagnetic pulse effects and near misses; and smart, able to talk easily to each other using a variety of encrypted signals, so that the enemy could never crack the global communications network.

"It was a highly secret project. It had to be. That was why it was able to obtain huge funding for a long time, even though anyone who looked at it objectively could see why it wouldn't work. It needed tens of millions of computer instructions, lines of program code that could only be tested when the actual war was declared. It assumed a static world order, with a single well-defined enemy. It bypassed every civilian chain of command. Worst of all, it assumed that one side or the other could *win* an all-out nuclear war, and be all set to fight again. No mention of hundreds of millions of casualties, or disabled food and water and sewage and transportation systems, or a totally collapsed economy that couldn't pay ten cents for a military budget.

"Well, we were lucky. MILSTAR came out from behind its veil of secrecy, little by little. That doomed it. It couldn't stand the sunlight. Finally, after years and years of staggering along when no one really believed in it but kept it going as a source of jobs and a political pork barrel, the money was cut off and the development ended. MILSTAR never became a working system —on Earth. But something like it was developed, and is still in operation"—Drake indicated the galaxy ahead of the ship—"*there.*"

Drake had been carried away, in time and space and in a depth of feeling lost to him for aeons. He knew he had spoken for Ana, more than for himself. Those had been *her* voiced fears, her indignation, her relief at an earthly doom avoided. He also realized, for the first time, that existence in a purely electronic form could admit emotion and passion and longing.

The ship had absorbed the facts of his message, if not its intensity. "So although an S-wave signal system exists in that galaxy," it said, "the original creators and owners are long vanished. Therefore no moral or practical impediment exists to our taking over its use. We should find it possible to inhibit the encryption system. As soon as we have done that, and our own type of S-wave signals can be sent and received—"

"We can't do that."

"I believe that I possess the necessary analytical capabilities, even though you may not be aware of them."

"That's not the problem. The problem is in going there." Drake again indicated the galaxy ahead of them.

"We are only twenty-one thousand light-years away. We have traveled forty thousand times that distance already, without difficulty. The remaining journey is negligible."

"No. It's the place where we can expect trouble. Look at them." Drake displayed an array of blackened and silent worlds for the ship's attention. "We can't say what did this, and for all we know it may still be working. Maybe it's waiting for something new that it can hit. The weapons ran out of *targets*. We don't know that they ran out of anything else. Just because a galaxy is dead of life doesn't mean it's safe to go there."

"Then I request that you propose an alternative." The ship turned its imaging equipment, swinging slowly from the island of matter ahead to the great ocean of space that surrounded it. "The next nearest galaxy is two and a quarter million light-years away. It showed no evidence of S-wave transmission. Do you suggest that we change to it as our target? I am ready to follow your instructions."

And that was the devil of it. There *was* no better alternative. No other galaxy, in a search that stretched halfway across time, had displayed superluminal signals. It was a poor moment to decide that the ship had left the big detection system, laboriously constructed over so many years, prematurely. But it was true. The smart thing would have been to survey every galaxy in the universe for S-wave transmissions, before rushing off to tackle the enigma of the one that lay ahead.

It was Drake's fault. He should have thought harder and longer before he acted. The price of mindless action was high: they had to return to their detection system, a billion years away, and follow that with another interminable search.

That was the price. But he was not willing to pay it.

Surely *something* could be done with the facilities that lay ahead of them, so temptingly close? Compared with the other option, twenty thousand light-years was like stepping to the house next door. He knew, with absolute certainty, that a full superluminal capability existed here, in perfect working order. Nothing like it might be found again before the universe itself came to a close.

As the field of view of the ship's sensors performed its steady turn in space, Drake watched the grand sweep of the galaxies. They had not changed. *He* had changed. When had he lost his will and daring? When had he become so cautious?

Long ago, without a second thought, he had risked everything. Now, no matter what he did, he would be risking less than everything. Other versions of him surely still existed, even if they happened to be at the far edge of the universe. They did not know that *he* existed—they would think that he had died fifteen billion years ago, when the ship was swallowed by the caesura. But what of that? They should still be there. Did he have anything to lose, if now he risked the dark menace ahead?

"Aye, but to die, and go we know not where . . ."

Was that all it was? Simple fear of death?

"Are we still heading for the galaxy?"

"Yes. We have not changed our course."

"Then forget the alternative. Hold our path. Take us to the nearest world where you are detecting a source of S-wave messages."

There are many events in the womb of time which will be delivered.

And how long since he had thought of *that*? It was time to take a chance, and test the kindness of reality.

Taking a chance on one thing did not mean abandoning caution in everything else.

Drake elected to remain conscious, though not embodied, through the whole slow approach to the galaxy. The ship's speed had to be subluminal. Meanwhile, the S-wave messages flashed and flickered ahead from spiral arm to spiral arm, as enigmatic as ever. At Drake's suggestion, the ship's brain assumed that the messages were deliberately encrypted and tried to decipher them. The effort consumed the bulk of the ship's computation powers for twelve thousand years. There was no useful result for either type 1 or type 2 messages.

While this was going on, Drake constantly monitored the galaxy ahead. He had no idea of the range of weapons that remained there. At any moment, the ship's approach might be detected, and an alien force could reach out to consume them. He was ready to power the ship down totally and hope that silence would end the attack, or if that failed to turn the ship around and try to outrun the destruction.

The thirteenth millennium brought the change. It occurred while Drake and the ship were analyzing the comparative freedoms and restrictions of their two mentalities.

"What would you have done, in a similar situation?" The ship was dissatisfied with its own performance.

"Assuming that I were a ship, with your history and your inorganic intelligence? The first thing I would do, after Drake Merlin insisted on being sent as a superluminal signal to this galaxy, is tell myself that embodied humans tend to be impulsive and make decisions too quickly. We evolved that way, because the old human body rarely lasted a century. We were always in a hurry, we had to be. So as a ship I would have spent a long time evaluating my own possible actions. Then I hope I would have asked what could be done at the S-wave detection structure we built and nowhere else. When all those things were done, I would have headed this way."

"And what would you have done as a *human* in the same situation?"

"If I could see no possible further use for my existence—"

Drake's comments on suicide, an idea alien to the ship's intelligence, were interrupted.

A-W-A-W-A-W-A-W-A-W-A-W-A-. The ship's S-wave detector screeched and warbled in overload as a message blared into it.

A-W-A-W-A-W-A-W-A-W-A-W-A-W-A-W-A-.

"Is it coming from the galaxy?" Drake had to send his own thought at maximum volume to penetrate the curtain of incoming noise.

A-W-A-W-A-W-A-W-A-W-A-W-A-W-A-W-A-.

"I do not know." The ship's own signal was barely intelligible. "The source is so powerful. It comes from everywhere. Wait." The ship de-tuned its receiver, and the volume of signal suddenly dropped to a tolerable level.

WARNING. YOU ARE ENTERING A DANGEROUS AND QUARANTINED AREA. DO NOT PROCEED FARTHER WITHOUT INSTRUCTIONS. REPEAT, YOU ARE ENTERING A DANGEROUS AND QUARANTINED AREA. HALT, AND DO NOT PROCEED WITHOUT INSTRUCTIONS. WORKING S-WAVE COMMUNICATION PROTOCOLS ARE CONTAINED IN CARRIER WAVE. VISUAL AND REAL-TIME INTERACTION FOLLOWS.

"I'm sending our identification and reply." The ship was already transcribing protocols. "It is safe to do so. That signal can't be coming from the galaxy ahead."

"How do you know?"

"Because there is no encryption. More than that,

the signal is in *standard form.* It must be coming to us from our own form of mentality."

Drake did not need that last piece of information. The promised visual and real-time information flow was beginning, and pictures were already flowing in. The first frame was very familiar. It was Drake Merlin, staring at something right in front of him. A puzzled voice was saying, "Please transmit that identification sequence again. There appears to have been a transcription error. According to our records, you don't exist. You haven't existed for fifteen billion years."

Drake was not embodied, so he could not send an exultant real-time image of himself. The best that he could do was to provide his own stored and smiling icon, as it was preserved in the ship's memory.

"What you have received is not a transcription error. We exist, and you have the right ID sequence. We've been heading for home all this time. I'm sorry that it took so long." And then, the only thing that really mattered, the question: *"Did you develop the technology needed to restore Ana? Is she there with you?"*

While Drake waited for answers, he realized that everything else made sense. A rogue galaxy, devoid of life but sending out S-wave signals and filled with weapons of destruction, was a menace to every intelligence in the universe. A region around that galaxy was needed as a quarantine zone. All the approach routes had to be monitored. Like a dangerous reef in a peaceful sea, the galaxy must be surrounded by warning bells and lightships. It was a beacon for the whole universe, the best possible place for lost travelers, like Drake and the ship, to arrive at.

And arrive they had. They were on the way home.

In an infinite universe, anything that can happen will happen.

One of those things, now and again, was a little bit of luck.

Chapter 29

Homecoming

With Drake's return to human space, his problems seemed to be in the past.

The feeling of euphoria did not last. It ended when his question about Ana remained unanswered, and when the image of the other Drake Merlin vanished suddenly from the screen. It was replaced by the face of Tom Lambert. Tom's features, hair color, and expression varied wildly for a few seconds before they stabilized.

"Unfortunately, Ana has not been resurrected." Tom's mouth shrank to half its size, then enlarged again. Drake had seen the effect before. Some strong emotion, fear or joy or rage, was distorting the presentation. "The problem of resurrection will be worked on."

Will be worked on, after so many aeons? Drake wondered what they had been doing all this time. What could possibly be left to do?

But Tom Lambert was continuing. "I'm sorry." His

face writhed with worry, then took on a lopsided smile. "We have not used this particular form of presentation for more than fifteen billion years. We never thought it would be necessary. A return such as yours was never anticipated, although we knew that the theory showed it to be formally possible. Now, of course, we understand exactly what happened. You and your ship remained in this universe, but you passed through a noncausal path in the caesura. Before you reemerged, you traveled seven billion light-years in space and eight billion years forward in time."

"And then I couldn't find you for umpteen billion more. But here I am. So what is there to be sorry about?"

"We are sorry that you encountered the warning concerning your approach to the Skrilant Galaxy."

"I assume that I needed it." Drake was not convinced by Tom Lambert's explanation. "I presume I would have been blown apart otherwise."

"That is most probable. But our warning included a representation of yourself."

"So I met myself. Big deal. I survived."

"But it was *not* yourself." Tom glanced sideways, away from Drake. "You, as you are now, did not encounter the full present form of Drake Merlin. I should add that I form a minor subset of that whole. Very soon you will meet."

"I think you'd better tell me what's going on. This isn't the sort of homecoming I was hoping for. What do you mean, I haven't met my present self?"

"Drake Merlin, in all the universe except on your ship, you are no longer a single entity. The mentality of Drake Merlin, except for you, is a composite."

"I don't believe it." Drake sensed coming disaster. "It's the one thing I knew I could never afford to do. If I merged to a composite with anyone else, I knew I might lose sight of my goal."

"But we did merge, in a different way. We regret that

now. Sit quietly, Drake Merlin, for one moment more. We are opening an S-wave high-data-rate linkage with you and your ship. Prepare for an update of many billions of years, since the time that you vanished from our horizon. Be prepared for strong coupling, then all your questions will be answered. The link is opening . . . now.''

Drake submerged beneath a torrent of data, a million parallel sources streaming in. . . .

The struggle with the Shiva was ending. He saw new composites, part human, part Shiva, controlling the interaction between the two forms of life. Humans and the giant sessile plants might never understand each other, but with the right intermediaries they could coexist.

With success came a new problem. Through the endless years of battle, Drake had remained aloof. He dared not allow himself to become part of any composite, organic or inorganic, within the interconnected webs of consciousness. Nor would he share his personal data banks with anyone or anything. His logic was simple and invincible: He alone was willing to make the awful decisions of death and destruction needed to defeat the Shiva. He dared not risk any dilution of that will. But there was also the secret agenda: if he ceased to be a single individual, the drive to restore Ana might be lost.

For what seemed like forever, versions of his individual self had been downloaded and sent out on the warships, to meet their fiery or frigid end on planets at the edge of the Galaxy and beyond. With the Shiva ascendant that had been a one-way process. But in some of the spiral arms, humans at last began to hold their own. As they carried out their programs of counterattack and advance into the space between the galaxies, and then on through to other galaxies, human ships began to survive.

And now . . .

He was coming back, Drake Merlin in his billions; each of him was different, each had his own unique experiences, each was undeniably Drake.

He had held himself apart from all others. But how could he remain aloof and refuse access to himself?

He could not. Drake formed a composite, an unusual one: Every component would be Drake Merlin.

At first it was total chaos. His element selves numbered beyond the billions; he had long ago lost count of the number of times he had been downloaded, and the total constantly increased. Parts of him were close by, parts were separated from the rest by millions of light-years; some had been partly destroyed in combat and become maimed or incomplete versions of a whole Drake Merlin. All, without exception, were now different. Time and events produced changes in form, perspective, even in self-image. Drake struggled to understand, to assimilate, to integrate, and to maintain or create a single personality among that teeming horde of selves.

He was no longer essential to the struggle with the Shiva. A truce, incomprehensible to any entity but one of the human/Shiva symbiote framers, was signed. The need for oversight by Drake slowly diminished. As the threat of the Shiva receded and the need for his continuous involvement decreased, the Drake composite became increasingly consumed by introspection and by his own process of reconstruction. He took no interest in external events unless they were relevant to a substantial fraction of his own components.

Those components were linked to other composites and to other data banks. They stretched out across the galactic clusters and the great rifts, on toward the edges of the accessible universe. Drake Merlin had become guardian and caretaker of the cosmos.

With the growth of his composite came something else: slowly and imperceptibly, his driving willpower weakened. Old desires, needs that had propelled him forward from the farthest reaches of the past, dwindled and faded. Old longings no longer mattered. . . .

Until one day, unexpectedly, on the monitored boundary of the dead but malevolent Skrilant galaxy, a new but very old Drake Merlin appeared that formed no part of any other.

Within the vast extended composite of Drake Merlin, the

news of the encounter stirred a curious uneasiness. The stranger was asking questions. The attempt to answer them called for the use of memories so far removed in time and space that they carried no physical impressions. The composite had to sift deep within its own data banks before it found answers.

The result was shocking. Drake Merlin had somehow, somewhere, lost the way. He had forgotten his own most solemn vows. Now he had to change—and wonder if there was time enough, before the end of the universe itself.

Drake emerged, to find Tom Lambert silently waiting. The data flood had ended as suddenly as it had begun. Drake realized something else. He was no longer on board his own ship, and he had become inexplicably different.

Tom Lambert nodded. "Your perception is correct. You were uploaded while the data transfer was proceeding, and superluminally transmitted here."

"And embodied?" Drake worried about the long-lost feeling of a tangible self.

"That is no longer necessary. In fact, if you are to understand what we are doing, many parallel inputs continue to be necessary. In such circumstances, material embodiment is no longer possible."

"Something has gone wrong, hasn't it?"

"It has. We became distracted. What we are doing to correct it—if we can—is this."

If the previous data flow had been a torrent, the new one was a tidal wave. It washed over Drake and carried him along without a choice.

First came a different sense of self. Drake Merlin had multiplied, a million, a billion, countless trillions of times. He was on every planet, in orbit around every star, present in every galaxy (even the lost Skrilant Galaxy had its corps of Merlin mentalities). The distinction between organic and inorganic forms no longer meant anything. Changes from one to the other took place constantly. Drake felt his other self extending steadily across the whole universe. Even if he and the ship had done nothing but sit and wait after they passed through the caesura, eventually the extended composite would have discovered and recovered his lost individual self.

That individual self was in danger of drowning. He expressed his fear and heard the rest offering reassurance.

You can join us safely. You can never be lost. We are you.

"What are you doing?"

What we should have done long ago, and what we now must do. We are concerned not with individuals, but with universes. Remember this.

The trillions of voices became one:

In a closed universe, a final point of collapse lies at the end of time. The eschaton, the Omega Point, the c-point—the space-time final boundary has been given a variety of names. Its main properties have long been defined. One of those properties is of paramount importance: close to the c-boundary, all information—everything that ever can be known—becomes accessible. Everything that ever can be known, and everything that has ever been known.

And the implications . . .

We went astray, but now our task is clear. We must survive. We must gather, absorb, and organize information as fast as possible. Near to the end, that accumulation will, we hope, become sufficient. Ana, our true Ana, will by our efforts be restored to us. Thanks to you, we have again become aware of what must be done. Will you become one with us and join our efforts?

Drake knew that the goal was infinitely desirable. It was possible in principle. But was it possible in practice?

The mentality that Drake Merlin had become sprawled across the universe. It had near-infinite resources of data and processing. But it was far from omniscient. How much information was enough? Had the effort started too late?

Drake could not answer those questions. Perhaps there would never be enough information. However, he knew one thing: if the effort failed, it must not be because of the lack of even a single component or individual.

That made the decision easy. Decisions were always easy when you had no choice.

Drake sighed, and nodded. "Merge me in. Join me to all the rest of you. I'm ready to go to work."

Chapter 30

Love and Eternity

All the imagined analogies were wrong. When Drake agreed to merge with the universal Drake Merlin composite, he had seen himself as a tiny ant in a cosmic anthill, his every action subordinate to the common need.

It was not that way at all. He *was* the composite, the whole thing. And it was he. There was no sense of loss, but of enormous gain. He walked a carpet of tiny pink-petaled flowers on the surface of Eden, a garden world in a galaxy so far from Earth that it had never been named or even observed in Earth's lifetime. At the same time he maintained perpetual watch around the dead, deadly, and insane galaxies—Skrilant was not the only one. Sometimes he saw life there, indomitable as ever even in an aging universe, creeping back to blistered dead hills or ravaged ocean beds.

That was rewarding. Some things were not. Some things were close to intolerable. On a world of a remote globular cluster, he saw a species far more intelligent than humans rise to artistic triumph and technological power in just two centuries. He was present when the Lakons announced that rather than joining the combined human mentality, which had been offered to them, they would for reasons beyond human understanding choose self-immolation. He looked on helplessly as Lakon adults and children walked into the sacrificial flames. The babies, left behind, died of starvation.

He could have interfered—and done what? A being can more easily be killed than made to live. But he knew he would carry the memory with him to the end of time.

The universe did not care. That was the important point. *Humans* cared, but the universe was indifferent. He was present, ten billion light-years away from the Lakons, when two galaxies collided and hard radiation wiped out a thousand potential intelligences. He watched a black hole, invisibly small to human eyes but massing as much as one of Earth's great mountains, run through its last second of evaporation. An observing party, too curious and too close, died with it. After the final burst of elementary particles and hard X rays, nothing remained. That seemed symbolic. It suggested to Drake the nihilistic end of the cosmos itself.

Present conditions offered few clues as to that violent end. The universe seemed peaceful, moving toward a quietus that, if it came at all, suggested not a bang but a whimper. The blue shift was more pronounced, but still it seemed innocuous. Not observation but physics and abstract mathematics promised the final fiery doom, certain and implacable and unavoidable.

Drake forced himself away from introspection. There was a job to be done. He must collect, store, and organize information. He must remain intact and integrated and keep in touch with all of his myriad components. Computation power grew linearly with the number of units; coordination problems grew exponentially.

As time went on communication itself became easier. He soon realized why: The universe was shrinking. Contact between far-separated elements was easier. Increased problems of coordination more than cancelled that gain. He found himself scrambling, working nonstop and harder than ever to hold a single focus and a single goal.

Collect, collate, compare. He slaved on, sometimes wondering if there would ever be a recognizable end point to his labors. Would he still be serving as data clerk to the universe, when everything melted and fused into the infernal fireball?

The end crowns all, and that old common arbitrator, Time, will one day end it.

Collect, collate, compare. Drake worked on. The sky became brighter. The more distant galaxies glowed bluer. Constantly, he was forced to create more copies of himself to deal with the increased volumes of data. The number of his components grew, and grew again: trillions, quadrillions, quintillions. How many? He no longer attempted to track the total. Contact with some elements of himself, riding in as S-waves from far across the sweep of galaxies, were pure conundrums. They were indisputably Drake. Yet these components of his own self felt more alien than any strangeness of the Shiva or the Snarks. The effort of assimilating all his divergent personalities became ever greater.

As the universe comes close to its ultimate convergence, the density of mass-energy will increase and so will the temperature. At the end comes a singularity of infinite heat and pressure.

Words, theories, that was all they were. They had no basis in reality. *This* was reality, the toil of information collection without an end.

Except that finally, after a span so great that it was easy to believe that it could never happen, an end seemed in sight. The long downward curve steepened. The cosmos was shrinking faster—noticeably faster. Work for Drake became a frenzy, a blur of action. Energy densities were running higher. Information transfer was faster, over diminishing distances. Processes could proceed more rapidly.

And then more rapidly yet.

The microwave radiation was microwave frequencies no longer. It had shortened to visible wavelengths. The space between the stars crackled with energy.

Stand still, you ever moving spheres of heaven, that time may cease and midnight never come.

But midnight was approaching. Time moved on. The sky was falling, imploding toward its final singularity, and the firmament had become a continuous actinic glare when Drake became aware of a new presence, a different voice speaking from among his endless sea of selves.

It emerged from the white noise that formed the edge of Drake's consciousness and steadily approached his central coordinating nexus. He did not know where it had come from, but as it neared it seemed to touch and merge with every one of his components. It interrupted the rhythm of his frantic work, and as such it was dangerous. Somehow he must stop its action.

He reached out toward it. Even before full contact was established, there was a curious exchange of energies like a fleeting touch of fingertips. It destroyed his processing powers. All his work froze, and in the same moment he sensed who it might be.

A mixture of emotions—hope, joy, fear, longing, love—spread through his extended self and thrilled him with wild surmise.

"Ana?"

"Who else?"

"But where did you come from? Can you be real? I mean, to just appear . . ."

"We've really got to stop meeting like this, eh? I certainly *think* I'm real." The cosmos filled with quiet laughter. "I think therefore I am. I think I'm me, Drake, I really do. But you know the theory as well as I do; as the universe converges toward the eschaton, there's no limit to what you can know about anything. We're getting close to the end now. So it's not beyond question that I am your simulation, a construct of your mind. *You* think, therefore *I* am."

"You are not a simulation." Drake hated the suggestion that Ana might not be real, even though it had come from him. "You can't be. Don't you think I would know if I was creating a simulation?"

"You might. But maybe you have powers that you don't know about. Mm. That doesn't sound consistent with being omniscient, does it? Let's put it another way, with a question: Is self-deception possible, even for an omniscient being?"

"I don't know." The gentle touch had come again, closer and more intimate. "All I can say is it doesn't *matter*. When you are with me, nothing else is important. It never was, and it isn't now."

"All right, let's avoid an argument by agreeing that I'm here and I'm real. So before I do anything else, let me say thank you. Now I have another question. How much time do we have?"

She had always been the practical one, the clear-eyed realist, raising issues that Drake was happy to push under the rug. And as usual she was asking the right question.

Drake looked beyond himself, to the universe that he had been ignoring. It roared and blazed with energy. The cosmic background had become as bright as the stars around which most of the composites clustered. And still the pace of collapse was accelerating, rushing giddily on to the final singularity.

"We have a few more years of proper time, at most, before the final singularity." He found it impossible to worry. Ana was with him, never again would she leave him.

"Is that all?" The visual construct that she had chosen was her old self, and she was frowning. "Just a few years? I mean, it's more than I ever expected, but it's not much of a return on investment for *you*. Think of all your efforts!"

"I had it easy. It's enough. We'll stretch it subjectively. We can run multispeed in electronic mode and make it seem as long as we want."

"But it won't be *real*. I still don't like it." She was inside his mind, gently feeling her way around. It was the delicious touch of knowing fingers, exploring his most private regions. "A few years isn't nearly enough time. We need to get to know each other all over again. I know what I've been doing—nothing—but I want to hear all your adventures. And don't pretend you haven't had any. I know about the flight to Canopus, and Melissa, and the Shiva. I even know about the other Ana. But I want to hear it all from you directly. And you're telling me we won't have time. Don't you think you ought to *do* something about that?"

"Ana, you're talking about the end of the universe." Drake laughed, delirious with happiness. He could feel music swelling inside him, for the first time in aeons. "It's the end of everything. The Omega Point. Finis. There's no *da capo* marked in this score. That's all there is."

"I remember a different Drake. It was you, wasn't it, who once had a quite different opinion?"

Drake knew it was no question. She was teasing him. Ana was well aware who had thought what. And she must have been happily plundering his data banks of memories for longer than he had been aware of her presence, because he had never spoken aloud the words that she said next. " 'Science has come so far. Surely no one believes that it can go no further.' Remember thinking that?"

"That was when there was time, what seemed like an infinite amount of it. Now there's no time. Not for new science, not for anything but us."

"Once you knew next to nothing, Drake, and you were able to work a miracle. Now that you have all the information in the cosmos available to you, who knows what you'll be able to do. The universe is ending because it's closed, right? It doesn't care—but we do. So *open it*. The knowledge you need already exists. We just have to look."

Ana picked him up and carried him with her. He found himself cascading through space in all directions at once, while ghostly data banks swirled to him and through him, an accumulation of knowledge unimaginable at any earlier epoch. He recognized within them a million bare possibilities; but they were no more than that.

"We can't avoid the eschaton, Ana. It's there. It's a feature of our universe, a global reality."

"I thought the eschaton only existed in a closed universe."

"It does. If the mass-energy density had been below the critical value, this universe would be open. But the density is too big."

"So. Reduce it."

"That's impossible." Except that before the thought was complete, Drake had seen a way to do it. The caesuras, created so long ago in the struggle to contain the Shiva, sat as scattered and forgotten relics across space-time. They could still be used to receive any amount of mass and energy.

She was inside his mind, and she had caught the idea as it came into being. "Well, Drake. What are you waiting for?"

He could not reply. He was engaged on a dizzying involution of calculation, every one of his selves operating at its limit. The answer, when he had it, was not one that he wanted her to hear.

"It's still no, Ana. We can dump enough mass-energy into the caesuras to form an open universe. A tiny fraction would reemerge into this universe, although not enough to make a difference. But we would have to go far beyond that to do any good. We need enough structural bounce-back to avoid a final singularity here."

"So that's what we do. You say the caesuras can handle any amount of energy and mass."

"They can." The irony of the situation was revealing itself to Drake. "But there's one insoluble problem. Information is equivalent to energy. And I—with all my selves and all my extensions and all my composites—represent enough energy equivalence to make the bounce-back impossible. It's the ultimate catch: Any universe that I am in must be closed."

"You mean with the physical laws that apply in *this* universe. What about other universes, the ones that form the end point for caesura transfer? Look at those, Drake."

He was already looking. There was speculation in the data banks but no solid information.

"Ana, it's still no. Even if we had all the information possible in this universe, it would not be enough to tell us what lies in other universes. There's no way to find out."

"Not true. There's one very good way. We go and see. Come on."

Suddenly they were hurtling through space, faster and faster. Dangerously fast. Relativistically fast. At this speed, a few subjective minutes would bring them months closer to the eschaton. The little time they had together was melting away. Drake coordinated his countless selves. All would have to fly, exactly in unison, into the myriad caesuras that gaped black against the flaming cosmic background.

At the edge of the caesura horizon, he slowed and hesitated. Mass and energy was swirling past them into the infinite maws, draining from the universe. But as long as he remained there, the final singularity could not be avoided.

"Second thoughts?" Ana was tugging at him, urging him on toward blackness. "Bit late for those."

"Not second thoughts. I was thinking, it would be just our luck to emerge into some place where the laws of physics are too different to permit life. Or some of us might find ourselves right back here."

"What's so bad about that? If we do come back here, won't it be to an open universe? You worry too much." She was bubbling within his mind, an effervescence that he could never resist. " 'Life is a glorious adventure, or it is nothing.' You were the one who first quoted that to me. Have you changed so much?"

"I don't know. I can't bear to lose you again."

"You won't lose me." She was reaching out, enfolding him, confident as he was nervous. "This universe or another one, wherever we go, we go together. You'll have me for as long as there is time. Come on, Drake. You always said you wanted to live dangerously, now's your chance."

They were on the brink of the spiraling funnel of oil and ink, close to the point of no return. Ana was laughing again, like a child at the fair. "Here we go," she said, "into the Tunnel of Love. And don't forget now, make a wish."

"I already did." It was too late to turn back. Ahead lay total, final darkness. Behind them he imagined the radiance dimming, easing with their departure away from the hellfire of ultimate convergence. The universe they were leaving would become open, facing an infinite future. Not bad, for a man and woman who only wanted each other and had no desire to change anything. "I wished that—"

"Don't tell me, love—or it won't come true!"

"Won't matter if I do tell." They were passing through, heading for the unknown, the last question, birth canal or final extinction. Was it imagination, or did the faintest glimmer of light shine in the vortex ahead?

Drake reached out to embrace Ana, squeezing her as hard as she was holding him. "Won't matter if I do, love. Because it already has."

Appendix

Science and Science Fiction

$\mathcal{A}$ story that takes as its domain the rest of time must be fiction. However, many parts of the cosmological backdrop of this novel are not fiction at all but current theory.

This appendix sets forth the ideas on the structure and long-term future of the universe that play a part in this novel. Such a discussion turns out to require an analysis of the universe's past. What will be given here is a "conventional" treatment, in that it presumes the validity of most of modern physics, especially the notion of the Big Bang and the theory of general relativity. It also assumes that the basic physical laws of the universe, governing events on the smallest scale (atoms and subatomic particles) and the largest scale (stars, galaxies, and clusters of galaxies) have not changed since its earliest days and will not change in the far future.

Stars. Humans were surely studying stars long before recorded history. Mankind must have looked up and wondered about those points of light in the sky for tens, and probably for hundreds of thousands of years. However, until four hundred years ago no one had any idea of the sizes, distances, and composition of planets and stars.

The modern view, that stars are giant globes of hot gas, developed after 1609, when Galileo turned his homemade telescope upward. He found that the Sun was not the perfect, unmarked sphere that traditional teaching required, but a rotating object with lots of surface detail, like sunspots and solar flares.

Over the next couple of hundred years, the size and the temperature of the sun were measured. It is a ball of hot gas about a million miles across, with a surface at six thousand degrees Celsius. What was not understood at all, even a hundred years ago, was the way that the sun *stays* hot.

Before 1800, that was not a worry. The universe was believed to be only a few thousand years old. Archbishop Ussher of Armagh, working backward through the genealogy of the Bible, had announced in 1654 that the exact date of the Creation was 4004 B.C. Through the eighteenth century, that scriptural timescale prevented anyone worrying much about the age of the Sun. If it started out very hot in 4000 B.C., it probably hadn't had time to cool down yet. If it were made entirely of burning coal, it would have lasted more than long enough.

Around 1800, the geologists started to complicate matters. In 1785, James Hutton had read his *Theory of the Earth* to the Royal Society of Edinburgh, advancing the idea of uniformitarianism in geology. He published it in the *Proceedings* of the society three years later. It did not make great waves, but after Hutton's death, John Playfair in 1802 published a shorter and more accessible version.

Uniformitarianism, in spite of its ugly name, is a beautiful and simple idea. According to Hutton and

Playfair, *the processes that built the world in the past are exactly those at work today:* the uplift of mountains, the tides, the weathering effects of rain and air and water flow, these shape the surface of the Earth. This is in sharp distinction to the idea that the world was created just as it is now, except for occasional great catastrophic changes like the biblical Flood.

The great virtue of Hutton's theory is that it removes the need for assumptions. The effectiveness of anything that shaped the past can be measured by looking at its effectiveness today.

The great *disadvantage* of the theory, from the point of view of anyone pondering what keeps the Sun hot, is the amount of time it takes for all this to happen. It is no longer plausible to say that the universe is a few thousand years old. In so short a time, mountain ranges could not form, seabeds could not be raised, chalk deposits could not be laid down, and solid rocks could not erode to form soil. Hutton and Playfair, and later Charles Lyell, who developed and promoted the same ideas, needed many millions of years for natural forces to work. It is clearly preposterous to imagine a sun orders of magnitude *younger* than the Earth that orbits around it.

A sun made of burning coal would not do. Hermann von Helmholtz and Lord Kelvin independently proposed a solution that could give geology more time. They suggested that the source of the Sun's heat was not burning but gravitational contraction. If the material of the Sun were slowly falling inward on itself, that would release energy. The amount of energy produced by the Sun's contraction could be precisely calculated. Unfortunately it was not enough. While Lord Kelvin was proposing an age for the Sun of 20 million years, or at the very most 100 million, the geologists, and still more so the biologists, were asking for a much older age. Charles Darwin's *Origin of Species* came out in 1859, and evolution to do its work needed hundreds of millions of years at a minimum, and preferably a few billion.

No one could offer that much time during the whole of the nineteenth century. A scientific revolution was needed before a multibillion-year age became plausible for the Sun and thus for the Earth.

The revolution began in the 1890s, when in quick succession Röntgen discovered X rays (1895), Becquerel discovered radioactivity (1896), and J. J. Thomson discovered the electron (1897). Together, these discoveries implied that the atom, previously thought to be an indivisible particle, had an interior structure. It could be broken into smaller pieces.

The next thirty years showed that atoms could be split to form smaller atoms and subatomic particles, and light atoms could combine to form heavier atoms. In particular, four atoms of hydrogen could fuse together to form one atom of helium; and if that happened, large amounts of energy could be produced.

Perhaps the first person to realize that nuclear fusion was the key to the sun's longevity was Arthur Eddington. Astronomy, mathematics, and physics formed Eddington's life, and he was a superb theoretician. But even he could not say what processes were at work to fuse one element to another. That insight came ten years later, with the work of Hans Bethe and Carl von Weizsäcker, who in 1938 discovered the "carbon cycle" for nuclear fusion.

However, Eddington didn't have to know *how*. He could calculate the amount of energy released when four hydrogen nuclei changed to one helium nucleus. All he required was the mass of hydrogen, the mass of helium, and Einstein's most famous formula, $E = mc^2$.

From that, Eddington worked out how much hydrogen must be converted to helium to provide the Sun's known energy output. The answer is about 600 million tons per second.

That sounds like a huge amount, but the total mass

of the Sun is about 2×10^{27} tons. The conversion of 600 million tons to energy each second for one billion years would amount to only 1 percent of the Sun's mass. The Sun is about 65 percent hydrogen. To keep the Sun shining as brightly as it shines today for five billion years[1] requires only that during that period, less than 8 percent of the Sun's hydrogen be converted to helium.

The period of five billion years was not chosen at random. Other evidence suggests an age for the Earth of about 4.5 billion years. Nuclear fusion is all we need in the Sun to provide the right time scale for geology and biology on Earth. More than that, the Sun can go on shining just as brightly for at least another five billion years, without significantly depleting its source of energy.

It is appropriate to ask if the Sun is typical. It certainly occupies a unique place in our lives, but is it unusual or unique in the universe? The astronomical evidence suggests that the Sun is a rather normal star. There are stars scores of times as massive, and stars tens of times as small. The upper limit is set by stability, because a contracting ball of gas of more than about 90 solar masses will oscillate more and more wildly, until parts of it are blown off into space. The lower limit is set by the ability to initiate fusion reactions. Below a certain size, about one-twelfth of the Sun's mass, a star-like object cannot generate enough internal pressure to initiate fusion and should not be called a star at all.

The Sun sits comfortably in the middle range, designated by astronomers as a G2 type dwarf star. It lies in what is known as the main sequence, so named because most of the stars that we see can be fitted into that sequence.

---

[1] The Sun has actually been getting brighter. Over the past 3.5 billion years it is estimated to have increased in energy production by 30 percent.

The life history of a star depends more than anything else on its mass. That story also started with Eddington, who in 1924 discovered the mass-luminosity law. The more massive a star, the more brightly it shines.[2] This law does not merely restate the obvious, that more massive stars are bigger and so radiate more because they are of larger area. If that were true, since the mass of a star grows with the cube of its radius and its surface area with the square of its radius, we might expect the brightness to vary like the mass to the two-thirds power. (Multiply the mass by eight, and expect the brightness to increase by a factor of four.) In fact, the brightness goes up rather faster than the *cube* of the mass. (Multiply the mass by eight, and the brightness increases by a factor of more than a *thousand*.)

The implications of this for the evolution of a star are profound. Dwarf stars can go on steadily burning for a hundred billion years. Massive stars squander their energy at a huge rate, running out of available materials for fusion in just millions of years.

We can model mathematically the evolution of our own sun. In the near term (meaning in this case the next few billion years) the results are unspectacular. The Sun is a remarkably stable object. It will simply go on shining, becoming slowly brighter. Five billion years from now it will be twice its present diameter of a million miles, and twice as bright. Eventually, however, it will begin to deplete its stock of hydrogen. At that point it will not shrink, as one might expect, but begin to balloon larger and larger. Eight billion years in the future, the sun will be two thousand times as bright, and

---

[2] *Shines,* rather than appears to shine, because the brightness of the stars we see depends on how far away they are. The *absolute magnitude* of a star refers to its brightness as it would appear from a standard distance. The mass-luminosity law works in terms of the absolute magnitude.

it will have grown so big (diameter, 100 million miles) that its sphere will fill half our sky. The oceans of Earth will long since have evaporated, and the land surface that is left will be hot enough to melt lead.

In studying the long-term future of the Sun, we have as an incidental dealt with the future of the Earth. It will be incinerated by the bloated Sun, which by that time will be a type of star known as a red giant. The Sun, as its energy resources steadily diminish even further, will eventually blow off its outer layers of gas and shrink to end its life, ten billion years from now, as a dense white dwarf star not much bigger than today's Earth.

The Sun, as a midsized star, has a long projected lifetime. Massive stars when their central regions no longer have hydrogen to convert to helium have a more violent, and in many ways a more interesting, future. Detailed models, beginning with Fred Hoyle and William Fowler's work on stellar nucleosynthesis in the 1940s, allow the future course of such stars to be calculated.

Like a compulsive gambler running out of chips, massive stars coming to the end of their supply of hydrogen seek other energy sources. At first they find it through other nuclear fusion processes. Helium in the central core "burns" to form carbon, carbon burns to make oxygen and neon and magnesium. These processes call for higher and higher temperatures before they are significant. Carbon burning starts about 600 million degrees Celsius. Neon burning begins at about one billion degrees. Such a temperature is available only in the cores of massive stars, so for a star less than nine solar masses, that is the end of the road. Many such stars settle down to old age as cooling lumps of dense matter. Stars above nine solar masses can keep going, burning neon and then oxygen. Finally, above three billion degrees, silicon, which is produced in a process involving collisions of oxygen nuclei, begins to burn, and all the elements are produced up to and including iron. By the time that we reach iron, the different elements form spherical shells about the star's center, with the heaviest (iron) in the middle, surrounded by shells of successively lighter elements until we get to a hydrogen shell on the outside.

Now we come to a fact of great significance. *No elements heavier than iron can be produced through this nuclear synthesis process in stars.* Iron, element 26, is the place on the table of elements where nuclear binding energy is maximum. If you try to "burn" iron, fusing it to make heavier elements, you *use* energy, rather than produce it. Notice that this has nothing to do with the mass of the star. It is decided only by nuclear forces.

The massive star that began as mainly hydrogen has reached the end of the road. The final processes have proceeded faster and faster, and they are much less efficient at producing energy than the hydrogen-to-helium reaction. Hydrogen burning takes millions of years for a star of, say, a dozen solar masses. But carbon burning is all finished in a few thousand years, and the final stage of silicon burning lasts only a day or so.

There are obvious next questions: What happens to the star? Does it sink into quiet old age, like most small stars? Or does it follow some new path?

We have one other question to ask. We can explain through stellar nucleosynthesis the creation of every element lighter than iron. But more than sixty elements *heavier* than iron are found on Earth. If they cannot be formed by nuclear fusion during a star's normal evolution, where do they come from?

They were not, as you might think, "there from the beginning"; in order to prove that assertion, we need some additional facts. To obtain those facts, it is necessary to discuss another class of celestial objects: galaxies.

Galaxies.   The ancient astronomers, observing without benefit of telescopes, knew and named many of the stars. They also noted the presence of a diffuse glow that extends across a large fraction of the sky, and called it the Milky Way. Finally, those with the most acute vision had noted that the constellation of Andromeda contained within it a small elongated patch of haze.

The progress from observation of the stars to the explanation of the hazy patches in the sky came in stages. Galileo began the process in 1610, when he examined the Milky Way with his telescope and found that he could see huge numbers of stars there, far more than were visible with the unaided eye. He asserted that the Milky Way was nothing more than stars, in vast numbers. William Herschel carried this a stage further, counting the stars he could see in different parts of the Milky Way and building the modern picture of a great flat disk containing billions of separate stars with the Sun in the plane of the disk but well away (about thirty thousand light-years) from the center.

At the same time, the number of tiny diffuse patches visible in the sky went up and up as telescope power increased. Lots of them looked like the patch in Andromeda, which had long been known as the Andromeda Nebula.

A dedicated comet hunter, Charles Messier, annoyed at the constant confusion of hazy patches (uninteresting) with comets (highly desirable), had already plotted out their locations so as not to be bothered by them. This resulted in the *Messier Catalog:* the first and inadvertent catalog of galaxies.

But what were those fuzzy glows identified by Messier?

The suspicion that the Andromeda and other galaxies might be composed of stars, as the Milky Way is made up of stars, was there from Galileo's time. If individual stars cannot be seen in most galaxies, that is only because of their distance. The number of galaxies, though, probably exceeds anything that Galileo would have found credible. Today's estimate is that there are about a hundred billion galaxies in the visible universe —roughly the same as the number of individual stars in a typical galaxy. Galaxies, fainter and fainter as their distances increase, are seen as far as our telescopes can probe.

In most respects, the distant ones look little different from the nearest ones. But there is one crucial difference, and it is the main reason for introducing the galaxies at this point.

Galaxies increase in numbers as they decrease in apparent brightness, and it is natural to assume that these two things go together: If we double the distance of a galaxy, it appears one-quarter as bright, but we expect to see four times as many like it if space is uniformly filled with galaxies.

What we would *not* expect to find, until it was suggested by Carl Wirtz in 1924 and confirmed by Edwin Hubble in 1929, is that more distant galaxies appear *redder* than nearer ones.

To be more specific, particular wavelengths of light emitted by galaxies have been shifted toward longer wavelengths in the fainter (and therefore presumably more distant) galaxies. The question is, what could cause such a shift?

The most plausible mechanism, to a physicist, is the Döppler effect. According to the Döppler effect, light from a receding object will be shifted to longer (redder) wavelengths; light from an approaching object will be shifted to shorter (bluer) wavelengths. Exactly the same thing works for sound, which is why a speeding police car's siren seems to drop in pitch as it passes by.

If we accept the Döppler effect as the cause of the reddened appearance of the galaxies, we are led (as was Hubble) to an immediate conclusion: the whole universe must be expanding. It is probably doing so at a close to constant rate, because the red shift of the galaxies corresponds to their brightness and, therefore, to their distance.

Note that this does *not* mean that the universe is expanding *into* some other space. There is no other space. It is the *whole* universe—everything there is—that has grown over time to its present dimension.

And from this we can draw another conclusion. If that expansion proceeded in the past as it does today, there must have been a time when everything in the whole universe was drawn together to a single point. It is logical to call the time that has elapsed since everything was in that infinitely dense singularity *the age of the universe*. The Hubble galactic redshift allows us to calculate how long ago that happened.

Today's best estimate ranges from 8 to 20 billion years, with most cosmologists favoring values between 12 and 15 billion years.[3]

It is quite remarkable that the observation of the faint agglomerations of stars known as galaxies leads us, very directly and cleanly, to the conclusion that we live in a universe of finite and determinable age. A century ago, no one could have offered even an approximate age for the universe. For an upper bound, most non-religious scientists would probably have said forever. For a lower bound, all they had was the age of the Earth.

Answering one question, How old is the universe, inevitably leads us to another: What was the universe like, ten or twenty billion years ago, when it was compressed into a very small volume?

In particular, can we say if the sixty and more ele-

---

[3] Eight billion years represents a younger age than the oldest stars. This is a nasty problem that cosmologists favoring this age for the universe have yet to solve.

ments heavier than iron that we know today were created in the distant past?

Before addressing these questions, let us return to the question of the fate of fuel-depleted massive stars, poised on the brink of nuclear burnout.

The Early Universe. After Albert Einstein developed his theory of relativity and gravitation, he and others used it in the second decade of this century to provide simplified theoretical models of the whole universe.

Einstein could construct a simple universe, with matter spread through the whole of space. What he could *not* do was make that universe sit still. The equations insisted that the model universe had to either expand or contract.

To make his model stand still, Einstein introduced in 1917 a "cosmological constant" into his own general theory. With that, he thought he could build a stable, static universe. He later described the introduction of the cosmological constant, and his refusal to accept the reality of an expanding or contracting universe, as the biggest blunder of his life.

When Hubble's work showed the universe to be expanding, Einstein at once recognized its implications. However, he did not undertake to move in the other direction and ask about the time when the contracted universe was far more compact than it is today. That was done by a Belgian, Georges Lemaître. Early in the 1930s Lemaître went backward in time, to when the whole universe was a "primeval atom." In this first and single atom, everything was squashed into a sphere only a few times as big as the Sun, with no space between atoms, or even between nuclei. As Lemaître saw it, this unit must then have exploded, fragmenting into the atoms and stars and galaxies and everything else in the universe that we know today. He might justifiably have called it the Big Bang, but he didn't. That name was coined by Hoyle, the same man who did the fundamen-

tal work on nucleosynthesis. The odd thing is that
Hoyle himself does not believe in the reality of the Big
Bang, preferring an alternative theory that argues for a
universe of infinite age.

Lemaître did not consider the composition of his
primeval atom—what it was made of. It might be
thought that the easiest assumption is that everything
in the universe was already there, much as it is now. But
that cannot be true, because as we go back in time, the
universe had to be hotter as well as more dense. Before
a certain point, atoms as we know them could not exist.
They would be torn apart by the intense radiation that
permeated the whole universe.

The person who did worry about the composition of
the primeval atom was George Gamow. In the 1940s, he
conjectured that the original stuff of the universe was
nothing more than densely packed neutrons. Certainly,
it seemed reasonable to suppose that the universe at its
outset had no net charge, since it seems to have no net
charge today. Also, a neutron left to itself has a 50 percent chance of decaying radioactively in about thirteen
minutes, to form an electron and a proton.[4] One electron and one proton form an atom of hydrogen; and
even today, the universe is predominantly atomic hydrogen. So neutrons could account for most, if not all,
of today's universe.

If the early universe was very hot and very dense and
all hydrogen, some of it ought to have fused and be-

---

[4] So after twenty-six minutes, three neutrons out of four will
have decayed; after thirty-nine minutes, seven out of eight,
and so on. You might think that would mean that neutrons
ought to have disappeared early in the history of the universe.
However, that rapid decay only happens to *isolated* neutrons.
Bound inside a nucleus, a neutron is quite stable. Most elements have more neutrons inside the nucleus than they have
protons.

come helium, carbon, and other elements. The question, How much of each? was one that Gamow and his student, Ralph Alpher, set out to answer. They calculated that about a quarter of the matter in the primeval universe should have turned to helium, a figure very consistent with the present composition of the oldest stars.

What Gamow and Alpher could not do, and what no one else could do after them, was make the elements heavier than helium after the Big Bang that began the universe.[5] In fact, Gamow and his colleagues proved that heavier element synthesis did *not* take place then. It could not happen very early, because in the first moments elements would be torn apart by energetic radiation. At later times, the universe expanded and cooled too quickly to yield the needed temperatures.

Heavier element formation has to be done by *stars,* during the process known as stellar nucleosynthesis. The failure of the Big Bang to produce heavier elements confirms something that we already know, namely, that the Sun (and with it the whole Solar System) is much younger than the universe. Sol, at maybe five billion years old, is a second-, third-, or even fourth-generation star. Some of the materials that make up the Sun and Earth derive from older stars that ran far enough through their evolution to produce the elements up to iron, by nuclear fusion. Note, however, that elements heavier than iron cannot be formed during stellar nuclear fusion and remain unaccounted for.

Apart from showing how to calculate the ratio of hydrogen to helium after the Big Bang, Gamow and his colleagues did one other thing whose full significance probably escaped them. In 1948 they produced an

---

[5] This is a little bit of an overstatement. Actually, a smidgen of deuterium and lithium can be produced, too, but not enough to make a difference.

equation that allowed one to compute the *present* background temperature of the universe from its age, assuming a universe that had expanded uniformly since the Big Bang. Perhaps Gamow was skeptical of his own equation, since he never sought experiments to look for the background radiation. That was discovered, with an effective temperature of 2.7 degrees above absolute zero, by Arno Penzias and Robert Wilson in 1964.

Hydrogen fused to helium when the universe was between three and four *minutes* old. Before exploring even earlier times, we will resolve the fate of the massive star, ten or more solar masses, that has run out of fusion fuel and seems to have nowhere to go next.

Stellar Collapse.   Consider a star of ten or more solar masses that is running out of energy. The supply provided by the fusion at its center of silicon into iron is almost done, radiating away rapidly into space. In the middle of the star is a sphere of iron "gas" (technically, a *plasma*) about one and a half times the mass of the sun and at a temperature of a few billion degrees. It *acts* like a gas because all the iron nuclei and the electrons are buzzing around freely. However, the core density is millions of times that of the densest material found on Earth. Outside that central sphere, like layers of an onion, sit shells of silicon, oxygen, and carbon; helium, neon, and hydrogen; and smaller quantities of all the other elements lighter than iron.

When the source of fusion energy is exhausted, iron nuclei capture the free electrons in the iron gas. Protons and electrons combine. The energy that had kept the star inflated is sucked away, and the core collapses to become a ball of neutrons, only a few miles across.

That near-instantaneous gravitational collapse unleashes a huge amount of energy, enough to blow all the outer layers of the star clear away into space. What is left behind is a neutron star: a solid sphere of neutrons.

How much is a "huge" amount of energy? When a star collapses and then blows up like this, in what is known as a supernova, it shines as brightly as a whole galaxy—which is to say, its brightness can temporarily increase by a factor of one hundred billion. If a single candle in Chicago were to "go supernova," you would easily be able to read a newspaper by its light in Washington, D.C.

The explosion of the supernova creates pressures and temperatures big enough to generate all the elements heavier than iron that could *not* be formed by standard nucleosynthesis in stars. So finally, after a long, complex process of stellar evolution, we have found the place where substances as "ordinary" as tin and lead, or as "precious" as silver, gold, and platinum, can be created.

If the nearest stellar system to us, the triple star complex of Alpha Centauri, were to turn into a supernova (it can't—at least according to current theory), the flux of radiation and high-energy particles would probably wipe out life on Earth.

Supernovas are rather like nuclear power stations. What they produce is important to us, but we prefer not to have one in our local neighborhood.

Back to the Beginning. We will now run the clock backward, toward the *real* Big Bang, as opposed to the trifling explosions known as supernovas. The universe in some ways appears more and more interesting, the closer we get to its origin.

When the universe was smaller in size, it was also hotter. In a hot enough environment, atoms as we know them cannot hold together. High-energy radiation rips them apart as fast as they form. A good time to begin our backward running of the clock might then be the period when atoms could form and could persist as stable units. Although stars and galaxies would not yet exist, at least the universe would be made up of familiar components, hydrogen and helium atoms that we would recognize.

Atoms could form, and hold together, somewhere between half a million and a million years after the Big Bang. Before that time, matter and radiation interacted continuously. After it, matter and radiation "decoupled," became near independent, and went their separate ways. The temperature of the universe when this happened was about three thousand degrees. Ever since then, the expansion of the universe has lengthened the wavelength of the background radiation, and thus lowered its temperature. The cosmic background radiation discovered by Penzias and Wilson is nothing more than the radiation at the time when it decoupled from matter, now grown old.

Continuing backward: Even before atoms could form, helium and hydrogen nuclei and free electrons could be created; but they could not remain in combination, because radiation broke them apart. The form of the universe was controlled by radiation energetic enough to prevent the formation of atoms. This situation held from about three minutes to one million years A.C. (After Creation).

If we go back to a period less than three minutes A.C., radiation was even more dominant. It prevented the buildup even of helium nuclei. As noted earlier, the fusion of hydrogen to helium requires hot temperatures, such as we find in the center of stars. But fusion cannot take place if it is *too* hot, as it was before three minutes after the Big Bang. Before helium could form, the universe had to "cool" to about a billion degrees. All that existed before then were electrons (and their positively charged forms, positrons), neutrons, protons, neutrinos (a massless, chargeless particle), and radiation.

Until three minutes A.C., it might seem as though

radiation controlled events. But this is not the case. As we proceed further backward and the temperature of the primordial fireball continues to increase, we reach a point where the temperature is so high (above ten billion degrees) that large numbers of electron-positron pairs can be created from pure radiation. That happened from one second up to fourteen seconds A.C. After that, the number of electron-positron pairs decreased rapidly. Fewer were being generated than were annihilating themselves and returning to pure radiation. After the universe cooled to ten billion degrees, neutrinos also decoupled from other forms of matter.

Still we have a long way to go, physically speaking, to the moment of creation. As we continue backward, temperatures rise and rise. At a tenth of a second A.C., the temperature of the universe is thirty billion degrees. The universe is a soup of electrons, protons, neutrons, neutrinos, and radiation. As the kinetic energy of particle motion becomes greater and greater, effects caused by differences of particle mass are less important. At thirty billion degrees, an electron easily carries enough energy to convert a proton into the slightly heavier neutron. Thus in this period, free neutrons are constantly trying to decay to form protons and electrons; but energetic proton-electron collisions kept right on remaking neutrons.

We will keep the clock running. Now the important time intervals become shorter and shorter. At 0.0001 of a second A.C., the temperature is 1,000 billion degrees. The universe is so small that the density of matter, everywhere, is as great as that in the nucleus of an atom today (about 100 million tons per cubic centimeter—a fair-sized asteroid, at this density, would squeeze down to fit in a matchbox). Modern theory says that the nucleus is best regarded not as protons and neutrons but as quarks, elementary particles from which the neutrons and protons themselves are made. Thus at this early time, 0.0001 second A.C., the universe was a sea of quarks, electrons, neutrinos, and energetic radiation.

We can go further, at least in theory, to the time, 10^{-35} second A.C., when the universe went through a superrapid "inflationary" phase, growing from the size of a proton to the size of a basketball in about 5×10^{-32} seconds.[6] We can even go back to a time, 10^{-43} second A.C. (called the Planck time), when according to supersymmetry theories, the force of gravity decoupled from everything else and remains decoupled to this day.

We are far beyond the realm in which the physical laws that we accept—and can test—today can be expected to apply. It is reasonable to ask, Does the early history of the universe make any difference to *anything* today?

Oddly enough, it does. That early history of the universe is crucial in deciding the whole structure of today's universe and its long-term future.

The times mentioned above are summarized in table 1. Note that all these times are measured from the moment of the Big Bang, so $t = 0$ is the instant that the universe came into being.

Table 1 displays one inconvenient feature. Everything seems to be crowded together near the beginning, and major events become further and further apart in time as we come closer to the present. This is even more apparent when we note that the origin of the solar system, while important to us, has no cosmic significance.

Let us seek a change of time scale that will make important events more evenly spaced on the time line. We make a change of the time coordinate, defining a

---

[6] "Superrapid" is an appropriate description. During the inflation period the universe was expanding in size millions of times faster than the speed of light. This does not violate the theory of relativity, since no signal is being propagated.

new time, T, by $T = \log(t/t_N)$, where t_N is chosen as 15 billion years, the assumed current age of the universe.

That produces table 2. All the entries in it are negative, since we have been dealing so far only with past times. Also, the entries for important events, in cosmological terms, are much more evenly spaced in T-time.

We will return to table 2 later. Note, however, that we cannot get all the way to the Big Bang in T-time, since that would correspond to a T value of minus infinity. However, a failure to reach infinite pressure and temperature is no bad thing. In T-time, the Big Bang happened infinitely long ago.

The time transformation that we made to T-time has no physical motivation. It gives us a convenient time scale for spacing past events, in terms of a familiar function,[7] but there is no reason to think it will be equally convenient in describing the future.

A value of $T = +60.7$, which is as far ahead of the present on the T-time scale as the Planck time is behind us, corresponds to a time of 7.5×10^{70} years from now.

Does the long-term future of the universe admit such a time? We will see.

Origins.   We have discussed the present state of the universe. We have discussed the early state of the universe. Before we discuss the long-term future of the universe, we ask the most basic question of all: Where did the universe come from?

---

[7] Writing these words leads to a slightly depressing thought. Maybe the logarithm is no longer a familiar function. Fifty years ago, every worker in the physical, biological, or social sciences worked with logarithms daily. They had to, or face multitudes of tedious long multiplications. The hand-held calculator has made logarithm tables a thing of the past. Today's necessary tool is a knowledge of computer programming. What will replace that, fifty years from now?

The answer, until twenty years ago, was probably, Nobody can say. The most popular modern answer, perhaps not much more satisfying, is, even it came from nothing.

That statement is explained by an idea from quantum theory. One of the best-established concepts of that subject, and one of the most famous, is the Heisenberg Uncertainty Principle. In its most familiar form, this states that one cannot know both the precise *position* and the *velocity* of a particle simultaneously. A more general formulation is that one cannot specify the values simultaneously of any pair of "conjugate variables," such as position and momentum; or, to pick the pair that we want, of energy and time.

This means that there can be a large uncertainty or fluctuation in energy, provided only that the *duration* of the uncertainty is short enough. Conversely, if the energy fluctuation has zero *net* energy, then it can be around for an indefinitely long time.

The first person to suggest in print that the whole universe might be nothing more than an energy fluctuation with zero net value was Edward Tryon, in a paper published in 1973. At the time, his suggestion was apparently ignored.

It certainly sounds ridiculous on first hearing. We sit in a universe that fizzles with energy, everything from gigantic stellar furnaces, like our own Sun, pumping innumerable gigawatts into space every second, to supernovas, briefly shining a hundred billion times as bright. How can anyone propose that the universe has zero net energy?

To see that, we have to go back to Lord Kelvin, and his suggestion that the Sun shone because of its own contraction. If solar contraction releases energy, then moving the atoms that compose the Sun farther and farther apart must *require* energy.

How much energy would it take to move the atoms of the Sun from very close together to indefinitely far apart? The answer to that is a curious one: the total energy needed is exactly the amount that would be produced were the Sun's mass totally converted to energy. In the language of the physicist, the rest mass energy of the Sun is equal and opposite to its gravitational potential energy.

Exactly the same argument can be applied to the whole universe, to show that the total material energy (matter plus radiation) is equal and opposite to the total gravitational potential energy. The net energy is thus exactly zero. And a fluctuation of zero energy, according to the Heisenberg Uncertainty Principle, can sustain itself for an indefinitely long time.

The universe may have been created out of nothing, by a zero energy fluctuation. And one day it may simply disappear, when the vacuum fluctuation that created it pops out of existence.

Future Options for the Universe. The standard model of the cosmos begins, as already mentioned, with a vast explosion. The whole of the universe—space-time itself —then began a great expansion that continues to this day. The speed of recession of any pair of galaxies is proportional to their separation from each other. The expansion of the universe is continuously being slowed by the mutual gravitational attraction of everything, mass and energy, in it. It is like a shell fired upward from a gun on the Earth's surface. Depending on the speed of the shell, there are two likely outcomes. If the shell is traveling too slowly, Earth's gravity pulls it until it stops rising and begins to fall. If the shell is traveling fast enough, it will escape from Earth completely and head to infinity. There is also a third, and unlikely, possibility: that the shell's speed is just on the dividing line between escape and return.

The central question of cosmology today can be simply stated: Will today's expansion of the universe continue indefinitely, or will it one day slow, and then reverse itself?

The first possibility leads to what is known as an "open" universe, ever bigger with time and with an infinite future. The second leads to a "closed" universe, which will end after finite future time with a collapse of everything back into a superheated, superdense fireball just like the one in which the universe started.

Infinite, open universe, or Big Crunch?

Actually, for theoretical reasons the preference of many astronomers is for something that sits exactly on the fence between those two situations. This third possibility is usually termed a flat universe, or more accurately, an asymptotically flat universe. Such a universe continues to expand, but it does so more and more slowly, balanced on a knife edge between continued expansion and eventual collapse.

It might be thought that the far future character of the universe is something that is completely unknowable within today's science. Actually, the overall nature of the universe—open, closed, or flat—is decided by the value of a single number, which in principle we can measure today. That number is the average density of matter in the universe; or, since matter and energy were shown by Einstein to be interchangeable, the average combined mass and energy density of the universe.

Clearly, we have problems making direct measurements of the amount of matter in distant galaxies; but we can make local estimates, and use those to extrapolate. The situation is made more complicated because there seems to be a considerable amount of "dark matter," too cold to reveal its presence to us by its emitted energy, and too diffuse to see directly by reflected energy. The principal evidence of its existence is in the way that it affects the general rotation of the galaxies.

Measuring what we can measure, and making other inferences as to the nature and amount of dark matter, the answer seems quite definite: There is not enough matter in the universe to close it. The value is too small by at least a factor of ten. The expansion must continue forever. We live in an open universe.

This is not the answer that many cosmologists want to hear. The problem comes because one popular cosmological model tells us that if the density today is as much as one-tenth of what is needed to close the universe, then in the past it must have been far closer to unity. For example, at one second A.C., the density would have had to be within one part in a million billion of unity, in order for it to be 0.1 today. It would be an amazing coincidence if, by accident, the actual density were so close to the critical density.

The amount of matter needed to stop the expansion is not large, by terrestrial standards. It calls for only three hydrogen atoms per cubic meter.

This raises a question: If there is missing matter, what is it?

We will not go into that subject, beyond commenting that there are two suggested types of matter that might offer enough mass to close the universe. They are usually termed "hot dark matter," which consists of large numbers of neutrinos with a small rest mass; and "cold dark matter," consisting of exotic (and still undiscovered) particles known as axions, gravitinos, and photinos. Neither cold dark matter nor hot dark matter seems to provide a universe with just the right evolution and properties. Almost certainly, something is wrong with the theory.

Most cosmologists say that, today's observations notwithstanding, the density of the universe will prove to be exactly equal to the critical value. In this case, the universe will expand forever, but more and more slowly. This "unlikely" case of exact balance between too much mass-energy and too little mass-energy—the shell with exactly the right speed to just escape from Earth—is the one preferred by theorists. However, the question is far from settled. The universe is open, closed, or flat. No one knows which. Take your pick. Choose your universe.

Here are three alternatives:

The Big Crunch.

We begin with the case of the closed universe, since this is the one in which Ana and Drake Merlin live and ultimately change to open form.

The Big Crunch could happen as "soon" as 50 billion years from now, depending on how much the average mass-energy of the universe exceeds the critical amount. We know from observation that the mass-energy density is not more than twice the critical density. In that limiting case we will see about 17.5 billion more years of expansion, followed by 32.5 billion years of collapse. A smaller mass-energy density implies a longer future.

Not surprisingly, T-time is inappropriate to describe this future. The logarithm function has a singularity at $t = 0$, but nowhere else. An appropriate time for the closed universe contains not one singularity ($T = -\infty$, the Big Bang), but two ($T = -\infty$, the Big Bang, and $T = +\infty$, the Big Crunch). As the universe approaches its end, the events that followed the Big Bang must appear in inverse order. There will come a time when atoms must disappear, when helium splits back to hydrogen, when electron/positron pairs appear, and so on.

A reasonable time transformation for the closed universe is:

$$T_c = \log(t/(C - t))$$

where C is the time, measured from the Big Bang, of the Big Crunch.

Table 3 shows how this transformation handles significant times of the past and future. In this case, we have chosen $T_c = 0$ as the midpoint in the evolution of the universe, equally far from its beginning and its end. For past times, the values are very similar to those obtained with T-time. For future times close to the Big Crunch, T-time and T_c-time are radically different. As the universe is collapsing to its final singularity, T_c-time is rushing on to infinity, but the hands of the T-time clock would be hardly moving.

T_c is a plausible time to describe the evolution of a closed universe. When t tends to zero, T_c tends to minus infinity, and when t tends to C, T_c tends to plus infinity. Thus both end points of the universe are inaccessible in T_c-time. The transformation is symmetric about the "midpoint" of the universe, $t = C/2$. This does not mean, as is sometimes said, that time will "run backward" as the universe collapses. Time continues to run forward in either t-time or T_c-time, from the beginning of the universe to its end. Note also that T_c has no real values, and hence no meaning, for times before the Big Bang or after the Big Crunch.

Since the collapse applies to the whole universe, there is no escape—unless one can find a way to leave this universe completely.

Expansion forever.

Suppose that the universe is open rather than closed. Then it will expand forever.

Freeman Dyson analyzed this situation in 1979.[8] First, all ordinary stellar activity, even of the latest-formed and smallest suns, will end. That will be somewhat less than a million billion (say, 10^{14}) years in the future. After that it is quiet for a while, because everything will be tied up in stellar leftovers, neutron stars and black holes and cold dwarf stars.

---

[8] "Time without End: Physics and Biology in an Open Universe," *Reviews of Modern Physics* (1979).

Then the protons in the universe begin to decay and vanish.

That requires a word of explanation. A generation ago, the proton was thought to be an eternally stable particle, quite unlike its cousin, the unstable free neutron. Then a class of theories came along that said that protons too may be unstable, but with a vastly long lifetime. If these theories are correct, the proton has a finite lifetime of at least 10^{32} years. In this case, as the protons decay all the stars will finally become black holes.

The effect of proton decay is slow. It takes somewhere between 10^{30} and 10^{36} years for the stellar remnants all to become black holes. Note that on this time scale, everything that has happened in the universe so far is totally negligible, a tick at the very beginning. The ratio of the present age of the universe to 10^{36} years is like a few nanoseconds compared with the present age of the universe.

In terms of T-time, the stellar remnants collapse to form black holes between $T = 19.8$ and $T = 25.8$. The T-transformation still does pretty well in describing the open universe.

Long after the protons are all gone, the black holes go, too. Black holes evaporate, according to a theory developed by Stephen Hawking, because they have an effective temperature, and quantum theory allows them to radiate to an environment of lower temperature. Today, the universe is far too hot for a black hole of stellar mass to be able to lose mass by radiation and particle production. In another 10^{64} years or so ($T = 53.8$), that will not be true. The ambient temperature of the expanding universe will have dropped and dropped, and the black holes will evaporate. Those smaller than the Sun in mass will go first, ones larger than the Sun will go later; but eventually all will go.

In this scenario, the universe, some 10^{80} years from now ($T = 69.8$), will be an expanding ocean of radiation, which has scattered within it a sprinkling of widely separated electron-positron pairs.

The idea of proton decay is controversial, so we must consider the alternative. Suppose that the proton is *not* an unstable particle. Then we have a rather different (and far longer) future for the universe of material objects.

All the stars will continue, very slowly, to change their composition to the element with the most nuclear binding energy: iron. They will be doing this after some 10^{1600} years (T = 1,589.8).

Finally (though it is not the end, because there is no end) after somewhere between 10 to the 10^{26} and 10 to the 10^{76} years, a time so long that I can find no analogy to offer a feel for it, our solid iron neutron stars will become black holes.[9] Now our T-time scale also fails us. A t-time of 10 to the 10^{26} years corresponds to T = 10^{26}, itself a number huge beyond visualization.

Is this the end of the road? No. The black holes themselves will disappear, quickly (on these time scales) evaporating. The whole universe, as in the previous scenario, becomes little more than pure radiation. This all-encompassing bath, feeble and far diluted, is much too weak to permit the formation of new particles. A few electron-positron pairs, far apart in space, persist, but otherwise radiation is all.

Tables 4, 5, and 6 show the calendar for the future in "normal" t-time, for the closed and open universes with the unstable and stable proton. Time is measured from today, rather than the beginning of the universe.

Life in the Far Future   There is something a little unsatisfactory about the discussion so far. A universe, closed

---

[9] We have raised the stakes again. 10 to the 10^{26} is the number 1 followed by 10^{26} zeroes. The possible future is not just longer than the past. It is *unimaginably* longer.

or open, without anyone to observe it, feels dull and pointless. What are the prospects for observers, human or otherwise? We will not equate "intelligence" with "humanity," since over the time scales that we have encountered, the idea that anything like us will exist is remotely improbable.

Let us note that, on the cosmological scale, life as we know it on Earth has a respectable ancestry. Life emerged quite early in this planet's lifetime, about 3.5 billion years ago, so life is now about a fourth as old as the universe itself.

Land life appeared much later, 430 million years ago for simple plants. The first land animals came along a few tens of millions of years later. Mammals have existed for maybe 225 million years, and flowering plants about 100 million. Recognizable humans, with human intelligence, appeared a mere three or four million years ago. We are certainly upstarts, in a universe where ordinary turtles have been around, essentially unchanged in form and function, for a couple of hundred million years. Perhaps that is why we lack the calm certainty of the tortoise.

Humans have a short past, but we could have a long future. For starters, the Earth should remain habitable (unless we ourselves do something awful to it) for a few billion years. But in five billion years or so, the Sun will slowly swell until it is at last a hundred times its present size. Earth will be a charred cinder. Where will our descendants go?

We have already answered that question. Dwarf stars can shine for at least another thirty to a hundred billion years. They shine dimly, but a planet or free-space colony in orbit a few million miles away from one will find more than enough energy to support a thriving civilization; and of all the stars in the universe, the inconspicuous, long-lived dwarf stars appear to form the vast majority.

We are safe, not only as intelligence but even as hu-

mans, for at least another twenty billion years. The
Earth, however, will be gone—unless perhaps our descendants, displaying a technology as far beyond ours as
we are beyond the Stone Age, decide to take the home
planet along with them on their travels for sentimental
reasons.

If we are to consider longer time scales, beyond
thirty billion years, we must distinguish between the
cases of an open and a closed universe.

In the universe of the Big Crunch it seems obvious
that life and intelligence cannot go on forever, since
the future contains a definite time at which everything
in existence will be compressed to a single point of
infinite pressure and temperature. Life certainly cannot survive the Big Crunch, thus if we continue to measure time in the usual way, life exists for a finite time
only. However, we have already noted that in T_c-time,
even the Big Crunch is infinitely far away. Although the
transformation that we introduced seemed like a mere
mathematical artifice, it can be shown that there is
enough time (and available energy) between now and
the Big Crunch to think an infinite number of
thoughts. From that point of view, if we work with *subjective* time in which life survives long enough to enjoy
infinite numbers of thoughts, that will be like living
"forever" according to one reasonable definition. It is
all a question of redefining our time coordinates.

The open universe case has no problem with available time, but it does have a problem with available
energy. In the far future our energy sources will become increasingly diluted and distant.

Dyson has also analyzed this situation.[10] He has
looked at the possibility of continued life and intelli-

---

[10] Freeman Dyson, private communications, 1992–93. I am
not sure if *private* communication is the right term, since
some of these results came to me on a postcard. The postman

gence for the case of an asymptotically flat space-time, where the universe sits exactly on the boundary of the open and closed cases. I have not seen the details of his analysis, and to my knowledge they have not been published. Here, however, are his conclusions.

First, hibernation will be increasingly necessary. The fraction of time during which a thinking entity can remain "conscious" must become less, like $t^{-1/3}$. Also, the thinking rate must decrease, so that "subjective time" will proceed more slowly, like $t^{-1/3}$. To give an example of what this implies, one million billion years from now you will be able to remain awake for only ten years out of each million. And during those ten years, you will only be able to do as much thinking as you can do now in one hour. The good news is that you have an indefinitely long time available, so that you can eventually think an infinitely large number of thoughts.

Curiously enough, in an ultimately flat universe an infinite number of thoughts can be thought with the use of only a finite amount of energy. That's just as well, because in such a universe energy becomes less and less easy to come by as time goes on.

At the Eschaton.   The part of this novel that may appear least connected with physical theories is the idea of final human resurrection at the eschaton, or Omega Point. That is not so. Consider the following statement: The existence of God depends on the amount of missing matter in the universe.

That is proposed, as a serious physical theory, by Frank Tipler. It was the subject of a paper by him, *The Omega Point as* Eschaton: *Answers to Pannenberg's Questions for Scientists* (*Zygon*, vol. 24, June 1989), and expanded later to a complete book (*The Physics of*

---

could have read them. Maybe "personal communication" is better.

Immortality, Doubleday, 1994). The eschaton is the final state of all things, and it therefore includes the final state of the universe.

Tipler argues that certain types of possible universes allow a physicist to deduce (his own term is *prove)* the ultimate existence of a being with omnipresence, omni-science, and omnipotence. This being will have access to all the information that has ever existed and will have the power to resurrect and re-create any person or thing that has ever lived. Such a being can reasonably be called God.

The universe that permits this must satisfy certain conditions:

1. the universe must be such that life can con-tinue for infinite subjective time

2. space-time, continued into the future, must have as a boundary a particular type of termi-nation, known as a c-boundary

3. the necessary c-boundary must consist of a sin-gle point of space-time.

Then, and only then, according to Tipler, God with omnipresence, omniscience, and omnipotence can be shown to exist.

Conditions 2 and 3 are satisfied only if the universe is *closed.* It cannot be expanding forever, or even asymp-totically flat, otherwise the theory does not work. Ana's resurrection is possible only if the universe itself ends in inferno. The definition of *omnipotent* now becomes extremely interesting. Would omnipotence include the power to avoid the final singularity, by changing the universe itself to an open form?

I like to think so.

When the question of missing matter and the closed or open universe was introduced, it seemed interesting but quite unrelated to the subject of religion. Tipler

argues that the existence of God, including the concepts of resurrection, eternal grace, and eternal life,
depends crucially on the *current* mass-energy density of
the universe.

We already noted the surprising way in which the
observation of those remote patches of haze, the galaxies, showed that the universe began a finite time ago.
That was a striking conclusion: Simple observations today defined the far past of the universe.

Now we have a still stranger notion to contemplate:
The search for exotic particles such as "hot" neutrinos
and "cold" photinos and axions will tell us about the
far future of the universe; and those same measurements will have application not only to physics but to
theology.

Table 1

Event	t
Gravity decouples	10^{-43} seconds
Inflation of universe	10^{-35} seconds
Nuclear matter density	0.0001 seconds
Neutrinos decouple	1 second
Electron/positron pairs vanish	30 seconds
Helium forms	3.75 minutes
Atoms form	1 million years
Galaxy formation begins	1 billion years
Birth of solar system	10 billion years
Today	15 billion years

Table 2

$T = \log(t/t_N)$, where t_N is chosen as 15 billion years

Event	T
Big Bang	$-\infty$
Gravity decouples	-60.7
Inflation of universe	-52.7
Nuclear matter density	-21.7

Event	
Neutrinos decouple	−17.7
Electron/positron pairs vanish	−16.2
Helium forms	−15.3
Atoms form	−4.2
Galaxy formation begins	−1.2
Birth of solar system	−0.2
Today	0

Table 3

$T_c = \log(t/\log(C-t))$

Event	T_c
Big Bang	−∞
Gravity decouples	−61.31
Inflation of universe	−52.31
Nuclear matter density	−22.31
Neutrinos decouple	−18.31
Electron/positron pairs vanish	−16.83
Helium forms	−15.95
Atoms form	−4.81
Galaxy formation begins	−1.81
Birth of solar system	−0.74
Today	−0.52
"Halfway" point (32.5 billion yrs)	0
Helium dissociates	+15.95
Electron/positron pairs form	+16.83
Neutrinos couple	+18.31
Gravity couples	+61.31
End point (65 billion years)	+∞

Table 4

CLOSED UNIVERSE	
Event	t (billions of years)
Today	0
Sun becomes red giant	5
Halfway point, expansion ceases	17
Most dwarf stars cease to shine	30
Big Crunch	50

Table 5

OPEN UNIVERSE, UNSTABLE PROTON	
Event	t (years)
Today	0
Sun becomes red giant	5 billion
Most dwarf stars cease to shine	30 billion
All stellar activity ceases	10^{14}
Stellar remnants become black holes	10^{30}–10^{36}
Black holes evaporate	10^{64}
Only radiation remains	10^{80}

Table 6

OPEN UNIVERSE, STABLE PROTON	
Event	t (years)
Today	0
Sun becomes red giant	5 billion
Most dwarf stars cease to shine	30 billion
All stellar activity ceases	10^{14}
Stars are iron neutron stars	10^{1600}
Neutron stars form black holes	> 10 to the 10^{26}
Only radiation remains	10 to the 10^{76}

Charles Sheffield has published twenty-eight books ranging from bestselling science to horror to thrillers to hard SF, and over ninety of his short stories have appeared in print. He won the John W. Campbell Memorial Award in 1992 for Best SF Novel, *Brother to Dragons,* and the 1993 Nebula and 1994 Hugo Awards for Best Novelette, *Georgia on My Mind.* A mathematician and physicist by training, Dr. Sheffield has authored over a hundred technical papers, and serves as a science reviewer for several prominent publications. He currently resides in Maryland, where he is working on his next novel, *Aftermath,* to be published by Bantam in summer 1998.

And be sure not to miss

AFTERMATH

Charles Sheffield's
riveting new novel of
natural—and unnatural—disaster.

Our nearest neighbor star, Alpha Centauri,
goes supernova. And that is only the
beginning of the ordeal . . .

FIRST STRIKE. FEBRUARY 21, 2026; KIMBERLEYS PLATEAU, WESTERN AUSTRALIA.

It was evening, but it was not dark. Would darkness ever come again?

Wondjina crawled from the shadow of the rocks and peered north and west. No clouds were in the sky, and the Sun was on the horizon. Soon it should be night, cooling the desert and bringing longed-for relief.

But there would be no night; soon, again, would come the Rival.

Wondjina turned to face south and east. A hint of pink was already on the skyline warning that the Rival was alive in the heavens and about to rise in the cloudless sky. If Wondjina were to find water it was best to seek it at this time, in the cooler hour before the Rival usurped the Moon and evening turned again to day.

For twelve days, the Rival had risen as the Sun set. Between them, Sun and Rival seared the land and drew off every hint of surface moisture. Without dark there could be no night, without night there would be no midnight fall of dew. And the deep waters were running dry.

Wondjina took the trowel from his waist sling and started to dig in the gravel of the water-course. From time to time he laid down the tool, picked up the hollow reed, and pushed it deep. He sucked hard on the other end.

Nothing, and still nothing. Every day, the reed had to be pushed deeper. Dig again, dig harder. Finally, after ten minutes of hard effort, a few mouthfuls of warm, brackish liquid.

He straightened and stared again to the south. The Rival had lifted above the horizon. Now it was a dazzling blue-white point too bright to look at. There was no circle of light, like the Sun's disk, but when the Rival was high in the sky it threw down its own intense spears of heat.

And everywhere was reddish, powdery dust, worse than at any time in his long memory. He opened his woven bag, took out the necklace of dried bones and the bright-stained sections of emu shell. Let the youngsters speak of new ideas, of their belief that the Rival was nothing more than a star suddenly grown great. What did they know? Not one of them could recite a history of the family, not one had learned the modes of address to the spirits of autumn rains.

Wondjina began to ascend the course of the dried-out stream bed. He climbed slowly and carefully, leaning on his ironwood spear for support. Hunger had weakened his limbs, but he must husband his strength for the ceremony. The Rival lay directly ahead, its southern fire striking matching points of light from sharp-sided pebbles in the water-course. Was it imagination, or did the intruder to-night flame brighter yet, putting the vanished Sun to shame?

He reached the plateau and advanced to its southern margin. The desert land dropped away ahead. Far off, rolling dunes marched to the horizon. On his left the land rose to the distant hills, fading into the continental interior. Above, creeping higher in the sky, the Rival burned in Heaven. It threw the shadow of Wondjina stark behind him.

He laid out the pattern of eggshells and bones, slowly and carefully. The heat was fierce, sucking sweat from his body as soon as it appeared. His grizzled, tight-coiled hair was warm to his touch. The brief respite of evening was over.

Now, then, or never.

He removed his breech-clout and pouches and smeared the red ocher and white pipeclay on his body. Then the weaving dance began, turning steadily from right to left, following the line of shells and bones. The chanted invocation to the spirits of rain and cloud came without conscious thought. He had not spoken those words for many years—how many? He did not know—but they came easily.

The Rival rose higher in the sky, moving toward its own moon. The naked figure danced on and on, a solitary black mote on the great plateau. Danced, as his energy slowly faded. Danced, as his legs weakened. There had been a sign that he was to begin. There must be a sign that he was permitted to stop.

Nothing, though his legs were beginning to buckle. The dry south wind blew, and the Rival pierced his body with its daggers of heat. He decided that he would dance until he died. If his life were demanded as the condition of succor, he was willing to give it.

When the change came he at first noticed nothing. It was hot as ever, the wind blew still. Only when he stumbled and fell from sheer exhaustion, then made the effort to regain his feet, did he see it.

A new line of hills rose above the southern horizon. He stared at them for seconds, before his tired brain told him that what he saw was impossible. Not hills, Clouds. As he watched they crept closer, changing from that single indistinct line to lofty mountains and dark feathery canyons.

Not just clouds. Rain clouds.

Wondjina whooped in triumph. Rather than trying to stand up, he fell forward and lay prone. With his left cheek on the dry, gritty ground, he gave thanks. He watched the steady advance until the wonderful moment when a rearing thunderhead swallowed up the Rival's fire. The wind fell to nothing, then came back as veering random gusts. The air was no longer lung-searing hot.

As the first drops of rain spattered the parched soil, he stood up. He left the eggshells and bones where they lay, a tribute to the spirits. The rain was changing from a shower to a downpour to an astonishing cloudburst. He cupped his hands in front of his mouth, turned his face upward, and drank.